I0545030

CONTROL THEORY

BY RICH RESTUCCI

SEVEREDPRESS

CONTROL THEORY

Copyright © 2025 Rich Restucci

WWW.SEVEREDPRESS.COM

All rights reserved. No part of this book may be
reproduced or transmitted in any form or by any
electronic or mechanical means, including
photocopying, recording or by any information and
retrieval system, without the written permission of
the publisher and author, except where permitted by law.
This novel is a work of fiction. Names,
characters, places and incidents are the product of
the author's imagination, or are used fictitiously.
Any resemblance to actual events, locales or persons,
living or dead, is purely coincidental.

ISBN: 978-1-923165-69-4

All rights reserved.

For my Dad: The strongest, kindest man I ever met. We miss you.
For my Wife: Same thing but with a bottle of wine.

Control: The power to influence or direct people's behavior or the course of events.

"There are more dead people than living, and their numbers are increasing. The living are getting rarer." —Eugene Lonesco

A DIFFERENT KIND OF PRISON

"Easy," the doctor told me. "Nice and slow."

I didn't want to nod, as I was terrified. I lifted the glass cap off the black, wax-covered steel of the bottom of the hazard box with the forceps. The tool was stainless steel and maybe two feet long with a pair of recessions near the end which fit the glass stopper I was lifting perfectly. I put the stopper on the top of the test tube, the green-yellow liquid now fully encased in glass.

"And now the test tube," she said like I didn't know exactly what I was doing. There would be bricks in my underwear by the end of this.

She took in a lungful of air. "Take your time."

I side-eyed her, my hands still inside the gloves of the hazard box, the gloves firmly grasping the tongs. "Doc, I know you're a very smart lady and all, but if you don't shut it, I'm going to see just how far up your ass I can get these forceps after I'm done handling this poison shit. I'm thinking about pinching your uvula." I had been itching to say "uvula" my whole life. Today was my day.

"Language," another voice behind me said. The sternness belonged to the head honcho, Dr, Gamboa, and while he seemed to like me, he did have a temper.

"My humblest apologies," I began, "but I don't need constant caution warnings while I do this. I get it. I drop this and we have to start over."

"If it doesn't kill us," the smart-assed doctor beside me said.

I side-eyed her again, "Yeah, that. Now, hush."

I used the tongs to pick up the tube, put it in a larger steel tube and pushed down on the stopper with the tool.

She let loose an audible sigh and said, "Good job." She pressed a green button, and I heard a whooshing sound as the air in the hazard box was sucked through a tube in the side of the acrylic. I don't know where that air went to, but I'm glad I wasn't on the end of it.

I pulled my hands out of the gloves, which were part of the box, and stared at Gamboa.

"*Hush?*" he asked, his eyebrows shooting toward the water-stained drop ceiling.

"*Language?*" I shot right back. We both smiled, then laughed at each other, the laugh infectious as the young doctor who had been telling me to go slow began chuckling as well. Her name was Doctor Baker.

Even the infected leaning against the desk in the corner began to laugh. It was a guttural sound which if I had heard a year ago, would have added more bricks to my skivvies. I knew the twitchy, feverish man with crimson eyes meant me no harm right here and now, but he still freaked me the fuck out.

They all did.

I glanced at the double doctorate standing in the room with me and thought for the thousandth time that even though Baker was a five-foot nothing younger woman with no chin, and Gamboa was a tall, pointy bearded, skinny dude, both had to have balls the size of Death Stars to do what they had done.

The two of them had domesticated Runners.

The scariest, most terrifying creatures in the history of the planet were now in the employ of one Doctor A. Gamboa, research scientist for USAMRIID. When there was US anyway. Now he worked on the third floor of the mostly-cleared Mission Bay Trauma Center in San Francisco. I say *mostly-cleared* because every now and then, we find a fucking zombie they missed when they cleared the building. He was some kind of colonel or something.

Gamboa was also a God damned kidnapper, to which I can personally attest. The prick had instructed his infected stooges to pilfer me from Alcatraz.

Baker had cautiously come around the hazard box with her prize. A recently Teflon-taped glass test-tube now inside a foam-lined steel cannister.

She smiled, holding the container out to Gamboa. "We've got this plague by the balls now, don't we?"

Scary noises came from the creature leaning on the desk and he stood. "*We go now.*"

I wanted to placate him with pizza and dick jokes but suddenly I was shit out of both.

I swallowed. The infected couldn't remember his own name, but he had a tattoo on his forearm of a rose with thorns, so that's what we called him: Thorne. Ironically, the tattoo had a piece missing. It was where he had been bitten by a dead one years ago.

Thorne's red eyes shifted to me. "*We go.*"

The infected was gruff and terrifying. I'd seen thousands of Runners in my time and every one of them would kill themselves trying if it meant murdering a stray squirrel. If there was a living breathing creature, the Runners needed to make it dead. Period.

Except these ones. The thing is, all the doctors had done was capture the damned infected and... *talked to them*. So, this whole apocalypse thingie could have been averted by stimulating conversation? Not exactly. There was also some drug therapy and weeks, sometimes

2

months, strapped to a hospital bed. Once they had some infected to help, they got more infected and talked them out of murder.

It didn't always hold, though, and on a few occasions, a newly domesticated Runner would try to kill one of the doctors. There had been three doctors and six military guarding them when they first got to San Francisco a year ago.

Now there were two doctors and me.

The only reason I'm with these two is that the doctors had sent out a Runner A-Team to capture the one person they needed to experiment on in order to make this plague go away. The one human who has been bitten by an infected and survived. I looked at the prisoner foot-chains around my ankles and sighed. I clinked across the room to the sink and dumped a bit of water over my hands to wash them. Faucets were a luxury we did not usually have in San Francisco. I regarded my chains again. I *might* be able to get past the doctors, I *might* be able to get past secured doors and the Runner sentries, but I would never be able to get past the throngs of dead people shuffling around outside. Not with these shackles on. So, I'm biding my time.

Thorne grunted, "*We go!*" in his "*my patience is spent*" voice. Apparently, I hadn't been fast enough with the hand-washing. Thorne wanted his daily time with the other captive here at Mission Bay, another victim of post-plague kidnapping. Thorne loved him and they talked all the time. Well, Thorne grunted.

The problem with the other captive was that he was totally enamored by a little girl on Alcatraz. Well, she used to be on Alcatraz. Not sure if she's still there, stumbling around, or if she made it out with the others who took the boats and the submarine. I'll get back to that in a minute.

So, this other captive? He and I had been Shanghaied from The Rock during an attack by the undead. Thorne and his gang of infected assholes had knocked me the fuck out and taken both me and my new buddy across the bay to this damn trauma center. In the interim, the uninfected humans who had been calling Alcatraz their home had beaten a hasty retreat and escaped to who-knows-where. There had been talk of moving the colony to Angel Island, but I don't know if they went there.

I'll find out when I break out of this dump and go looking.

Thorne and I moved down the hall, me clinking the whole way. My shackles were longer than standard prison shackles (I would know), but I still wouldn't be able to run. The Runner pounded on a white door, *shave and a haircut* and was rewarded with *two bits* by the occupant on the other side of the door who had kicked his response. The door was pushed wide, and my friend sat on his ass on the floor, his knees drawn up with his wrists on them, staring at the dingy linoleum with what was likely

3

angry eyes. A quick glance around the room told me that he had destroyed everything in here that he could in the little time we'd been incarcerated. The room was total carnage.

"*Billy,*" Thorne growled.

The kid on the floor sighed, looked up for a moment, then continued his stare. "Yup, still ugly."

Thorne slapped his knee. He actually slapped his knee. "*HAR HAR HAR!*" he guffawed. He had meant to laugh, but what came out of him was a rasping hack, more like what you would think someone gargling with acid and broken glass would sound like.

Thorne loved Billy.

I stared at his chain. It was attached to a thick pipe that ran inside the wall next to the shattered window. I was thinking of ways to get through the chain when I greeted him with, "Hi pal."

"Hey," he answered without looking up.

"Gonna get cold in here with that busted window, buddy."

He simply shrugged. I had only known this kid for a while, and while he was certifiably bat-shit crazy, he was also the happiest person on earth. Being chained up was killing him slowly.

"Thorne, can you please get the doc?"

The infected looked at me and there was absolute murder behind his eyes. Thorne liked Billy, Dr. Baker, and sometimes Dr. Gamboa. He would casually eviscerate me and use my pancreas as a tea bag if the doctors told him it was ok.

A feral snarl fell across his visage. "*You don't tell me what to do,*" he said with as much menace as he could muster. His voice was such that I can neither confirm nor deny a code brown at that juncture. I would need to check my skivvies for smears later from multiple assaults.

He knew he scared the crap out of me just by being near, but he didn't use that in opposition. Thorne didn't give a shit about politics or bravado. I think those ideals were completely alien to him. He looked like he would kill me at any moment because he would. It was that simple.

"I *asked* you, Thorne. I didn't tell you."

Confusion pushed its way through the rage briefly. "What I meant was, it would be nice if you would get the doctor for Billy if you wouldn't mind, but nobody is telling you that you must."

He nodded once, curtly. "*Want to stay near Billy.*"

"Ok, I'll get the doc," I told him.

"*You get.*"

I had wanted to correct Thorne on his usage of interrogative adverbs, but I also very much enjoyed my larynx on the inside of me, so I kept quiet.

4

I shuffled off and clinked back down the hall. "That was fast," Gamboa told me as he and Baker took turns with their eyes plastered to a microscope.

"You need to let Billy go."

Gamboa sighed, "Not this again. Look, I've told you —"

"You have me. You don't need him."

"We might. The last subject we had whom the dead didn't want to eat killed herself."

I scoffed, "Wonder why. How many tests have you run on me since I've been here?"

"Eighty-three."

Baker pointed at the current sample on the microscope. "Eighty-four."

"Eighty-four," he self-corrected.

I nodded. "And how many on Billy?"

"None, but that—"

"You're killing him, Doc. He's not the most stable guy to begin with, and he can't deal with the chains. Let him go. There are others out there who are unpalatable to the rotters. Get one of them. Let Billy go," I repeated.

He shook his head. "I simply can't do that. He could be important to the research."

The doctors knew that I had been imprisoned in a government run facility as a lab rat before, but they didn't know all the specifics. I had an epiphany and thought about a tactic I had used on those government douches at Baldy Mountain. It had worked then. "Then from here on out I fight you. Every time you need to draw blood, every time you want to take my temperature, any test you want to do, I'll make it difficult. I'll punch and kick and bite you. I'll knock shit over and break stuff, starting with that," I pointed at the sample on the microscope.

"I don't think you understand the complexity of—"

I strode forward, chains clinking and backhanded the microscope off the little silver cart it had been on. That shit hurt like hell, but the thing crashed to the linoleum as did the sample clipped to it, and I smiled through the pain in my freshly smacked hand.

"No!" Baker screamed and scrambled to save the sample.

Gamboa yelled too, "Don't touch it!" Baker drew her hands back at lightspeed. She had almost touched the raw sample of the shit they were brewing mixed with some of my juice with her bare hands. Nobody knew what that could do to a person. Not yet.

"Are you out of your God damned mind?" Gamboa yelled at me. He took two steps toward me and tried to loom, but I was taller.

I slapped him across the face. Hard. Hand to cheek he just stared at me. Then he looked over my shoulder, his eyes going wild, and I just knew shit had gotten real.

A dead woman lunged the last two feet she needed after sauntering through the doorway. She tried to latch onto me, but I backpedaled quickly. Unfortunately, I was shackled, hadn't taken that into consideration during the backpedal, and as such went on my ass.

I still had two good arms to fight with, but so did the dead lady, along with lots of good teeth, and she decided to use them by falling on me, snapping.

She stopped halfway, my eyes locked onto hers, and suddenly she was jerked backwards. Thorne stood her up and smashed her head into the door jamb until her cranium came apart. Actually, he kept going for a few more whacks *after* it had come apart, the rancid, gooey shit inside the thing's noggin spraying all over.

He let the lifeless corpse drop to the ground, both the door jamb and his hand dripping with gore.

"Don't yell," the Runner admonished. He spun around and stormed away.

ONE FOR THE ROAD

"*Door broke,*" Subject Nine told us.

Subject Nine used to be a woman. I think she had been a beautiful ebony goddess, extremely fit and tough as nails. Her name had been Janice Stroud and before the infection took her, she had been a personal trainer and Ju Jitsu instructor. She was the only Runner who had been caught and successfully "re-educated" who had possessed a full set of credentials in a wallet in her back pocket. She still had her gym ID as well as a driver's license, both with photos of what was once a striking woman.

I didn't know ladies carried wallets, I thought they all used purses. I guess that's sexist of me, but I digress.

The funny thing is, Subject Nine didn't want to be called Janice or J-bird or Stroud. I had even tried Niner. She wanted to be called Subject Nine. The only Runner who had irrefutable proof of their name and she wanted nothing to do with it.

Where Thorne had taken a disliking to me, Subject Nine liked to be around when I was there. I think she has a crush. What's not to love, really? I'm the fucking bomb, and a sweet apocalyptic catch to boot. Greater than ten feet of awesome in a six-foot two-inch frame. Unfortunately for young Janice here, I have a strict and unwavering No-Dating-Infected-Broads policy, and even if I didn't, I'm apocalypse hitched. I've got me a wife 'n kids. Well, we aren't married in the strictest sense of the word but try telling her that.

So, that was a rabbit hole…

Anyway, Subject Nine brought Thorne and another Runner downstairs and they sealed the busted door. Kind of amazing that only one of the dead bastards made their way in here. All it takes is one bite or sometimes a scratch and you're playing for their team in a day at most. Everyone bitten either dies or begins to run around eviscerating people. The dead don't stay dead though, and they get up and do some eviscerating of their own.

Everyone dies. Everyone. Except me. I probably should have mentioned this earlier, but I'm immune to this whole zombie thing. I've been bitten a few times now and I haven't kicked the bucket. But there are… side effects. My eyes start to bleed when I get pissy, and I want to break stuff. So far, the only things I've broken were a chair and a couple of infected. And maybe a microscope.

Three guesses as to why a USAMRIID virologist wants to experiment on me.

"Thank you, Subject Nine," Dr. Baker said. "Why don't you get a Coke?" Nine reached her shaky hand into a Runner's-only fridge and yanked out a Pepsi. We didn't have any Coke, but the doctor was from Mississippi, and every soft drink down there is a Coke. S9 tried to get her fingernail under the pull tab but couldn't do it with the shakes. She started to get angry and let a small snarl escape then glanced up sharply at Baker.

The infected took a deep breath and kept trying, but she just couldn't do it. I extended my hand to her. "Can I get that for you?"

Baker piped up, "I think Subject Nine should—"

It was my turn to growl, "Shut it, you squirrely, chinless, gaslighting, dickwad." Nine passed me the can and I popped the tab for her. She guzzled the dark liquid down and let loose with a tremendous belch.

Her reward for sealing the door against intruders who would kill us had been a fucking test. Doctor Douche strikes again.

Subject Nine said something to me and hurried out of the room, looking at her feet as she left. I was learning a lot about Runners. They had way more emotional range than I had previously thought.

Baker hurried over to a notebook on the table and began scribbling furiously. I shook my head and clinked down the hall to Billy's room.

"Go Fish," I told Billy.

He grabbed a card from the pile. "So, what's the plan? When do we make like a tree and get out of here?"

"Working on it. Any threes?" He scowled and passed me two cards.

"How hard are you working on it? Any queens?"

The deck we were playing with was missing the queen of diamonds and the eight of clubs. "Go Fish. You're not the only one in chains, pal. I've searched high and low for the keys and nada. I have an idea though."

He looked up, his eyes hopeful. We heard footsteps and Gamboa stuck his head in the door. "An idea for what?"

I didn't even turn to regard him. "On what we should ask for in the next drop."

"I put in for the pudding and the Pepsi," the doc told us, like he was some kind of hero.

Now I did look at him. "Mountain Dew, Doc. Mountain. Fucking. Dew. While you guys all get what you want in the damn supply drops, I haven't had a swig of my stuff in a long damn time. We've gotten three supply drops in the two weeks I've been here and not one bottle of green in any of them." I spun back around. "I thought you had some pull, Doc." I winked at Billy. Billy didn't do subtle and winked back.

The doc noticed. "I'll see what I can do. Billy, is there anything you would like?"

Billy clinked his chains and before Gamboa could answer I piped up, "He'll see what he can do."

Billy smiled and I turned to glare at the doc, but he was gone. He sighed and asked me, "So, what did you do all day?"

"Not much. Just made some anti-zombie juice, watched Thorne bash a zombie's brains out, and clinked around some in my anklets." I was thoughtful for a moment. "Ya know, the doctors are pretty lax when it comes to security."

Billy harrumphed. "What are you gonna do? Run through a swarm of dead with those on?" He pointed at my shackles.

I sighed. "I guess you're right. My point was, if they had been watching, they would have seen me searching through old drawers."

"Got any threes?" I had just asked for threes. Story of my life.

I handed him a three of spades, surreptitiously glaring at him across the top of my cards to see if he would notice the cheat. "So that idea I was working on? It involves the lax security I mentioned, you and me getting the hell out of Dodge, and this." I pulled an item from my sleeve and passed it to Billy. "It was in one of the drawers. There were four of them. This is the weak point." I tapped the outside of the cuff portion of the shackle on his ankle which was attached to the chain.

He stared hard at me for a moment and then smiled a knowing half-smile.

"We don't kill anybody, right? Especially me," I demanded.

He kept the half-smile going. "Not with this." He tucked the hacksaw blade I had handed him under the dirty pillow on the floor.

"Be ready at midnight," I told him.

I'd always wanted to say that.

I glanced at the G-Shock watch I had appropriated from a dead guy a while ago. The illuminated blue hands told me it was just after midnight when I took a big breath in front of Billy's door. I pushed the door open and saw him sitting on the bed. In the darkness. He held up the foot-shackles in triumph, stood up and gave me a huge hug.

"I don't forget things like this," he whispered as he pushed past me into the hallway.

We did a fair amount of slinking, but we positively skulked past the open door to Dr. Baker's room. She was talking to someone via her laptop, the light from it illuminating her silhouette. "Yeah, he wants

Mountain Dew. Apparently, he's too good for the stuff we have here and needs better. Maybe you should send some nail polish and a pair of Gucci shoes, too."

Billy and I regarded each other with wide eyes. I mouthed, *Bitch*! And he mouthed *Jerk*! at the same time. We continued to sneak down the hall and came to a corner. Our salvation was to the left and down a long flight of stairs. The only problem was that the stairs were guarded. Subject Nine twitched and jerked, making some of those weird coughing noises that the Runners sometimes make. She stood between us and the stairs.

You know, it's amazing how many thoughts you can have in the span of a microsecond. She immediately reminded me of a girl I had a crush on in high school. There was little resemblance. This Runner was black. My girl had been Asian. Both were fit and hot, but where this girl was infected and fast, the other one was likely significantly more chewed with a top speed of about one mile per hour. I thought about the time I asked my girl out and she laughed at me. She told me there was no way she would go out with a "freak" like me. It had taken me three weeks to work up the nerve to ask her. I had done it while my favorite song was playing at the local arcade we had both been at. I never listened to that song again.

On the flip side, I think I could ask out Subject Nine and she would readily accept my offer. Perks of having a pulse in the apocalypse.

She whipped her head around and glared at both of us, a silent snarl on her face. The snarl instantly dissolved when she saw it was me. Slowly, ever so slowly, her red eyes dropped from my face to where my shackles should have been, then back up to my eyes.

"*Leaving*," she said. It hadn't been a question, but a statement. She stared at the floor.

I sighed, "We have to. Eventually, they're going to hurt us, or maybe kill us."

She didn't look up when she said, "*Yes*."

I still couldn't get past the voice of a Runner. It was fucking terrifying. I mean, they still have the same basic anatomy as us, right? Why would their voices be so messed up?

She turned and crept down the steps in front of us. Soon we were at the bottom of the stairs staring at the barred exit door. It was barred with wood, but it had held out most of the inquisitive undead in the area.

"*Bag*," she said. I had no idea what she was telling me.

A green army pack, definitely worn during the Tet Offensive, plopped down in front of us from absolutely nowhere. Now, I don't normally piss myself, but this was a special occasion. I expected Gamboa to be there with his sidearm pointed at my face, and I started raising my hands, but it was Thorne who stepped out of the shadows. My nuts shrank so far up into me I could taste them.

The big Runner moved past me and removed the door braces. He stuck his head outside and looked in both directions, then stood aside. He nodded and pointed at the olive drab bag.

I picked up the pack. There were two flashlights, a case of MREs without the case, and two canteens. Subject Nine passed me a crowbar and Thorne thrust his arm forward toward Billy, a sword in his hand.

"Muramasa..." Billy whispered, and I had no fucking idea what that meant.

"*Don't die, Billy,*" Thorne growled and crept silently up the stairs.

"I won't."

"I'll try not to either," I told Thorne, but he didn't care.

I reached down into my hip pocket and pulled out a Pepsi. I popped the top and handed it to Subject Nine, who immediately guzzled the contents and let loose with a belch. She dropped the can and stared at me, tilting her head.

I stepped forward and put my arms around her. She tensed and I thought she was going to scream, but she relaxed. She didn't hug me back, but I knew she liked the contact.

"*Go,*" she said, and we did.

I looked at Billy and shrugged. The son of a bitch began to skip down the street, whisper singing "You and Nine, sitting in a tree..."

WHAT THE HELL IS A SECNAV?

When you're traversing an apocalyptic landscape, one of the things you always forget is how dark it is at night. No apartment lights, no cars, no cellphones. The darkness isn't absolute, but it's just... more. I regarded Billy through the night. The kid had survived, on his own, in a damn city, for the entire plague. I mean, I had survived as well, but I almost always had help, and I was almost never in a city. I usually had a ton of firearms on me as well. Billy had lived through this whole zombie thing with a sword and his crazy since the start.

He did have a superpower: the dead didn't want to eat him. I'd seen it before. I watched him as he casually strode down the sidewalk, seemingly without a care in the world. He took no precautions and seemed totally unafraid. I had been shitting myself since the door to the medical center had opened.

I guess when the dead don't care about you, you don't need to care too much about them. Me? I needed to care. I could get nibbled on and not turn. That was my superpower, but you need to think it through, Dear Reader.

I looked at my left arm. The appendage still worked, but I had a nasty scar. I was bitten by a dead friend of mine a few months ago, and it still hadn't healed all the way. Compound that with the other bites I've received, and you have a dude with holes where they shouldn't be. If I were to keep getting bitten, that shit would add up and I would lose function someplace. While Billy doesn't have to run from the dead, I do. They can still kill me, and often try.

I glanced back up to see Billy's stance had changed. He had his head cocked to the left and was listening for something, searching with his ears. He drew his sword, and I went on high alert. Yeah, so, I had already been on alert, but now I was on *high* alert. Sweat dripped down my back and I clutched the crowbar a bit tighter.

The dead don't try to be stealthy. They just up and bite you if they can. The good part about the dead is that they are constantly falling apart. The bad part is that we are going on four years of this shit, and they still haven't rotted away. Maybe it was all the MSG in our food and these fuckers are preserved. Not important. What was important were the six or seven dead bastards who turned the corner right then. Usually, groups of dead were loud, but these ones weren't. The silent, stupid asses went the wrong way, and I heaved a sigh of relief. They step-dragged and shuffled away from us down the San Francisco cobbles.

They hadn't seen us.

That is until Billy snuck up behind them and started swinging his steel. Then they got loud. Hissing, screeching, that rasping hack.

Fuck.

The kid was efficient. He slashed and stabbed until there weren't any left. He wiped his blade on the rotten pants of a dead UPS lady and stood there thinking.

"I lost count." He gawked at me. "Those jerks in the medical center made me forget!"

Billy had a tally of zombies he had destroyed.

I shrugged. "Imprisonment does a lot of nasty things to a person. We should be quiet, though."

"Oh, yeah. Maybe I'll just call it two thousand?"

"I like it." I could hear the sounds the dead make, and they weren't far off. "Do you think we should get inside?"

Billy started to answer but was interrupted by the sounds of bare feet running on pavement. I had time to turn halfway around before something hit me like a freight train and we both went to the ground. The back of my noggin conked the ground pretty hard, and I was dazed for a moment. The thing astride me, now throwing downward haymakers, had no such problems. I threw my arms in front of my face to protect it, but the creature just kept hammering until ten inches of Japanese folded steel abruptly jutted from her sternum. The look on her face was comical, all the hate gone and replaced with surprise.

She grabbed the blade, trying to figure out what the hell had happened to her, and Billy withdrew it, cutting her fingers. She stared at her hand for a sec, looked at me, back at her hand, then she was all rage again. She threw her head back and sucked in a shitload of air to scream that scream that they scream and her melon sort of toppled from her frame. Infected blood spurted from her severed arteries in great gouts of crimson. It looked like the death from a really bad horror movie. I bucked her off me and stood, my arms stuck out for inspection, both they and my blue Johnny shirt dripping with gore.

I had been attacked, yet again, by a Runner who couldn't possibly be sixteen years old yet. Why did kids want to kill me?

"I'm sorry," Billy said as he wiped his sword.

"You saved me, man. A little blood on me is ok."

"Wasn't talking to you."

Our fifteen second battle with the infected had drawn some unwanted attention, and a few of the curious decided to shuffle in our direction.

It was dark and we were still in the city. Shit could go from bad to Fucktown in a microsecond, and we didn't have much more than that to make a decision. I glanced right and saw the wide-open maw of a building I couldn't identify. "What about in there?" I thumbed.

"Any other time and I would say we should stay on the street, but I can't see anything. Yeah, let's head in there."

Billy strode forward and I followed him. I was used to making the decisions, even though of my entire group, I was the biggest idiot. I guess that's debatable if everybody listens to me. I rather enjoyed Billy taking the reins for a while.

He sauntered into the building like he was going into a 7-11 for a Hershey bar. Listening to the amount of dead people coming our way made me go in right on Billy's heels. I quickly closed the heavy door behind me.

Have you ever woken up in the middle of the night and it was really dark? So dark that you put your hand in front of your face just to see if you can see it through the gloom? I did that in this place. I stuck my hand up in front of my face and couldn't see shit. I had thought it was dark outside, but the darkness in here was absolute. It also stunk. The door had likely been open for years, the mold and mildew securing a dank and permanent foothold. With dead people wandering in and out through the open door over the years, we had the stench trifecta.

I was more worried about any of them who had seen us duck in here and more to the point, any of them in here with us already. I almost shit myself when I heard a thump a few feet to my left.

"*Sorry!*" Billy whispered to me. "Can't see!"

"Not sure if we should use a light. They might be able to see it from outside, I can't tell if there are any windows." I glanced left and right and nope, couldn't see anything.

"Smells..." he told me. I had to agree.

I could hear the horde as it passed by the building. It was loud, which meant there were a lot of them. There was no way we couldn't have heard it before, so that means the fuckers hadn't been making noise.

Something warm and wet dripped onto my cheek from above. My other cheek had a fresh bandage on it from where a dead asshole had grabbed me by the face a while ago. The thing had torn me up pretty good, but between my medic girlfriend and the two douche doctors, my pretty was coming back. None of that mattered right then, but it still poked its way into my head.

I wiped the stuff off my face with my hand and took a sniff. It didn't smell, but that didn't mean anything. It could be blood, swampy rainwater, infected goo, bird shit... I didn't know. Either way I wasn't staying in that spot.

I shifted left, stepped on what could only be a glass bottle from 1939, slipped and went on my ass. The bottle shot away from me hitting every single fucking piece of everything in that room until it came to rest, spinning. I know it was spinning because as I sat there on my ass contemplating the universe, I could hear that glass fucker winding down. Oh, and my ass hurt where I had landed on it.

It was about to get chewed off anyway, as the dead fuckers both inside and outside the door had heard the commotion and wanted to know what it was.

"Um…" Billy said, and he went down tussling with something.

Smacks and thumps started on every inch of the front of the building, and it got loud quickly. That noise that the things make increased as well, with at least a few of the rasps coming from this side of the door.

If I couldn't see them, they couldn't see me, but they already knew we were in here and would be in here with us in a moment. Eventually one of the dead bastards would just bite me in the dark. Fuck that noise. The Runners had thoughtfully added a flashlight to each of our packs, and I had hung mine on the outside using one of the lanyards. I clicked that bitch on and to my utter dismay, provided a beacon to the three dead sons of bitches in the lobby of whatever business this had been. They wasted no time in coming for me, but hey, I had a crowbar.

Number one had been a kid. Maybe sixteen, and she had a filthy, formerly pink crop-top hanging off her neck. The whole left side of her body had been savaged and her head was at an angle as the muscle was gone from that side of her throat. No matter how many of these things I destroy, I always pity the kids. I don't know, I just think of their deaths as less fair somehow. The pity was fleeting, and I put her down with a sideways smack that sounded like someone had dropped a cantaloupe.

Number two looked like a gray version of Wilt Chamberlain. Enormous, almost as tall as my bestest buddy-pal Ship, but not as wide, this thing just waded through office furniture like it were dandelions. Two chairs and an empty water cooler went flying as it strode toward me. It hit a desk with its thighs and sort of fell forward across it. Good thing too because I likely would never have been able to brain him unless he was brought down a peg. I smoked this one with a downward swing as his head was now at waist level when he started reaching for me.

Somehow, I had turned the steel around in my hand and the crowbar stuck in his damn head. The hooked end of my weapon was a few inches deep as number three, a big woman with her belly eaten away and insanely long curly blonde hair, came at me. She wasn't as big as the gray one I was frantically attempting to free my weapon from, but she had not been small in life.

She would be dining on my innards before I would get this thing loose, so I abandoned my attempt at the crowbar and swung my pack at her. I caught her in the shoulder, and she stumbled. Before she could right herself, Billy took her out with his sword. I was thankful until he casually reached down and extricated my crowbar from the dead basketball player's dome with two fingers.

Showoff.

"Let's make like a tree and beat it," he whispered, and we did.

The beam from my flashlight sliced through the thick darkness, driving shadows into corners. There were tons of bones scattered about with brown stains liberally distributed as well. Must have been a shit show in here during the first days of the outbreak, a last stand or something. We found the stairs to the upper levels of the building. An attempt had been made to block the steps off with anything the poor, trapped souls could muster. Chairs, desks, lamps, computer monitors, even a big carpet had been tossed hastily down the stairs, but it hadn't held. There were a couple of bodies entangled in the mess, and I can only assume because they hadn't been eaten that these had been dead trying to get to the living upstairs.

There was no fucking way we were going up there. I could hear stuff banging around overhead and judging by the way the barricade in front of me had caved, we would just be trapping ourselves anyway.

Then I had an epiphany.

"Billy, why are you running? Can't you just wait for them to get in here and walk right past?"

He looked at me like I had a pair of boobs growing out of my head. "Yeah, but you can't."

I really did like this kid.

Another large room was behind the first, and this one had about a dozen cubicles, most with wide brown stains of what could only be conical arterial spray on them. There was movement at the back of the room, but it was about forty feet away. I would leave it until it came after us or we had to go that way.

Billy found a metal side door just as something crashed down the stairs in the room we had just left. Whatever it was, it was trying to extricate itself from the debris which had been set up as a barrier. Unlikely it was my favorite porn star with a bottle of tequila and a box of Trojans. Between the rattling of that thing and our bobbing flashlights, every dead asshole outside knew there were vittles in here and they wanted in. There were no windows back here and I was wondering if that was up to code when Billy pushed the door open.

He wagged his head at me, and we shut our lights off, moving cautiously and quietly into a small alley between structures. One end of the alley was a brick wall and the other had hundreds of hungry dead filing past it trying to get in the building we had just left. We couldn't go back inside, or we'd be trapped for sure, but if even one of those things looked this way, we were equally as fucked.

We hugged the stained wall as they just kept streaming past fifty feet away. I was torn between wanting to keep the door open in case they saw us and knowing that an open door was something the dead would certainly find. There was nothing in the alley to hide behind other than some trash which included another glass bottle and a rat who stared curiously at us.

Not frantic yet, I searched in all directions, but there was nothing but bricks and a rat. Then I looked up and realized what a douche I was. Thirty feet up or so something spanned the gap between buildings. It was dark as hell, so I couldn't be sure what it was, but I could see the shadow it threw on the brick. Didn't I just write how dark it was in the apocalypse up above? My eyes had adjusted a bit, and I could see stars where I couldn't before.

Yup, it was some kind of bridge across the alley. There were no fire escapes, and I wasn't Spider-Man, so I was never getting up there from here. We had to go back into the building. I mean unless the dead in front of us never looked left.

I got Billy's attention and pointed up. He instinctively ducked while throwing his arms up to protect himself like there were bats attacking, but noticed our sky-bridge and said, "Oh."

We moved back inside at about the same time the front door gave way. It had been a pretty solid door, but with the weight and might of the horde outside, it had been a short matter of time before it crumbled. It got loud quickly as the dead poured in, stumbling and smashing everything in their path. Don't forget the horrible sounds they make, Dear Reader. Those were loud too.

Billy and I had seconds to reach the stairs before the dead, so we hurried back through the cubes and got to the steps at the same time the infected did. They were very interested in our bobbing beams, and one of them actually latched on to me as my boot hit the first step. Steel flashed and two hands fell to the ground. I vaulted up the stairs three at a time with Billy behind, and he started kicking and moving the fallen barricade into the path of the oncoming dead. It wouldn't stop them, but that wasn't the plan.

A dead man greeted me at the top of the stairs. It was a crawler and as my head crested the top step, he was waiting. This one was icky, with shreds below both knees, no face, and one arm. My crowbar thumped into his head and the bone squished easily. Billy had finished his death-dam and made an appearance next to me. We needed to find roof access.

There was finally some good news as the wet shit that had dripped onto my cheek a few paragraphs ago was revealed. A hole in the roof above had let rain in enough to damage the floor to the left of us in the middle of a short skinny hall. The stuff that had pelted me had been dirty water, but just water. I looked closer and it wasn't a hole in the ceiling, it was a hatch with one of those aluminum ladders extending down from it.

"That was easy!" exclaimed my partner and he strode toward the ladder. The floor beneath him started to creak like crazy and he stopped moving, holding his arms out a little. He shot me a wide-eyed, terrified glance as the creaking reached a crescendo. A few years of neglect and being open to the elements had damaged the floor enough that my crazy comrade plunged right through without so much as a fair thee well.

Soft footfalls on the dank carpet behind me forced me to assess my situation first rather than the friend-through-the-floor. It was another kid. This one had been a little boy, maybe six. He stared at me for a moment and when he let loose with one of those growls, I knew that all the little boy that he would ever be had fled the building. I smashed his little head right the fuck in.

The whole escapade had taken five seconds and when I shined my flashlight down through the hole Billy had fallen through, I could see him starting to get up. His light had rolled away, and it illuminated shadows moving toward him. Hopefully they wouldn't find him appetizing as there was no way he could jump the ten or so feet between us and I had almost nothing to dangle through for him to climb up. Almost. I stripped my pack off quickly and held on to the top strap. "Come on!"

Billy wasn't big, but he wasn't a toddler, maybe 165 pounds? I had only one arm to dangle as the other was being used to brace myself. None of that mattered as Billy stood, glanced about, and darted out of sight.

I mean, what in the actual tree-hole fucking hell was he doing?

Unpleasant sounds from behind me made me abandon my life saving plans and I rolled onto my back to see a few of the dead bastards rounding the corner down the short hall. They must have successfully negotiated the feeble stair barrier and had made their way up the steps. They kept coming and I realized there was no way I could get to Billy.

I spun and tested the floor in front of me with my feet. If I fell through the hole, I'd be sloshing around in the rotting stomachs of who knows how many undead. "Fuck it," I said, and leapt across the four-foot chasm, the toe of my right foot briefly touching the edge of the broken flooring before I was able to latch onto the steps of the ladder. It creaked like hell, and I thought for sure I would be re-visiting the first floor, but the old girl held, and I wasted no time in climbing her.

I was halfway out of the roof access, with my legs still on the steps behind when the dead guy on the roof grabbed me. I smacked him with the pack, just as I had the dead lady downstairs, but this guy was having none of my pack-attack and shrugged it off like a true champ.

He really wanted a taste, and I didn't have time to talk turkey because the state of California was on the floor below us. He dropped the pack, and I thumped him with the crowbar. A wicked dent appeared in the side of his dome, but apparently noggin tunnels were in this year because he didn't give a shit and charged me. It was completely unfair and against the rules that this dead asshole didn't drop to the ground when I smacked him.

The cheater latched on to my shirt and leaned his stinking face in for a nibble, but I brought the pry end of the bar up under his chin for all I was worth. I'm guessing my total value is in the dollar-twenty range, because I wasn't worth shit.

The crowbar did not rip through his palate and enter his brain, it went through his jaw and came out the front of his face. I did the only thing etiquette demands when confronted with this situation. I used the pry bar to pry. I pushed against his chest and yanked back on the hooked bottom of the bar. Fucker's jaw came right off in my hands and twisted its way down the steel until his chin was resting on my fist.

He didn't seem to miss the lower half of his mouth too much. He continued his attempts to bite me, so I swung the crowbar again, his jaw flying off and the steel connecting in exactly the same spot as before. That did the ticket, and this jawless fuck collapsed. I thumped his melon into jelly just to be sure.

Loud noises were coming from the hatchway, so I moved quickly to whack any heads that came through.

I smiled. Each and every dead prick who surged forward looked up at me and each one of them fell through the hole in front of the ladder. It was a bit funny. The bottom step of the ladder rested on two inches of floor before the hole, so none of them would ever get up it. They would fall through like lemmings for eternity.

I ran to the edge of the roof to see if Billy had made it outside and when I cautiously peered down my nuts crawled up into my belly. If all the ones outside were trying to get in, they were going to exceed fire code by quite a few. The street was, literally, wall to wall with dead folks.

In the sea of dead, I caught a glimpse of a live one. It was pushing, pulling, and fighting its way toward the front. It would never get there as two-thousand dead ones were in between it and the door of the building I was perched on.

I boogied over to the plank and did the same cautious peek. The dead were filing out of the side door just as we had a few minutes ago. If Billy was in the building, he was going to have to wait a week or two to get out. If I yelled for him, I would end up starving to death on the top of one of these buildings while those dead fucks waited me out. Of the two of us, I would probably survive a bite, but he was more likely to survive being crammed into a thousand or so infected as they didn't like to nibble on him.

The whole point of these shenanigans had been to slip across the boards to the next rooftop and make our escape quietly while the dead were focused on where we just were. Looking down I could see that would never have worked. The dead were wall to wall outside in front of the structures a hundred yards away in either direction. Do the math on that one. There was no way I could go out the front door.

Sighing, I tentatively put my foot on the boards spanning the buildings. There were two of them and they looked to be some type of 2x10 barnboard. The distance between the sides of the structures was, maybe, ten feet, so looking at the boards, they were about twelve feet long.

I may have mentioned previously in another journal that while I am somewhat intelligent, I also took several classes in stupid. Aced 'em too. I am not an engineer, but I can judge weights and distances pretty well. What I couldn't possibly know is the tensile strength of these boards when they were stretched across this distance with 181 pounds of me on there. I know I am 181 pounds because of the repeated scale-stepping I did when I was a guest at the medical center recently. They weighed me once a day.

Should I really go across this chasm armed with all the knowledge of the past few paragraphs? I wouldn't be able to go out the front and there was only a side door in this building. Was there a back door in the one across the boards? Had to check. Had to. Otherwise, I'm stuck here until all these assholes move on. I'd be pretty skinny and weak before they did unless they reacted to some other stimuli.

I reached up and touched my face. It still hurt from where one of those dead dickweeds gouged me a couple days ago. I put my other foot on the board, took three steps, and was across to the other building before I could talk myself out of it. The boards didn't creak or bend at all. They felt like they could have withstood Ship riding a hippo.

I hurriedly moved to the back of the roof and once again stuck my head over the side. Lo and behold there was a steel door which emptied out into a little courtyard next to another street. Finally, some good news. The bad news was the only reason I could see the door when I was looking down was that it had been propped open. The worse news was that a dead douche shuffled out the door, looked around briefly, and shuffled right the hell back in. It was like some higher power was actively trying to screw me. The terrible news was that four dudes, all in black, in single cover formation, were taking short, quick steps toward my current location.

Initially, I thought them to be Triumvirate. The Triumvirate was a trio of assholes who grabbed power back in the early days of the plague. They had way better resources than most groups including attack helicopters and transport planes. While those dicks were a nuisance, and very much wanted me, they were not what I was seeing here.

These guys moved with perfect precision. The kind of precision you get when you train together for years. The moonlight showed them for what they were.

This was a SEAL team, and they were sent by SECNAV. What's a SECNAV, Dear Reader? That would be the Secretary of the Navy. The Big Kahuna. The dude who controls all the other military dudes in the area. I had met him before on an oil rig in the Gulf of Mexico and he had been a douche. He wanted me because I'm immune. He had tried to get me on a container ship in the Gulf, and then again at a ranch in Texas and had killed some good folks and a couple of good dogs in the attempt. He must be in cahoots with Gamboa and Baker.

He wasn't getting shit today. Fuck this guy.

GRAVEL TASTES LIKE SHIT

There was nothing for it, so I looked for a roof entrance. Where the last one had been a hatch, this one was one of those full-sized raised door jobbies that you see all over San Francisco. All I had to do was get into the building, make it to the ground floor, go out the back door, make some noise without getting taken by the SEALs, and come back for Billy, all without getting eaten, then escape with Billy without alerting the SEALs or the dead and live happily ever after.

Fuck it. Piece of cake.

I miss cake. Pizza, beer, the movie theater, and my parents too. All of those are gone unless I get really lucky. My parents were in their seventies and lived in a major city when the dead got up. No way they're alive. The other stuff can be had, but with great difficulty. We had pizza and movies on that oil rig I mentioned in the last chapter. That was great, but a bunch of dicks blew it up, movies and all. But a beer? An ice cold, fizzy, mass produced, American beer in a can? It had been a long while.

I was thinking about Bud Light when I yanked the roof door open, shining my flashlight into the darkness. One of them had been right on the other side and it wasted no time in trying to taste me. It lunged and because of the beer, I wasn't in the right state of mind for a zombie attack. Stupid, really, as zombies are kind of the point of this story.

It was a kid. Another dead kid. I don't like the dead in general, but the kids are the worst.

Anyway, the little bastard grabbed me and darted right in for chow. Muscle memory taught from Remo and practiced over the past few months kicked in and I brought my forearm down on this dead kid's forearms to break his grip. I heard a couple of snaps, waited for pain to lance through my arm, then realized the angle on the boy's arms was all wrong.

Undeterred with the paltry effect of a couple of broken appendages, the dead thing realized its mouth was closer to me than it had been before and the little fucker bit me on the hand. He pulled his head back and again I had to wonder where the pain was. Somebody in the pain department was getting fired, because other than a quick thump, there had been no pain at all. He tried for another nibble, but I chucked him to the side and his arms ripped away from his body. I got some of his fluids on me and that was icky, but icky is better than being bitten. Fact.

How did he still have fluids? I mean the kid must have been dead a couple of years. Shouldn't he be all desiccated and shit? I was thinking of other fluids than beer when the boy looked up at me from where he had landed in a heap. The thing had no lower jaw. I'd seen this a few times, but you still shit yourself when one of them grabs you. I lashed out with my boot, once, twice, three times and he was released. I checked my hand and there was no blood, no flesh missing.

I heaved a sigh of relief, but it was short lived as something grabbed me from behind. I spun and it spun with me, but miraculously, it let go and went sprawling right next to the re-killed kid. This one had been an adult female when it died, and it was enormous, or had been. She had a fully excavated midsection, disgusting bits of her hanging into and out of it in stringy nastiness. I kicked her too, but it took six kicks and a thump from my crowbar to put her down for good. I hoped it was the kid's mom. At least they would have been together in death.

I gave her a stab in the eye with the chisel end of the tool for poops and laughter. She would never bite anyone again. I was wiping the crowbar on her rotten pants when I heard suppressed gunfire from inside the building.

They would eventually come up here and they would capture me. I had to move into the building and confront them there as there was fuck-all to hide behind up here. I could get up on top of the door thing, but I might get one if I was lucky before they got me. I would have to get past them or take them all out quickly. They were totally unprepared for the fuckery I was about to unleash. I am a badass now and would not go quietly.

Except if I made a fucking sound we were all lunch so, I literally had to go quietly. Also, these are SEALs and no matter how tough I am, they eat nails for breakfast and spit bullets for dinner. Come to think of it, I'm not even that tough. A bit of a bitch, even, but I will deny that to anyone not reading this journal.

Shit.

I moved through the door, shining my three-dollar Walmart flashlight into the darkness below. There was nothing on the stairs or near the closed door at the bottom. The mom and son must have been trapped in here or afraid to leave, one or both died and turned, and they had been here ever since.

After creeping downward, each step sounding like a gunshot on the creaky old wood, I put my ear to the door at the bottom of the stairs. I couldn't hear anything at all other than the far-off sounds of scuffle and the occasional suppressed shot. It wasn't enough to bring the horde down on us, as that amount of dead people made a ton of noise, but I could hear it from this side of the door.

I pushed the door open slowly and to my chagrin, the hinges sounded like chainsaws that needed oil. I pushed faster to make the sound go quicker, but that shit was loud. Nothing showed up, hungry or armed, so I had that going for me. I made it past a bunch of rooms with closed doors before I got to a wide stairway leading down.

"*Copy,*" I heard someone whisper. "*SITREP as follows: Wolf Platoon Detachment Charlie proceeding to target. Moderate resistance but the bastards are sneaky. Wolf-Charlie two and three down, Wolf-Charlie one infected but mission capable. Target is one level up and eight meters east of current position. Will confirm when target is acquired. Comms going dark. Charlie out.*"

One level up and eight... Motherfucker. They bugged me. They had friggin' bugged me again. When was I going to cease with the dumbassery and remember the diabolical nature of these fuckers? Gamboa and Baker had taken tons of fluids out of me, but I hadn't watched those assholes to see if they had put anything *in* me. I ran my hands up and down myself but searching for a tiny bug which was probably under my skin while in the dark was pointless.

I had no guns to shoot these dicks, and they knew exactly where I was, likely down to the angstrom. I'm sure I had my own fucking satellite by now. The bitch of it was these SEALs were only doing their job. As it happens, their job was to bring me in, and I had had enough of that lab rat garbage. Fuck that noise. The good news is they wouldn't shoot me.

I didn't wanna kill them, but it was them or me. Somehow, I doubt they would want me talking at all, let alone listen to what I had to say. Hell, me going with them was probably best for humanity, but you know what, Dear Reader? Humanity was doomed anyway. Not because of this plague, but because we simply can't get along. At least the dead didn't kill each other because somebody liked ketchup on their hot dog and somebody else doesn't.

I couldn't see any lights bobbing up the stairs but that was because these dudes had night vision. Night vision is cool. You know who doesn't have night vision? This guy. (I just pointed to myself.) I did have a flashlight, though, and placed it on the moldy carpet pointed at the stairwell.

Although I couldn't see them, I knew the hunter on point threw his fist into the air when he saw the light. I knew it looked really cool. I rolled the torch to the edge of the wall and opened a door with a big glass window in it and stepped inside. The door hadn't made so much as a squeak and no undead were waiting with salivating jaws to bite me.

Lucky for me the top step squeaked when one of their black booted feet stepped on it. At least I hoped it was the top step. I leaned out the door and chucked the crowbar hoping the night vision was compromised by the flashlight beam. Remember that part about not shooting me? Yeah, I had been woefully inaccurate with that statement.

Four suppressed shots shattered the glass and punched through the sheetrock near where I had been standing, but I had juked back the moment I had tossed my only weapon. It definitely had hit one of them, but I was unsure as to the damage done. Using whatever confusion I may have sown, I bolted down the hall, awaiting that shot that would catch me in the lung or the leg, but it never came as I reached the stairs and climbed them towards the roof.

There was nowhere to hide. I could perch behind the roof access, but they would find me in seconds. No chance I could jump from this high, it was a forty-foot drop. I quickly searched the kid and his maybe-mom, but other than a pair of nail clippers, there was nothing on either of them. But... I had an epiphany. The kid weighed, maybe, sixty pounds. A bit heavy, but heavy was good.

I dragged him to the left side of the open door and waited, my hands wrapped around his little ankles. My plan was to smack a motherfucker with another motherfucker. I heard a creak right next to me, saw a rifle suppressor poke through the open doorway and swung that dead little boy as hard as I could. The kid impacted the door frame with an awful crunch, but there was no SEAL. He had rolled through the door and was now pointing an exceptionally large rifle at me. It was just a short-barrel M4, but when you're on the business end of one of those, it looks like a damn cannon.

"Fuuuuck," I whined.

"Damn skippy," the douche agreed. "On your knees." He motioned with his rifle toward the roof top.

"No," I said and folded my arms.

His eyes were pretty much the only part of him I could see with his balaclava on, and his eyebrows shot skyward. He had expected neither resistance nor tomfoolery. Fucker got both. They had shot at me downstairs, but I was guessing it was because they hadn't known it was me.

He took neither his gaze nor his rifle off me when he spoke into his radio. "Wolf-Charlie actual to Barricade. Doc, where can I shoot this asshole so he can both walk and know I mean business? Copy that."

Oh fuck...

I heard the suppressed shot, and it pushed me back a step. Prick had put one through my side, just above my right hip. It was exactly where a buddy of mine had accidentally shot me a while ago. Probably went through the same hole.

I went down on one knee when the pain decided to make its presence known. It hurt. A lot.

"You dick!" I said, clutching my side. Blood flowed freely through the hole.

"You want another one?"

I shook my head and gritted my teeth. "No thank you."

"Both knees," he commanded, and I complied.

He moved cautiously to my wounded side and fumbled for a second trying to extricate a pair of zip-tie handcuffs from his vest. The second he looked away, before he could do anything else, I shot forward, knocking his rifle aside with my head as I bowled him over. I had no illusions that I would be able to win a fight with this guy, but I wasn't going down without one, even with a hole in me.

I carried him forward for about ten feet before he got the upper hand. He flipped me around so that I would land first when we fell, and fall we did. Right on top of the dead lady I had re-killed a few minutes before. It was squishy and stinky and in all ways nasty, but had I landed on the gravel of the roof, the end of this fight would have been different.

His rifle was pinned between us, and I wasn't about to let him get a bead on me, so I kneed him in the nuts. He grunted and I knew I was screwed. He thumped me in the side of the dome, which hurt way too much, then the fucker punched me in the boo-boo he had just given me. I screamed on that one, but it was a whisper scream because I knew what screaming would do for all of us. I grabbed his vest with my right hand and pulled his face into my rising forehead, his nose exploding in a shower of warm wet. A true fighter, this guy kept going, but I rolled right, trying to unbalance him.

In a moment of genius, I hit the magazine eject button on his M4, caught the falling magazine, and brought it around into the side of his face. His hand slipped and the poor bastard's forearm went directly into the mouth of zombie lady. I knew she wasn't going to bite him, and we were in the perfect position, so I elbowed her in the jaw as hard as I could. The SEAL yanked his arm from her mouth and did everything he could to get away from the dead woman and me. I punched him in the face and was able to get his rifle sling over his head.

He stood up staring at his forearm, now on the deadly side of his own gun.

Blood trickled down into his glove, and he yanked back the sweater thing he was wearing. One of those semicircles of death was looking right at him. Teeth marks and broken skin. He swallowed and looked at me. "Do you think…" he trailed off and stared at his arm again.

"Dude, I dunno." I felt terrible. I had bitten him with somebody else's mouth, and he was likely to die because of it. I didn't want to feel shitty, because this guy was going to bring me to a horrible place, but I did feel bad.

He reached slowly for his sidearm. "Whoa! Hold on!" I whisper-yelled at him.

"It's for me," he answered.

I let him pull his weapon, a worn but beautiful Sig Sauer that I was absolutely going to appropriate, and he placed the suppressed barrel against his temple.

"Hey, man," I said, "We don't know if that—"

He interrupted, "Yeah, we do." The sound of the single suppressed shot made me jump, even though I knew it had been coming.

Son of a bitch. I hadn't wanted this guy or any of those SEALs to die. For what? Me? A possibility even though those assholes at Baldy Mountain had run tests for months? There was no cure for this. Even if they were capable of using my blood to stop someone from turning, there would still be a few billion dead people walking around looking for nosh.

I stooped down to retrieve the SEAL's Sig. He had a couple of extra mags in a MOLLE, and I grabbed the whole pack from his vest. I heard a barely audible crunch on the gravel behind me and tried to roll away, but something thumped me in the dome, and I was suddenly tasting rocks. Part of me tried to get up, sparkling motes dancing across my tenuous consciousness, but another whack and everything was dark.

CRASH

The wind blowing across my face and through my hair woke me. Wherever I was it was loud, and I was thoroughly confused.

And my fucking head hurt. My eyes tried to open of their own volition, but I knew opening them would send tendrils of agony shooting through my broken head, so I sent an override to the eyeball guy, and we kept them closed. It only took a moment before the pain said, "Hey bro, vacation is over!"

The pain came and he stayed. I wanted to put my hands to my head because everybody knows you cradle your dome when it hurts, but it seems I was to be denied that simple pleasure as well. My hands were tied firmly together between my knees with a zip tie.

Another wave of pain crossed my mind, this time his buddy nausea showed up with him. There needs to be a concussion protocol in the apocalypse. Everyone, literally everyone, wants to stove my roof in. They all hit me in the head and it's bad form. Eventually, that shit is gonna kill me or worse, turn me into a cabbage. My side hurt too, but I could feel a taped bandage there. The head was worse.

I had figured out I was in a helicopter before I opened my eyes, but I still needed to look around. Two guys were working on another who was laying on the floor... deck?... of the bird, and two other guys were looking at me.

One of the dudes said something and all four of them glared directly at me before the two administering aid went back to work. I wasn't fortunate enough to have the headphones that the other guys had so I couldn't hear what they said to each other.

The guy on the floor was naked except for a pair of OD green skivvies and he didn't look good. One of the medic dudes stood and spoke into his microphone, then the other three guys kneeled, stood, lifted the mostly naked guy up by his shoulders and ankles, and pitched him out the fucking open door.

I got the stares again and two of the guys sat on either side of me. The other two sat on a bench across from us and it was easy to tell that they all wanted to make me dead. The guy that just took a nose-dive must have been the prick that knocked me senseless on the roof. He also must have been bitten.

The dude sitting on my right put a pair of white ear-muff things on me so I could hear what they were saying.

"Half our squad. A whole fucking fire team, lost."

"We could chuck him out the door like we did to Savvy. We're only a couple hundred feet up, he might live."

"Stow that shit. We kill him and they died for nothing."

"I didn't ask to be kidnapped," I added, and the guy who had given me the headphones elbowed me in the ribs so hard I'm pretty sure my spleen *did* join their buddy, Savvy.

"Our squaddies are dead because of you," the first guy said.

"Bullshit," I shot right back, "they're dead because your stupid SECNAV told you to come get me and you don't even fucking know why. So, you can lovingly caress my boys while your head bobs, you fuckstick."

Headphone douche's elbow shot towards the same spot on my side, but I beat him and held up my own elbow to intercept. It was difficult because my hands were zipped to my feet, but I was able to reach. The elbows collided, and for fuck's sake that hurt worse than when he had gotten me in the ribs, but the grunt and subsequent cursing from this asshole was worth it.

"We're SEALs, asshole, it's what we do."

"You mean in addition to always having balls on your chin?"

The wind from the open doors was refreshing, but it started to get cold and one of the guys stood up and closed them. They slid like the doors in a mini-van. I don't know helicopters, but I know this one. It was a Blackhawk.

One of these asshats had a map, and he spoke to one of the pilots, "We'll fuel up at China Lake and then head southeast to Connor." The guy looked at me. "Then your ass gets put on a plane and I don't have to worry about you anymore."

I shrugged the best I could with my hands zip tied. "You could just drop me off, I don't want to be a bother. Be nice if you landed first though."

Guy was gonna elbow me again. Fucker just didn't learn. I growled and flashed my teeth at him. "Try it, fucker! Maybe I'll bite you and see how you do."

This was the first time my voice had changed. The growl was old hat, I had perfected it, but my voice sounded a little like Thorne's and that scared me as much as it did this fucking SEAL. He couldn't get away from me fast enough, but was buckled next to me and couldn't move far. I couldn't see them, but I knew the whites of my eyes were full of red.

"He's turned!" the shithead screamed while fumbling for his weapon. "Shoot him!"

I screamed back at him, "Stupid, fucking SQUID! What the hell do you think they want me for?" I sat perfectly still while they all pointed weapons at me. Prick would never elbow me again, of that, I was sure.

The dude who looked like the leader looked deadly, but he wavered. "Say something!"

"SEALs have little dicks."

They all exchanged glances and lowered their weapons. Even headphone douche.

"What the hell is wrong with you?" one of the guys across from me asked.

"That list is long, but currently my biggest fault is that I'm being kidnapped and escorted who knows where, by a gaggle of shitheads following orders they don't understand."

The medic looked at me in awe for a few moments, I get that a lot. Awe. "Why exactly do they want you?"

"Probably because I've been bitten half a dozen times and haven't turned. They think they can use my blood to synthesize some kind of anti-virus, but I know a few things they don't."

"Like what?"

"First of all, this isn't a virus. At least not one like you're thinking. It has nothing to do with blood, so mine won't help. Secondly, I was a guest at a facility which studies things exactly like what's going on and you know what they found? Nothing. They couldn't find any type of foreign organism at all either in me or any of the reanimated dead. They didn't know what's happening or what's making it happen."

My voice had changed back from evil monster to me as I had spoken to them. It was cool to listen to myself as I explained. I was about to launch into a long-winded explanation of how the current situation on earth was actually due to a computer virus instead of some DNA, but God decided to step in and fuck with stuff, so I never got to finish.

"Strap in!" came screaming over our headphones.

"Check him," the leader guy told the dudes to my right and left. Both of them began to ensure I was neatly tucked away.

Leader guy leaned backward and shouted into his mic, "Pilot, SITREP!"

"Master Caution is on. Transmission light is on. Probably a gearbox failure because of our maintenance schedule. Gonna have to set her down! Swiss cheese!"

I shrugged my eyebrows. I love Swiss cheese. When the pilot had been talking, I could hear a vicious beeping going on over the comms. It was that same beeping you hear in any airplane or helicopter crash in the movies.

There was a grinding sound, and something popped above, metal tinkling as it cascaded loudly down the hull behind us and into space. The bird started making funny noises and we slowed way down so quickly I felt myself shift forward. I could smell electronics burning too.

Terrific. It had been a while since I had been in an aircraft crash. Memories...

A NAME TO REMEMBER

Something's on fire. I can smell it. Taste it too, but the taste is mixed with copper. I can hear something beeping, but it sounds far away. My wrist hurts, but my head hurts worse. It's hot.

My right eyelid literally scraped across my eye when it opened. It was like dragging my eye across a sandy road. Left eye decided to stay shut even though I should be in charge of that decision. Once again, I should have kept my eyes closed.

Guy across from me has half his face missing. There's blood everywhere. Like, everywhere. It's dripping from the ceiling, or whatever you call a ceiling in a helicopter. Actually, the ceiling is the door because we're on our side. The guy's face and arm are gone because the other guy has chewed them away. The second guy is reaching for me, having given up on the first guy. First guy must be too dead to eat anymore. Oh, yup, first guy just opened his eyes. Too dead. Now there are two of them in here with me.

Well, at least two. Elbow-douche is above me, strapped in, and he looks to be dead, but I can't tell. His arm and head are dangling where I could reach if I wanted to chew on him, but my head hurts and he doesn't look appetizing. The other guy's head and right arm are nowhere to be found. Nope! There they are! On the door below me. His eyes are also open, and he looks a might peckish, but he'll never be able to do anything about it.

My eye won't open and there's blood dripping from my head. Did it finally happen? Did something hit me in the head so hard there's a new hole? The universe has been smacking me in the dome for a while now, so why not?

"Screw you, Universe."

"Screw who?"

I almost shit myself. People say that when they get startled. They don't really mean it, but they wish to convey how startled they were by using an exaggeration. This is not an exaggeration. I felt the turtle push his way out to assess the situation and then retreat when he realized his escape route had been compromised. I'm super happy about that too, but there would need to be an emergency session very soon or things would get messy around the brown-eye.

Elbow-douche was staring at me with *his* brown eyes, and I burst out laughing. It really hurt.

"I'm glad you're alive," I told him.

He answered by drawing his suppressed sidearm and pointing it at me. The aim was brief, though, and he re-directed it towards his buddies. Three pops later and there were only living in the compartment. He unbuckled himself before I could protest and hit me pretty hard on the way down when he fell past me. He had tried to hang on to the belt, but gravity won, and he dropped like a rock.

He didn't move for a moment, and I thought he had killed himself. He looked up at me, wincing, and stood. "C'mon."

I was closer to the ground when I released, but he still caught me. It hurt him too, I could tell. I sighed. "And now we gotta climb back up." He cut my zip ties with his knife and we did. The guy didn't utter a sound of complaint. It had been burning hot in the chopper, but the sun out here was ferocious. We were in a desert, but I could see mountains that looked not too far off. He passed me a bag and then I helped him out. He was drenched in gore. The guy had his gun on me the moment our boots touched the sand.

"I still have a mission," he told me and coughed. He held his hand out for the bag, and I passed it to him. The effort must have been too much to extend his hand, because he fell to one knee, his focus decided to leave the building, and he crashed backward on the sand. "Don't eat me," he said and passed out.

He came-to about five hours later. I checked his watch as I was unfortunate and no longer had one. I had thought the mountains were only a couple of miles off, but I had vastly underestimated the distance. They still looked a couple of miles off and I had been pulling this asshole across the scrub on a make-shift stretcher I had fashioned out of a piece of broken helicopter and a hunk of netting.

I had found the only tree in the whole of the desert, and we were currently sitting under it, although the sun was almost down. It had dropped twenty degrees at least, and that made me happy. I had a fire going when the guy opened his eyes.

"Where…" he started, and I brought him some water. I put the water bladder to his mouth, and he took a hefty gulp. "Thanks."

I nodded and watched him search furiously for his sidearm before his eyes locked on me. I drew the weapon and pointed it at him. "Sucks, huh?" I asked before I reversed it and held it out to him by the suppressor. "You were pushing the can into the sand when you were sleeping. I cleaned it."

He was staring at me funny and ejected the mag for inspection. "All there," I told him. I had already eaten a pimento loaf MRE, and I passed one to him. He reached for it but stopped his hand halfway and I could see he was in pain.

"The bruising on your side tells me you probably have a couple of busted ribs, Chief. Likely internal bleeding, but I'm not a doctor. Could just be you being a pussy." I tore the MRE open with my teeth and dumped some water into the heater. "The pilots didn't make it," I added.

"My mission—" he started, but I cut him off.

"Is fucked. You shoot me and you fail your mission. Same thing if you die. You need me to get you out of here, and I might need you to shoot some dead people or bad guys. What do *you* think, Todd?"

"My name isn't—"

I cut him off, "I was talking to him." I pointed at the skeleton next to him. He started a bit, but to his credit took it in stride. "He was under the tree, broken leg and a hole in his skull when we got here. Didn't seem right to drag him off if he was here first. He must have popped himself when he realized he wasn't going to make it." Elbow-douche didn't fail to notice the two rifles propped against the tree next to Todd. Both were well within reach.

"You gonna kill me?" he asked.

"Bruh, are you alive now? Why the hell would I pull you out of a helicopter and drag your fat ass across the desert if I was going to kill you? I'm not interested in your death. But I'm very interested in my continued, un-imprisoned life. You and I will have issues if you try to take me wherever it was you were trying to take me. On that day, yeah, I'm gonna kill you. More likely I'll make you kill me. I'm not a SEAL."

He swallowed some water. "Where are we?"

"The fucking desert."

"Are you always such a pain in the ass?"

"Yes."

I held up a broken little transceiver by the short antenna and wiggled it at him. I had found it in my boot sewn into the underside of the tongue and had smashed it immediately upon finding it. "Your dick buddies won't be finding me this way."

I pulled the MRE away from the tree I had leaned it against. "You'll have to eat it out of the heater. My bowl is on Alcatraz likely covered in zombie goo." It was at that point I realized I would never see my SOG again. It might seem trivial to you, Dear Reader, that I would think of a lost knife instead of friends and family, but I would see my family again, of that I was certain. That knife had been with me longer than most of the people I knew. It was a SOG Seal Pup, and I loved it. I love it still. Not only was it functional, not only had it destroyed dozens, possibly hundreds of the dead, it was sexy. Razor sharp and battle scarred, that knife was just like me. A two by four. A fucking stud.

I just had to get back to my family. After I figured out where they were.

"What's the plan?" he asked me as I was thinking up a plan.

I pointed, "We walk that way until we can appropriate a vehicle. Then we drive until we can't anymore, rinse and repeat until I'm standing with my family. You're welcome to come... What's your name?"

"Chauncy."

"You're fucking kidding me."

"Nope."

A SEAL named Chauncy. Earth is well and truly fucked.

"It was my great-grandfather's name. His father was a slave who was given the name Chauncy when he got to America. My dad wanted to honor him. He said that—"

"Wow!" I interrupted. "Great story. A-typical." I stood from my haunches and noticed something odd. It was a dust cloud about a mile out. It was either a tiny sandstorm or... I reached into the pack I had dragged along with Chauncy... poor bastard... and yanked a pair of binoculars. I sighed and dropped them back into the pack.

"Our secret is out, One with the Lame Name. The unliving are upon us. Can you walk?"

"How many?"

"More than one. Can you walk?"

He nodded and I helped him stand. He winced, but I realized you could remove this guy's appendix with a plastic spoon, and he would never utter a word.

He put his palm over his eyes and stared back the way we had come. "Pass me the glasses."

In short order he was peering through the binoculars at what I had just seen.

He sighed, and while still looking said, "Fuck."

"Fuck?"

"Fuck."

"Fuck, like, how many?"

"Too many to count. They're about two thousand meters out." He glanced at the sky and ran his eyes back and forth across it. "It'll be dark in two hours, but they'll be here long before then."

"Alright, so let's book. You can walk, yeah?"

"Damn right."

I made to kick the fire out, but he stopped me. "Leave it. They might be drawn to it and by the time they get here we'll be gone. Maybe it will distract them."

Solid point. I shouldered the pack and one of the rifles I had appropriated from the crash. I passed the other rifle to him, and he immediately checked both the load and the action on the rifle. We had three hundred and eight rifle rounds total and eighty rounds a piece for the sidearms. There was a standard med kit, six MREs, four grenades, two small bricks of C4 explosive with a detonator, and some breaching charges. Two extra knives but no radios, as the one in the pack was non-functional. I had brought the radio anyway in case the SEAL could fix it. The big find was a pair of night vision goggles. These things were the bomb.

He was breathing heavily, and we hadn't taken a step yet. I started packing up the litter I had carried him on, and he asked me what I was doing.

"You're tough," I told him. "But you look like you're about to take a dirt nap so this could come in handy if I have to drag you. Really, I should leave you for the dead, especially after that elbow shit you pulled on the bird, but that isn't me. I don't leave good people. I know you were only doing your job, but that job is over. Done. I'm no terrorist or drug kingpin. There are no cartels or Bin Ladens here for you to strategically eliminate. I'm immune and the fucking idiots in charge think they can use my blood to fix everything. The problem is for all their education and time in the military or whatever field they're in, they know precisely dick. My blood can't cure this virus because this is a fucking computer virus."

And that's where I lost him. I could immediately tell he either didn't believe or couldn't wrap his head around the problem at hand. Honestly though, can you? I mean it's tough for me and I know it's fact. I didn't have all the minutiae, and I wasn't about to mansplain shit I wasn't one hundred percent on to a guy who could kill me with an eyelash. Besides, I was cold, and my fuck-it meter was pinning in the red.

We started to leave, and I looked back at my cozy fire and the skeleton leaning next to it. "See ya, Todd."

PLANTS AND BIRDS AND ROCKS AND THINGS

Chauncy (still can't write it without a giggle) and I headed northwest across the desert. We had gone, maybe, four miles when it was evident he could go no further. It was pretty cold, his watch said forty-six degrees. He was coughing steadily and shivering. I shined the light in his face, and his lips and chin had blood on them. When I got closer, I could hear him wheezing through every short, heavy breath.

"Lung's punctured," he rasped. "Must be the broken ribs. Breathing is hard now and very painful." He took a horrible breath for emphasis, his face a rictus of agony. "Tension pneumothorax. It's when—"

"I know what it is. The med kit in the pack doesn't have any needles, how do we fix it?"

He drew his big-ass knife, and my nuts were once again tickling my epiglottis from the inside. This guy wanted me to perform delicate, life-saving surgery on him using a fucking pig sticker with no anesthetic or medical training. I mean the wife had showed me the best way to suture a wound and I could figure out the tabs on a Band Aid, but what the fuck? Seriously?

"Seriously?" I repeated, this time out loud.

He passed me the blade. Even that small action caused him pain, but I could tell it was downright agony when he lifted his shirt. "Stick it in a half inch then turn it a quarter inch. Here," He touched a spot on his side between two ribs. Holy Jesus H Christ in a chariot driven side car, was I going to stab this man?

My mouth had already been dry, because of the hot and cold of the desert, but every molecule of moisture took the evaporation train right out of my pie hole at that juncture. Resigned, I searched the med kit for a bottle of antiseptic, but all I came up with was swabs. I wiped the end of his knife down and he put his arm up as high as he could.

"Do it."

I put my hand on his side to steady myself, the knife point pressed against his skin. "Ok, on three, ready? One…" I jabbed the knife in and turned it clockwise. There was a sound like PFFFFfffff and blood blew out the hole then dripped down his side. He could immediately breathe and started nodding.

He moved his arm up and down a bit, grimacing. "Good work. What happened to two and three?"

"Stupid numbers, really. Overrated."

We were smiling at each other through the moonlight when an emaciated infected stumbled from the darkness, grabbed him, and bit into his shoulder.

He reacted swiftly, and as previously noted, the guy was good with elbows. He brought his right one up into the jaw of his attacker and the thing's head snapped back. I jumped it and drove the knife I had just stuck him with into its eye. It dropped without much complaint.

"Let me see!" I yanked his shirt over his shoulder by the collar. That semi-circle of doom was barely oozing blood.

He had been watching me and noticed the look on my face. "Well, shit."

At this point in the plague, it did nobody any good to theorize whether he would survive or not. He wouldn't and we both knew it. I was going to say something witty when we heard more of the things around us in the darkness. We were prepared for a few of them, but a few dozen would take us down for sure. The first one stumbled out of the scrub and Chauncy shot it with his suppressed sidearm. My handgun had no suppressor, so I rushed forward and gave another of the things a downward stab. A third grabbed my arm, but I spun out of it and drove the blade into its temple.

We dispatched two more of them before we ran out of infected. That was when we heard another odd sound in the gloom. We glanced at each other as a horse casually strolled into the area where we were as if looking for a cold beer. He was saddled but riderless and stopped to glare at us. He regarded us with that same disdain an animal displays with new people. I pulled a water bottle from the pack and when I unscrewed the cap the horse perked right up. I held the bottle to his lips, and he astoundingly drank without spilling much. He took the whole bottle, but there were only two more plus my water bladder.

"Can you ride?" I asked my compatriot.

"I'm from Brooklyn."

It was a bitch getting him on the horse with his ribs, but he made it. I put him in front of me so I could both hold him on and use the reins. We rode at something between a trot and canter for about two hours before he asked me to stop.

"I'm infected," he told me and vomited. He didn't get a drop of puke on the horse and together we were able to get him down to the ground. We had made good time on horseback getting away from the horde, and I estimated they were about three miles behind us. "I can't ride anymore."

"Yes, you fucking can."

"I'll only slow you down."

"Listen, shithead, we have literally just been through the desert on a horse with no name. I'm not leaving you behind to get eaten by those things!"

"The horse can't carry two for much longer, look at him." I did. I threw him a glance and he did look exhausted with his head down and a bit of sweat on his chest. It was cold and I didn't know if horses could get sick like a sweaty person in the cold would.

"I'm not leaving you," I said with less conviction. We both heard it.

"Thanks for helping me out. I wouldn't have made it out of the helicopter and I sure as shit wouldn't have made it this far without you."

"Yeah, enough. Let's blow this one-horse taco stand."

He drew his Glock and pointed it at my face. The action chilled me to the bone. "I would have completed my mission. I would have brought you in even though you saved my life over and over again. What does that say about me?"

"That you're a good sailor."

He lowered the weapon. "Thanks," he said, put the suppressor to his temple, and put his brains on the sand.

Just like that I was alone again. Except for a horse.

It took me an hour to dig a hole and bury him. In the end I took everything he had and either put it in the pack or on the horse. I had folded his hands on his belly, covered his face with his shemagh, and left him under four inches of California scrub. I didn't think I had time to dig deeper and all I had was an entrenching tool I had found on the horse. I hope Remo will forgive me.

I regarded my newest pal. "We good?"

He didn't answer but did look away from me. I put my foot in one of his wooden stirrups and he walked forward like an asshole. I hopped to catch up with him with one foot in the stirrup for a moment and fell on my ass.

So, it was gonna be like that.

I grabbed him by the reins and glared into his eyes. "Listen up, shithead, I'm about as thrilled over this as you are. I don't know where your rider is, but if we don't get out of here, a horde of those dead pricks will be dining on us posthaste. I just lost what I thought was my friend, but who ultimately would have served me up to the bad guys who think they are good guys. Confused? Yeah, me too. Now I'm going to get back on you, and if you piss me off, you can expect a bullet to the junk. You feel me?"

I had dealt with a dickhead horse before and what you had to do was let them know who's boss. He weighed 1100 pounds, and I was 180 soaking wet. He had his size, but I had a friggin' gun. Four guns, actually, and a couple of knives.

He let me get up on him and I made a clicking sound that my buddy in Texas had shown me a while ago. We moved forward at a walk, and I glanced back at the ground over Chauncy. Poor kid. He was probably a decade younger than me and had served his country even through an unimaginable plague.

I used the NVGs to peer through the darkness and was surprised to see the mini-swarm had caught up to us. They were about a half mile back and heading in our direction with that plodding gait. I guess the campfire we had left burning hadn't done its job. I coaxed the horse into a trot, and we moved northwest.

We walked and trotted until 5:20 am. The sun would be up in an hour, so I thought it a good time to make a quick fire and have something to eat. The water situation was good for me, but I would need more for the horse, or he would drink us dry. In our haste to get out of the gore-drenched helicopter, neither of us had thought to take a map and there wasn't one in the bag. I mean, it was stupid of me not to grab the map, but how stupid were these SEALs to not have one in their go bags? Bitching about it wouldn't help and I was hungry.

The horse had a sack of food tied to him and I put some in a feeder I found in a small pack on his ass. My shit was heating up in the MRE heater and I could hear him munching greedily on his oats or whatever the fuck they were.

We had to have at least four hours on the pus bags and the only shut-eye I'd had in the past sixty hours or so had been when I was unconscious during travel. I figured I would grab some sleep while I could. The sun would wake me up. I kept the saddle and bridle on the horse in case we had to vamoose quickly, and I tied him to a big branch on the ground. No tree, just a big branch. Go figure.

The horse also thought that sleep was a good idea and crashed down right next to me and the fire. He looked like a big dog.

"What's your name I wonder? Trigger? Ed? Artax?" He snorted. Prick actually snorted at me and closed his eyes. "How about Big Dog?" He opened his eyes briefly and closed them again.

"Yeah, I like Big Dog." I closed my eyes too.

CHILD'S PLAY

Click

"Oh shit."

"You got that right, asshole. Get up."

I was looking up at the exceptionally large barrel of a cocked lever action rifle. Beautiful thing. Blued barrel, dark walnut furniture. Bit of brass where the black rear sight aperture attached to a short picatinny rail. It was so close to my schnoz that I had to cross my eyes to see the business end of it. The hole this thing would put in me could easily fit a golf ball, and that was going in. Coming out would be... messy. Two men and a woman, all with their guns on me, were looking either smug or angry, I couldn't tell. Either way, Dear Reader, it wasn't looking too good for our hero. I had slept straight into very early morning and the sun that was supposed to wake me had been up for an hour or so.

The dude with the rifle up my nostril looked like that grizzled short order cook you see in the movies saying, "Order up!" with that broken glass voice as he slams his palm on a counter bell. He wanted to shoot me. The woman behind him used to be heavy-set but had thinned out due to hunger. She had curly salt and pepper hair and definitely wanted to shoot me. The guy behind her, with his hand holding four horse's reins scanned in all directions. He was tall and wore a balaclava. I couldn't see his face, but I'm pretty sure he wanted to shoot me.

Big Dog was standing idly, getting his neck scratched by a fifteen-year-old girl, also armed, but her gun was holstered. She glared at me with an unmistakable hatred, and I *know* she wanted to shoot me.

"Where were you on that one?" I asked the horse with a side eye.

The guy with the rifle looked confused, "What? Get up! Reeeeaaaal slow!" He had drawn out the 'real' to ensure I got his meaning.

I put my hands up and realized that was stupid as I needed them to push off from the ground. I stood, then I did put 'em up.

"Easy," I said.

The woman raised her AR-15 to firing position. She had one of my stubby CQBR M4s slung over her shoulder, "Where'd you get that horse?"

Well, shit. I had my apprehensions on whether they would believe my story, but this wasn't my first rodeo with that. I snickered at my use of the word "rodeo" what with all the horses around us, even if it had been in my head.

"Something funny?"

"Yeah. My story. I was in a helicopter crash yesterday about fifteen miles back. Everybody died except me and another guy."

Two of them looked around, "Where's—"

"I'm not finished. The two of us trekked across the desert but he was hurt bad. Last night some dead found us, and they got him. This horse literally walked out of the desert during the fight."

"And where's Chuckie?"

"Sorry, I don't know Chuckie or where he is."

The guy with the beautiful rifle looked confused. "Chuckie wasn't on Pie?"

I had no idea what he had said to me. None. He had spoken English words but had compiled them into a sentence that was indecipherable. I just stood there with my hands up not knowing anything.

"Just shoot him!" the young girl said.

Here I am, just winning over the hearts and minds of our youth.

"We need to find Chuckie before we shoot him."

"We been trackin' you all night," one of the dudes said. "That horse's name is Pie, and he had a rider when he left yesterday."

"The inimitable Chuckie?" I asked.

"What? Yeah, Chuckie. He's with us."

I shrugged. "He's likely with them," I told him, throwing a thumb toward the oncoming horde. As if to punctuate my statement, a voice came over the woman's radio.

"Harriet, you got ten minutes and them dead ones'll be on ya. Best high tail it outa there. Still no sign of Chuckie out here."

"Gotcha, Carl. We'll be long gone by then."

The one with the lever action stood up from his crouch. "Tie him up and get him up on Pie. Julie, you're lightest so you go with him. If he pulls any malarky, kill him."

Malarky. Dude had said malarky. Nobody says malarky. My grandma said malarky once. Once.

I stuck my hands out and the kid wrapped a rope around my wrists three times, then overlapped crossways. I flexed my arms and spread my hands apart as far as possible without showing her what I was trying to accomplish while she was doing it.

I heard a low whistle behind me and glanced back to see the dude who hadn't spoken pulling a brick of C4 from the pack. "Now what in the hell do you need this for?"

"To blow shit up."

He nodded and put it back in the pack, then shouldered the pack. I guess the boom was coming with us. I used the saddle horn to leap up into the saddle with my tied hands and offered them to the kid. She slapped them away and hopped up behind me. "I know you killed Chuckie," she told me. "Can't wait until they cut you down."

"Hate to disappoint you, kid, but I haven't killed anybody lately. Your horse found me, not the other way around."

"Liar." She grabbed the reins, made that same clicking sound I had made, and we took off at a canter. Two minutes later, Harriet called for a stop.

"Carl says there's two groups heading our way, one from the east and one from the south. They look to converge in a half hour, but I don't wanna chance riding through them. North is 180 degrees in the wrong direction, so we gotta go west. We can hole up in Baker until they pass. Maybe they'll even head off in a different direction."

Ha, Baker. They had named a town after that shitty scientist lady?

I had been down this road before. Trudging through the desert and all of a sudden there's a thousand desiccated dead eating one of your best friends. I clearly didn't have any friends here, but I still didn't want to be eaten. I could overpower the kid, chuck her off the horse and gallop into the wide blue yonder, but not before half a dozen bullets caught me in the back. I would have to go with these assholes to Baker, whatever that was. I was really hoping it wasn't that bitch doctor they were talking about.

Turns out Baker *is* a town. A shitheel town of about seven hundred people before the plague. Now it was just another dead town. We saw one infected and the guy with the lever action, whose name was Harlan, put it down from two hundred yards with no optic. Glad I didn't try to make a break for it. The shot had been unbelievably loud, and it echoed across nothing like a guy with a broken, baritone yodel.

Baker was a hick desert town that lived and died by interstate traffic. I15 runs southwest to northeast just to the south of the town. I'm riding down the center of Baker Blvd (stupid not to call it Baker Street after the song) and to my left we just passed a Burger King and an Arby's. There's a Denny's, an A&W Root Beer, a Subway, and a TCBY. There was a sign for Carl's Jr and Del Taco and I'm looking at a Jack in the Box. I just have one question; WTF?

A billion restaurants and 700 people? How much traffic can the interstate provide? I asked these questions to the kid, but she ignored me, so I asked Harlan.

"Vegas is only 90 miles northeast of here. This place was busy as hell all the time. I met my wife in the Dairy Queen further down on the 15 extension." He pointed down the street.

I looked back at Harriet, who was talking on the radio. "Is she your wife?" Both the kid and Harlan snorted.

"Naw. Ellie, my wife, got bit in the first couple days during the outbreak. My daughter bit her. She got bit by Chuckie's daughter and we dunno where she caught it."

"Shit, I'm sorry."

"You're gonna be, if Chuckie's dead."

I sighed. "Is there a chance that he could have lost the horse somehow?"

"Pie? Nope. Pie woulda gone back for him. S'why I'm havin' a hard time believin' your story."

"Finding the helicopter would be easy," I told him with a shrug.

"Doesn't mean you didn't kill Chuckie."

Shit. He had me on that one. I mean I didn't kill Chuckie, but how the hell was I going to convince these yokels of that? Speaking of yokels, we passed the World's Tallest Thermometer on the way to wherever we were going. It was actually pretty cool and was at least fifty feet tall. I stared up longingly at it, thinking sadly for some reason of the spinning clock on the top of a pedestal in a long dead Faneuil Hall in Boston.

Harriet's horse sidled up to ours. "You'd be surprised how many people came here just for that thermometer."

"Are you guys from here?" I asked.

"Harlan and Julie are. The rest of us are from towns in and around here. Doesn't matter, every town is as dead as this one."

"The rest of you?"

"Yeah, you didn't think it was just the four of us, didja?"

Our four horses pulled into Baker Firewood, an enormous set of white buildings with boarded-up windows. I had no idea why this town would need a firewood store, but there were stacks of wood, both full logs and cut. The building we pulled up to had three huge garage doors, and we pulled the horses right in after Harlan undid a padlock. He pulled the doors down, and we dismounted. I could feel the hate coming off the girl, and I had to wonder if she was going to kill me in my sleep.

"Keep your gun on him, Julie," Harriet said, and the kid drew her sidearm.

I had been in similar situations before. Ya know, situations where someone who had a gun wanted me dead. I had gotten out of all of them, but this one was different. These people didn't seem like bad people, and I didn't want to kill any of them, but I sure as shit didn't want to die.

We all sat on three bench seats from three different trucks. They had been bolted to the concrete floor and honestly, after sitting in the sand or on the back of a horse for the past day, my ass was grateful. Harlan spit brown shit into a black and yellow Chock Full of Nuts coffee can and started the questioning.

"Tell us where you're comin' from and where you were goin'."

"I was shanghaied in San Francisco." Julie huffed when I said that. I glanced at her but continued. "A fireteam of Navy SEALs captured me and were bringing me by helicopter to a plane at an airfield near here, but I don't know which one. From there on, I would have been brought to the Secretary of the Navy. The helicopter had some mechanical difficulties, and we crashed. Me and one other guy made it out, that guy was busted up, so I carried him for a while. I fixed him up some, then he was bitten by one of the dead and took his own life. That was when the horse showed up. Alone. No Chuckie astride him. I've been riding him ever since."

"You're a deserter, then?"

"What? No. Do I look Navy to you? They wanted me for something else."

"What?" Harriet asked. "What did they want you for?"

The last thing I needed was for someone else to know my little immunity secret. For fuck's sake it's getting to be widely known. I was unsure if these people, no matter my take on them, would turn me in for some Saltines and Gatorade. I could only think of one reply.

"That's classified." I had never said that before. Well, not with any meaning behind it. I sounded pretty damn cool.

The three of them looked at each other. The other guy was off doing who knows what.

"Where's Chuckie?" Harlan asked.

"Look, man, I dunno where Chuckie is or even who he is. I told you the truth about everything I can talk about."

He passed his rifle to Harriet, stood from the blue and white bench seat and sauntered over to me. He backhanded me across the face, then drew his sidearm. It was a silver snub nose .38. "That was me bein' nice. Next time I smack you with this." He brandished his weapon. That shit would hurt, and my face was already fucked up from a nasty set of undead fingernails.

"Where's Chuckie?"

"I told you, I don't—"

He didn't wait for me to finish. He brought the revolver around in a sideways arc, not enough to dislocate my jaw, but enough that it would open up my already damaged face.

I grabbed his wrist with my bound hands, jerked him off balance and leapt up with lightning speed, kicking his back leg out further. I twisted his wrist enough to be able to get the gun from him and then stood there, pointing his own weapon at his head with his right arm pinned against his back with my knee, his face pressed against the puke-green bench seat.

His face was directly over an ancient tear in the seat with equally as ancient duct tape attempting to cover it. Yellow foam stuck into his mouth.

"Holy sh—" Harriet started, but it was my turn not to let someone finish.

"Don't. Don't move a fucking muscle or his brains will be in a tiny fucking puddle on this decrepit seat."

Julie and Harriet swallowed, and I did a quick search for the missing guy but came up empty.

"Weapons down."

Julie started to protest, but I cocked the hammer on the revolver, and she shut up. Without another word they both lowered their weapons and put their hands up.

"Good. Now let's talk without this idiot smacking me."

"I knew you killed Chuckie," Julie sobbed. "And now you're gonna kill us."

"Wrong on both counts, kid. I did not kill Chuckie and have no intentions of killing you unless you pull some monkey shit." I leaned down to Harlan, who also had his hands up as best he could with his face pressed into the seat. "Don't move. Not an inch." I leaned back a bit, took the gun from his head and the pressure from his arm and he visibly relaxed. With the gun in my hand, I pushed my wrists together and in two seconds the rope that bound me was on the floor.

"Much better. You two, sit. Harlan, you can sit up." I strode over and grabbed my new M4, pulling the bolt back a bit to check the load. I stuck the revolver in a pocket and nonchalantly aimed the gun at the floor between the seats.

Harriet looked scared when she asked, "What now?"

"I try to convince you idiots that I didn't kill your friend. Because I didn't. Like I said the horse just showed up."

Julie huffed and turned her head away from me, "You're a liar. You said you came from San Francisco, but everybody knows the cities are full of the dead."

"They sure are. They're also full of the living and not all of them are nice. My family is there and I'm going back. Actually, you remind me of one of them. She's full of piss and vinegar too. We lived on Alcatraz for a while, but that place just got overrun. I'm not sure if the military was able to fend off the dead. I was kidnapped as they were being attacked. Oh, you can put your hands down."

Harriet frowned. "Kidnapped? Kidnapped by who?"

"Let me guess," Harlan interjected, "classified?"

"Probably. That I would tell you, but you straight up wouldn't believe me. Actually, now that I think of it, the assholes who took me and delivered me to the doctors were the nicest of the bunch. Same dicks who took me also work for the doctors, who work for the military, who work for the new President."

We heard something from far off. It grew loud quickly and suddenly the whole building shook. It was a giant helicopter. One guess why they were here. They all looked up and the bird flew off, searching. Harlan said dumbfoundedly, "I thought the military were all gone."

"Alive and well. There's a nuclear submarine anchored off Alcatraz and half the Pacific fleet is off the coast of Panama."

"Harriet! Harriet, do you read?"

The guy sounded frantic, and we all heard it. I pointed at her radio. "You can answer it."

"Copy, Carl. What is it?"

"The two groups have met up and they're already pouring into Baker! If you're at the wood shop, it's already too late to get out. Shore it up and we'll try to lead 'em away. That damned helicopter is dragging them in for miles! Second helicopter I've seen today, but the first one was all busted up."

I raised my eyebrows as if to say, *Told you.*

"Copy that, Carl. We'll dig in. Big Mike, you copy that? Big Mike?" She looked at me. "Mike is the other guy with us. He went to do a perimeter walk."

They had sent Big Mike to walk the perimeter alone. WTF had they been thinking? I searched around the place looking for access points. The boarded windows were chest height and whoever had boarded them had done a great job and cut the boards to fit perfectly. Not really a problem there. That left the three garage doors, two of which were steel, and one wood. The wood looked solid, but still. Two other doors, both in the same wall, did not look as sturdy. I sighed and regarded my captives.

I grabbed the beautiful lever action rifle and passed it to Harlan. "Grab your weapons, all of you."

Harlan pointed his rifle at me. "Shoot me later," I told him and turned to check those two doors.

BAKER

The good part was that nobody had shot me. They all had their weapons, but I was still relatively unperforated. I had holes in me, but not from them. They told me the building had been cleared, but what they didn't say was what was on the other side of those human-sized doors. Business offices with a dozen tall windows stopping at about knee-level. Those windows might stop a mosquito, but not a throng of dead folks. These hadn't been boarded up and I didn't have time to ask why.

Harlan and I used a dolly to move some heavy file cabinets into the other room, then we put them against the doors. There were three cabinets of about three hundred pounds each pressing against the wood and both doors opened in. We stacked some other shit against the file cabinets as well. An ancient metal stairway switchbacked up into a loft. We could get up there, but the horses couldn't. That would be our primary fallback position. There was no roof access from in here and it was a hangar style roof anyway and I didn't want to fall off.

It didn't take long for the fuckers to figure out where we were. We were silent, the horses were silent and there was no power so there were no lights on for them to see. The skylights and high windows in the place threw enough light to see by. No idea how they knew where we were, but they were pounding on the wood and metal of the building in short order, and they were fucking loud. Not the banging, although that was unnerving as well, the noises they make.

"Don't worry," Harlan said to Julie, "they can't get in here. Them walls are strong."

"Yeah, I've heard that before. Let's figure out a way to get rid of some of those stairs so they can't follow us up when they get in."

"But... but the horses!" Julie blurted.

"I'm being pragmatic, kid. They're gonna get in here and we can't get the horses up high enough."

"No!"

"Then tell me what to do."

"I... we can... I don't know!"

"Harriet," I asked. "Can you get on the horn and ask your people to lead the dead away? Even a distraction so we can get gone?"

She tried to make a call, but nobody responded. She made another call to Big Mike with the same result.

"Nobody's coming," I told them. "It's just us."

One of the windows in the wooden garage door shattered. The windows were about seven feet up and I couldn't for the life of me understand why windows would be installed so high in a door like this. Dead hands from some of the taller infected grabbed at the empty window but that wouldn't do anything. The windows were about a foot across each and there were eight of them in a row with big spaces at the end. I estimated the three garage doors had to be about sixteen feet wide by thirty feet high.

I didn't want the horses to die like this either. I had a horse buddy in Texas and even though he was a douche-coward, afraid of his own shadow, I liked him.

"Shit! Alright, listen up! We go to the other end of the building, make as much noise as possible, and then high-tail it out this door. There's no way we get them all to bite on the distraction, so we'll need to build up some steam before we plow through the leftovers."

Harlan was shaking his head. He rubbed his chin and said, "Door's gonna take ten, maybe fifteen seconds to get it all the way open."

"Harlan, we're gonna go out in tandem. Julie, you ride with Harlan and Harriet rides alone. Tie that horse," I pointed at a chestnut-colored beauty, "to yours, Harriet, and I'll ride Pie, even though that's a ridiculous name for a horse. I'll get the door. If there's a million of the damn things on the other side of this door, just power through them. I'll be right behind you. We can meet up where you met your wife at the Dairy Queen."

"I don't like this…" Harlan said.

I was also shitting myself. "I am very open to options right now."

Apparently, he didn't have any because he tied one horse behind Harriet's, got on his, and helped Julie up behind him. I went to the far end of the room, knocked the file cabinets over and ran into the offices. A few of them were outside, meandering about, but most were over by the garage doors. I put two rounds through one of the glass windows, then shot one of them in the head and started yelling for the rest. This was where I was really terrified. I plugged a couple more who tried to gain entry, then heard the rest before they made the corner. As the horde came into view, they got exponentially louder. I shot two of them, then ran for the doors. They were already climbing in through the broken window and pounding on the other glass when I made it back. I slammed the door and pushed one very heavy cabinet against it.

Thumps came from the other side before I was finished. I ran over to the rope-thingie to pull up the door. "Shoot as many as you need to get away. Ready?"

"Hell no!" Harlan said and swallowed.

I counted down from 3 and started yanking on the rope. Nothing else on earth mattered at the time so the only thing I could think of was how much I wanted a strawberry Tootsie Roll as I yanked that thing hand over hand. Several of the dead crawled through the low opening, Harlan and Harriet shooting them as necessary.

It seemed to take about 3 weeks to get that door high enough, but when Harlan yelled, "Yah!" and the horsed kicked into high gear, I knew it was time to vacate the premises.

I watched Harlan and Julie bolt through the door, both ducking as they did. Harriet did the same, towing Big Mike's horse behind her. I made to jump on Pie, but that fucker sprinted right after his horse buddies, his hooves clacking on the concrete.

Fuck.

I didn't want to get trapped here. I could wait up in the rafters for a rescue that was never coming because these redneck assholes might have still thought I killed their friend. I ran through the door and into Hell.

A hundred or so of the shitheads shuffled after the horses, all of them facing away from me except the ones coming back around the corner of the building. They saw me for sure. The ten-foot road that the horses had plowed was beginning to fill back in when I saw Julie get pulled from her horse. One of them had grabbed her and it had a better hold on her than she had on Harlan. He kept going, not realizing she had taken a tumble.

She landed hard but got up and shot the dead thing in the face. She was forty feet from me, surrounded, but the horde in front of her had thinned out considerably. It was at this moment that I did the stupidest thing in the history of stupid things. I sprinted down the collapsing field of walking corpses, the dead filling in behind me. She was shooting into the crowd in a panic, not scoring headshots when I miraculously got to her. I grabbed her by the shoulder, and she pointed her weapon at my face and pulled the trigger. She pulled it about five times, but the slide on her weapon was already back.

"Come on!" I screamed and fired my M4 into four of the things in front of us. She followed me as I sprinted right into the edge of the cleared dead, bowling three of the things over. I went down in a heap with them clawing and biting but was able to extricate myself and get the kid past most of them. I fired two quick shots with the stubby rifle to get the one off me who was holding on to my pack, and we were free.

I yelled in her face, "Run!"

She sprinted and I followed her. The dead followed us. There were stragglers to the main party that were still streaming toward the place we had just been in, but we avoided them and kept running. We rounded the corner of a small church and stopped to take a breather. I was in the best shape of my life, helicopter crashes notwithstanding, and I was wrecked from springing a quarter mile.

We both heaved, me leaning against the church and her bent over with her hands on her knees.

"You saved me," she breathed.

"Yeah, I do that."

"Why?"

"Because it was the right thing to do. Also, you really do remind me of someone I love. What kind of tyrannosaurus-douche would I be if I just let them have you? I'd never be able to look her in the face again."

"So, you didn't kill Chuckie?"

"Nope. Do you believe me?"

"Jury's out," she said, and I liked her immediately. She pointed to our right, and I saw a slew of dead things crossing the church parking lot. We started to jog away.

"Which way is the Dairy Queen?"

The kid thumbed back behind us. Literally 180 degrees in the opposite direction. There were several hundred infected cannibals between us and the DQ, so we had no choice but to keep going. We hopped a broken-down stockade fence, clearly done in by a horde of the dead, and passed a house surrounded by another fence and some trees. It would have been a great place to hide except for the dead people trapped in the yard. We jogged toward a little roundabout with a flagpole in the center but a crowd of three of the things stumbled into our path from the corner of the fence. It was my turn to get dragged to the ground.

I fought them hard, punching and shoving because my rifle was pinned to my chest, the whole time suffering from a testicle shriveling terror. These things were all dry and dusty, having been in the desert for a while, but they weren't any less heavy, which is weird. Or maybe I was just being a bitch. Either way it was tough to fight them off and I had to wonder why the kid had just let them have me. I was able to knock one aside while the other two were snapping at me and draw my sidearm. I plugged one, elbowed the other in the face then shot her. Goo flew everywhere on that one, it was nasty. The third one grabbed my leg and bit my foot, but my toes were covered in boot and the disgusting thing couldn't get through it.

Not for lack of trying though because that shit hurt. I kicked it a couple of times and shot it in the face. All these shots were going to bring every dead thing in the vicinity even with the suppressor. I heard scuffling behind me and spun to drop the next threat, but it was way worse than that.

Two more of the things had the kid and while she was fighting like a tigress, they were bigger. I fired a shot at one of them, but the fucker moved, and I missed, the slide on my HK remaining back. I holstered the pistol, the suppressor sticking almost to my knee, and brought the rifle to bear, but the three of them were doing this fucked up dance and I didn't want to hit the kid.

They were only a few steps away, so I rushed over and thumped one with the butt of the rifle. It let go, which they never do, and focused on me. It reached for me with both hands in that classic zombie style. I thumped it again, and again before it fell to the ground. I smashed its head to pulp, the spray getting on my face. Heaving, I looked around for the kid; she had somehow gotten another dead thing attached to her and that wouldn't do.

There were more coming from several directions, so this had to be settled most ricky-tick. Julie gave a great shove, and I clocked one of the douches with my dripping rifle stock. This just pissed the thing off and it tried even harder to bite her, repeatedly snapping so hard a tooth flew from its mouth. I reversed the rifle, put the fluid-covered stock to my shoulder and blew its brains out. Apparently, this thing had an overabundance of brains because it kept up the attack. Etiquette usually demands that the living dead drop when you shoot them in the head. This asshole didn't get that memo or was extremely rude. It fell on the second shot, but it didn't let go and the three of them, living, living dead, and just dead, dropped to the scrub.

Julie was starting to panic, and I could hear it in her struggles. I grabbed the thing on top of her and pulled it away as best I could. This one wasn't snapping, but it had its mouth open wide in anticipation of a bite.

"Push," I told her calmly, but calm had left the building, and she frantically beat against the thing's chest. Pistol empty and with no way to use the rifle after I had grabbed the thing, I let go with one hand, drew Chauncy's big ass knife and stabbed the prick in the temple. This one had the good manners to fucking die.

Julie scrabbled back across the scrub leaving skin on the dirt. She rolled, stood, and ran blindly.

Shit.

I chased after her as she sprinted who knows where. She was damn fast, too. She ran over the roundabout thingie and toward a chain link fence, which she was up and over in a split second. Why did this place have so many damn fences? She disappeared into some trees on the other side of the fence, and I lost her. I put a hand against the flagpole and noticed half an American flag hanging from it. I had to be thankful that

Remo and Alvarez weren't here, or they would get eaten trying to take the flag down and do it justice.

I had a conversation once with Alvarez, a former private in the army, about the importance of the flag in post-zombie-apocalypse America. I told him I didn't think it meant much anymore as the country was gone. He chastised me and told me that now is when it mattered the most. Now was when the living needed to come together, and the flag stood for unity above all else. It was a symbol of hope and perseverance, and all those who had shit on it in the recent years before the plague would benefit from those ideals as much as those who loved it right now.

I could hear the dead behind me. They were a bit back but would be here in minutes. I followed the kid and climbed the fence. My rifle somehow got caught in one of the links and ended up poking me in the balls. I didn't like that. I dropped to the other side and one of them was there, but it was only half a guy and wasn't going to chase me too far. I had a sec, so I reloaded the HK. This was a .45 caliber, and I had six more magazines. I really liked the action on this larger handgun, it was smooth when I pulled the slide to get a round in the chamber. I liked my old 9mm Sig Sauer better, but this was nice.

Half-a-guy was reaching for me and making those noises they make. I wanted to end him, as ankle biters are every bit as deadly as a horde of Runners. I stabbed through the top of his head with the big blade and his face fell into the dirt. That was another thing I didn't like about this place; there wasn't a single fucking blade of grass in this entire town that I had seen so far.

I was cleaning the blade with the guy's shirt fragments when I heard Julie screaming. I bolted around the round structure in front of me, staying away from the broken windows until I spied her. She had shimmied up a tall pole in the middle of what looked like a playground, eight of the things scratching the metal reaching for her. I understand she had been in a panic, but this was literally the worst thing she could have done. A professional rock climber with the grip strength of the Hulk could only hold onto that pole for so long. I had to wonder how she had survived up to now.

I used the rifle to dispatch the critters, the last one finally understanding that there was easier food around and turning toward me. It had been a little girl, and I drilled her in the dome, blowing her out of the one shoe she had been wearing.

"Come down!" I whisper-yelled at her. Ridiculous to whisper after I had just fired a dozen unsuppressed shots. The whole world knew where we were. Probably heard the shots in Kansas.

She wouldn't even look at me, just squeezed that pole, eyes clamped shut, her feet just out of reach.

"Julie, come on! I'll get you back with Harlan and Harriet, but we have to go now." She sobbed and squeezed harder if it were possible. I was done fucking around with this kid. "Move your ass, you little shit, or we're both fucking dead!"

She opened her eyes, blinked rapidly, and glared at me. This kid still hated me even though I had saved her life about 600 times and was currently trying to do so again. I was at once angry and terrified. Although I couldn't see the swarm, I knew it was a matter of moments before they crashed through the myriad of fences I had just navigated.

"Now!" I yelled and she slid down the pole. I grabbed her hand, and she let me.

"We're going to die," she said in a tiny voice.

I gently grabbed her chin in my hand and forced her to look at me. "Not today."

I pulled her a bit and soon we were running toward the white brick building in front of us. Most of the windows were busted out and I could tell that it had been a school. The tac light on my M4 bit deeply into the inky darkness of one of the classrooms and other than it being dirty, it looked ready for class. A dead thing ambled around the corner outside, and we left it and crawled through the glassless window. It was about chest height. I helped the kid through, and she pulled me in after. The dead guy stuck his face where I could stab it, so I did. I stuck him through the eye, and he fell to the ground, smacking his chin on the sill on the way down.

It was extremely unlikely that a building like this would be devoid of the dead but being inside when there were hundreds of them outside was preferable. I mean unless they just knew where we were like a half hour ago. Julie seemed to have checked back in, and I was quite grateful for that.

"Do you know this building?"

"I went to middle school here."

"How do you get to the roof?"

She frowned. "I dunno." I looked at her and was about to say something snarky when she put her hands on her hips and scrunched her eyebrows. She looked so much like Kat I took a step back because I knew shit was about to go down. "Do you know where your middle school roof access is? Yeah, I didn't think so."

I felt like Alderaan just before that Death Star douche with the fucked-up helmet pulled the last handle down. I put my hands up in

54

supplication. It was either that or melt from the furnace of wrath. "Easy, Killer. I just meant—"

She pointed behind me, so I spun to check out the hubbub. Half a continent's worth of dead people were streaming onto the school grounds, and I doubt any of the fuckers had a hall pass.

"Can they get in?" She sounded like a little lamb ten seconds after she had displayed Hannibal Lecter face.

"Damn skippy they'll get in. We just need to be in a place where they can't reach us or in another place altogether."

I was no longer in favor of going to class and I wanted out of this school posthaste. We bolted through the open door of the classroom and directly into the waiting arms of a dead thing. It was big, very big, and wasted no time in trying to eat me. I put both hands on its neck trying to push its teeth away, but the neck just sort of gave up and the mostly rotten skin came away in my right hand. It leaned back in to take a hunk out of me, but I juked, and it missed. I re-grabbed the nasty bastard by what was left of its throat, but this was not a battle I was destined to win, and the bastard bit me in the shoulder. He didn't get much, and the sling on my rifle stopped the teeth from ripping out a larger chunk, but he got me. He pulled back, the sling, a bit of me in his mouth, and tried to chew. The sling stopped him, so he opened his mouth to spit it out and to my horror, a wet piece of my T-shirt tumbled from his face to the floor. He was going for another bite when a ridiculously loud shot sounded and he jerked to my right, his head in pieces.

Julie's revolver was smoking, and her eyes were wide. We didn't have time to fuck about though, as two more of them were coming down the hallway. Both looked to have scrubs on, and I drilled them with my M4. With the sound of the firearms still echoing in the hallway, there was little chance the swarm outside hadn't figured out where we were.

I grabbed her and spun her around. My boots squeaked down the linoleum tiles while we ran for the front doors. I pushed one open and lo and behold there were infected dead people ten feet away and starting up the steps. I yanked the thing closed not a moment before a dead woman's face smacked against the little window with the chicken wire in the side of the door. Her face moved up and down and shit leaked from her orifices as she was crushed into the door by the horde behind.

There was fuck all to chain or bar the doors with, but these were heavy fire doors, and they opened out. As long as the shitheads pressed against it, these babies would never open. The frame though… that could collapse under the weight of hundreds of bodies pushing against it.

We booked it back into the school and I asked her where the best place to hold up would be. "This way!" she told me, and I followed her like a puppy. We made it through the side door of an auditorium, musical instruments on chairs or stands on the stage. I kept up with her when she vaulted up on the small stage and ran for a side exit past an impossibly tall black curtain. A body lay on the floor in a fetal position. It was a kid, and it was mostly a skeleton. She didn't even look at it and rushed to the door.

This was also one of those heavy steel doors that you would see on any school or municipal building in the country, with that push-bar type opener. This one was devoid of windows though. She put her hand on the bar, and I told her to wait. I put my ear to the steel but couldn't hear shit. Hopefully the dead were not on this side of the building.

I'm one of those people where if there's a fifty percent chance, I'm wrong one hundred percent of the time. I pushed the door open and there were dozens of them right outside. I tried to pull it closed but infected fingers wrapped around the edge. There were a lot of fucking fingers, and the noise of the creatures entered through the crack in the door. Julie grabbed the bar attempting to pull it closed with me, but there were too many hands on it and one of the more industrious assholes now had his upper torso poking through and made a grab for the kid.

"Let it go!" I yelled and we bolted back the way we had come. The door fought the press of the things against it for a moment, but I heard the screech of it opening and knew they were in here with us. One of the shadows across the stage moved and came toward us. It was dressed in robes that reminded me of a Jedi, and it stumbled on a cello. Before it could right itself, I grabbed a still shiny silver saxophone and clubbed the fucker once, twice, three times with the wide end. Hey, I knew I would need the ammo later for crowd control and didn't want to waste a bullet right now. Also, I didn't know silver saxophones were a thing.

I dropped the sax, and we screwed up the aisle toward the front doors to the auditorium. We burst through the open doors into a lobby of sorts, the whole front of it fabricated from glass. There were two sets of glass doors set in frames with a glass wall in between and above. A window into another room in between the partitions was likely a security checkpoint when the kids who attended school weren't all dead. *These* dead were ten deep smacking on the exterior glass, and I was fortunate enough to see the center partition come crashing in, spilling half a dozen of the things into the atrium. They still had another glass wall to penetrate before they were on us, but it wouldn't take long.

This shit was getting old, and I was tired of running, but not wanting to be in the gullets of several dead people, I thought it best we keep on keeping on. Julie didn't say anything when she ran through the atrium to a set of stairs going up. We moved up the stairs quickly and through another set of doors. We were on the top level of the gymnasium, looking down on the basketball court. There was a fifteen-foot-wide corridor which ran all the way around the gym about twenty-feet up. Four dead people gawked at us from the court and began their slow amble toward us. Julie ran forward a bit and then angled around going the long way down the side of the gym.

How the hell did a rinky-dink, pissant little town like this get a top-notch half a million-dollar gymnasium like this for their damn middle school on the corner of no and where? I thought back to the Parlin Junior High School in Everett Mass. Step the wrong way on that ancient, unpolished parquet, and the rats would be nibbling at your ankles when your foot went through. And those fucking ropes! Remember those damn ropes we had to climb 25 years ago? F that noise. I was skinny and strong, and I still hated those things. One of the shackles pulled from the ceiling when my buddy Chug was forced by a sadistic gym teacher (Mr. Reynolds) to climb the damn thing. He went to the hospital with a broken leg and needed stitches. Chug, not Mr. Reynolds.

That is what was passing through my noggin as I ran down the elevated corridor of the gym in whatever damn school we were in at the time.

Julie ended up at another push-bar type fire door and I thought she was going to just burst through, but she pulled her hands back like the bar was made of lava. She swiveled her head and stared at me, wide-eyed.

"What is it?" I demanded. "What's wrong?"

She looked at the door then back at me. "What if they're outside like they were at the last door?"

"They might be."

She stepped away from the door and regarded me weirdly. "So, who opens it?"

I immediately put my thumb on my forehead.

Her look went from terrified to quizzically terrified. "What is that? What are you doing?"

"What the fuck are you talking about? This is the *Not It* sign. Everybody knows this is the not it sign. You do this when you call not it."

She was dumbfounded. Literally no idea what I was telling her. "I don't... I don't..."

"Means you do it!" I pointed at the door. but she didn't move. "For fuck's sake!" I yelled and pushed past her. I kicked the door open, and we looked out into the heat of the day from twenty feet up. It had been freezing last night, but it was hot AF outside now. Stupid desert.

We were on some kind of metal fire escape landing with a single long flight of stairs attached to the side of the building. There were a couple dozen shitheads, but they were dispersed nicely so I told her to come the fuck on and we clunked down the steps, our feet ringing on the steel.

Kicking the door had been loud and subsequently had gotten all the dead to look at us and seeing us made them come in our direction. So, we had that going for us. None of them were close, so I grabbed the kid's hand, and we booked it past outstretched arms. When we had a bit of breathing room, I asked her which way the Dairy Queen was.

"Southwest!"

How in the absolute hell does everybody know which direction is which simply by knowing? Was there a class I missed on knowing directions? Should I have been an Eagle Scout? Can you assholes navigate by the stars in the day time? In addition, why does everybody also assume *I* know which way is southwest? I have no fucking clue. None.

"Fucking point!" I growled and her finger extended. She pointed exactly the way we had come and exactly back at what was shuffling after us.

"Follow me!" she whisper yelled, and we ran across a packed earth parking lot. The ground beneath us was stone dust and it was damn hot. We had to juke a couple of reaching pus bags, but overall, the journey to the road was uneventful. We hooked a right onto Stadium Road, and I had to wonder where the stadium was and what they played there. We booked it down the paved street, and where the parking lot had been hot, this was like magma. I could feel the heat through my boots.

The junior high was on our right as we followed Stadium Road towards the rest of the town. The dead were there too, and they looked pissed and hungry. Hangry? Crossing over Hillview Drive, we ran into scrub and hooked another right. The dead were coming at us from most directions now, but directly in front of us was the best way to run. They were there too but spread out. Not like the hundreds in the concentrated swarm which was now behind us. Julie led on and we jogged between a... a... is that a house? Hell, I don't know, between whatever the hell that thing is and a field of dark blue solar panels.

Death Valley Road, cracked all to hell with pieces of asphalt jutting up all over the place, looked like a dried-out riverbed. One of the legless assholes was dragging herself across it and I could hear and smell her cooking on the tar. I am not even kidding. It was nauseating. Almost as nauseating as when we entered Clarks Mobile Home Park with all six of its mobile homes. Yeah, there were six of them stacked about twenty feet apart three across from three the long way. WTF? Six?

For six trailers, there were a hell of a lot of dead here. Maybe twenty, and they reached from broken windows and stumbled at us from shadows. One was seat belted into a car with the windows up and I had to wonder if it was still stinky in there or if the stench had dried up like the creature had.

We spirited past these dickheads and kept moving southwest (I think) until we ran into the desert proper. They were out here too in ones and twos, but the threat didn't seem imminent, so I called a halt to the running. I think she was as grateful as I to stop because she heaved an enormous sigh. A huge V-shaped sweat stain covered the back of her pink tank top, and I shuddered to think how much water I had lost running. She had a tan, but she was going to cook under this sun with nothing on her bare shoulders and arms. I had nothing to give her for cover, either.

Up ahead there looked to be a wall of Conex containers. As we got closer, I could see that it was, in fact, an actual wall. Other pieces of metal and wood had been interspersed in the gaps to make an efficient barrier. I had seen something like this in Montana once and I asked Julie about it.

"Naw, that's the junkyard. It was all sealed up like that before the dead came."

It seemed the perfect place to hole up and I was wondering why we didn't meet there instead of a Dairy Queen, so I asked her that too.

She shook her head, "We don't go in there."

Clearly not wishing to elaborate I had to ask, "Why not? It looks pretty safe."

"Cannibals," was all she said.

"You mean more dead? Too many to clean out? Look at the walls, this would be great for you guys!"

"No, cannibals. Not dead people, living people who eat other people."

I stopped and switched magazines on my M4. I could see the red sign for the DQ a couple hundred yards in front of us. "Are you people crazy? Why the hell would you take us into a town full of cannibals and then want to meet up right next to their fucking house?" We continued walking.

"They won't come out in the day," she stated, shaking her head. "We didn't expect to get surrounded by a group of the dead. I just wanted to shoot you in the head and not come to Baker at all, but Harriet wanted to know if you killed Chuckie first."

"Right, so, assume I'm a murderer, torture me to prove it, then kill me?"

"Yeah, that was the plan."

"Shitty plan," I told her. "At least for me. Still think I killed Chuckie?"

"I don't know. You were ridin' Pie."

"Right. Back to the cannibals. Why haven't you cleaned them out?"

"There's too many."

I was about to get high and mighty, but we found a radio on top of a newspaper dispenser out in front of the Dairy Queen. There was a note attached to it upon which was written *Channel 13.* Julie grabbed the radio and made a call. "Harriet, come back?"

Harriet came back instantly. *"Julie, we found Big Steve. He's in the junkyard. Big Steve is hurt, and we need help getting him out of here. Them rats that was in here are gone, you can come get us and Steve."*

The kid looked right at me when she answered, "Copy that, Harriet. We're a bit surrounded by the stiffies right now, but they don't know where we are. We'll wait until nighttime, and we'll come get you guys."

"Alright, Julie, see you then."

Julie looked scared. "They're in trouble."

BOOM?

So, it seems these idiots who let a man do a perimeter check solo, were smart enough to have a panic word. Apparently, Big Mike had been captured by bad guys and Harriet had let Julie know this via the code word "Steve". We didn't have panic words in our group and that shit was going to change. It was genius and the measure of respect I had lost for these folks was restored back to zero with the code word.

Nothing better than a fresh start.

Julie switched the radio to channel nine and called Carl, but nobody answered. She tried a couple other frequencies and two more names with the same result.

She shook her head, "Nobody's answering."

"Then it's you and me. Let's go get your friends."

She blinked. "I... I don't..."

"Yeah, I get that a lot. We'll go tonight, but we have to get my bag. I dropped it by the place you guys were going to torture me in."

She stared at her sneakers. Oh man had I shamed her. It was great. And before you get all high and mighty about me shaming a kid: Fuck you. Fuck you and these people. What would they have done to me if I hadn't had the foresight and wherewithal to escape their bonds? Exactly. I'd be short a few digits and have a smashed in face if I were lucky. Then there's the fact that I was about to put my life on the line for people who were going to cut pieces off me. I like me better than these assholes. Sorry, not sorry.

There it sits. Maybe a hundred feet from where we're hidden in this little trailer that is actually a house. This place is so damn dirty I was worried about scabies or herpes or whatever you can catch from a nasty place. The kind of filthy that warrants a tetanus shot just for looking at it.

Julie and I are kneeling on a bed peeking out a side window at the firewood place. Bed is a bit generous as it's an ancient, stained mattress with cigarette burns. Looking at the charred edges of the little holes it's a Christmas miracle this place isn't cinders.

My bag is right there, accidentally dropped when I had to save the kid. It's sitting upright and it looks like someone gently placed it there with reverence. It's raining, and I didn't think that happened too much in the desert, it being a desert and all, but it's really coming down. Julie says the rain will last fifteen minutes and I have to wonder where her meteorology skills come from.

There are about thirty pus sacks aimlessly stumbling around the bag. I know what you're thinking: Hey, create a diversion! Isn't that kind of your thing? Diversions? Yeah, but you're forgetting the bigger issue: If I do something loud, the swarm of half a thousand dead will be on us.

Speaking of 'on us' dusk had arrived. Between the darkness of the rainclouds and dusk itself, I can just make out the bag. Guns aren't viable as they'll draw the swarm, I'm gonna have to get up close and personal. I told Julie the plan of how she was going to stay here, and I was going to get the bag, and she had the audacity to ask me, "How?"

"I'm gonna stab 'em in the noggin."

Before she could protest, I parted the curtains (yeah, this shithole had icky, thin, yellow curtains) and took a final glance out the window. Bag still there. Zombies still there. Ok I... wait, what the fuck was that? There was furtive movement across the parking lot. Two people, dressed in raggedy ass ponchos, were eyeballing my bag of goodies. They had slipped behind a stack of pallets, not ten feet from the nearest shambler. They too were a bit put off by the number of dead in the area and seemed to be looking for the perfect moment to grab my stuff.

"Are they friends of yours?" I asked the kid, pointing.

She struggled to see who I was pointing out, but her squint changed rapidly into wide-eye, her mouth turning into an O, and she told me that these people were not only not friends, they liked to eat people.

"Perfect," I told her. "Stay here."

I slipped out the rickety aluminum screen door and was soaked to the skin in seconds. I hunch-ran to my left, circled around and ran into a dead woman. I used Chauncy's knife to end her before she could make a sound and continued my roundabout run. I was behind the ponchos in short order. It had been a minute since I had murdered anybody, and I still wasn't ok with it. That said, these people ate people and it's unlikely the food was a willing participant in the meal.

I was twenty feet behind them on the other side of a three-foot high wooden fence in the pouring rain and I could see they were holding hands. Fuck. Hopefully the hand-holding was a safety thing and these two weren't in love. I didn't want to kill lovers but cannibal lovers... maybe. With a bit of effort, I stepped over the fence. I crept up behind them and could hear them whispering but couldn't make out what they were saying.

How the hell did it get so bad that people were willing to hunt and eat other people? Seriously, the thought had never entered my mind. I had eaten some nasty shit since the start of all this, and there were times where I was well on the way to starving before I lucked out, but I drew the line at dining on my fellow humans.

I could tell from their voices that it was two dudes. I glanced at their hands again and sighed. I really wanted to kill these assholes if they were cannibals, but the hand thing was putting me off murder. I would run past them, grab the bag, and juke the dead ones, leaving the two people-eaters wondering what the fuck happened as I twinkle-toed my way out of this shit storm.

But alas, that was not to be. They started talking about killing someone. Then they started talking about doing it slowly and what they would do, giggling a little. Then they mentioned Julie by name and that was enough. They were going to eat that girl if the chance was given them. Don't worry, Dear Reader, it wouldn't be.

I sidled up to the bigger one, yanked his poncho hood and hopefully his hair back, and stabbed down into the prick's throat, ripping the blade backwards. Fucker was dead before he knew I was there. The other one looked when his buddy started to gurgle, and I shoved the big blade into his chest. He made an *ooaahh!* sound that didn't go unheard by the living impaired, and they glanced in our direction. I stood, took the fuck by his poncho and spun hard, throwing him out in front of the pallets almost into the arms of the things. The poncho ripped away in my hands. It had been some type of weak plastic.

They fell on him quickly, but he was either too injured by the knife wound or too overwhelmed to scream, because he never made a sound as he fought briefly and weakly. A large crowd fought for the choicest pieces, and I could hear his clothing and other things being ripped. I casually walked around the gorging morons and even the ones too far away to get a nibble seemed to ignore me. They just kept reaching at the puddle that was a man not a minute ago.

I hoisted my bag, shouldered it, and strode toward the trailer without a care in the world. The fuckers would be done with the cannibal in moments and the rain would wash away his blood stains. The only evidence he had been there would be bones and torn clothes.

Fuck him.

I got to the trailer and Julie opened the door. She was aghast at what I had done until I reminded her that these dickheads were going to eat her and only a few short hours ago she and her pals had planned some torture for me.

We stole into the night, heading for the junkyard.

So, the junkyard. It was a fucking fortress. End to end Conex containers the like of which you would see on a big ship. I was quite familiar with these things. Someone had been super intelligent and cut angles into the inside of them, then tac-welded the outsides of the things together, because there wasn't a seam to be had. It was beautiful, and if they had a good gate, it would take tens of thousands of dead to break this shit down.

I was both impressed and pissed off. Ship would love this thing. Remo would hate it. There didn't seem to be any watch towers, and that was weird, but getting inside this thing wasn't going to be that difficult. It would stop an infected, to be sure, but I could just climb up the side of this bitch and be free to cause whatever mayhem I saw fit.

"Wait here," I told Julie. I was the toughest son of a bitch currently wearing my pants, and I was about to prove it. I would save her friends, and we would all ride off into the sunset and then I would be on my merry way.

I crept up to the rust-stained red steel on the balls of my feet. In the history of sneaking, nobody had ever snuck this quietly. I listened as hard as I could, and I did hear some stuff over the wall, but it was far off. I'd be up and over this thing in just a sec. I nodded my superiority to Julie, who was well hidden behind the husk of a burned-out car, and gently placed my hands on the steel.

"Twenty-one, two, three, four, five." Somebody kissed me. "One, two, three, four…" Why was somebody pushing on me? "Thirteen, fourteen…" I coughed.

The kid was crying. "Oh my God, you scared the shit out of me!" she blurted between sobs as she sat in the mud.

"Language," I coughed. It was the only thing I could think to say, then the pain hit me. I was walloped by an all-over ache that seemed to emanate from my bones and travel into everything else. I tried to sit up, but the little guy in charge of nerves screamed, *"Fuck that!"* and I collapsed onto my back. I blinked as the light rain hit me in the eyes. "Ow. Whahapn?"

I hadn't meant to have it sound like that, but my shit wouldn't work correctly.

"You touched the container and then flew back five feet! You weren't breathing!"

"Lectrified."

"What?"

"The container. It's electrified." Pretty fucking ingenious, actually. Look, I'll be the first to tell you I don't know shit about electric perimeters. How this thing sits on the ground in the rain and doesn't just fucking zap a bitch eludes me. Ship would know and would launch into a twenty-minute tirade using sign language on how it was possible, but when he was done, I still wouldn't know shit because I only ever get about twenty percent of what he's telling me.

So, I got mad. Not so much at almost being electrocuted, but that compounded with the fact that I just couldn't master sign language, and I should be home with my family, and cannibals, talking Runners, SECNAVs, and FUCK IT!

I stood. The nerve guy could suck it because I was pissed. Except I fell right back down on my ass in the mud. Apparently getting shocked does shit to you because nothing was working properly. I collected a bunch of thoughts and stood again. This time I stuck the landing and was able to go inspect the container. Sure as shit there was a wire running sideways the whole way around the thing it extended past the next one and was connected to each box with screws. I searched the ground for a stick to throw at the wire before realizing how ridiculous that was.

I needed a cape because I was super angry. How was I going to get over this thing? I couldn't touch it and there was no going under it, so how was I getting over it? I know they are eight and a half feet tall, but I don't know how wide they are. Ten feet? Eight? Fuck. I would have to get higher than the thing and jump down over it.

"Lotta meat on this one," I heard from behind me, and I almost pissed myself.

I spun, drawing one of the suppressed sidearms I had appropriated from the SEALs. I was having a hard time focusing, but I could see that one dickhead had Julie in a rear forearm choke and a second asshole with a hand-fabricated edged weapon like you would see in The Road Warrior stood looking smug. Prick nonchalantly had his weapon on his shoulder like he was waiting for batting practice.

"Drop your gun and we don't kill the kid," Mad Max said.

I blinked hard a couple of times as I tried to focus. "Um… no," I told the asshole, reacquired, and shot the dude holding Julie between the eyes. Speaking of eyes, Max's got huge before I shot him in the chest. He clutched at the wound and stumbled back in the rain, falling on his ass in the mud.

The guy was wheezing and rolling around on his back. I harrumphed. "What, no witty repartee now, pus nuts?"

He just kind of gurgled for a sec and died. I stuck Chauncy in the dead guy's eye and scrambled for a sec to be sure he was done.

"You shot him!" she stared down at the guy missing the top of his head.

"I did."

"What if you had hit me?"

"I didn't." I grabbed my bag and rummaged around until I found what I was looking for.

"But you could have!" She stomped her foot, a bold move in that at any other time I would chide her for being a spoiled brat. Not too much spoiling in the apocalypse.

"I also could have hit him. I did." I found what I was looking for and tucked one under my arm. The other I turned over in my hand looking for instructions. There weren't any.

She looked enraged and confused at the same time and she pointed at the brick in my hand. "What's that?"

"It's a can opener." I saw the blank look on her face and thought I should explain. "C4. It goes boom. Hopefully there will be enough boom to open up one of these containers so we can sneak in the front door."

Confusion won out over anger. "The front door?"

"Yeah. When these things go off, they're going to be loud. Like, stupid loud. If my plan works, the bad guys will come running to check on this, abandon their posts at the front gate, and we slip in, grab your friends, and slip the fuck out."

"What if the guards don't leave the gate?"

"Then we shoot 'em and take our chances."

The only thing I wasn't sure of, well, let's face it, there were a shit-ton of things I wasn't sure of, but in this instance, it was whether or not the explosives would go off when I put them on the electrified metal container. I hadn't thought of that up front and I must admit it was a pants-shitting terror question. I had seen this stuff explode and there was no way to get far enough away from the blast unless I threw it and ran like hell. I mean I had two bricks, so why not? We needed to be on the corner of else and where when these went boom though, or we'd get caught or blown up.

A dead thing stumbled upon us, and I dispatched it quickly. As I write this, I'm thinking this has become commonplace. Five years ago, I wouldn't have been able to be so nonchalant about killing, but did this thing count? It was already dead.

Julie was about fifty feet further away than I was to the blue container in front of us. I was about twenty feet away when I chucked the brick of C4 and ran like a baby backed bitch.

It was all for naught. Nothing happened other than a slight thud when the plastique hit the metal. So, I tried it again. And again. A wicked smile came over my face as I realized the electricity coursing through the metal wouldn't set off the explosives. I set both timers for eight minutes. These timers had little tabs that clicked instead of a digital readout and that was new for me. I leaned the bricks against one of the containers and we ran like hell.

We set up about a hundred yards in front of their gate. Two dudes dressed in trash bags stood on top of two shipping containers with cutouts so they had their whole head above the metal and could see a decent distance. It would be damn difficult to get through this gate with them there. Julie and I had gone over the plan several times. I wanted her to stay back in the trailer, and she gave me shit about it, but eventually went back to wait. She would wait two hours, then run home to her people and tell them what had transpired.

I looked at the watch I had appropriated from the dead SEAL, then at the guards, then back at the watch. I started to count down under my breath, "eight, seven, six..." BOOM! The friggin' earth shook. The worst part of it was that I had fucked up my countdown and would have gotten me or somebody else killed if the time had been critical.

Every living and dead creature in North America had heard that. I pictured the horde that we had ditched at the school turning in unison and beginning their arduous march toward the sound. Toward me.

True to form, the douches on guard duty fled their posts to check the boom. My mind's eye is on Remo and Alvarez when they read this, both will be shaking their heads. I sprinted toward the front gate, a marvel of steel and chains, and climbed up one of the chains and over the barrier like a spider. Hey, I'm in good shape and I had shit to do. I dropped over the side and into the cannibal camp, my nuts clenching in fear.

The place was a disaster. I have no idea how they had done it, but they had preserved garbage that couldn't possibly be around at the current date and time. It looked like the remains of a concert in a field after a bunch of teens had brought beer and pizza and left the trash. Discarded boxes, rotting bags, rusty car parts, a broken aluminum ladder. Which would have come in super handy a few minutes ago, by the way.

The place had been a junkyard, but they had turned it into a dump. A dead man on the end of a chain looked at me. The other end of the chain was attached to a pole driven into the ground and the thing had no lower jaw. It was covered with little somethings, but I couldn't figure out what they were. I moved a little closer and then it moved. Bells. It was covered in bells, and they jingled like Santa's sleigh. More jingling came from my left, and I saw a dead boy crawl out from behind an old Jeep with no tires. The jingling got louder when another of them came from behind a wretched blue mailbox. Soon enough I realized my mistake because the whole area sounded like it was Christmas in Times Square. I began to wonder where the cannibals had gotten all the bells when pain exploded in my head and my lights went out.

DONNER, PARTY OF 40

I had banged my head some prior to the apocalypse. Like everybody else I guess, you just do it. You don't mean to do it, it just happens. Post apocalypse though, everybody wants to cave my roof in. Everybody. From zombies to rednecks, to military douches, helicopter crashes, to cannibals, everybody wants to take something heavy and acquaint it with my dome at high speed.

As such, my head is almost always in agony. Today was no exception. I had already been in a bit of pain from the copter crash, but now... this was next level. No doubt I was going to be a bowel movement in a few hours but until then my head would continue to hurt. Nobody would ever know what happened to me. Would they look for me? Billy would tell them what had happened in San Francisco with the doctors and shit, but that's where we parted ways. I got a bit sad then and then I got angry. Angry doesn't do well inside a splitting noggin.

I opened my eyes and there was a dead woman not three feet from me. I tried to shrink away from her, but I was bound. Didn't matter anyway because another dead woman was behind me. In fact, I was surrounded by the dead. I was inside a yellow circle painted on the asphalt and the dead were chained on the outside of the line. I was also chained to a spike driven into the ground in the middle of the circle. Ingenious incarceration system when you think about it.

I had five seconds of *holy shit* before the chains were pulled back and a guy wearing a familiar garbage bag poncho strolled in and got on his haunches in front of me. He cocked his head a bit and his blue eyes pierced into mine. He shook his head in disgust and three more similarly clad assholes showed up, one with a key. They unlocked me and dragged me to my feet. I didn't like it. We filed toward an opening in the garbage, my three-foot chain dragging in the dust in front of me. I had been in a procession like this before, and just like before one of the assholes gave me a push on my left shoulder. I didn't like that either. He pushed me again on the next right step, and on the right step after that I dipped my left shoulder. He missed the push, took an elongated step, and I spun and kicked him directly into the waiting arms of one of the chained up dead people. He made some undignified noises as he fought the thing off and he was successful as he wasn't bitten. Can't win 'em all.

"Clearly, you have plans for me," I told them through the pain in my dome. "If you fucking push me again, I will kill you or make you kill me." The guy just threw hate at me, heaving like he had gone twenty rounds with Ali. An affirmation of their plans for me. If they were going to just eat me, they could kill me at any time, so I had that going for me.

We strolled into a big open area completely surrounded by crushed vehicles and trash. A table off to the right had half a dozen guns on it, two of them being mine. Two of the larger idiots stood blocking the only exit with their hand-made weapons. Why didn't they have the rifles? It was absurd. Forty or so trash bag wearing shitheads were standing or sitting in a circle and they marched me into the center of it. Higher than the rest, on a throne of trash, sat an enormously fat woman with two dead men on chains struggling on either side of her. She had a weird smile that I thought might be perpetual, and she wore a torn and stained Mumu. No trash bags for the queen. A wide scar ran from the left side of her mouth up into her hairline and split her greasy black hair with a wide swath of white. The most interesting part of her were her eyes, though. They were a deep red because she was infected as fuck.

A Runner.

"Who's this then?" she asked at great volume and then hacked and spat. While she did have a terrifying broken glass voice, it wasn't the same as the other infected I had heard, and her words were perfectly pronounced. Not like Thorne or Subject Nine. This thing was five hundred pounds of infected eloquence.

Nobody answered her and she raised an eyebrow and her smile vanished. "You," she said pointing at me.

"You made the mess."

I remained silent and she stood. It was an effort. She thundered down the three trash steps and emptied out onto the dirt, Mumu a-jiggle. She leaned in, putting her face two inches from mine, expecting me to shit myself because of her red eyes. I could tell by the smirk on her face she had done this before and that bothered the shit out of me. The other domesticated infected I had been around didn't give a shit about scaring people. They did it naturally. This thing was getting off on it.

She looked confused and pulled her face away slowly. Then her fat knee came up into my balls and she lifted me off the ground a couple of inches. She had mostly missed, but the force of the kick was enough to drop me to the ground in a fetal position, chain clinking and coughing my balls out. I might need an X-ray on my pubic bone, too.

She put her hands up in the air, her lumbering mass completing a circle, legs obviously straining. This woman was probably in her early thirties and her heart would fail before forty. I had no idea how she could be so huge and still be alive, then I remembered she was infected.

I stood slowly, the agony in my crotch begging for me to do anything but move. She put her hands down and approached me with a huge toothy grin. I hauled off and kicked her in the crotch as hard as my damaged nuts would allow. It had not been my best kick, but it was up there, screaming testicles or no.

She did exactly what I had done. She put both hands to her crotch and dropped to the ground. She was too rotund to go into a fetal position, but she tried like hell.

"Right in the piss flippers, bitch!" I yelled at her.

One of her trash bag cronies sprinted at me and I took the chain in both hands and swung it. It connected with the side of his dome and wrapped halfway around the side. He collapsed like a dropped sack of shit, and if he wasn't dead, he was gonna wish he was tomorrow.

My nuts hurt, my head hurt, fuck, *everything* hurt, but if I was ever going to get out of this one, I needed to kick Ruth to the curb. I would need to be absolutely ruthless. As such, I swung the chain down on the back of the downed behemoth, who spasmed a bit and cried out in pain. Two more of the garbage pail kids stood, so I cracked the big bitch across the back of her legs, and she screamed again.

"Stay the fuck back or she gets another one!" I twirled the chain over my head once and brought it down hard on the dirt next to her head. I felt wet around my eyes and knew what was happening. I pounced on her then and I saw something I had never expected to see: fear. Stark terror. I snarled and she screamed, throwing her hands up in front of her face.

What in the actual fuck was happening? I reached down and grabbed her hair. She screamed again and I brought her face to mine to examine her. Her eyes were blood red, but there were no feverish twitches. She didn't snarl or try to kill me, and the dead giveaway was her terror.

This was no fucking Runner. Bitch was faking it.

But I wasn't. I let a little more of the rage consume me and threw my head back. I took a deep breath and screamed. It scared me because I sounded exactly like one of them. More importantly, it scared everybody else because they couldn't back away fast enough. Problem was, I was between most of them and the only exit.

She was crying now. Sobbing like a toddler who didn't get a cookie. I don't know how she did the eye-thing, but everything else told me she was a damn charlatan, and these rubes had fallen for every pound of her.

A young woman tried to run past me, and I whipped the chain and caught her in the ankle. She screamed as well, and I howled again.

"This is your queen?" I yelled, my voice not my own. "This is who you take orders from?" One of the guards thrust his spear at me and I grabbed it and pulled, throwing him off balance enough that he fell face first into the dirt. I jumped on his back, pulled his arm to my face, and ripped off his left triceps with my teeth. I spit it back at him.

Now everybody screamed. They panicked but they had to get past me to get out. Several of them began climbing up the trash and cars and some made it, but most rolled back to the dirt.

Ankle girl and arm guy were holding their wounds, and the boss lady was lying there, sobbing. I could have just left. I could have turned around and strolled out of that trash canyon without a care in the world, but I didn't. I grabbed the spear that arm guy had dropped and thrust it into the fat woman's ample belly. Ripping it out, I swung it at the other guard, the edge flaying off a bit of his face.

Cowards. A bunch of cowards. All they had to do was have three guys rush me and I was dead, but they just ran in every direction but at me. I threw the spear and took a younger guy in the back, then lashed out with the chain and hit a dude in the arm. I spun and launched myself at ankle girl, yanking her head up by her filthy, matted hair. "Where are the prisoners?" I demanded, my voice frightening even to me. She was fully crying now, her foot shattered. She wouldn't run anywhere for a long time and that may well be a death sentence now.

"Where?" I screamed, but she had checked out. I threw her head into the dirt and moved to the next person who tried to get past me. It was a kid. Sixteen or seventeen at best. I grabbed him by his long hair and his trash bag and threw him hard into one of the crushed cars. The impact jarred him, but I could see some blood where the trash bag had ripped away and the edges of the car had cut him. He fell to the ground naked, and I kicked him in the ribs. I put my face right down to his and growled deep in my throat. He screamed and threw his hands up between our faces. I smacked his paws away and he just crushed his eyes closed.

"Where are the people you took today?"

His eyes shot open, and he focused on mine. Both of us had liquid in our eyes, but I could tell by the look on his face, the colors were different. He glanced toward the single exit, where trash bag wearing cannibals were fleeing.

"I know they're not in here, asshole. Where are they?"

"In the jail," he stammered. "Out and to the left."

I grunted. All I wanted to do was kill this kid. I wanted to hurt him in any way I could. I had done some vile shit to people since this whole apocalypse thingie had gone down, but I wanted to make an example of this little shit to the rest of the little shits in this place. My hands closed around his throat.

But this wasn't me. I wasn't like these people. I didn't hurt or maim just to do it or, for fuck's sake, because I was hungry. They had been playing with their food. I hurt people to save people. I looked at the Queen. She was bleeding out in the dirt. My eyes darted right, and I saw the guy whose face I had flayed off. He had passed out and didn't even look human anymore. Ankle girl was weeping and rocking back and forth, holding her leg. The guy I bit was nowhere to be seen, but I'm sure a bite was a death sentence to these assholes. They didn't know I couldn't pass this shit on. Hell, I wasn't even sure.

While I had been surveying the damage I had done to this group, the entire time I had been doing the stuff in the paragraph above, I had been unknowingly squeezing the life out of the kid beneath me. Deep furrows had been dug into my hands and forearms where he had struggled to free himself and cut me with his nails. His face was purple. I released him and he sucked in a huge gout of air. He looked at me, terrified, and I just stood.

This wasn't me. I know I said that above, but it's true. Whatever was in me did this. I looked at my hands. Not because of the blood dripping down my arms but because it was like I was seeing them for the first time. I had killed when I hadn't needed to. The fight was over, and to my everlasting shame I had carried on.

If Richy or Chloe didn't listen to me, would I flip out and kill them? Would I bite Remo's nose off if he told me my tactics were poor? If Donna and I had a baby, would I fly into a rage and kill it because it was crying? Jesus, would it be born infected?

I was like the Hulk, but with none of the good stuff. A time bomb that could go off at any time and kill those whom I love. It was at that moment that I realized I would not go back to San Francisco. I had tried running away before, but that was so the government stooges who were looking for me wouldn't hurt anybody close to me. Now I was the one who was a danger.

Deep thoughts, none of which helped in saving my new friends from becoming bowel movements. I picked up the spear and glanced at the kid. He had scooched away from me and sat naked against a crushed car, holding his throat with both hands and trying to be as small as possible.

I stormed out of the trash arena and took a left down another corridor. It was pretty dark for such an open area. Two guards, each holding pike-like weapons, stood to either side of what looked like the same type of entrance that the last place had. I snarled at them, and when they saw my eyes, one just cowered against the crushed vehicles. The other one thrust his spear, but I knocked it away with mine and thumped him across the face with the butt end. His nose exploded and blood showered his naked chest. This fucker must have been an elite because he was wearing filthy pants. He dropped to his knees, and I kicked him out of the way.

"You come in behind me and I will tear you to pieces," I told them with that inhuman voice, and picked up their weapons. I was wary when I entered the area, but there were no dead folks on chains and no guards waited to impale me.

Six people were in six dog cages. They were naked and terrified and when one of them saw me they lit up.

"You found us!" Harriet whisper yelled. "Was that explosion you?"

"Yeah, Jill and me. Remember that C4?"

She smiled and I strode over to her dog cage. I was never getting that lock off without a key, but I was able to use the spear to pry the door and bend it open from the top. The lock would be there after our sun faded out, but she was able to squeeze through the opening we had made together. I reached down to help her, and she was out in just a sec.

"Thank you," she said and looked into my eyes. She backpedaled so fast I thought she would suck in light until she collided with one of the crushed vehicles. "You... you're..." She reached for a gun on her hip that wasn't there.

"Glad you're unarmed. Look, don't sweat it, I'm not like them. Well, not in any sense where I can transmit it to you or think you look tasty."

I got the other five out of their cages, two bolted immediately at the sight of my eyes, but Harriet, one of the newbies, and Harlan stayed. I didn't know the other two people, but I hope they made it. Between cannibals and undead, everybody was on the menu around here.

Harlan looked wary until I threw him the makeshift spear. "There's a fast one leading the others," he told me.

"Not anymore. She's bleeding out a few rows of trash over." I thumbed to my left. "She was also full of shit and not infected."

The new kid hadn't seen my eyes yet when she asked, "How do you know?"

I rounded on her way faster and harder than I had wanted to. My voice was all gravel when I snarled, "Because I'm infected!" That was enough for her. She screamed and bolted, her naked ass sprinting out through the crushed cars.

"Oops."

Naked Harriet and Harlan were to my left, the spear I had given Harlan levelled at me. "I'm not going to eat you, Harlan, you're not my type. Come with me if you want your guns back." I made for the exit, and they warily followed.

MISTER AMERICAN PIE

"And here," I pointed to a scar on my calf. Clearly healed after a few years of traversing our infected country. "But this was the worst one," I told them, showing them my arm.

I pointed out that all the bites had occurred months ago and that the scratch on my face had been there before they met me two days ago. Even the scratch should have killed me or turned me into a Runner by now. The three of them looked like they were about to shoot me anyway.

"How are my eyes?"

Harriet and Harlan exchanged a quick glance. Harlan rested his hand on his sidearm. "Still red."

I sighed. I couldn't blame them. They had learned that the only thing these creatures do is kill. No remorse or guilt or feelings of any kind from the dead and only rage from the Runners. These people believed nothing else, even with me standing in front of them red-eyed and talking.

"He saved my life," Julie told them. "He saved all of us." She started crying and attempted to run to me, but both of her friends grabbed her. She fought briefly, but I put my hand up.

"Stop. I'll just go. It's ok."

"Look," Harriet began, "we just can't—"

"I know," I interrupted. "It's fine. I'll just grab my gear and go."

Harlan nodded, never taking his eyes off mine. "Prolly for the best."

I shouldered my pack and stuck the HK in the holster on my hip. I missed my Sig, but this was still a nice sidearm. Big holes. Chauncy was in a sheath above my ass.

I glanced around the firewood shop and sighed, "You take care of yourselves."

Harlan kept his eyes on me when he replied, "You too, Mister." Julie started to sniffle.

"I'll be fine, kid. This is what I do."

I started moving toward one of the garage doors when Julie said, "Let him take Pie!"

All I could think of, in that moment, was my mom's homemade cherry cobbler. Not a pie per sé, but still, it was a fond memory.

"Now, Julie…" Harlan started.

"If he didn't risk his life to save you, you'd be sitting in a cage with your arms and legs sawed off right now!"

And that's how I ended up with another horse. As I was mounting the big fella, I couldn't help but think of Shaitan, the last asshole I rode.

Well, fuck, *that* came out wrong.

The last horse I was on.

Another thought pervaded my mind, and I glanced down at the three humans. "At some point, the military is going to be knocking on your door asking about me. Tell them the truth. All of it. Everything. They might give you some supplies." I shrugged. "Of course, they might shoot you too. Fifty-fifty."

Harriet strolled over to me, she looked embarrassed, but she passed me a parcel. I checked and inside were 3 MREs, 3 bottles of water, and a very used roadmap of California.

"Thank you," I said, and kicked gently at Pie's sides. We started to walk away from the firewood store at a good clip. I was heading northwest, so I was literally riding into the sunset. I threw up a hand in a good-bye wave but didn't look back. I hoped they would make it.

The horde that had been traversing the town of Baker would make things hard for my new friends, so when I reached the outskirts, I jumped off of Pie and tied him to a stop sign. I had a hundred yards clear around me in all directions, so I fired three rounds over five seconds to catch the ears of the horde and waited. A Runner came screaming out from between a mail truck and a rickety stockade fence. I got a bead on him immediately, but when my finger started to tighten on the trigger, I hesitated. Thorne, Subject Nine, and the other domesticated Runners had proven that, while they would never be who they were before, they could be new and useful... *people*. This thing sprinting at me wasn't domesticated, but it could be. What if me and this guy could get beers and talk about the inconsistencies of cooked venison or how to crack safes?

The barrel of my rifle lowered ever so slightly, and I stared at the face of the thing coming for me. It had been a man. A man who probably had a job, a car, and a family. Maybe he had an Australian Cattle Dog running around his back yard getting treats for sitting when told. All of that was gone now and the only thing this creature had was its hate.

When it was thirty feet away, my eye snapped back to the optic and I plugged the dude center mass. He faltered but kept coming so I double tapped him. He lost balance and slid the last few feet toward me on his chest. He looked up at me then, his face pleading, but he wasn't pleading for me to let him live. His split second of pleading was for me to step closer so he could kill me with his hands and teeth before he bled out. I felt pity. I hadn't felt pity for these things since I shot one who jumped at me off an old Airstream trailer in the woods of New Hampshire.

Ammo was worth way more than gold or diamonds right now, but I still put one in his dome. I would never let a Runner suffer again. I would be merciful for Thorne and Nine. For whomever the Runners used to be. For whom I am now.

It took about a half hour for the vanguard to show their gray faces. By twos and threes they came, stumbling and shuffling toward me until suddenly there were hundreds. Pie was getting nervous, so I untied him and climbed aboard. I made that clicking sound you make when you want a horse to move, and he did. He wanted to trot, but I kept him at a walk. We dragged the horde out into the desert and away from Baker, hopefully forever. We kept the swarm of dead things about a quarter mile back, but Pie was getting more nervous by the second. The sun was high, and it was steamy before I let the poor guy trot. We had been moving for about six hours by then and we trotted for another after we had lost sight of the dead. That's when I turned his nose to the left and we ran hard for three minutes. I slowed him to a stop and gave him some water from Chuckie's water bladder which had been affixed to Pie's saddle.

He greedily drank and so did I. We took ten minutes then galloped for five minutes, then I slowed him to a walk. We had to have five miles on the rotters by then, and hopefully they would just keep travelling northeast while we moved northwest.

In another hour or so I heard something in the distance. It was coming from behind us, so I stopped Pie, stood up in the saddle, and shaded my eyes with my hand as I peered in the distance.

It was a helicopter, and it was far off, but coming this way.

I was in the middle of the California scrubland. There was nowhere to hide. We galloped anyway, like our asses were on fire. It was damn hot by now. It only took a few minutes for Pie to start to tire and his neck was foamy with sweat. The good news is there were some big rock formations up ahead to the north, so we ran for those.

"Come on, Pie," I urged. "They'll take me in the copter, but there won't be room for you. What do you think they'll do to you, buddy?"

I swear to everything he heard me, because we made those rocks which were a minute away in less than twenty seconds. We weaved between a few pillars of stone, and I dismounted, pulling him with me by his face with the reins. There was a set of hills next to us and that was the only thing of any altitude for miles. These hills were more like bumps of rock, the biggest maybe thirty feet high, but most were about ten feet off the scrub. This was the only place to hide and I'm hoping the bird wouldn't see it the same way I did, or worse, have some kind of optics that made me glow.

I clutched my rifle tightly as the sound of the rotors got louder. Did they have infrared? Heat vision? Whatever the hell that white shit on the screen was that you saw on TV when there was a world, and an attack helicopter was shredding bad guys in a far-off desert country? I don't know what it's called but did they have that?

Fortunately for me, but unfortunately for you, Dear Reader, the helicopter noises began to fade. This wasn't going to be one of those times when the bird just buzzed right over us, hovered, and attacked. They hadn't seen us and just flew the fuck away.

Pie was jumpy and nodding his head. He made undignified horse sounds, and he had every right to be afraid of that helicopter; they would shoot him or leave him in the desert to die. What I didn't consider was the horse's sense of smell. He could smell the dead before I could, and that information was paramount in this particular situation. I was tired and had my attention elsewhere when something grabbed me with one hand and thumped me in the neck between my shoulder and my head. I spun, seeing something made of black and silver, but the thing wouldn't let go and its black-clad head came in for another attempt.

I broke its grip, and I kicked it away. It turned toward my horse, but Pie lashed out with his front hooves and knocked the thing's head almost off. It went flying, landing against one of the rock pillars. It made feeble movements for a moment and then expired.

I stared at it for a long minute. We were in the middle of the California desert, so what the hell was this thing doing out here in a gimp outfit? All in black vinyl with little chains, it was missing its left arm and had part of its side gnawed away. A bloody, red, rubber ball gag kept its mouth open and more importantly, unable to bite.

I put my hand to my neck. I might have a bruise, but if not for this undead guy's sexual proclivities, I would be bleeding out in the sand. He had gotten close enough to sink his teeth into my carotid, but his pervert ball gag had saved me. Thank God for BDSM.

Then I thought about this poor fucker. He must have been tied to something and the dead broke in and killed him while he was restrained. He had thought he was going to have some weird sex, and it had gone to a level he hadn't anticipated. Can you imagine being dined on while tied up? So horrible.

I looked at the ball gag. It was almost bitten through. I felt my neck again but mostly I felt lucky and relieved. And stupid. Fucking dumb for not paying attention to my new buddy.

I put my forehead on his long nose. "You just saved me, you dumb horse."

He snorted and nodded. We both had a new buddy, and we would need to protect each other. I would start by letting the helicopter keep flying away for an hour. I busted out an MRE from my pack and filled Pie's nose feeder.

He got oats or something that looked like oats, and I got pimento loaf. What the hell is an oat anyway? I had only ever seen them in meal, granola, or in front of a horse. Where did oats come from? Trees? A bush? Does it look like wheat? Fuck, I dunno. Lots of questions flooded my mind while we both munched, but the one that really pervaded my thoughts was where the fuck did a BDSM zombie come from? I mean, we were in the middle of the damn desert!

I looked at the pathetic thing, then back at my food. I was completely comfortable with eating while there was a dead thing not fifteen feet away. When the hell did that happen?

Pie started making noises and nodding his head. I dropped the gum from the MRE (because ew) and pocketed the crackers and the drink mix. I pulled the empty oat bag from Pie's nose, and he started looking in multiple directions. He was nervous and that made me nervous. We had hidden in these pinnacles because the helicopter wouldn't be able to see us, but the downside was that I couldn't see shit either.

But Pie could smell. He could smell much better than I could, so I trusted him. We needed to be gone, that much was apparent. I hoped the bird had flown far away in the fifteen minutes we had hidden in here, but while I couldn't see, hear, or smell the dead, I knew they were almost on us.

Screw pulling the horse by the face, I jumped up on him using an expert cowboy move, and we started to trot through the rocks. "Let's went, Cisco," I told him.

Our hidey-hole was behind us in just a minute or two, and we headed for the mountain range to the left and in front of us. I glanced over my shoulder to see what had been in the rocks with us, but nothing emerged. I would chalk this up to Pie having a superior sniffer, and we moved on.

In a half hour we hit a highway and ten minutes later a sign saying Entering Death Valley National Park, but it was facing away from us, so we had just come from there. I looked at my map and realized we were either crossing over the 190, or I didn't know how to read maps.

Not wanting to stay on a highway in case the helicopter, the dead, or bad guys came around, we headed due west toward the mountains and what a monumental fuck up that was. I couldn't see on the map what kind of mountains they were, but they were impassible by horse, that's for damn sure. They rose up out of the ground and said, "Fuck you!" because we all knew Pie wasn't climbing those.

There were a ton of towns north, but only one on the southerly road which cut through the mountains. So, in order to go northwest, I had to go southwest. For the next hour we saw nothing. Not a bird or an infected, not even a bug. Then we saw a sign for Panamint Springs Resort. It was five miles in front of us.

We clippity-clopped out of the mountains and back into desert. There were more mountains in front of us, but this next stretch of road snaked due west and we followed it. There was nothing here. Very few scrub bushes and mostly just hard-packed dirt. There would be nowhere to duck and cover until we hit the mountains on the other side of this valley. I thought against moving forward, but really, there was no other way to go, so we went.

The sun beat down on us hard, and I was thankful for the shemagh I had appropriated from one of the dead SEALs. Pie was covered in hair, but he would still overheat if I didn't get him shade soon. I couldn't run him either, or the heat would kill him. It was a hundred degrees easy. I stopped at what I considered halfway through and let him have a big drink. He took a quarter of his water bladder, but he needed it. I took a swig too, but only enough to swish around in my mouth.

Twenty minutes later I could see a structure through the haze and heat of the highway. Twenty minutes after that and I could make out what it was. Not that I needed to, there was a sign. Panamint Springs Resort, next left.

"Well," I told Pie, "it ain't Club Med."

"Resort" was a straight up bullshit lie. It was a crappy gas station with a restaurant attached to it. A sign atop a pole just read BAR so I figured there were either tons of Browning Automatic Rifles, or at one point there had been drunks here. There were what looked like campsites behind the main structure with some trailers and abandoned tent paraphernalia. Typical of early plague setups where everybody died.

I glanced back up at the sign on the pole. I mean, there was no way there was any booze left in there, right? I shifted and grabbed the binoculars attached to Pie's saddle. I scanned the area but didn't see anything. Of course, if there were bad guys, cannibals, or undead, it was unlikely they would announce their presence or intentions until it was too late.

Any other time, and I would have gone far, far around the Panamint Springs Resort, but it was hot as balls, and I needed out of the sun.

We ambled up to the sign and stood in the shade a moment. I looked through the binoculars again, checking out what was behind the establishment. If there were dead here, they were quiet. If there were bad guys, they likely already had me scoped.

I climbed down from the horse. I couldn't tie him up, if I got dead, then he would be helpless. At least he could run away if something came for him. But still...

"Dude, do not leave me in this place. I need you to keep me alive and I'm thinking you need me. I'm going to check the place out and if there's water, food, or shade, I will come back and get you. You feel me?"

Not a snort, not a nod, not even a side eye. Nothing. So much for being the horse whisperer. I checked the load on both my rifle and my sidearm. I didn't know whether to go in with the suppressor or the rifle, so I opted for the rifle. At least it would give me 30 rounds before I had to switch to the sidearm. But it would be loud. I mean, the suppressor wasn't completely silent, but it was way better than the rifle in the noise department.

Fuck it. Sidearm it was.

The front doors to the restaurant were closer than the gas station and they were those old style, glass jobbies in a metal frame with the push bar. One door had no glass, but I don't know about the other door because it was missing. The whole door was gone. This was the third time I had seen a place in the middle of nowhere missing a door. Like, completely gone. Was there an odd door collection hobby I was unaware of? I had to think about it, but not now. Now we needed water and shade. There were also bullet holes in one of the front windows and another window was shattered and gone.

I stepped through the doorway, my suppressor leading the way. There had been a stand here, but I don't know if it had been against infected or breathers. Bullet holes and casings all over the place, brown stains on the linoleum that had to be blood. Full breakfast plates with desiccated food still on them were on a few of the tables and the bar. Chairs, stools, and some of the tables had been upended. I hadn't seen any casings outside, so I assumed the dead had assaulted this place. That was confirmed when I peeked behind the breakfast bar and saw gnawed piles of yellowed bones missing every scrap of flesh on them. There were too many bones for it to have been one person and there were two skulls. The skulls had been broken open and the good stuff removed.

Suddenly I didn't want to be in the restaurant at the Panamint Springs Resort any longer. It was creepy and there were way too many shadows for so close to noon. Too many places for dead things to go unseen. Even with all the shadows, a glint caught my eye as I drew my head back from peeking over the bar. I checked again and the one bit of sunshine that had made it into the back of the restaurant had glinted off a bottle.

Hey, this had been a bar. I moved cautiously around the end of the bar and noticed a bunch of broken stuff and a full bottle of brown whiskey on this side of the bone pile. Keep in mind this was a breakfast bar. I'm not a hard alcohol type of guy, but this could come in handy. Trade maybe? Disinfectant? I thought you could only use clear alcohol for disinfectant, but I had seen Alvarez use whiskey, so maybe. I grabbed the mostly-full bottle and rooted around behind the bar. There was a lever-action shotgun on the bar shelf next to a half a box of shells. I grabbed both, checking the load and action on the shotgun and stuffing the dusty box in my pack.

I wanted to make haste and get back to Pie, but I stopped and put my hand on the faucet handle over the deep dish-sink behind the bar. I shrugged and turned the handle, but no water flowed. No cheeseburgers flowed either, just sayin'.

I spun hard when I heard a thump through a set of those Western saloon type doors that led into the kitchen. I felt a bead of icy sweat trickle down my back and perch at the crack of my ass. Hey, I was clenched, and it was hot. I moved forward quietly, the suppressor on my sidearm out in front as I took slow, furtive steps.

Another thump and I almost went full code brown. I didn't know why I was so scared. This was old hat for me. I shook my head a bit to clear it and peeked over the rustic saloon doors. Standard kitchen, except for the carnage and the blood smears on the yellow tile wall. The third thump had me direct my weapon at the walk-in freezer.

I may have told you prior to now, Dear Reader, that while I am definitely better than when these whole undead shenanigans started, I am still not high speed. That is likely why I kicked a pot when I moved again, sending it clattering into every fucking thing in the state of California, then doing that incredibly loud rattle as it completed its circular rolling motion and slowed to a terrifyingly loud stop. The crescendo echoed through the shadowed kitchen for what seemed like an eternity, but really had been half a second.

Dead silence for a moment as I crushed my eyelids closed in self-loathing. Ship's stink eye could reach across the world and I felt it boring into me right then. There was nobody here to see it, but my face burned with disconcerted chagrin. The silence ended when something crashed against the walk-in door hard enough to move it a bit. Fists started pounding on the door and walls of the freezer. More than two fists.

Personally, I am of the school that every living dead that can be destroyed should be destroyed. Shoot 'em, stab 'em, thump 'em on the dome. Get rid of them because a destroyed infected is infinitely less likely to bite someone, specifically me.

But fuck that noise. There was no room to move around in here and there was a ton of shit on the floor that could trip me up. No matter how horrible it was for the folks who died in that freezer, they could stay in there. Sorry, not sorry.

I holstered my HK, the suppressor reaching almost to my knee, and pushed a stainless-steel food prep table between the freezer door and the wall. The table was flimsy, but it would keep that door closed indefinitely wedged as it was.

The creeps had fled my psyche, and I did a more in-depth search of the kitchen. I was able to snag an unopened first aid kit, two D batteries, still in the package, a red Bic-style lighter that worked when I tried it, an unopened jar of half-sour pickles, and a huge can of tapioca pudding. Like, enormous. There were other cans of food items, but they were on the floor covered in crusty blood, dented, or swollen. I ain't got time for no botulism.

I was about to leave the kitchen when I saw a blue-handled chef's knife just sitting there on the counter. It was in a plastic clip-on sheath, and I clipped that shit right the fuck on. I would never see my SOG Seal Pup again, but I hoped to dice and filet many an infected with my knew Dalstrong, 8-inch, Shadow Black Series, Titanium Nitride coated, Razor Sharp Chef Knife with All-New Finger Guard. That was what the beautiful box next to the knife told me. The box was sexy AF too; wood with red felt inside, but WTF would I do with that? It had to stay behind.

With this thing I would be the envy of chefs world-wide. Both of them. The rest were likely dead. The kitchen held no more booty, but upon further inspection I found two bottles and a can of some microbrew beer I had never heard of, several full salt and pepper shakers, and… wait for it… a twenty-ounce bottle of Mountain Dew prepared by Zeus himself atop Mount Olympus as he looked down upon a crumbling humanity with disdain. I saw the green bottom nipples of the bottle poking out from under an overturned table at the far end of the dining area. Caffeinated, sugary, citrus deliciousness with a side of brominated vegetable oil was in my future, and no you fucking barbarian Reader, I would never insult the Dew by mixing it with the whiskey.

The only thing left to do in here now was explore the restroom. I could use a porcelain sit-down, and with a recently cleared diner, I was finally going to get my wish. No squatting in the California scrubland today, my dudes.

I stared hard at those saloon doors, not being able to see the walk-in from my position but hearing those dead dickweeds thump the door. They had been in there who knows how long, so it was unlikely they would escape their formerly frosty prison in the time it took me to drop the kids off at the pool.

The door to the men's room opened with the squeal of unkept hinges, the cacophony sounding to me like a howitzer shell fired out of a jet engine. That sound alone would have been enough to bring every dead thing in the men's room out for a snack. Nothing came. Three sinks on the left with a full-length wall mirror, four stalls and three urinals on the right, one at a smaller height than the other for the kiddies. Other than two hand dryers on the wall and a red drink cup complete with cap and straw on the floor, the place was empty. I checked the stalls anyway, one at a time, but they were devoid of things wanting to eat me.

I moved back to the first stall, inspected it like a quality control expert, and found it to be both clean and stocked with single ply toilet paper. Deplorable, cheap-ass sons of bitches and their single ply shit tickets. The barbarous heathens of Panamint Springs had copped out and gone cheap for the hundreds of travelers who visited this resort stop on their way to whatever vacation debauchery they were up to. The good thing was that all of it, every soft, single ply square of virgin wood pulp tightly rolled into a pleasurable toilet fantasy, would now lovingly caress my bum as I finished my business.

I unbuckled, dropped ye ole pantaloons, and sat down with a blissfully contented sigh, the coolness of the plastic seat nuzzling that most sacred of places. I laid the recently reloaded lever-action shotgun across my naked thighs feeling its coolness as well and got to work. Fire in the hole!

All I needed was a magazine. Failing that, I pulled out something I hadn't touched in months. No, you pervert, not that, my wallet. Through all my travels, all my trials and tribulations, every battle, every time I was submerged, sometimes in zombie-infested waters, I had held on to my wallet. A philosophical need to keep it had pervaded my psyche since I had gotten the worn leather bifold returned just prior to getting onto a prison bus several years ago. One of the guards had grabbed a box of our personal effects when we had evacuated, the dead on our heels, and to my utter surprise my wallet had been in there.

So, I did what every guy does when he's on the can with no means of entertainment: I started reading the cards in my wallet. Funny thing is, Dear Reader, through all the stuff I had listed above, I hadn't opened my wallet, other than to dry it out, since that prison bus escape. The first thing I took out was a library card. Now what in the fuck did I have a library card for? I don't think I had ever been in a library before or during the apocalypse, so why the card? But there it was, with my name, former address, and an illegible number. It was unlaminated and...

I lifted my head, listening. Dead silence. But there shouldn't be silence. There should be... the thumping had stopped. The pounding on the walk-in — the door to the bathroom smashed open so hard I heard a piece of something metal hit the ground. I couldn't see how many because, as etiquette demands, I had secured the stall door, but I could hear at least a couple of zombies thunder into the shitter.

Then, a palpable gust of breath-stealing stench enveloped me, forcing me to bend over and dry heave, informing every one of those dead fuckers where the vittles were housed.

With a hearty clench, I pinched off what had been in the process of release and yanked my drawers up at lightspeed. I grabbed the shotgun in one hand and the webbing of my belt in the other, the buckle of which had suddenly become a fucking Rubik's cube. Thank God, Jesus, Mary, Joseph, and all the little cherubs the porcelain walls of the privy had secured that which had plunged into the landing zone.

These particular infected needed no knack for extra sensory perception as they immediately launched a thunderous melee against the precarious portal which I stood behind. The lock snapped without further ado, and I was face to face with no less than three of the dead ones. Not wanting my pants to fall back around my ankles, I held on furiously to them with one hand while aiming the shotgun into the face of a dead man in what used to be a white apron with the other. Black tar coated a decent portion of the room-length mirror, and the sound nearly deafened me when the blast of the scattergun took apron-guy's head off.

Dear Reader, it is impossible to lever a shell into your lever action shotgun with one hand. This is a fact. You know it now and I was baptized by fire right then. I let go of my pants, not to charge another round, but to grab the blued barrel of the weapon with both hands and thrust it sideways into the faces of the oncoming two dead people. I shuffled forward, pants restricting my movement, and pushed the assholes back out the shitter door. One of them, a woman with one arm and a skull for a face, used her single hand to latch onto my weapon and try to yank it from me. Gagging, I tried to bring my knee a bit forward to deny gravity's grip on my pants, but fall they did and suddenly my forward momentum was halted that much more.

The dead onslaught persisted, the woman pulling and the other thing, not sure of the sex, reaching over the gun. I gave a final, mighty heave, and let them have the weapon, pushing myself back as I pushed them away. The unforgiving grip on my now fully restrained ankles made itself known and suddenly my lily-white butt was tasting the cool tiled floor of a rest stop bathroom.

I felt extremely confined as I sifted through the coils of my pants attempting to yank my sidearm from its holster. The suppressor made it a long draw, but I succeeded just as the no-sex thing had righted itself and reached for that which was, to my utter dismay, unabashedly displayed. Of course. Of course, the dead thing would home in on my spaghetti and meatballs and those decrepit, filthy, nailed fingers seemed to stretch to the breaking point in doing so. Losing all semblance of control, I crushed my finger down on the trigger and emptied the magazine into both approaching figures. One fell back and the other fell forward, but I rolled my unwiped ass under the sinks, and it missed me.

First thing I did was perform a systems diagnostic to ensure the boys and their buddy were still there and undamaged. After that, I ejected the sidearm magazine, the metal box clattering away under one of the stalls, and slapped in my last mag, ripping the slide back to charge a round after my tantrum had consumed everything. Aiming my weapon at the restroom door, I heaved, gulping great lungfuls of air.

If I could have shit myself, I would have.

I sat on the floor for thirty seconds or so, listening but hearing nothing, then yanked my pants back up, toilet paper be damned. I'd sort that out later. Nothing else stormed the door, and with the commotion we had made, had there been others, they would have come.

I did grab some toilet paper then, but even that was a fight. The untrusting bastards of Panamint Springs Resort had secured their TP in those little roll locks such that you could use the stuff to wipe your ass but couldn't pilfer any paper. I solved that problem with a single kick and was rewarded with two rolls that went into my pack.

A smallish red puddle coated the floor where I had fallen on my ass. The hole put in my side by that douche SEAL had opened during the battle, and I could feel a bit of pain there now, but it wasn't awful.

I peeked out the door, but nothing waited for me. I made my way past the carnage in the diner and exited into the burning sun, noticing Pie looking at me strangely.

The gas station was next on my exploration list, but Pie needed some water. He perked up when he saw me coming and walked halfway to meet me.

He got a nose rub, and I scratched behind his left ear. "Good boy." I got the water bladder off him and, wiggling the shotgun blast out of my ear with my pinkie, gave him a huge drink. I would save as much water for him as I could because I would be enjoying my newly acquired Mountain Fucking Dew. Sacrilege they couldn't put the F word in the title. I checked the bottle anyway. Nope. No F bombs.

Stowing the bladder, I climbed up into the saddle and rode a stalwart Pie to the gas station. It was attached to the restaurant by an overhang to prevent the sun from pelting folks on the head as they moved between the buildings. It would be rain protection anywhere else, but it is likely that the last rain these parts had seen had been accompanied by an ark full of critters.

No dead people were inside the gas station and the single bay had a Chevy Tahoe up on the lift with the bay door wide open. I walked Pie right into the bay and pulled the door down with the attached rope. A steel back door and another push-bar type half-door with chicken wire safety glass that led into the station, were the only other entrances. High windows, well beyond the reach of any dead hands, let in a bit of light.

A pot-bellied stove adorned the back wall of the bay. I could use that tonight to keep us toasty if I could find something to burn. Toilet paper came to mind, and I took care of the clean up right there in front of Pie, the resulting trash going into the stove.

I covered the half-door glass with a couple of pieces of cardboard, set Pie up for a meal of oats, and gave him a big drink.

Speaking of drinks, there was no need to save that one can of beer, so I fired it down. I followed it with the two bottles, and I had a pretty spiffy glow going. I'm no lightweight, but I don't have time to drink much in the apocalypse. The label on the bottles said Death Dealer, and I found that apt. I glanced at the green plastic of the Mountain Dew bottle. No. No, I would save that for the trail. It might save my life. But the whiskey...

Nah. I'm not a hard alcohol drinker.

I filled the stove with some newspaper and there were two pallets against the side wall that I broke up and I was able to get the hardwood into the stove. It was burning merrily in moments, and none too soon. The cold had set in. I glanced at my pack, the neck of the whiskey bottle poking out of the top inviting me to hang out.

I did have a nice buzz going. It had been forever since I had a beer, and three micros certainly had done the trick. The whiskey beckoned.

Maybe just a sip...

ASSHOLE

I'm never drinking again. Ever. My mouth is so torridly parched it would give the desert a run for its money, and someone replaced my eyelids with 50 grit sandpaper. Everything hurt, from the top of my head to the tips of my toes, but my stomach and the inside of my head were vying for the prize of being most uncomfortable.

Also, I needed to piss. An ocean of the yellow stuff had expanded my bladder like on over-filled balloon. I shifted and that was a bad idea as my stomach contents, more or less nothing but bile and whatever whiskey wasn't digested, threatened revolution.

I would have slept another twelve years or so, but Pie had decided he needed to nudge me awake. He stood over me, nodding his head, clearly laughing at my predicament. I said above that I needed to piss, and I did, but it seems that I had also done that while I had been passed out as well. I was hungover, wet, and super uncomfortable. My pantaloons had been hit by a torpedo and Jesus, Captain, they had taken on water.

The light that streamed into the garage bay assaulted my retinas in an unrelenting attack, my rods and cones retreating back into the depths of my eyeballs, but when my lids came down, they scraped across my dry eyes, which seemed to be the only thing that wasn't soaked in human processed whiskey.

Pie was still nodding, and he grabbed me by the pantleg and dragged me a couple of feet.

"Da fuck, bro?" I grumbled. "Leave a bitch in peace."

He was nodding his head furiously and quietly making horse noises. His sounds were eclipsed by... fuck.

I stood up quickly, every part of my body complaining, but the fear guy had sent requests to the dude in charge of adrenaline and while my hangover didn't go away, it felt a bit dissipated.

The noises of the dead were all around us. Not that rasping hack of theirs, although that was there too, but the sounds of dozens of feet trudging past in the dirt just outside. Hordes were usually much louder than this, so I had to wonder how many were out there. An ancient, five-rung, painting ladder sat dusty against the wall near the stove, and I carefully leaned it up against the side wall to peek out the high windows.

The light hurt my eyes but not nearly as much as the scene outside. I had been wrong about dozens. There were hundreds. Maybe a thousand or more. They were milling about, and I hoped they were just passing through, but I'm not that lucky.

But they weren't talking. Usually they make that undead hiss-growl noise as they trudge around looking for a snack, and while some of them were doing just that, most just soldiered on. The whole area was full of them, and if they found out we were in here, that much weight could tear this building down. I climbed off the ladder and moved to Pie, who was visibly shaken. He was doing that nod, and I knew what it meant.

I mean, I do now. Twice he had done it and twice I had been too human to listen to what he had been telling me. I put my forehead to his and told him it was going to be fine. I did my best to soothe him, rubbing his neck and chin and blowing gently up his nose. That last part was a trick my buddy Matt had taught me in Texas a while back. Matt could also talk to horses, a skill I sorely lacked.

Pie didn't like being here and while he wasn't totally silent, he was quiet. He knew there were predators about, and he knew we were the prey.

"Good boy," I told him. "Good boy." I hoped he was thinking the same thing about me. I looked at my watch, 08:16. I had slept until almost 8 am. That never happened, but I also never got drunk, or at least not in the past few years. I looked around and realized that while it got pretty cold during the evenings, we were in a steel box, and this shit was gonna heat up today. I looked at the big thermometer on the wall, and the mercury told me it was already north of 85 degrees.

If we didn't get out of here in the next few hours, there would be a zombie eating a cooked horse in this oven. I searched the walls and ceiling, but there was no roof access. I glanced at my watch again and then at the thermometer. 08:23 and just under 90 degrees.

So, it was like that.

How the hell did people with no air conditioning live in this type of blistering heat? It was cooler out of the sun, sure, but how hot would it get? People died in cars all the time because of the heat, so would we cook or not in this cinder block and aluminum oven? Would the air be charred away, leaving us nothing to breathe but horse shit and human piss as we gasped our last?

At 09:00 it was 96 degrees. At 10:00 it was 113 and we were literally in the shade. I took a small drink, then gave Pie the last of our water. He gulped it down greedily, chewing on the end of the bladder cap.

I had an epiphany and looked around for my Mountain Dew. It wasn't in my pack, so I searched the surrounding area. There! By whatever the fuck that rusty piece of metal is, I found my...

No. No fucking way. The bottle lay on its side, a little green demon taunting me. It was pointing right at me, a horrible travesty of spin the bottle, because the fucking cap was gone. Stunned, I stood there staring at the plastic before I picked it up. Empty. Empty as a whorehouse on Sunday. I upended the bottle, trying to snatch those last couple of drops that always collect in the little nubs on the bottom, but in true demonic fashion, it was dry as a bone.

I had fired down the whole damn thing in a drunken stupor and I didn't even get to remember enjoying it. I made to throw the empty, useless plastic bottle against the wall in fury, but Pie took one step and put his chin on my shoulder. Damn horse was smarter than I was ever going to be.

I gently placed the bottle back on the concrete floor, getting dizzy because I was still very much hungover. "You're right, buddy, that would have been stupid."

Something smashed into the garage door and the thing rattled like a son of a bitch. Nothing beat on the metal, so I figured it was just an accident. Any of them that figured out we were in here would drag the rest of them and then we'd be fucked. They'd tear the whole building down.

Jesus fuck it was hot. I sat down and started writing all that shit you just read, sweat dripping onto the pages, some of the ink running. It was unbelievably loud too. The silence of the horde had ceased, and they had reverted to that dry hack they do.

My head started to hurt, and I realized there was more to this than just being hungover. Thanks to me being a booze bag on top of the current weather inside this concrete box, I was dehydrated as hell. All I could think of was those prison movies that used to have some guy in the hot box. Pie and myself were in the box.

We couldn't get out either, not with so many of them so close. It would take a solid ten seconds to get the door up, and in that time, there would be a hundred of them in here.

It was 12:21 when I decided we would run at 13:00. The huge thermometer needle was past 125 degrees, and I was feeling dizzy. I saddled the big guy, and we stood in front of the entrance. I had put the painting ladder next to the pull rope on the garage door. I was able to look out and see that there was a gap in the horde about two-hundred feet down. The damn infected seemed to be circling around as opposed to trudging through the area. They must have seen a rat or were just stumbling through the buildings one zombie at a time until everybody gets to go inside. I had an image of infected who had sidled up to the diner, the line for flesh forty deep. *Ding, ding ding!* Order up! One almost cooked moron with slightly pissed pants. 'Slightly' may be an exaggeration, but I digress. Oh, and don't forget I was unable to completely cleanup immediately after the restroom debacle yesterday, so there's that.

My plan was to get as high up the ladder as possible, grab the rope as high as I could, and jump. Hopefully my momentum would open the roll-up door enough that I could quickly get on Pie and get the fuck out of Dodge. The gap was coming. It was sixty feet away, fifty, forty.

"You ready, buddy?"

Twenty... ten...

I jumped at five and that fucking door shot to the roof. Every single dead eye shifted to look at us. Not just the ones here, all of them. The entire world. The infected of planet Earth knew what we were about and every one of them asked in their stupid minds, "Are you shitting me?"

I scrambled to my horse, who hadn't moved a muscle, and got up on him as fast as I could. "Hyah!" I yelled but he hadn't needed the encouragement once I was aboard. He was full gallop in half a second and the fucker was fast.

Straight and right were not options, so we ploughed left into the thinnest part of the group near us. Undead assholes went flying or were trampled, but I knew they'd be up again in posthaste. One of them grabbed a harness on Pie's saddle and hung on for a sec before its arm tore loose at the elbow. Others grabbed at us, and I can honestly say piss wasn't the only excretion that would compel me to acquire new pants.

We made it quite a way before the amount of them in front of us would have bogged us down, so Pie took control and just hooked another left. He reared and lashed out with his hooves, but I had been ready and took it like a champ. The last time I had been in this situation, a different horse had chucked me in the middle of the horde.

Fuck that noise, my feet stayed in the stirrups.

Pie kicked backwards and forwards, spinning and kicking again. He was athletic as fuck and if you've ever had an image of a bucking bronco in your mind, this was that.

But I'm no cowboy. He kept that kicking shit up one second too long and before I knew it and to my everlasting shame, my ass was tasting dust. What had I just thought about feet and stirrups? The wind got knocked out of me when I hit the ground and one of Pie's kicking rear hooves came so close to my face, I felt it pass.

I coughed and was helped to my feet by one of the dead things. It leaned in for a nibble, eager to sample bits of me I needed to keep, but I used one of Remo's tactics and punched up under its arm, the desiccated appendage coming away at the elbow for the second time in half a minute. I spun and gave the fucker what I call "the hangover kick" which

90

is when you drank too much fucking whiskey last night and then try to do pretty much anything.

My boot went right through its rib cage, bone splintering into yellow shards. Although the outside of it was as dry as the desert, the inside remained gooey, with the consistency of rancid melted chocolate. Regardless, the thing went flying and me and my gore covered boot ran like a bitch, zombie shit kicking every which way. Pie continued to kick, and I realized that only one of us was going to make it out of this.

It wasn't gonna be me.

I remember thinking of the kids then. With the dead surrounding me and closing in, all I could think of were my kids. Kat was twenty-something and tough as nails. She was a handful. The twins, Richy and Chloe were equally as capable and equally as hands-fully. They would be fine. I knew it. They were on a submarine or a boat on the way to a better place than the shit show that had been Alcatraz. They would be kept safe by Donna, Ship, Alvarez, Remo, and each other. They would be fine. I knew it and I smiled. They would never know exactly what happened to me, but they would get the gist. That made me a little sad, but the fact that those who protected Donna and the kids were the stuff of legend in the apocalypse made my grin widen. I thought of my parents too, and a vacation we took to New Hampshire once, but that was a time best left not revisited. I had shit to do right now.

I brought my rifle up and calmly took aim. I popped domes, counting rounds and moving slowly between targets as they came toward me. Slow is smooth, smooth is fast. I ejected the mag after twenty-eight shots and slapped in another. I had two left, one mag for my sidearm, and the Chauncy. The dead were about six deep in front of me and I knew I could never get through them all, but Pie might. I spun and acquired targets near my horse. Animals would die when bitten as quickly as a human would, but they didn't come back.

Nobody was biting Pie today, and I fired and fired until he was free. He busted out and took off and I smiled harder. The dead had reached me, but I knew he would be safe. Until the prick circled around with a head of steam and came galloping back to me. I fought off the two who had grabbed me, shooting as many as I could before the big, four-legged bastard plowed through the dead like a freight train, knocking the hissing assholes in all directions including five feet in the air. He let out one more kick and I let my rifle dangle and leapt at him.

As previously stated, I am not John Wayne. I can ride a horse, and I don't even suck at it, but I'm no pro. So, when I tell you I got my foot in that wooden stirrup first try, and chucked my leg over the horse, please imagine my pride. Oh, there was relief, too, plenty of relief as Pie took off like a bullet and we mowed the shitheads in front of us down until we were both free. We got about forty feet before I fell off again. No more pride. I had struggled and failed to get my second foot into the second stirrup.

Pie stopped immediately and he had the same look the dead had had a few minutes ago: *Are you fucking shitting me?*

The good news is that we were clear of the horde, the bad news is I had fucked up my arm. It was the same damn elbow boo-boo I had suffered with the last horse. It was a bitch to climb back up on Pie, but he remained patient until he didn't. His head was doing that nod again and he pawed at the dust. I got one foot up, same as last time, and he started to go, but I *WHOA*-ed him. He stopped immediately, and I threw my leg over him and stuck my other foot in the stirrup.

"Alright, let's boogie!" I told him and he did. We shot out of there at lightspeed, those dead, flesh- gobbling dickheads left in the dust.

MINE ALL MINE

I'm thirsty. Pie is thirsty. It's hot. My elbow is fucked. I want a pizza. The pain in my elbow is vying with the pain of thirst right now. You've been thirsty before, we all have, but right now, my arm won't close all the way at the elbow. Ever jam your finger on a basketball and have the joint swell up so much that you couldn't touch your finger to your palm? Yeah, this is the same. I can get the lower arm a little lower than ninety degrees of angle with the upper arm, but it won't go any further than that. I'm afraid if I keep trying, my arm is gonna pop off like the prick who grabbed me a few hours ago. And my side hurts.

Oh, yeah, and that horde is following us. I can't see them anymore as we've followed the 190 into the foothills, but the dust cloud they are kicking up as they trudge through the scrub can be seen for miles. It looks like a tornado heading right at us at about two miles per hour. I think they are probably about four or five miles to the southeast.

I pulled Chauncy out of his sheath and looked him up and down. Deadly. That was the word for this thing. Big and gleaming, I caught the sun with him and twisted my wrist back and forth to flash the reflection on the ground. Fuck, I had nothing else to do.

"You're a big bastard, Chauncy, and I'll bet you've seen some shit. Been across the throats and into the heads of some bad dudes. And not just zombies," I added. "*Bad* dudes. The kind that would wrap you in rubber and light you on fire or torture a kitten. That kind of bad. I bet you've killed a bunch of them. Dozens, and I bet you loved it."

"Damn right I did," Chauncy answered in a voice that was a cross between a Southern drawl and a guy from that movie Fargo.

At this point a talking knife did not surprise me. Pie didn't stop walking, but he threw me a glance, then shifted his eyes to Chauncy.

"Relax, Pie. Me and Chauncy are a team and you're part of it. We don't stab horses. Unless they're asshole horses," I added quickly. "Right Chauncy?"

"Damn right," the shiny bastard replied.

As I sit on this horse, both of us slowly dying of thirst, I can't help but ponder what comes next. I can't possibly bring Pie into San Francisco. Chauncy, yes. Pie, no. He would be devoured before we made it off the interstate in the suburbs. Equally as cruel would be to leave him out here. He'd die slowly, thirst and hunger getting him or making him weak enough for the dead to take him down.

Get your head out of where it is too, Dear Reader. I'm not going to shoot him and put him out of his misery. I'll die before I let my guy Pie die. He saved my ass, and that shit doesn't come around too often. The last nag I rode would have chucked me off and headed for the hills, gleefully listening to my screams as the infected tore me apart and I wouldn't have let him die, either.

"My Guy Pie Die," I said again and smiled, my lower lip developing a crack that would make the Grand Canyon blush. "My Guy Pie Die. My Guy Pie Die."

In a couple of hours I could no longer see the dust cloud. The horde had either left the desert or had seen a jackrabbit and slogged off in a different direction, everybody trying to get some hasenpfeffer.

Yes, I have seen a Bugs Bunny cartoon. Thinking about Bugs Bunny ultimately brought me around to Billy. Kid was always quoting that damn rabbit. I started to worry about him. Billy, not Bugs. The kid was alone in the apocalypse, likely with Navy SEALs chasing him in addition to having the living dead scampering about. That douche Doctor Gamboa would never stop looking for him, and his sidekick Baker probably wanted to stick needles in us for fun. Shit, I wonder if he sent Thorne out to find Billy. Furthermore, what would Thorne do when he found Billy? Thorne loved Billy, but he did what the doctor said. Would he snag Billy and bring him back like last time or just laugh at his jokes and let him go? I mean, he already let him go, right?

I think Thorne likes Billy because they are cut from the same cloth. They are both fucking nuts, but where Billy is still human, Thorne is something else. He's not *not* human, but he's not human either. Maybe it's a good thing that humanity left him because if the past few years have taught me anything it's that humanity kind of sucks. Don't get me wrong, there are good people, but when it comes down to feeding your kid or not killing someone to steal their food to feed your kid, what do you do?

With Thorne you know exactly where he stands, and that is usually on your throat while he rummages around in your chest cavity. Billy will only kill you if he's having a bad day. Or if you steal his Pepsi.

FFS doesn't southeastern California have a single fucking tree? It's a million degrees out here and there's fuck-all for shade. I dragged my forearm across my forehead and it stung. It stung a bit more when Chauncy, who was still in my fist, smacked my nose with the back of his blade. I was still wearing this shemagh, but somehow my forehead (which, let's face it, was more like a five-point-three head) still received a sunburn. I put my palm on Pie's shoulder, and it felt like a furnace. We both needed shelter soon.

We still had several hours of sun, but I think we might be cooked by then. Our stint in the brick oven followed by the last few hours out here in the sun would have at least one of us shuffling around looking for nibbles before the sun went down.

Pie would need a shitload of water soon, and a shitload we did not have. I dared a glance behind us, which turned into a long look. If the shitheads were back there, I couldn't see them or their cloud of whatever.

Grass. There was actual grass on one of the little hills in front of us. Not scrubby bullshit or crabgrass. Real Kentucky Blue Grass. I glanced further down the road and could see some hills and shit. I looked into the sky. Didn't grass mean rain? We both know, Dear Reader, that it hasn't rained in these here parts since the Pleistocene Era, so WTF?

The hills in front of us were green too, but that was scrub and bushes. There were mountains past the hills on my left and I found out that I wasn't, in fact, on the 190, I was on route 395 about five miles outside of Independence, California. I busted out the map, but I'll be damned if I could find the town. The road sign I was currently staring at told me that Independence had a population of 700 and was the county seat of Inyo County.

Whatever the hell that means.

There was another sign fifty feet or so down the road. It looked like a piece of barnboard nailed to a 2x4, but I couldn't read it until I was on top of it.

Turn back now, was scrawled on the board in black paint.

I glanced at the scrub behind me and to the right, and the hills to the left. There was a swarm of infected behind me, of that I was certain even though I couldn't see them. Hills and scrub were unlikely to yield any water, and we had about half a day before we were both dead, so the only way forward was actually forward.

I'm sure Independence was just as dead as every other town with signs like this.

Half a mile down the road I saw another sign, *Trespassers will be shot.*

My horse and I were dead if we didn't get some water soon. Hopefully any survivors wouldn't shoot Pie. The third sign said, *Not shitting you, go away.* This one sold me on the fact that there were people in the next town. I knew this because a quarter mile in front of me, parked across the highway, was an MRAP and it was not unmanned. MRAP stands for Mine Resistant Ambush Protective vehicle. It's a big, armored truck. The top turret swiveled in my direction and the engine started up.

95

This MRAP was different and smaller than the one I had driven halfway across the country, but it still would be impossible for me to stop whatever these assholes had in mind to do to me. It was that coyote tan color you saw in all the desert conflicts of the late 20th century, and it had that same throaty, diesel growl that made my nethers bulge in all the right ways. It was sexy as hell.

The truck stopped thirty feet from me, and two guys dressed in the same color camo as the truck jumped out with rifles and approached, business ends of the guns pointed my way. I sighed as I knew where this was going. I glanced at the sun but didn't make any motions with my hands. As it turns out, I'm glad I didn't.

"Hands up!" the guy on my left shouted.

I wanted to spit like Josey Wales and look all cool and shit, but every drop of liquid in my mouth had been redistributed to more important places by my body.

He tightened the rifle to his shoulder. "I said, hands up!"

I rolled my eyes. "I'm too fuck'n tired to put my hands up. I have a sidearm in addition to my rifle and a big ass knife as weapons. I also realize that your horse is bigger than mine, so if you're here to rob me, get on with it. I've got another few hours before I die from heat stroke and thirst, so if you try to turn me away from the town and some water for my horse, I'm just gonna make you shoot me."

The two guys glanced at each other and then back at me. The guy on the right and the guy in the turret were chuckling. The guy who had spoken was not.

"The fuck are you laughing at?" Left-Guy demanded of his buddy. "This guy is—"

"What?" Right-Guy asked. "Sun baked? Dying of thirst? He doesn't talk like one of the crazies, and he sure as hell doesn't look like he has any friends close enough to save his ass if we decided to put holes in him. Lighten up, Francis."

I chuckled at the Stripes reference and knew I was about to get some water or get dead.

"Put the gun down, Joe," Right-Guy said, and Joe lowered his rifle. "Can you climb off the horse? Nice and slow, ok?"

I got down and I have to tell you it was work to do it. There was an audible sigh from Pie, and I knew he was glad to have my heavy ass off him. "I'll put my weapons on the ground and then you can search me, ok?"

"Sounds good," Right-Guy agreed. "What's your name?" he asked. I told him and asked him his.

"Otter. And this is Joe and the guy on the 30 cal is Brent."

Joe came over and frisked me after I had put my weapons on the million degree black top. How this shit didn't melt I have no idea.

Otter came over and passed me his canteen. It was one of those ancient, metal canteens that you would see in a WWII movie. I smiled and I felt my lip crack again. I moved to Pie and let him take a quick drink before I did. He didn't spill a drop. I took a hefty sip, but didn't want to drain this guy's water, so I passed it back to him with some thanks. It was very warm and tasted like metal. It was delicious.

Joe picked up my weapons, slinging my rifle. His demeanor toward me had taken an upgrade and he used his hand to indicate I should follow them to the truck. I grabbed Pie's reins and we ambled on over. There was a fourth guy who stepped out of the back of the vehicle and looked me over before speaking into a police style shoulder radio.

"Bill, this is Randy out at post one. Yeah, we got a stray out here. He don't look like he's gonna make it much further if we don't get him some water."

The response was immediate, "*Is he babbling like a whack-job and covered in blood or shit?*"

"Nah, he ain't one of the crazies. He's just..." he looked me up and down, "Cooked."

"*Alright, bring him in. Put a hood on him, though, just in case.*"

"Will do, post one out."

"A hood?" I asked. "Really?"

"Really," Randy told me and helped me into the truck.

INDEPENDENCE

They checked me head to toe for bites, asking about my scars, then they started to drive. It had only felt like a few minutes when we came to what must be a gate. I couldn't see shit because I had a black hood over my head, and when they took the hood off, I could see that the sun was setting. They hadn't bound or cuffed me, but they clearly hadn't wanted me to see their defenses or how many people were in the town. I can't blame them, for all they knew I was an advanced scout who would relay just such information to a group of armed shitheads looking for trouble.

Otter pulled the hood off me, and we stepped out of the MRAP back into the inferno that was the central California desert. I glanced at a sign that said Independence Sheriff, but the building was just a house. Then I remembered my horse.

"Where's Pie?" I demanded.

Randy and Otter side-eyed each other. "You want some pie?" Randy asked, his face scrunched up in incredulity.

"No, no, my horse. Where's my horse?"

Otter raised his eyebrows in a look that was every bit as non-believing as Randy's, "Your horse's name is Pie?"

"Yeah. I didn't name him. Where is he?" I looked around, searching for the big fella.

"He'll be along directly," a new voice said from the direction of the house. An older man, perhaps in his early sixties, but clearly quite fit, was strolling down the concrete walk from the house. He stuck out his hand when he got close enough.

"Sheriff John Hicks."

I stared at his paw for an elongated moment. Great. Terrific. Another sheriff in another walled off, hick zombie-town. I can't wait for him to ask me to save somebody or get something.

I sighed and shook his hand. "Sheriff, I could use some water, and some food if you could spare some. I don't want to get in anybody's way and I'm not here to hurt you or take anything that's yours. If you could give us some water, we'll be on our way."

"Us?"

"Yeah, me and my horse. We met in the desert a few days ago and now I can't get rid of him. Truth be told, I'm a bit enamored with the big asshole."

I am a comedic genius. Witty AF and fun to be around when the comedy strikes. That last little sentence should have elicited at least a smile, even though I was shooting for a chuckle. Otter laughed a bit, he gets it, but Sheriff Dudley Do-Right over here didn't.

And yes, I know Do-Right was a Mounty, not a sheriff. Shut it.

"So, you don't want to stay?"

"Can't," I shrugged. "I have people in San Francisco I need to get back to."

"Son," he said with a look, "that's almost 350 miles from here by road. See them mountains?" He thumbed over his shoulder behind him. There were, indeed, mountains. I nodded. "Them mountains is what protects us from the dead on the other side. They occasionally stumble in our direction, but most of 'em go north or south because that's where the dinner is. There's more 'n a million of 'em just on the other side of them mountains. Right between us and San Francisco."

"My family is there," was my answer.

It was his turn to nod and sigh. "Alright. We'll get you 'n your horse fed 'n watered, and you can go get eaten."

My left eyebrow shot to the sky. It's kind of my thing. "That's it? I don't have to catch a chicken or save a bunch of assholes at an overrun hospital?"

The sheriff looked confused, "Huh?"

"Never mind. I'll take whatever you can give, and I appreciate it."

He nodded "C'mon in." Hicks turned and I strode up the pink bricks behind him. We entered his house/sheriff's station, and it was modest and cool inside. "Have a seat," he told me, waving at a set of chairs around a kitchen table that was also obviously a desk. So, I sat. Otter sat next to me, and Hicks sat across. He reached into an unpowered fridge and passed me a bottle of tepid water. I greedily gulped it down with some thanks, and the sheriff launched into his interrogation.

Where was I from. Boston? *Bullshit*! How did I end up in San Francisco? Whose horse was that? Why was I out in the middle of the California desert and did I know anything about the helicopters that had been zipping around for the past few days?

In my extensive travels, Dear Reader, I have painstakingly learned that I should keep my mouth shut when it comes to who I am and why the government wants me. The problem is that I never think up a good lie beforehand and when I am questioned, I ultimately give myself away with an overly dramatic pause. They don't know my secret, but they *do* know what I am about to tell them is total bullshit.

"I was in one of those helicopters and it crashed. I'm trying to get home."

Hicks and Otter side-eyed each other, then focused back on me. Points had been lost with my statement. I held up my hand and continued. "I was not on the bird by choice. I was kidnapped for reasons I will not discuss, but I promise you that I am not a bad guy. I haven't killed anybody in the apocalypse who didn't need killing, and I did not crash the helicopter."

I chugged the rest of the water in case they either tried to take it back, cuff me, or shoot me. The next question took me by surprise.

"Who was flyin' the bird?"

"That would be the US government, or what is left of them. They think I can provide them with things I cannot."

Both men crinkled up their faces, but Otter spoke first, "What things?"

"You guys have been very kind to me. I appreciate that and the last thing I want to do is be an asshole or get shot, but those are the *none-of-your-business* kind of things. I'm really sorry about that last part," I added hastily.

Hicks' radio blared to life, "*Sheriff, we got about thirty crazies attacking the northwest perimeter fence. Can we shoot 'em?*"

He grabbed his radio, "Light 'em up, Jesse. You need backup?"

"*Naw. Me 'n Stern'll handle it.*"

"Copy. Sing out if you need a hand."

"Crazies?" I asked.

"Yeah, 'bout a year back we started seeing these sunburned folks with crazy eyes and wearin' rags. Tried to help 'em, but they ran off. Then they started attackin' folks, so we shot a few of 'em. We got some livin' in one of the mines to the west. They were grabbin' travelers for a while, and now they hit the fences a couple times a week. Thirty is a lot, though. Usually, it's just three or four."

"Infected?"

"Nope. Just whack jobs."

"What happens to the people they take?"

"Dunno. Likely they eat 'em, but we ain't never been over to the mines to check it out. I don't have enough fighters to go to war with a bunch of crazies. We can keep 'em out of Independence, but a full-on frontal assault might lose us too many people. We used the MRAP to get close to the mine and some dynamite to blow up the entrance once, but them mines is all connected and there are a hunnert ways in 'n out. But, we're gettin' off topic. You said the US government? There's still a government?" He had pronounced it "gove-mint."

"Of sorts, yeah. I had been living in a gated community for a couple of weeks when I met my first government representative. He was with a bunch of military guys. Didn't matter because the dead came knocking and everybody joined the enemy. They came for me when I was living on an oil rig in the Gulf. They asked nicely and then we were attacked by a group called the Triumvirate. Different government assholes with lots of people and resources. Not the kind of people you want at a tea party. Bad dudes."

"So, how'd you end up out here?"

I didn't want to tell them about Gamboa, Baker, and Thorne. They might believe the stuff about the docs, but they were never going to buy domesticated Runners. As luck would have it, I was saved by the bell. In this case, the radio.

"Sheriff, we shot six and the rest ran off. Do you want us to pursue?"

"No!" he shot back. "That might be a trick to get you off the wall and out into the desert. Stay put and shoot 'em if they come back."

He put the radio on the table, and it blared back at him immediately. *"Sheriff, this is Post Two. We got deaders eight miles out."*

"How many?"

"Can't tell with the sun almost down. They're moving past us on the road toward town in ones and twos. You want we should take them out?"

"If it's more than fifty, run 'em down. Any less and we can get 'em when they hit the walls."

"We're in the Tacoma, Sheriff."

"Dang it! Alright, if it's just a few, take 'em out. More'n ten, you hightail it back here."

I had told Otter that there was a horde behind me in the desert someplace, but I didn't think they would have caught up to me by now, and he hadn't seemed concerned.

Otter looked embarrassed. "Sheriff, this fella told us about a bunch of dead in the desert following him."

"And you're tellin' me this now?" Hicks looked at me. "How many?"

"Couple hundred, anyway."

"Jesus…"

"They couldn't possibly be here yet," I told him. "They were miles behind me. It would take half the night for them to get here, and I thought I lost them in the hills."

"Guess not!" the sheriff almost shouted. "Ya brought 'em right to us!"

"There's no way they could be—"

He grabbed his radio but spoke to Otter. "Otter, you grab Jeran and Clarke, get in MRAP 2, and get out to Post Two. Go see how many of them zombies is comin'."

Shit, if these things were about to attack the town, that was on me. I couldn't live with that. "I can help, Sheriff. I know how to drive an MRAP and I'm not terrible with a rifle."

The sheriff looked at me when he asked, "You trust him, Otter?"

"I do," Otter told him after the briefest of pauses.

"Give him his gear back and get out to Post Two, then. If he misbehaves, kill him."

I smiled. Hey, I was getting my stuff back. Ten minutes later and my still-thirsty ass was zipping due east in an MRAP exactly the same as the one that picked me up earlier, except this one was all black and had SWAT in yellow letters on the sides. We were driving down a bumpy dirt road as the only paved ones ran north and south.

"I can't raise Post Two," one of the new dudes said. I didn't know if it was Clarke or Jeran because in an epic faux pas in etiquette, we hadn't been introduced. The guy kept trying to get them on the radio to no avail, and that bothered me.

The headlights on the front of the vehicle bumped and jostled as we moved forward. It wasn't awful, but this road needed work. I almost flew forward when Otter slammed the brakes on, and we skidded on the packed earth.

He pointed forward through the MRAP's window. "That's Mike!"

A guy was running at us full sprint waving his arms as best he could while maintaining his run. He was illuminated by the headlights maybe two hundred feet in front of us. Two human forms sprinted after him and I could tell that Mike was not going to make it. One of the things, a younger woman, leapt at him and they both tumbled to the ground. Mike tried to get up, but she grabbed him and threw haymakers while also trying to bite him until the second thing caught up and joined her. Two more sprinted from the darkness into the twin beams of the headlights, then a few more. Soon there were a dozen, then a dozen more which quickly turned into a hundred. Mike had been engulfed by then and there was no coming back from that. They kept coming, all Runners. Most of them stopped where Mike had fallen, pulling other Runners off, and tossing them aside in an attempt to tear into the man on the ground, but some barreled directly at us, knowing in their broken minds that the lights in the darkness probably meant something to kill.

I had been in a huge battle with the dead at an Air Force base in Mississippi a couple of years ago where tens of thousands of the things had attacked the fences in a horde. I had seen maybe twenty Runners that night and until right now, that had been the most I had seen at once. Back then there had been tanks, Bradleys, attack helicopters, planes, and five-thousand armed people to fight back.

Now there were the four of us in a truck.

What in the infected fuck was this?

"GO!" I screamed. "Turn this thing around and get the hell out of here!" The first of the things impacted the front of the truck with a thud and tried to scramble up on the front, but the thud had set Otter into motion, and he threw the gear shift in reverse. The moment he did that the song from an ice cream truck blared over loudspeakers followed by huge lights shining in four directions a quarter of a mile in front of us. The ice cream truck was surrounded by the shuffling dead. Hundreds of Runners formed the vanguard of an infected army that seemed to span the entire earth from left to right.

As the creatures materialized out of the gloom, I knew Independence was doomed. These things were on a direct intercept course and there was no stopping a force this size. I could see no end to them. There had to be a hundred thousand.

I heard several other thumps and thuds, and in the ten seconds it took Otter's mind to register the absurdity of the situation, the things started trying to scratch their way through the steel of the armored vehicle.

"Go!" I screamed a second time.

Otter reversed down the road a hundred yards, then cut the wheel and threw the shift into drive. Pro job, but it was all for naught if we didn't get back soon.

The guy who had been on the radio called this in and the sheriff said he understood. Apparently, Independence had a contingency for just such an event.

As we bumped down the road at forty miles per hour, I heard the sheriff ask if we could slow the infected down. The guy told him there were too many.

"Copy, Sheriff, we'll meet you there," was how he ended the radio call.

Otter sighed, "Shit."

"What?" I demanded. "What is it?"

"We're falling back to the mines."

"The mines? You mean the place with all those crazies you were talking about?"

"This mine is different. It's a mile north of the old copper mines and was used for data storage before everybody died. It has a vault door, concrete walls, and... amenities."

"Then why the hell weren't you guys living in there the whole time?"

"Cuz it's a mine," Otter answered with a shrug. "One way in, one way out. And who wants to live underground, anyway?" he added.

"Is nobody going to say anything about that truck?" Not Otter and Not Radio guy asked.

"Yeah, that was new," I said. I pointed at him, "What's your name?"

"Clarke. Clarke Morris," the dude answered. I deduced that the other guy must be Jeran.

Jeran was shaking his head. "How could you not tell us about this?" I noticed his finger move to the trigger of his shotgun.

"Whoa, dude! This is not the group that was chasing me a couple of days ago. This is way bigger and coming from a different direction. Also, I did tell you about the horde on my ass." I thumbed behind us, "But that ain't it."

It took about twenty minutes for us to cover the almost nine miles back to Independence. I was flabbergasted. The place was lit up like a Christmas tree and the gates were opening as we got there. Not to let us in, but to evacuate the town. An armored school bus, an MRAP, and a couple dozen other vehicles began filing out the front gate. In twenty minutes, the sheriff had gotten the entire town ready. Remo and Ship would love this guy and I had to admit to an increase in fondness as well. Most of the trucks and Jeeps were bristling with rifles poking out every which way. Reminded me of some rednecks from Tennessee I had met once.

As I watched this logistical marvel unfold, I had but one question nagging me. "Where's Pie?" I demanded.

"You want Pie now?" Clarke asked me and Otter smiled.

"My horse! Where's my horse?"

I glared out the bullet resistant MRAP glass, but nobody seemed to have my horse. "Sheriff, where's the new guy's horse?"

There were some questions on the other end of the radio and then Joe, the douche who had ridden Pie back to this backwater, shithole town, piped up. *"I, uh... I left him tied to my trailer."*

"Sheriff," Otter began, "We're gonna take this fella to his horse and join up with you at—"

"The hell you are!" Hicks yelled through the mic. "We're gonna need that MRAP with us! You follow and be rear guard, understood?"

Otter sighed loudly, "Yessir."

I sighed right back, knowing where this was going. "Where's his fucking trailer?"

Clarke pointed, "Down the main drag, take a left at the diner and it's two houses up on the right. Want me to come with?"

"I don't want Pie to carry two. Just open the door and I'll run for it." I saw a little boy's face peer out at me from one of the trucks as it rumbled past. There were a bunch of kids.

They opened the door without me having to threaten them, and I hopped out. "Hang on, Otter!" Clarke yelled. He leaned in and whispered to me, "Mine's about three miles northeast of town dug into the hills. There's a huge parking lot across from it, but the mine's hard to spot even if you're looking for it. The vault door is covered with fake rocks, and it looks just like the side of the cliff face. The horse will fit fine if you can get there. Take this," he passed me a flare gun. "Fire it into the sky when you get to the parking lot. Watch your ass."

With that he pulled the door closed and I felt extremely alone. Moreso when the MRAP pulled in behind the last piece of shit Chevy pickup and all I could see was the ass end of the convoy pulling away from me in the dark.

What kind of asshole leaves a horse tied up and defenseless against a horde of undead creatures? Seriously, what a rat-fuck son of a bitch. I wanted to punch him and might sort that out later. But first I needed to find Pie and ride him the hell out of here without being eaten.

I checked the load on my rifle, having checked it half a dozen times already, and felt for Chauncy and my sidearm even though I knew them to be there. I hurried down the street at a jog remembering that I had almost died of heat stroke not a few hours ago. I felt fine. Amazing what a couple of liters of water and some shade can do for a person. I saw the diner, also lit up with every light imaginable, and had to wonder why the place looked like Las Vegas. The generators were on as was every light I could see. Wouldn't they want to save the fuel? Shouldn't the place be shrouded in darkness to try to make the horde miss it?

Fat chance on that last one, but still. As I contemplated all the what-the-fucks, I saw two loping shapes about sixty feet in front of me. They ran low across the street, trying not to be noticed. No way the infected could have reached town that quickly and even if they had, they don't do stealth very well. They would have sprinted right at me, screaming the whole way. I slowed a bit and felt rather than heard something coming at me from behind. I side stepped and spun like Barry Sanders, an ape-dog thing missing me by inches as it swiped its paw at me in anger. It wasn't an ape-dog, it was a filthy man, and it threw itself at me, snarling.

What the fuck? What in the actual fuck? Why had I come across so many crazy assholes? If folks like the Independence people could be at least human, why couldn't these people? It was like a damn Lovecraft novel up in here.

All of this ran through my mind as fast as the bullet that went through this douche's shoulder. He spun and fell, whimpering.

"Please," he begged with his palm outstretched as he inched away on his ass.

"And what were you gonna do to me?" I raised my rifle.

Something struck me in the shoulder, and I saw three forms sprinting in my direction. Something else sailed past my head and all I could think was that people were throwing rocks at me. I lifted the barrel of my rifle a bit higher and yelled, "Stop!" They didn't.

These poor fools had rocks as ammunition, and I had military hardware. I felt so bad for them. They had been nurses and stockbrokers and mechanics and moms. This stupid plague had converted humans into monsters and not just the infected. The sickness had brought the dead back to life but also the worst out of humanity. I pitied them.

When I was done with all the pity, I riddled them with holes. Fuck 'em. Pity or not, these pricks had likely committed murder when they could have helped instead. They sure as shit weren't in this town to assist the elderly. They were here to steal and kill. The long and short of it is that I am better than them. The people in this town were as well, at least I think so. The crazies could have come in here and helped build and protect this place but instead they chose... this.

So again, fuck 'em.

Two were mortally wounded, two would survive unless infection got them. Shoulder guy had one through and through, and another woman had one through her abdomen, but far enough to the left that she would be ok, and one in her left leg.

I harrumphed, re-thinking the situation. None of them would live. That horde would be here within a few hours, and they would eat these assholes alive. I shook my head. What a waste.

I leaned down and looked into shoulder-dude's eyes. "All you had to do was ask, and these folks would have taken you in." I shook my head again and moved off to find my horse. "Fuk'n Sleestack," I added over my shoulder.

I took a left at the diner like I had been told and saw Pie in a few seconds. He was tied to the end of a trailer which I thought would be a filthy dump but was actually quite nice with some pretty flower boxes and a white gravel walkway.

"Hey, buddy."

He sneezed, looked at me, and nodded furiously.

I was immediately on edge. Well, *more* on edge. I knew his nods meant trouble and he could smell much better than I could. I spun and panned my weapon around, but there was nothing there. No infected, no crazy probably-cannibals. No werewolves or tax assessors.

The place was pretty well illuminated, but a pair of NVGs wouldn't have gone amiss. I lost the ones I had appropriated from the helicopter back when the *other* group of cannibals was trying to eat me.

I untied Pie and climbed aboard. I patted his neck, and it felt cool in the evening air, not like the blistering hair he had while we were in the desert. He pawed the ground nervously, and I had to wonder if he could smell the vast horde that was bearing down on us from the desert.

I had hoped to carry some supplies with us out of here, but the only thing we had was my weapons, some ammo, and the will to live. I contemplated just heading out to San Francisco. I mean, what was one more gun going to do to help these people? Besides, they were inside an impenetrable mountain fortress, right? I could just go back to Alcatraz and be with my people.

Except I couldn't. Forgetting the fact that Alcatraz was swarming with the living dead the last time I was there, what was I going to do with Pie? I couldn't bring him into the city, he wouldn't survive. He can't hide behind a Subaru like I can when a group of thirty of the things shamble past. Even if I were to somehow get him past the throngs of dead and infected, and Alcatraz was completely cleared, how would he live there? There was no room for him. No barn or any place for him to just be a horse.

No. No, he had to go somewhere else, and that somewhere else was here. Independence could take care of him, and he could take care of them. He had to stay, but not if there were no Independence. If they got wiped out by the horde coming, then all was for naught.

Fuckers were coming down that bumpy, potholed path that passes for a road right now at whatever top speed the undead have, but the Runners were three times as fast. And what was up with that ice cream truck? I hadn't forgotten about that shit, Dear Reader. It had been leading the dead. For absolute sure it had been leading them.

I was walking Pie back to the wide-open front gate, trying to do mental math on when the things would hit the town when I realized trotting might be a better plan. I nudged the horse, and he didn't need to be told twice. He could sense the fear and trepidation that must have been seeping out of my pores.

I had seen the horde about an hour ago and it was nine miles from where we saw them to the town. Could Runners sprint at a consistent nine miles per hour?

I need to stop asking myself these questions, because every time I do, I get them answered. A Runner's scream sounded back behind us. Pie began that furious nod again and I wasted no time. Two other cries sounded and then a human scream. I guess the Runners had found the assholes I had put holes into.

I gently pulled the reins, but Pie was already moving. We went away from the screams, but the gate was on the other side of them, so we cut through a couple of trailer yards, and I could see the lights from the gate off to the left. In the middle of the street were a few of the faster Runners, who had begun tearing into the douches I had left behind. To this day I still didn't know if the Runners ate those whom they killed, or if they just needed to murder and move on. I had seen them take bites out of the dead, chewing and swallowing dead flesh, so it would make sense that they consumed the living, but I wasn't sure. I would have to ask Thorne or Subject Nine if I ever saw them again.

That is, if they would tell me. Thorne was a hair's breadth from returning feral, and Nine might be too embarrassed or just not remember. The other domesticated Runners... well other than Naruto, the young Asian kid who seemed as calm as a cucumber, I didn't know them very well. Enough to stay the hell away from them, but that was it.

None of these thoughts erased the fact that several other speedy infected had come screaming down the road to jump on those unfortunates I had shot. They came in ones and twos, but there were already fifteen or so, and that was enough to get me going.

"Hah!" I whisper-yelled and gave Pie a polite spurring with my spurless boot heels. He bolted, going from standing to gallop immediately. The nanosecond his shod hooves stepped from the grass and hit the asphalt, every fast, infected bastard whipped their heads around, stared for a brief second, then started off after us at a sprint. We clippity-clopped down the street as fast as Pie could go, leaving those chasing far behind us.

Unfortunately, more streamed into the town from in front of us. They just materialized slowly out of the darkness and into the light thrown from the gates. A half dozen or so came right at us, one with her hands raised above her head, screaming that awful scream that they scream. She ran directly into Pie's path, and I have never seen a horse so casually give less of a fuck. The infected woman bounced off the front of him like she had been hit by a road train. Must have flown fifteen feet and there is no way she was getting up again with a pulse. Pie never slowed down one iota.

What the fuck is an iota anyway?

We galloped into the desert, trailing twenty Runners I had seen and likely another hundred I hadn't. So, what did I not want to do, Dear Reader? I did not want to lead their infected asses to the front door of the place where the town had gone to hide.

As terrified as I was, holding on to a galloping horse for (literally) dear life, I still was able to get him to angle off to the right, which was east, directly into the oncoming horde. We circled right again around the town and headed southwest. I saw a few more Runners, but they either didn't see us or didn't care as they ran toward the lights of the town. Pie galloped for another minute or so and I slowed him down.

"Easy, big-boy. They're far enough behind us now, we can move a bit slower." I don't know if he was happy or upset at slowing down, but he slowed. I patted him on the neck, and he nodded. We slowed to a walk, and I thought I might need new balls. Not because they were thumping against the back of a horse, but because they had retreated inside the building in terror. My boys would be back but right now I was a eunuch.

I could see the lights from the town off to my right and knew that the horde would be reaching it any time now. I just didn't see how the townspeople could ever go back. Even when the dead just walk through an area, they leave bits of themselves behind. When an enormous horde moves through, some full specimens would remain as well, plus there would be crawlers. Everybody's homes would be destroyed or covered in fluids. Everybody's stuff, including gardens, would be trampled.

I shook my head, and we circled right again, heading northwest, hopefully toward the mountains and the mine Otter had told me about.

TUNNEL RAT

It took three hours to find the parking lot Clarke had described. Just as he had said, it was enormous. What he had failed to mention was the two hundred or so decrepit cars that were parked there, rusting away. Many had their doors open and there was evidence that a camp had been here. Tarps attached to poles or tied to open car doors hung loosely and rotten clothing littered the ground, as did some coolers and empty plastic containers. The place had been overrun by the dead, or marauders, or had fallen from within. The sun was coming up, and I could see skeletons hanging from posts in the waning darkness.

Nothing moved. No living and no dead. No animals either, but this was the desert.

You know what I didn't want to do, Dear Reader? I didn't want to tell every living and dead thing within a mile radius that I was here by firing a flare into the sky. I hadn't thought of that when Clarke had passed me the flare gun and apparently, neither had he. I could see the cliffs Clarke had spoken about, they were a couple hundred yards across, but nothing screamed *Door!* at me, which Clarke had also mentioned.

The sun was past reddening the sky, and the first rays of dawn hit us in our faces. We ambled on over to the cliff face and I did a search. I couldn't see shit. I was seriously considering calling it and just heading on back to the infected hell of San Francisco, when Pie started his furious nodding again. I panned my rifle in a 270 degree arc keeping the cliff face on my right, but even with the waxing sun, I couldn't find any threats.

Pie pawed at the ground... can a horse paw? It has hooves, so shouldn't it hoof the ground? Regardless, I searched the ground and found a pen, an empty chewing tobacco pouch, two empty water bottles, and the head of a stuffed duck. I could discern that the ground in front of the cliff in front of me had been disturbed, but I couldn't see footprints. Pie turned to his right, and we were both staring at a cliff face.

I expected a door to open with a whoosh like in a Star Wars movie and light to shoot out of the mountain with a bit of fanfare, but I got rock instead. Just rock in front of me. Also, now that I think of it, it might be Star *Trek* with the whooshing doors.

I was about to pull Pie's reins to the left to amble on, but I heard a repeated ticking sound and the cliff in front of me opened. The door was about fifteen-feet square, and it pushed toward us about eighteen inches and then moved to the left.

The sheriff and several of his stooges stepped out armed to the teeth to greet me. Hicks was pissed, I could see it all over him. Clearly, he still thought I had brought ruin upon his precious town by leading a large city's worth of infected to it. I think this is exactly what had happened, but I hadn't done it. That had been the driver of that ice cream truck.

"Get him inside," was all the sheriff said. One of the guys grabbed Pie's reins and we all moved into the mountain, me still astride this wonderful animal.

This was no mine dug by shovels. This was a tunnel made with machines. It actually got bigger and wider once we were inside. Florescent lights illuminated the thirty-foot wide and twenty-foot tall entry area so brightly that I could read everything in the room. There was an inlay on either side of the room with some type of clear material closing it off. Behind that glass or clear plastic were three rednecks on each side, all toting machine guns, all pointing at me through gunports. A heavy machine gun emplacement sat behind a sandbag semi-circle ten yards down the hall, immediately in front of several branching tunnels leading deeper into the facility.

Nobody was finding the front door, let alone getting through it, and if they did, all this firepower would turn them into hamburger damn quickly. There were a dozen or so unarmed folks moving supplies into the mountain and the place bustled with chatter.

Hicks rounded on me. "Found us, didja?"

"Yup. I was asked to meet—"

He cut me off, pointing his index finger at me. "You done brought them dead ones down on us!"

I was sick of his shit. I was sick of everybody's shit. If assholes would just leave me the fuck alone, I wouldn't have to constantly defend or explain myself. Why could the assholes of Earth not get that? I sure as shit hadn't asked to be here. I had been content fighting zombies on Alcatraz.

"The fuck I did, you dumb hick shit!" I yelled in his face from atop the horse. The place went deadly silent, everybody looking at me. I was just as angry as this douche sheriff, but I still felt bad they were about to lose their town. "I am sick and tired of assholes like you," I pointed at his reddening face, "telling me what a terrible person I am for trying to stay alive. That horde was not following me! It's a hundred times the size of the one I saw and it's coming from a different direction on the other side of the fucking mountains!"

I swung my leg over Pie and didn't fail to notice every weapon in the place swing my way as I did. I got to the concrete floor and towered over the sheriff as I glowered down at him. "Your problems are not my fault,"

I told him much more calmly. "Besides, look around. You're pretty fucking safe. You want me out? Say the word and I'll leave right now, but if you think I'm going to stand here and let you accuse me of bringing doom to your town, I'll fucking make you shoot me."

Sheriff Hicks of Independence California did the strangest thing right then. He shot me.

I woke up in the infirmary, and I felt like shit. There were no holes in me, and I remembered that the sheriff had used a taser. That had been my first tasing, and I need to emphatically tell you how much I disliked it.

I sat up and noticed the sheriff talking in low voices with a few of the rednecks. He was making hand gestures and ended the conversation by pointing at the door. Three of the five guys hurried off. My pack and gear were on a small stainless-steel table next to me. One of the guys noticed me sitting up and pointed at me.

Hicks turned, regarded me for a sec, then strode over. "Y'alright?"

"Fuck you."

He smiled and sat in the chair next to me. I started rubbing the back of my neck and he sighed. "I'm sorry, son. I know you didn't bring them dead ones. I was lookin' for someone to blame is all."

"The hell did you taze me for?"

He shrugged, "Didn't know what else to do. You had a bunch of guns on you and were all kinds of mad, so I diffused the situation."

I sighed again and lay back down. "You could have asked me to be quiet."

"But then I wouldn't have gotten to taze anybody..."

I know, Dear Reader, that this is going to sound ridiculous, but with that statement all my ire and dislike of this man melted away. I liked him. Anybody who could say something like that to a guy they had just put a few thousand volts through had a funny bone akin to mine.

"Prick," I called him, and he chuckled.

His mirth subsided and his face showed concern. "How did the town look when you left?"

"There were a few of those raggedy assholes in town going through houses when I grabbed my horse."

"How many?" he asked like it was tax day and he had to pay.

"Five or six that I saw, but I put holes in 'em. That's not what you're really asking though, is it?" It was my turn to sigh. "The Runners were hitting the wide-open gates as I was hightailing it out of there on the horse. The main body of infected has probably been inside your town for a couple of hours now."

He slapped his thighs with his palms and stood. "Well, we'll wait three days n' go take a look. They should have moved on by then."

He caught my look of *what the fuck* and asked about it.

"Hicks," I said nodding, "you can never go back there..."

"What the hell are you talkin' about, son?"

I kept nodding. "There were thousands of infected heading in your direction. Tens of thousands, maybe a few hundred thousand."

He wasn't getting me, and it was obvious, so I rolled my eyes and continued, "Forgetting the fact that a hundred thousand dead people will likely tear down every structure in town just by walking through there, the whole place is going to be covered in infected... *stuff*. Blood, fluids, bits of shit that drops off them. Just brushing up against it could infect somebody. Not to mention if half a percent of them stay behind, that's... well it's a lot of them to fight off. Besides, look around." I gestured to the walls of the tunnel we were in, "Isn't this place considerably safer?"

Hicks shook his head. "Yeah, but can a hundred and eight people," he looked at me, "a hundred and nine, be happy in an underground prison? How long before there are riots and dissention? Infighting and a stab wound?"

"The alternative to dissention is digestion. You'll all get eaten out there. In here, you're safe. Just have a system to stop the dead inside."

"Huh?"

"Eventually, somebody is going to die in here. You need a system in place for that."

"We have one."

"What is it?" I asked, my brow furrowed.

"Bullets. Lots of 'em."

"Good plan."

The next few days saw me up and around, looking at my temporary digs. I let it slip that I had a bit of mechanical knowledge and soon I was repairing an air exchanger with a bad rotor. As I used a twenty- eight-millimeter socket on the central hub bolt, I thought about the last secret underground facility I had visited. "Visited" is a euphemism, as I was carted away in a helicopter and imprisoned in an enormous military laboratory a couple hundred feet beneath the ground.

That facility dwarfed this one. Before it fell to the dead, Baldy Mountain had a thousand or so people working there with every state-of-the-art piece of equipment you can think of and a bunch you can't. It was multiple floors of the best minds in the world at whatever field needed fielding. There was a pool, a basketball court, a firing range... You get it, Dear Reader; it was big.

This place had been a copper mine. They widened it a bit and added a shitload of concrete and a hundred rooms or so, but a mine, nonetheless. Every room was a twenty-by-twenty box, sixteen feet tall, made for infinite document storage. There were exactly one hundred storage rooms, and then there were the facility rooms which housed air handling, moisture control, electrical and stuff like that. Only one floor, but it sloped sharply downward the further back you got. There was also a huge ashless/smokeless furnace for destroying documents, so the folks here had already destroyed the tens of thousands of boxes of paper that had been here since before the Cold War. It had taken a few guys the better part of a year, right when the infection started, to get rid of everything.

I learned that the whole town of Independence was created in the sixties to house people to look after the Document Storage Center. It had been government employees to start but had switched to private sector services in the late seventies.

I put the castle nut in a parts holder and pulled the rotor. The whole thing was cracked down the side, which was causing it to shake instead of spin true. The rotor was steel, which was weird. I would have thought it would be aluminum, but the unit was ancient.

"That's going to need a weld," I told Lisa. With average height, bright blue eyes, cornsilk yellow hair, and big toothy grin, Lisa Willie was my helper. She had been glued to me since I got let out of the infirmary. Truth be told, she was watching me as nobody really trusted me yet, but she also helped, and I was appreciative of that. She's also the one who gave me the history lesson on this place we were in. She had a Vietnam War era M16 slung with an equally as ancient green sling, and a sidearm on her hip. I had to respect that. Complacency would get you killed, and everybody needed to be strapped in the world we lived in now. "Do you have a competent welder and gear?"

"Uhhh..." she said.

I chuckled. "I can do it if you have the equipment."

She pulled a radio from her belt, "I'll ask Hicks."

While she was asking Hicks, a tremendous crash came from farther down the hall. The place shook and the only conclusion I could come up with was that there had been some type of explosion. Dust rained down on us and a chunk of concrete ceiling fell, missing Lisa by about two feet.

She had jumped to the right and tripped over a pipe bending up out of the floor. Landing hard on her side, the air was pushed fast out of her lungs. I reached down a hand to help her up but looked toward the high-ceiling when the lights began to flicker. She grabbed my paw, and I hauled her up in time for the lights to give out. Emergency lights on the wall came on, but whatever was causing the problem had to be pretty bad.

"You ok?"

"Yeah," she told me, rubbing her ankle. "Yeah, just banged my leg on that stupid thing." She pointed at the pipe in the floor, which I had to agree was pretty stupid.

The dust rain continued.

I squinted at her. "Any idea what the fuck the big boom was?"

She leaned her head to speak into that little speaker attached to her radio. "Hicks, this is Lisa, come in? Hicks, this is Lisa, what's going on, over?"

Then we heard the sound that is always followed by bad news. The sound that means you have crossed the line in the shit-pool to where your feet no longer touch bottom. Gunfire. Yelling and screaming came next, followed by more gunfire.

Guns didn't shoot by themselves, and locations like the one in which we currently resided, dictated that there were either bad guys or dead guys eliciting the bullets. Lisa's pistol grip was firmly in her palm when I thought of just how far away *all* my weapons were.

Lisa continued to ask Hicks to tell her something of value, but no response came. I looked around the room. It was bigger than the storage rooms, and there was only one way in; a steel fire door. No food or water in here and we were damn close to the end of the mine that ended in rock and dirt. This place was a death trap.

I grabbed Lisa by the arm, "We need to go, now!"

She yanked her arm away. A bit petty, but she was scared. "I'm trying to call Hicks!"

"He can't help us! We need to figure out what the hell is going on, but we can't stay in here, there's only one way out!"

She wasn't moving, so I ran to the door and pressed my hand up against it. I thought that if there were a fire on the other side, the door would be warm. It was cool, so I pressed my ear against it to listen. Yup, still guns and yelling.

I put my hand on the handle and just as my compatriot was asking *what the fuck I thought I was doing*, I opened the door and poked my head through. Not fifty feet down the hall, where the concrete floor ended and the rock began, was a thick dust cloud which obscured most of my view. I could make out a few staggering forms with a few kneeling and reaching into something on the ground. Really, I couldn't see much for sure.

But I sure as shit wasn't deaf. I could hear the dead, and they were coming.

DEAD PEOPLE

"Gimme a gun..." I said as the noises of the dead grew louder.

I couldn't see her as she was behind me and I was looking into the dust cloud, but I just knew she was shaking her head. "Hicks said—"

"I don't give a fuck what Hicks said!" I whisper-yelled. "Give me a weapon or we all die!"

I was standing in the corridor, squinting into the dust and reaching for a weapon. None was forthcoming. Lisa stepped into the hall with me, and the first dead woman materialized out of the cloud. She saw us at the same time we saw her, black drool spilled over her bottom lip and dripped from her grayish green chin.

Lisa gave a short scream and fumbled with her sidearm. She had a perfectly decent rifle slung, and she fought the sling to bring her handgun around. I couldn't fault her; she hadn't been in this type of situation before.

I had, and I grabbed the carry handle on the M16. Lisa looked at me, blinking. The sling was caught on her gun hand. "More triggers is more of a chance for us!"

She let me have the rifle and I brought it to my shoulder and flicked off the safety. I sighted the drooling woman's forehead and squeezed the trigger.

No bang. No bullet.

I yanked the charging handle, tried again, and was rewarded with a neat little hole in dead lady's forehead. She crumpled to the ground, but more shadows shuffled behind her.

"Headshots only, or that's your ass!" I yelled and I could see Lisa was terrified. I mean, so was I, but I had to put on a show of bravery, at least.

A little boy shuffled out of the dust, and I plugged him without hesitation. Even over my ringing ears I could hear Lisa's sob. I sighted on an old man, then a young woman with rotting tattoos. I shifted my aim to another old man with half a scalp, my weapon belching hot unlife, then another in the brown shorts of a UPS driver. Heads popped like grapes stepped on by a rhino. I side-eyed my compatriot and saw that her weapon was pointed at the oncoming dead, but she wasn't firing.

"How many extra mags do you have?" I was talking about the M16 because Lisa had a revolver. "How many?" I yelled.

"I don't have any," she said through tears.

Why would she? We were in a totally safe, completely impregnable, underground fortress. The only reason she had weapons on her in the first place was in case I tried to pull any monkey shit. Which was, in itself, stupid on a dozen levels. Anybody could die at any time down here, which would give us a dead person attacking the living, so everybody should be armed. Also, while not completely incapable of monkey shit, I hadn't been in the mood.

I had fired nine rounds. I had another twenty-one. My sensational computational skills told me we were fucked if we stayed here. "Let's go!" I grabbed her arm, and she squeezed the trigger. To my surprise, one of the dead coming at us dropped.

"Nice shootin' Tex!" I pulled her back toward the rest of the facility, yelling into storage rooms as we went. There was a fire door ahead and we made it with ease. It was a steel door with a handle on this side and a push bar on the other. She closed it behind us just as a bunch of dudes with guns showed up.

Rifles were pointed every which way when someone I didn't know asked, "What's going on?"

I pointed at the door, a bit winded from sprinting sixty feet. "Dead people."

"That's stupid!" the guy informed me. "They can't get in here! And you're not supposed to have a gun!"

So, I guess *he* knew *me*. Or rather, he didn't because he tried to take Lisa's rifle from me. Remo had ensured that I was at least a bit capable when it came to not letting folks take my stuff. I jutted forward with an elbow into his sternum, and he collapsed to the ground. I passed the rifle to Lisa.

"I was just borrowing it. Ya know, to save your stupid asses? Next douche who tries to touch me is drawing back a stump. Except you. You can touch this." I offered a hand to the shithead I had put on the floor so he could get up.

"I'ma sit here for a sec," the guy wheezed.

Thumps sounded on the metal door behind us and everybody, literally all of them, pointed their weapons at the door. Of course, Lisa and I were between the business ends of their guns and the steel of the door.

I rolled my eyes, "Somebody wake up Hicks."

"I'm here," Hicks said, pushing through the crowd. "What happened?"

All eyes turned to me. I glared back. "Yeah, you assholes didn't want to give me a gun, then tried to take it back when I got one of my own accord to shoot infected. Get your answers elsewhere." I folded my arms like a petulant little bitch.

"There are dead ones coming in through the cave section of the archives," Lisa told him. "I don't know where they got in."

"What about Terry and Jack? They were working on the new floor by the end of the tunnel."

"We heard gunshots and screams," I told him.

One of the guys who had shown up with the guy on the floor, yelled, "We need to get them!" and made for the door. I stood in his way and wrapped my fingers around his wrist when he reached for the push bar.

"Don't," I said very calmly. This asshole clearly wasn't picking up what I was putting down and he wrenched his arm from my grasp. He tried to get past me and as I had deduced his intentions, that was not happening. I threw an open-handed poke to his throat. Not enough to really hurt him, but enough that he would stop and have to think about it.

I repeated myself, "Don't," then reached behind me and turned the round deadbolt to lock the heavy door.

He gagged for a sec then reached for his sidearm, fumbling with the ancient, gunslinger flap.

"Don't be an idiot, Cletus. You open that door and we're all dead." I think it was Hicks who had said that, but there were a couple dozen armed people crowding the wide corridor now, all talking in low voices.

"But Terry and Jack—"

"Are probably dead," Hicks finished.

The dickhead Cletus rounded on me, "Funny how all this happened after *he* showed up!" His finger stabbed the air in my direction.

"Yes, you've sleuthed it out, Sherlock. I mind controlled a hundred thousand infected to destroy your shithole town and then let them into your secure facility that I didn't know existed while I was under twenty-four hour surveillance."

I'd had enough. "Mr. Hicks, I'm leaving as soon as we solve your little dead problem. Enjoy your life with this bunch. Come on, Lisa, I want my guns." I was going to push my way through the throng of people, but they parted when they saw my face. I checked to see if Lisa was behind me and she followed, sheepishly staring at the floor.

"Otter," Hicks said aloud, "go with them and get the man his gear. We may need his help clearing out what's on the other side of this door." Hicks and Otter moved toward me and the four of us started our journey back to the armory, where they kept my stuff.

We were, maybe, fifty feet down the corridor, the folks behind me now talking in authoritative voices, when the door holding back the dead exploded. It just fucking blew up. The blast shook the entire facility, and more dust rained down, but this time water started spraying from a crack in the wall. The concussion threw both Lisa and I to the cold, hard ground, and honestly, I was tired of explosions.

119

I glanced back the way the explosion came from, my ears screaming, but another cloud of dust obscured my view of the people back there. I could hear human moans and someone weakly calling for help. Then I heard the hacking rasp of the dead, then the obligatory gunfire.

"Here!" Lisa shouted and passed me the rifle back. She was already on her feet and running into the cloud of death.

"Wait!" I yelled at her, but she either didn't hear me or didn't care as she disappeared into the dust haze. With this undead plague thingie, I wondered if anybody thought about cancer anymore, because that cloud screamed cancer as soon as you took a breath.

I got to the side of the corridor and took to a knee, aiming Lisa's rifle toward the danger. People began to stagger or run out of the cloud, many bleeding, or dragging others. Lisa came out carrying Hicks by the arm. I could hear the dead now over my ringing ears. They were loud. So were the screams of the people who hadn't been able to get away from the hungry dead.

Literally everybody ran past me. None of them stopped to guard the passage, and just left one rifle (me) to shoot whatever followed them. Lisa and Hicks were, maybe, fifteen feet outside the haze when someone sprinted from the dust behind them. In the half moment it took to realize this was a Runner, it had covered most of the distance to the humans in front of me. I didn't have time to bark a warning, so I just fired a round. Most of the Runner was behind Lisa and Hicks, but I still managed to score a shoulder hit.

All for naught, as the thing was completely unconcerned about my bullet. It made an impossibly long leap and landed on Hicks, knocking him away from Lisa. I shot it again in the same shoulder and Lisa smacked her sidearm across its face. The thing, a teenaged girl, put its hands to its face and screamed. Lisa reached down and grabbed Hicks by the shirt but in doing so blocked my target again. The thing righted itself quickly, made another lunge, grabbed Lisa and bit into her shoulder.

Its head was now in perfect view, but they were moving all around as Lisa tried to fight it off. She pushed it away after a moment and plugged the little brat three times. Hicks stood and grabbed Lisa, both of them staggering toward me. Speaking of staggering, the cloud dispensed a couple dozen dead things, all of which wanted to eat us, and they staggered toward our position. The three of us ran back to another door and closed it behind us posthaste. Once again, I engaged the little lock.

Lisa pulled the shoulder of her shirt down and we could all see the semi-circle bite mark which had already begun to ooze some blood. She sighed, put her handgun to her head, and before we could stop her, pulled the trigger.

HOW TO TRAIN YOUR ZOMBIE

Click!

She pulled the trigger again.

Click!

Her revolver was empty.

"You can kill yourself later," I told her. "Until then, shoot the dead people."

I looked around. This section of the corridor was devoid of human beings. All those dickheads full of piss, vinegar, and bravado had flown the coop. What were they gonna do? Sit in their rooms and hope the dead weren't hungry? We needed to fight back.

Hicks held a palm to his forehead, then looked at the blood on his hand. "What the hell is happening?"

"Two possibilities," I answered. I held up one finger to start my genius, "One; there are living people among the dead who are blowing up your doors. Now start getting people back here. We need to open the door if we can and shoot those assholes."

"Wait," Lisa said, confused. "You said two possibilities. What's the second one?"

"How the fuck should I know? Hicks, get your people back here. Tell them to bring that heavy gun I saw at the entrance and all the ammo. Bring the sandbags too and be most ricky-tick about it."

The sheriff's eyebrows were threatening to pop off the top of his head. "You givin' orders now, son?"

I rounded on him. "Nobody else is! Get that shit down here or you're all dead!"

Hicks called his people back and got the stuff. We set up the machine gun, an M240, on the far side of the third metal door. We were about fifty feet from the other door and there were waist-high sandbags built up in a buttress design with the gun resting in a divot. Six of us with various weapons also waited in the corridor behind the sandbags and we had closed and locked all the doors to the storage rooms all the way up the corridor. When the dead came through, they would get funneled into bullets. We would mow them down until they got close, then fall back behind the door and rinse and repeat until we ran out of bad guys.

I had gotten my gear back, which was nice, but the weird thing was that the horde that had moved through Independence was already past it and there were only stragglers left in the town. There were cameras set up all over the town which were being monitored from this place and every one of them confirmed what I just wrote.

Whoever was trying to get into this mine was not with the horde, and I didn't know if that was good or bad. Either way, we had to shoot some assholes to make sure, because the dead didn't use explosives. This was an attack.

I checked my rifle for the fourth time. Still loaded. The thumps and pounding on the door at the far end of the corridor were a bit unnerving, but attrition through ammunition would hopefully win the day.

Two hours later I had to wonder if the bad guys had run out of explosives, or if maybe they were going to attack from a different tunnel. The general consensus was that it was the crazy people who lived in the other mines and that somehow those tunnels came close enough to this one that they were able to blow their way in. But that would mean that someone in their group either knew about this place or had gotten their hands on a classified map.

I had to wonder how many dead they had at their disposal too. Clearly, one of the assholes was the type whom the dead wouldn't attack. I'd love to know how that works. Gamboa and Baker had theories on it, but I thought they were kind of dumb. Something about—

The sounds coming from the far door changed from meaty thumps on the other side to a metallic banging. Someone was hitting it with a sledgehammer. "I guess they did run out of explosives," Otter said with a shrug.

Doors, man. I mean I understand that this place wasn't super crazy with security like Baldy Mountain had been, but still, get some good doors for your secret underground storage facility. The front door would withstand a nuclear blast. The one down the hall from us was a ghetto door clearly made from substandard steel and likely paper mâché. Rending metal sounds came from it then the top hinge fell into the corridor. The pry end of a crowbar poked through the lock side and the lock snapped like a toothpick. The press of the dead on the other side was such that it took a moment for them to figure out what to do, but the side of the metal moved back a bit, and a few dead arms poked through the gap. We could see the gap widening, and I could envision the press fighting the door opening. One dead woman was able to fall through the door and she stood up quickly for a dead person.

"Hold fire!" I yelled. "I'll shoot this one. Head shots only when the door gives way until they start streaming in, then cut them down with the machine gun at head level. Everybody else hold fire until I tell you to shoot!" I put a round through the dead lady's head, and the door peeled back revealing a throng of the dead fuckers on the other side. I could see

122

one smiling raggedy asshole holding a sledgehammer, but he frowned quickly when he saw me with a bead on him and stepped out off to the side in the group of dead before I could plug him.

The things poured through the opening door and the door continued to open.

"Machine gun only!" I yelled. "Light 'em up!"

Nothing happened and I screamed in the machine gun guy's ear, "Fucking shoot them!"

"Oh!" he yelled and opened fire.

Jesus, it was loud. Nobody had any ear protection, and we were in a ten-foot wide corridor. My ears were screaming after the first shot, and my hands covered them. The guy was pivoting the gun right to left, not really aiming at any one target, just pushing high-velocity lead at the dead things. Neither was he doing poorly. He kept the gun barrel trained high, using tracer rounds to keep the heads popping. The woman next to him was feeding the belt into the side of the machine gun and brass was raining down like... well... rain.

The gun ran dry, but we still had some dead crawling over their fallen brethren, so I yelled for the riflemen to fire. Idiots just belted out rounds on full auto out of their M16s, but the folks with bolt, lever, or semi did much better with ammunition conservation and popped domes as they could.

The dead stopped coming before the machine gun got reloaded, and the stinking pus bags never got more than fifteen feet past the smashed door. I couldn't hear much with my gun ears, so I don't know if there were sounds of the dead past the pile of them in the corridor in front of us.

We waited five just to make sure no more came through the far door. None did.

"Don't feel so good," Lisa told me. "How long do I have?"

I've seen a thousand bites. Every one of the bitten asks me that question. I must have some invisible sign on my forehead that proclaims I am an expert. "Not sure," I answered loudly over the din in my ears. "Five to ten hours." I shook my head, "Nobody makes a day."

She nodded in acceptance and sat on her heels against the cold cinderblock wall.

Crews of people moved forward to pull the dead out and pile them up. Others guarded them. The ringing in my ears was subsiding, but I would suffer from it at least until tomorrow. We all would.

Hicks and I chatted while everyone else worked. It was good to be the king, and Hicks was royalty to these folks. I was an outsider and had been treated as such. They could fuck right off if they expected help in removing the dead, but there were already talks about going into the tunnels to find bad guys or dead guys and I wasn't sure if these idiots could handle that. I didn't want to go in there, though, I had places to be. I figured they would ask anyway.

"Were you a soldier, son?" Hicks asked me.

"Nope. I was the type of guy you would have hated. I was a criminal." I could tell he didn't like hearing that, so I tried to assuage him quickly. "I wasn't a murderer, or a rapist. I did some dumb shit and got caught, that's all. Although, not for nothing, I've killed some assholes who deserved it since the dead started walking."

"So've I," the sheriff said. He said something else, but I didn't catch it because Lisa let out a raspy cough.

"You ok?" I asked her. "Lisa?"

She sat there on her haunches, trembling. I knew she didn't have long. Man, if only what I knew and reality were ever even remotely similar.

She whipped her head up, blood red eyes snapping onto Hicks. Already in a crouch, she leapt at him, shrieking. I was able to swing my rifle around and hit her with it, so she only gave the sheriff a glancing blow, but she rolled into another crouch and sprang at him again. This time she latched onto his cowboy shirt, metal buttons popping off like the machine gun rounds my ears were still ringing over.

Lightning fast, she began throwing haymakers and slashing with her fingers. I stepped forward and the butt of my rifle and the side of her head became close friends. Twice. The thing that had been Lisa lay there with a bleeding scalp, unconscious but very much alive.

I held a hand down to the sheriff and he took it, standing up. "Thanks." He drew his revolver with an enormous barrel and pointed it at Lisa's head. "Sorry, hon. You were one of the good ones."

"Wait," I said.

"Son, she don't want to be one of them things."

"Nobody does, but let me tell you a little bit about where I came from…"

Several of the people from the cave group wanted to go hunting for whoever blew a hole in their sanctuary immediately, but we needed an hour or two to get our shit together. Lisa was trussed up and had a wooden stick tied in her mouth so she couldn't bite anybody. She was firmly affixed to one of the gurneys in the medical room. Nobody would go in there except for me and Hicks.

There were about a hundred bodies just inside the facility, and a few mostly-skeletons of people who didn't make it away from the dead in time. Some tears were shed for those lost.

We passed the bodies and checked each of the rooms. Only four pus bags were not destroyed, but their bodies were so far gone they would never walk again, and one of the people in the hunting party took great joy in spearing their heads.

We proceeded through the broken wall and into the cave behind it. It was pretty wide but tightened up as we moved forward. Fifty feet in, the cave turned into a mine, with old wooden braces and metal buckets and such. It must have been the plan of whoever built the storage facility to tie into the rest of the mining system, but for whatever reason, that had never happened.

I was expecting to search through a bunch of caves that twisted and turned and branched off in a hundred directions, but it ended up being one tunnel. Right about the time it turned into the mine, we saw three dead men eating some leftovers. It was the guy who had ducked behind the dead when we shot at them. He must be like Billy, where the dead won't attack him, but the dumbass must have either given himself away somehow or cut himself and his army turned on him. Fuck him, I hope it hurt. Several other gruesome bodies were stirring, likely more like him.

The funny slash terrifying thing is that the guy was right next to an ancient crate with the word DYNAMITE stenciled in white letters on the side. Looks like we found out how they blew their way in, but how did they know where to put the explosives? That knowledge likely perished with the assholes in front of us.

There was some discussion on whether to keep this tunnel as an emergency exit, but in the end, Hicks decided to use the dynamite, which was covered in greenish gray goblets of stuff. That *stuff*, one of the guys told everybody, was pure nitroglycerin, and we gave that shit a wide berth. They put a timer with something on it right in the box, and in a few minutes the compound shook and dust rained. We had been assured that the hardened structure would be ok from the blast as it was far enough away from the facility so as it would only affect the tunnel around it. Unless the whole mountain came down.

It didn't.

I got back to the infirmary, and Lisa was wide awake. She was strapped to the gurney with hospital restraints, but I had been down this road before. Every time there was an infected in a place of safety, that fucker or fuckers broke out and killed everybody. That shit was not happening on my watch. In addition to the leather restraints, Hicks busted out some handcuffs and prison manacles, which we used as additional fastening to keep Lisa at bay.

She hadn't liked it. The second I walked into the room, she went ballistic and did everything she could to try to kill me. I pulled up a chair and started talking to her.

I did that for a few days, and she never once did anything other than scream and thrash. We tried to feed her with some old fireplace tongs and some cold hot dogs. Getting the bit out of her mouth had been interesting, and nobody would do it except me. Safest for me to do it anyway, but I wasn't telling these people my secret.

There were ampules of amobarbital and sodium pentothal in the infirmary, so I drugged her and continued to talk to her each day. I figured we would have to shoot her in the head within a week, but on day six, things changed.

Hicks and Otter were in the room with Lisa and I, speaking in hushed voices. They wanted her gone. I couldn't blame them, but I also wanted to try to help her. I injected her with a cocktail of both drugs, and she began to get drowsy. When she settled down and stopped her monkey shit, I spoke to her calmly, like I had seen Baker do with one of the new Runners they had been conditioning.

"Lisa, it's me again. I enjoy our little talks and was wondering if maybe you do too? We don't seem to be getting anywhere, and I really want to rub those asshole doctors' faces in my success if I ever see—"

"*No Lisa*," she growled. It had been clear as day, with perfect enunciation, even if the voice sounded like a sixty-year cigarette veteran who had a side job of gargling with broken glass.

"Holy shit," both Otter and Hicks whispered at the same time. It was comical as hell.

My shit eating grin could be seen from space. We continued our conversations with Lisa strapped to that gurney for a while after that. Other people started coming to speak with her as well, and while she wasn't the best conversationalist, she sure as shit had calmed down in the *I need to eviscerate you* category.

Her language came back fast. She didn't need to learn to speak again, she needed to remember she already could.

It had taken those quacks Gamboa and Baker four months to domesticate a Runner. I had done it in six weeks. With a lot of time, patience, unbelievable balls, and some expired sodium pentothal, I was able to get Lisa talking and not wanting to explore my abdominal cavity. She sat up, snarled, and looked like she was going to kill Otter and the other two guys who had rifles trained on her. Except she didn't.

We untied her on the first day of the seventh week. Even though we had discussed what to do at length, and there were two gurneys between her and them, one of the guys looked jumpy.

"*Hungry*," was all she said, and we gave her a pimento loaf MRE. She ate the meat and threw the rest on the floor. I would have done the same, unless there were those peanut butter crackers or that oatmeal cookie...

I picked up the package of Saltines, tore it open with my teeth, popped one in my mouth and offered the other to her. She stared at it, unsure of what to do.

I nodded to her and pushed the cracker a little further toward her. "You eat it."

"*Why?*"

"Because it's food."

"*You food!*" she almost shouted.

"No. I am not food. Not for you. We don't eat people."

"*Why?*"

"Because it's wrong."

She looked confused. "*Wrong.*"

We had discussed the intricacies of right and wrong, morals and convictions over the past few weeks. She understood.

"Wrong," I agreed. "Eating people is wrong. Hurting people is wrong unless they try to hurt you."

She looked at the marks and welts on her wrists and arms, then back at me. "*You hurt me!*"

Fuck, she had me on that one. I had to lie to her and suddenly I was nervous. "We did that to help you. If we hadn't have tied you down, you would have killed all of us."

"*Kill!*"

"No!"

She furrowed her brow again and looked at the floor. "*Kill is... wrong.*"

"Yes! Kill is wrong."

In another week the person who had been Lisa and I were standing outside the camouflaged front vault door of the storage facility. The people inside, even though they had known Lisa for a long time, would never allow her to stay.

It was hot as hell outside, and we could see heat rising from the scrub. Pie was there and he put his nose in my hand.

"You can't come, buddy. I can't keep you safe in the city. I'll meet up with you someday. I know I will." Lisa and I began to walk away from the small group assembled outside the door. Pie tried to follow, but Otter held him firm. I dared a glance back, and Pie had his nose lowered so far, I thought he would fall over. It broke my heart.

Lisa and I had a week's worth of supplies in our backpacks, and I had my rifle and six full magazines. My sidearm was on my hip, too. I strode off to the west in the California heat, one of the most dangerous creatures in the history of mankind as my travelling companion.

She definitely probably wouldn't eat me.

FORE

We sat off the road west of Route 395 about twenty miles north of Independence and its mines and crazy people. I was going to build a fire, then remembered the hundred thousand or so dead being led around by a whack-job in an ice cream truck that we seemed to have misplaced and decided against the fire. We would be out of Death Valley in the morning if we got going early enough, and we would branch left at a town called Bishop, head up to just before Lee Vining, and hang a left on Tioga Road. That would lead us through Yosemite National Park, a place I had always wanted to visit.

The last time I was in a national park a friend of mine had been attacked by lions. No shit.

After that our time in the desert would be over and we would be hitting the populated areas. Small towns, but lots of them. Then we would have to go around Stockton somehow and on to San Francisco.

One problem was that Bishop and every town north of it had fallen to the dead. The other potential problem sat in the sand five feet from me twitchy and sweating. The reason Independence had only had sporadic attacks from the dead was that none of the hordes had come this way. The mountains and the desert protected the little town until someone brought the dead on purpose.

Lisa was staring at me, her head cocked to the side. Studying was more the word, so I needed to know what was up.

"You're staring, Lisa. Did you need something?"

"*I want to kill you,*" she said, her fists clenching.

Well, fuck…

"*But it wrong. I not kill. Wrong.*"

I gave a relieved sigh. "Yes, killing is wrong." I poked at the fire I never started, it seemed like the thing to do. "Why do you want to kill me?"

She seemed to struggle.

"*Need. Need to kill. Hate.*"

"You hate me?" I asked, genuinely confused. "Why do you hate me?"

"*Not hate you!*" she spat, clearly frustrated. "*Hate… you!*" She balled her hands into fists and started smacking the sides of her head.

I reached over and put my hand on her arm. I was shitting myself as I didn't know where this was going to go. Ship and Remo would have shot me already for even considering taking this creature with me. Hell, they would have killed her the moment she turned.

She snarled at me when she felt the touch. I spoke to her softly and calmly, just like I had when she was strapped down in the infirmary. Just like I had seen Gamboa do. "It's ok." She was breathing heavily but stopped hitting herself. "What do you hate about me?"

"*Not same! Not same as me! Not same!*"

"You hate me because I'm different than you?"

She screamed in rage. I actually pulled my hand back. "*Not hate you! Not same... ME!*"

It was one of those moments that your brain hurts when you figure it out. It had been right there all the time. Right in front of everybody. In fact, we all already knew what it was. Knew why the Runners wanted to kill us and the dead wanted to eat us. It was because we weren't infected with whatever shit they were. Dead or alive, on a primal level, the infected needed to make us like them... or consume us.

I ruminated for a few minutes on that. Other than her breathing, and the occasional twitch, she remained silent while I thought. Finally, it occurred to me what to say.

"You are my friend," I told her. "I will protect you. We are not that different," I said, shaking my head. She started to say something, but I interrupted her. "The only difference between us is that you can't remember who you were. I will help you with that if you let me."

She stared at me, her red eyes burning deep into my soul. I was shitting myself, and that feeling would likely stick, but I was also extremely sad. So many people had died. So many had changed from good people into something else. Then I thought about all the Runners I had killed who may have been able to be saved and I thought I would go crazy.

She let out a low growl. "*Protect friend...*"

"Protect friend," I agreed.

She reached down into the sand and came up with a scorpion. It was a pretty big one, and it stung her at least twice. She bit it in half, and I could hear her crunching the creature between her teeth. So much for dinner...

I was going to have to sleep next to that. I had to wonder if I would be lunch soon.

Throughout our conversations, both while she was strapped down and not, I and others had told Lisa about the world, the end of the world, and what came after. We had tried to tell her that she was a product of the virus that had done what it had done, but she didn't care. All she wanted to do was live. Live and kill. These two things were pretty much on the opposite side of the spectrum, but she didn't care about that, either.

Lying there on my back, looking at the stars, I could hear her ragged breathing. I had taught her about being on watch and what it meant, and I think she understood, but I still couldn't sleep. If a friggin' zombie came upon us while I was catching some Z's, would she help or watch me get eaten? Would she eat me when she ran out of venomous arachnids?

Protect friend ran across my mind.

I had trusted her up to now. Why shouldn't I trust her from now on? I thought about what Remo, Donna, and the kids would say when they met Lisa. They would all immediately be on edge and draw weapons. But Ship? I didn't know anymore. Would he want to study her? Would he see the benefits of an infected in our group?

Much like Billy, she could walk through hordes of the dead with impunity. She could be a very useful asset to our group, but convincing the others might take a minute.

I thought about the twins. They had grown up so much since we had picked them up. Living in squalor in a boiling hot attic, to becoming absolute undead slayers, to teaching others how to fight. I thought about Donna and Kat. Two more heroes of the apocalypse, both of whom I love. I thought about Tim, one of the nerdiest people I had ever met. He died in the Texas scrub, killed by infected. Remo's buddies, who had become my buddies, Kinga, Brick, and Ray Ban. All dead. More victims. I looked at the stars again. It was a crystal-clear night, and those little pin pricks of light were beautiful.

I blinked and the sky to the east was on fire. Red as far as the eye could see. It was the sun coming up. I had fallen asleep, and Lisa hadn't eaten me. I heard water and spun to see her, five feet away, squatting and peeing. She stood and pulled her pants up, her twitchy fingers giving her trouble with the button on her jeans. Modesty was a human trait, and while she looked human, I couldn't say whether she was or not. Not yet.

That provoked a thought: Did all Runners drop their pantaloons to relieve themselves? Nobody had taught Lisa to do it, she just did. Did other Runners just go and then sprint after us with poopy drawers?

Ew...

I should also note that she didn't seem to sleep. When I was on watch, she just sat and stared at me. It had been a bit awkward, but what could I do about it? She had performed her watch well enough. I was still alive.

I got up and moved a bit into the scrub to leave my own wet marks in the sand. As I was finishing up, I heard her breathing behind me. She was close. I didn't want to freak her out, so I zipped up and turned slowly to face her. Her arm was extended, and she was passing my pack to me.

Her voice was full of shards when she said, *"Protect friend."*

It went like that for the rest of the morning. Small conversations, tasty critters for her, and free-range bathrooms.

We saw the first signs for Bishop as we trudged down the highway not long after waking up. Then we crested a big hill and saw the town itself not long after that. Nestled in a bit of a valley, the mountains on either side were a few miles from the town. It looked like one of those pretty Western towns with the old fashioned and rustic storefronts and one main thoroughfare. Side streets branched off into neighborhoods, but the place was concentrated and quite small. It was hot as hell where we were, but I could see white on the tops of the mountains to the east and west.

"Hang on," I told Lisa, and she jumped like she had been shot. It had been an hour or so since we had spoken aloud, and I guess it had startled her. I pulled the binoculars from the side pocket of my pack. There was a single dead man shuffling down the center of the billion degree street. Honestly, spontaneous combustion wasn't out of the realm of possibilities for any of us. It had to be a hundred degrees, but way cooler than the past few days.

I gotta tell you, a hundred degrees and a hundred and fifteen seem like three hundred degrees apart. It was a dry heat too, so if one could get out of the sun it was better than tropical heat. That said, it was fuckin' hot.

Except for the one dead guy, I didn't see any movement. That didn't mean there weren't a thousand shufflers in the town, but I couldn't see them. So, the question was, did we go in there and get the supplies that we would likely need, or go way around this town and worry about supplies later?

The sign we were standing in front of told me that Bishop CA had a population of 3,120 souls pre-plague. I'm guessing there were no souls now, but still a few things ambling about. Our water would hold out for another four or five days if we did it right, but if we could get some more in this town, or maybe a Mountain Fucking Dew, it would make foraging less of an issue later, and maybe we could go around the higher populated areas.

Yeah, we had to go into Bishop. Hopefully that dead guy would be the only one.

Moving down the hill in the highway, we lost sight of the town in a dip. There was a junkyard off to our left as we crossed over Warm Springs Road, then suddenly everything on the left was green. This was the goddam desert, there shouldn't be green. I was thinking that when I saw signs for Bishop Golf Club.

We strode across the highway and climbed a six-foot chain link fence. Moving through some privacy trees we were suddenly across from what looked like a... Sand trap? It was a friggin' golf course. A golf course that had been meticulously maintained. I checked my watch, and it was just before six in the morning. Hot as hell already, but something was weird. I reached down and touched the grass. It wasn't damp, it was wet. Someone had watered the grass.

I could envision the automatic watering system hooked up to a bank of solar panels. That would explain this. But the green I was standing on was tight as hell and the fairway had been mown recently. Even the rough was maintained. Whoever had done this had gone to school for it.

We moved northwest, hugging some trees between fairways, and I saw the club house. A modernish structure with wide steps up to a mahogany door. Floor to ceiling windows were on either side of the front door, with smaller but still large casement windows the length of the front and side walls. It was kitty corner to another building, which looked like a garage and storage. Several golf carts in various states of disrepair sat out in front of the garage.

The weird thing were the eight infected dressed in golfer's garb each chained to a separate bolt that had been driven into the mostly-empty parking lot. Every one of the dead had a golf club wired to its hand.

Lisa and I ducked beside a tree when we heard something coming. It sounded like a vehicle, but not gas powered. Two golf carts came into view, each with two people in them. It took a sec, but I was quickly able to deduce that only two of the four people weren't ambulatory deceased. Each cart had a dead guy dressed like the golfers with their hands somehow attached to the golf cart, and what looked like duct tape around their mouths. Two humans got out of the carts and made for the doors of the country club, talking and laughing.

We snuck up to one of the tall windows and I peered in. Five dudes sat or stood near the bar, each wearing the same golf garb the dead had been wearing and examining little pieces of paper. Assholes were comparing score cards after a game.

What in the actual fuck? I mean, I was never a golfer, but I could go for shooting a few apocalypse holes.

A pretty young girl, maybe eighteen, came into the room with five bowls of something on a tray. She was wearing a French Maid outfit that was so revealing it had to be a costume. All five guys leered at her when she put the tray on one of the tables. She put the bowls in five locations and used a pitcher to pour water into glasses. The guys came over and the fattest one pushed the girl's face down on the table, two of the glasses of water toppling over. He held her down with his left hand and spanked her bottom hard three times with his right. He yelled at her, but I couldn't hear what he was saying. Then he pointed back toward where she had come from and she hurried back that way, fighting tears.

She came back a minute later and she was crying. She held out a pair of handcuffs to the fat guy and he spun her around and put them on her. He pushed her to the ground while the other four douches laughed, dangling the keys before he put them in his pocket.

That wouldn't do.

The five of them sat down to eat and I turned to look at Lisa. "Do you remember when I said we shouldn't kill?"

"*Yes.*"

"Do you also remember when I told you that you need to defend yourself, and help people weaker than you?"

She struggled with that one, but answered, "*Yes.*"

"There are five men in there who might not be good people. There is a young girl who they are hurting. We are going to stop them. We are going to let the girl choose what she wants to do, stay with the men, or leave. We are going to try not to hurt the men, but if they try to hurt us or the girl, we will hurt them."

"*Kill? Kill the men?*"

"Only if we have to. I'm going to bring you around back. You'll go through the back door, and I will go through the front. Only hurt the men if they try to hurt me. Stay out of sight until you think I need you. Do you understand?"

"*Understand.*"

I got her around back and the morons didn't even have the ancient door locked. She went in through the kitchen and I moved around front. One guy leaned against the bar while the other four sat at the table eating their bowls of whatever.

I strode into the country club dining area, all 180 pounds of me spilling a confidence I didn't have. One of them at the table noticed me and stood up, pointing. The guy at the bar stretched for a shotgun that was just out of reach, the standing table guy started to go for the sidearm on his hip.

"Don't," I told them. My rifle was pointed down, but not at the floor. My finger was on the trigger. "Hands up or I put holes in you." One of the assholes looked like he was going to be problematic, so I fired a round at the floor, which ricocheted and buried itself in a wall.

All of them raised their hands. That was good. The girl, still in handcuffs, sobbed in the corner.

"What horrible transgression came about to put a kid in handcuffs?" I demanded. Several of them glanced at each other, and I raised the rifle a bit. "Don't get antsy. Antsy gets you dead, and I haven't decided yet if you're worth the ammunition. Why is she cuffed?"

The fat asshole harrumphed. "She don't know how to do nothin' right!"

"Yeah," another one of them said. "She's dumb as a post!"

Not sure what the big one could be eating in the apocalypse to keep him in the shape he was in, but there must be a lot of food around here someplace. He chin-wagged toward the girl. "You can have her for a couple of hours if you want."

I sighed. If he had said anything else, begged for his life even, I would have just taken the kid and walked out of there. That comment was enough to prove what kind of people I was amongst. I pointed the rifle at him but noticed all of them had devious little grins on their faces. Remo shouted to me in my mind, and I dropped to the floor, rolling left and bringing the rifle up fast. Two more golfers had come up behind me, one with a butcher knife and the other with a nine iron. I plugged them both. Even before they dropped, I spun to face the other five assholes, but shotgun guy was already aiming the big thing at me.

Lisa hit him like a freight train and all hell broke loose. The douche-kidnapper-rapists, as I believed them to be, all completely ignored instructions and leapt to their feet, going for their weapons. I mowed the whole table down with half a mag on full auto. Two guys would live and two were dead as hell. The guy who had pointed the shotgun at me was screaming and fighting a losing battle with Lisa.

It was very loud in the Country Club right then. The two not-dead guys were whimpering and crying, the handcuffed girl was shrieking and trying to push her back through the wall to escape everything, and both Lisa and the asshole she was battling were yelling stuff.

Lisa, on top of the douche, finally threw a haymaker that connected directly downward into the guy's temple, stunning him. She leaned in like she was going to rip his throat out, but then looked toward me, expectantly.

"Hurt?"

"No!" I pointed, snarling. "Kill 'im!"

The guy had started to rouse, and he weakly pushed at her with his hands. She grabbed one and gave it a vicious twist and a thrust of her palm, snapping the arm in half, then she batted his hands away and grabbed his head with both of her hands, sinking her thumbs into the guy's eyes. That woke him up and he started to scream in earnest, beating at her much harder with his unbroken arm. Lisa pushed her head toward his in what looked like a kiss but ripped off the corner of his mouth with her teeth. A big shred of lip tore off when she pulled her head back, and it flopped on her chin. She spat it out and went in for a second bite, crunching down on his larynx. The guy gurgled another attempted scream.

That was enough for me, and I stepped on one of the downed guy's hands as he reached for his revolver.

"Uh-uh."

My ears were ringing from the gunfire, but the terror-stricken girl's shrieks were going right through my head like nails.

Lisa stood, her entire chin and shirt dripping with shotgun guy. His face looked like bad chili, and his long game would probably suffer from the bones sticking out of his arm and the fact that he was dead as hell.

"Lisa, would you please watch these two? If they reach for weapons, rip them to pieces." She grunted and stood menacingly over the two downed assholes. I slung my rifle and made my way to the kid. She was way more scared of me than of the guys splattered all over the dining room.

"I'm not going to hurt you," I said but she continued to scream.

I sighed and shouted, "I'm not going to hurt you!"

She gasped and shut up. I showed her the handcuff keys and she tried to stand. I startled her when I grabbed her under the arm and helped her to her feet. She stood and I spun her a bit to get to the cuffs. She rubbed her wrists and blinked at me.

"You ok?"

She just blinked, her eyes wide.

"I'm sorry for what those assholes did to you, but I am not like them."

Her eyes darted to Lisa, and she pointed, "It... it's one of the monsters!"

"No, she's not like the ones you've seen. She's...different."

"It talks!"

"She can talk, yes. Are you ok?"

Her eyes focused back on mine and her lower lip started to tremble. "Are you going to kill me?"

"No. Absolutely not. I came in here to free you from those assholes." I thumbed over my shoulder. "You can do whatever you want. If you want to come with us, you can. If you want to leave, go for it."

She bolted. She ran through the open door, and I never saw her again.

"Alright then," I said and strolled back to the table. "What should we do with them?"

One guy had a hole in his shoulder and the other had two on the side of his chest. He might not make it. I leaned down and took their guns.

Lisa snarled, thick crimson dripping from her chin. She was going to need a new shirt. "*Hurt?*"

"We've hurt them enough." The fat guy, very dead with a hole in his shirt right where his heart would be, began to stir. So did one of the other dead dudes. The guy Lisa had ravaged tried to sit up pushing with his broken arm, but the bones snapped completely, and he fell on his side. I shot him through the head before I realized that was dumb.

"Let's go," I told Lisa, and she looked confused.

One of the dead guys looked at me, his eyes totally crimson. He began to get up. The guy with the injured shoulder began to stand and his buddy cried for him. "You gotta help me, Bobby!"

Bobby pushed with his feet, inching his ass across the carpet. He went right through the infected blood puddle of shotgun guy.

The guy screamed again, "Bobby!"

That got the attention of one of his dead buddies and the thing stared at him for a moment before deciding to crawl under the tablecloth toward his pal. The other thing sat up and Lisa and I made our way to the door, closing it behind us just as the guy on the floor began to scream. I don't know what happened to the second guy. There was a case of canned pork 'n beans, and a case of water by the front door. I grabbed the cans and told Lisa to get the bottles.

"Not all people are bad," I told Lisa as we made our way down the steps. "But not all people are good, either."

She grunted, then again. Then again. *"Who is bad?"*

"Most times you have to figure that out for yourself."

"You bad?"

We stopped at one of the golf carts with no dead guy in it and I put the beans on the back of it, opening the case plastic with my knife. I put six cans in my pack and six in hers. Same with the water. The packs were quite heavy when I was done.

"Depends on who you ask." I had an epiphany as we started walking again. "What do you think? Do you think I'm bad?"

"You help girl but kill men. Why girl good? Why men bad?"

Well fuck, she had me on that one.

"Because we should never hurt the weak. We should help the weak and punish those who would hurt the weak."

"Weak!"

"Yes. Anyone who can't or won't fight back. But there are limits. You can put yourself in danger to help someone, you can even die to help someone. But helping someone you know is going to give up and die is a waste of time. The problem is, you need to figure that out and it's not always easy."

She thought for a moment as we walked past the snapping zombie golfers. Their mouths were duct taped, but they still very much wanted to eat us. *"Girl weak. Men hurt her. Men bad."*

I nodded. "Exactly."

"You good."

"Thank you."

"I bad."

I tilted my head and asked, "Why would you say that?"

"I need to kill men. I need to kill girl." She glared at me and said with a voice full of glass shards, *"Need to kill you."* She looked at the sky and gave one of those Runner shrieks that make me shit myself every time I hear one. The scream was long and loud. I stepped to the side, my rifle barrel coming up imperceptibly. I immediately lowered it, and she stopped screaming and twisted her head toward me.

"Bullshit," I told her and realized she had no idea what that meant. "Not true," I added. "If you needed to kill me, you'd kill me. You would have killed me already. You haven't, which means you don't need to." I sighed, "Something in your... your... new *life*, wants you to kill me. It tells you to." I shouldered my weapon and put my hands on her shoulders. "But you haven't. You haven't because you are good."

"Good!" she growled as we crunched across the gravel toward the road.

"Yes, good."

She did the scream thing again. We were going to have to talk about that. Underwear was hard to come by.

138

BISHOP

Not surprisingly, there were undead in Bishop. The thing is, there weren't nearly as many as I had thought there would be, at least not out in the open. Were there thousands holed up in the buildings to keep the heat off? I had to hope not. This was the last smallish town we would hit before we hooked west on Tioga Pass Road about sixty miles north on the 395. There were other towns, but we would be going way around them. I didn't want to push my luck.

But we would need supplies. We had the beans and some water, but hey, I like variety. If the dead had ravaged this place quickly, there might not have been time enough for survivors to loot goodies before they were turned or eaten themselves.

I was just about to write *One can only hope* in regards to those people not getting the spam, but that would be me wishing death on strangers. It is my fervent hope that those people escaped with their kids and color TVs intact. No bad karma for me.

The good thing was that Lisa wouldn't touch the beans. I tried to give her some and she smacked the steaming cup away, the food splattering on the yellow dotted line of Interstate 395. I had to think of that last night. Not the beans, the fact that there was a dotted yellow line smack dab in the center of nowhere. I mean, who gave a shit about putting lines down? In addition, the dotted yellow line meant no passing. Why weren't we allowed to pass when the nearest car would have been miles away? Wait, the dotted yellow means you *can* pass, right? Shit, I don't remember.

The bad thing about Lisa not eating beans is that I had no food for her. How long would she go before she saw me as one of those chickens with the little white booties the Coyote dreamed the Road Runner was wearing?

Anyway, we waited until nightfall to move into Bishop. Having seen Runners sprint at people just to kill them, I thought I was going to have to teach Lisa how to sneak, but she was a pro. That scared the shit out of me. Could other Runners be sneaky? I had never seen one lie in wait... dammit, yes, I had. I had been in a building and one of the fuckers had waited behind a door.

Shit. I hadn't put that together until now.

Regardless, Lisa surprised me in how quiet she could be. We snuck by a huge lot of recreational vehicles, dark hulks that were rusting away.

I didn't want to go near them because there were too many ways in and out of the area and too many alleys between the vehicles.

Not surprisingly, an RV supply store was attached to the lot, and we passed by it and over East Jay Street as we hugged a wall of overgrown shrubbery. A Jack in the Box fast food restaurant sat basked in the yellow glow of a functional sodium arc streetlight. I wanted no part of being illuminated for anything hungry, so we kept away from Jack and crept further up the street.

Something else I should tell you: with no other lights on in the town it was damn dark everywhere but near that restaurant. Not pitch black because there was a mostly full moon shining on us, but it was hard to see.

A few dead things shuffled out of a building on our right, and we stopped moving while they ambled on to whatever destination they had in their feeble minds. We moved on, passing some indeterminate structures, a motel, a plumbing supply company, and a big parking lot. This is where we saw our first signs of trouble.

Several police cars had been parked in an arc outside a building across the street. I peered through the darkness and was helped by another sodium arc streetlight to discern that this had been a California Highway Patrol outpost. The cars had been there for years, so I had to believe the cops had made a stand here. I was standing next to a tree, on the corner of another parking lot, when I looked behind me. That was my huckleberry: a Speedway Express gas station and quick mart. The front door was closed, and that made me happy. It was less likely that the place had been looted. The bad thing was that those doors, and the entire front of the building, were made of glass. There were stickers and banners and shit on the windows, but unless those bitches were tempered glass, the first undead who banged on it would likely gain entrance, and that was if I could lock the doors. It was a little box that could be the death of us if we got caught in there.

The town was silent. Not a bird called, nor a bug chirped. We would have to be equally quiet. The place *looked* empty, but I didn't believe that for a second. I'd been in totally empty places before only to find out that a hundred hungry undead were lurking just out of sight.

We moved toward the gas station, the forgotten pumps dark sentinels standing guard over the possibilities awaiting us in the store. We were silent as ninjas until we had made it to the first bank of gas pumps, and I held up my fist for Lisa to stop.

"*What is that?*" she grunted. The volume of her voice had been kept low, but it still sounded like a rock concert to me.

"What's what?" I asked, looking at her over my shoulder.

She held her fist up as high as she could. It was almost to the point of injury, and I realized, yet again, that I was an imbecile. How the hell could she possibly know what hand signals meant? This version of Lisa had never seen a TV show where communication with hand signals had been shown and we had never covered it.

"It means stop and be very quiet. If I hold up my fist, like this," I showed her, "you should stop and be quiet. If I point with my hand like this…" Well, you get it, Dear Reader. I showed her several hand signals. Hopefully she would remember them. I slung my rifle and drew my sidearm. I had fired a ton of rounds through the suppressor, so I didn't know how long I had before it burned out. The last few shots hadn't been any louder than the first few, so I guessed I had a few more magazines before the sound dampening gave out.

I used another hand signal to tell her to follow me and she did. We slunk across the parking lot, its only occupant a truck of indeterminant make and model rusting away with the doors open, perhaps sixty feet away. We reached the doors to the Speedway without incident, and I peered inside. I couldn't see shit more than five feet in. I pulled the door open on silent hinges, and we stepped inside.

The closest shelves had been looted, but not picked clean. There were items on the floor that I could not make out, and stuff on the shelves getting more prevalent the deeper into the store they went, granted I could only see in about five-foot increments.

I did have a red filter for my flashlight, but I didn't know if that would still be a beacon of light in an otherwise deserted place, so I kept it on my belt. I stepped on something, and it crunched a bit. I reached down and picked up what could only be a human leg bone. Likely the skeleton of someone that, unlike the store, had been picked clean. Ok so, I did turn on the flashlight. I blocked it with my pack, but it was still quite evident. I shut it off quickly after seeing what was on the floor. More assorted bones and partial skeletons adorned the floor in this aisle. Looks like these folks had come up with the same idea as me but had been caught in the act. They hadn't been killed recently, either, as the darker stains on the floor were dry and I smelled nothing. Likely they were attacked and killed at the onset of the plague and their remains remained. The dead didn't care much for burials.

Even the skull was broken open and the gooey bits had been removed of the one closest to me. Two backpacks sat on the floor, but I couldn't tell what was in them as I had shut my light off. I reached into the first bag to check. Cans for sure, but full of what I couldn't tell.

I sighed. I could discern items but couldn't tell what they were. The simple fact was I couldn't see shit without the light. This wouldn't do. We would have to wait for dawn and hope we weren't spotted. In the meantime, we would have to hole up someplace.

But not here. Even if there was some room to hang out upstairs or in the back of the place, there was little I could do to prevent the entire store from filling with undead cannibals should they figure out we were in here.

I gave a couple of hand signals and then realized Lisa couldn't see me in the darkness. I was about to explain what was happening when something raced past the front of the Speedway. It wasn't a car or a horse, it was of the two-legged variety. I fell to my haunches, getting as low as I could, and Lisa seemed to follow suit. There were some low shelves between us and the window that we hid behind.

A second thing ran by, then a third. They had been fast. So fast I couldn't tell if they had been infected or not. My answer to that little conundrum came forthwith.

One of those underwear destroying screams sounded from somewhere outside. It wasn't on top of us, but it hadn't been in Paris France, either. Another scream came, followed by a third, and that last one had been way too close.

The three screams sounded again, but this time all three were much closer. It sounded like a coordinated attack pattern was being communicated through those screams. In addition, the noise would bring every dead fucker within earshot to the Speedway for a look-see.

A sound creeped into my ears. It was very close. Inside the store, not five feet from me. I strained to hear what it was, my pistol pointing in all directions and a turtle threatening to escape into my shorts. It was Lisa. She was breathing heavier than usual, and it was way louder than I liked.

"Easy," I whispered.

"*Calling,*" she whisper-growled. "*Looking for... you.*"

Scratch, scratch, scratch, scratch... came in rapid succession from the window behind and above me. *Scratch, scratch.* Two second pause, *scratch.*

A thud against the window was next and I shot a glance up. I was at an angle such that I could see the entire window. The two Runners that had their faces pushed up against the glass and were peering in didn't see me. But all they had to do was look down.

The one on the left, a skinny, twenty-something woman with filthy and matted long dark hair, twitching and jerking her head, reached her hand up and scratched at the window with her claws. It was fucking terrifying and that was her goal. To scare whoever was hiding into the fatal mistake of making a run for it.

Runners didn't get tired. They could outrun the fastest of humans not because they were faster, but because they would sprint until a muscle tore, or their heart exploded. Humans didn't have that luxury and always got caught when out in the open.

The second infected was a big, bald man. Not by any means fat, just big. He looked like the kind of guy that you knew would be scrappy if you got in a fight with him in a bar.

I stared at those two creatures, the man heaving, the woman scratching at the glass, both with their faces pressed against it, for another ten seconds or so until I heard the front door, which was ten feet away, begin to open. The moonlight barely illuminated the door as it creaked slowly forward, but there were enough shafts from the moon outside to show someone's hand curl around the metal of the glass doorframe. It opened a bit further, and a head stuck through the top as the first foot fell into the room. I glanced back up and both Runners were still peering into the darkness.

That meant there were three. At least three.

The creature, a mid-sized man with longish dark hair and broad shoulders, was halfway through the door when it sucked in a huge breath and screamed into the store. I had been wrong when I thought there were three... There were at least four because Lisa screamed right back at him.

Then the infected murderer did what any self-respecting infected murderer would do, he glared at us. His eyebrows shot skyward in surprise as he saw me, and my nuts shrank as I saw him. He sprinted toward us immediately, but Lisa was up and running at him like a bullet. They both leapt, he at me and she at him, at the same time, executing the most bone-jarring mid-air collision I had seen to date.

The guy hit the floor with Lisa behind him and tried to scrabble toward me on all fours, but Lisa was having none of that and grabbed his ankle. He kicked like a frog, but she was a Runner too, and as I've said before, they do not let go. She climbed up on his back as he tried to crawl toward me. She slashed his face to ribbons and the bastard didn't even fight back. All his energy and hate were directed at me and nothing else on planet Earth mattered, not even the thing on top of him ripping him to pieces.

She stuck her claw in his mouth and ripped back, tearing his gums and cheek open to the point where I was able to see his teeth. He did not care. That was when she decided to push his face into the floor. She did it over and over again, but I was more concerned with the other two Runners who had entered the building and immediately raced toward me.

I shot the male first, high in the chest, then the female one through the abdomen and another through the face. Her head snapped back, but she tumbled forward, her momentum carrying her. She had ceased moving, but the guy put his hand to his chest, looked at his hand, then tried to scream. Not a scream of pain, like you or I would have tried, but one of fury and hatred. The bullet had punctured his lung, so that was hard for him, and the scream came out as a croak. He fell to one knee, and I put one through his dome before he could stand back up, because he was trying. The shots, although suppressed, were way louder than I would have liked but also significantly quieter than shots from an unsuppressed weapon.

I was breathing heavily, almost to the point of hyperventilation. In the back of my mind, I could make out these meaty thumps and had to refocus before I could discern the source. It was what was left of the first Runner's face being repeatedly and viciously smashed into the floor.

The guy had been dead a solid thirty seconds, but apparently, Lisa was a closer.

"Lisa!" I whisper-shouted. "He's dead, you can stop!"

She stopped immediately and stood, looking at her hands. They were positively dripping with gore, thick locks of the dead Runner's hair acting like wicks for the blood to run down toward the floor. She heaved as I did, but then again, she heaved a lot because of her infection. Runners do not breathe like we do.

She brought her hands up, sniffing them. She opened her mouth, and I realized she was going to lick the blood and bits of other chunky stuff from her fingers.

"No! Don't eat that!"

"*Why?*" she asked, and I couldn't come up with a compelling reason not to, so I straight up lied to her.

"Because it's bad for you."

"*Bad? You said kill ok! Protect!*"

"Yeah, you can kill them, but don't eat them. I'll find food for you."

"*Food!*" she said, looking at the broken bits of skull covered in brain matter on the floor.

"I'll find you *better* food!"

She cocked her head, about to say something when something outside caught her eye. She jerked her head that way and gave a hiss that almost made me wet myself.

I also redirected my gaze toward the window. The good news was... well there wasn't any. The bad news was that we had found the undead in Bishop. All of them.

I FOUND IT

Thousands of the things bore down on us from the town and they were loud. They shuffled and shambled across the huge parking lot from the north and northwest. They crawled from cars and fell through open doorways, only to get up and plod on. Some stood in the tall grass of a vacant lot next door. Dozens stumbled from a road to the southwest as well, stumbling into the yellow glow of the streetlight by the police station.

In two minutes, escape would be impossible. A decision needed to be made quickly on which way to go, but I still had time to calculate that there were way too many dead things for this shitty, one-horse town. The population had been less than four thousand, but I was looking at at least that now. It looked like a sporting event had ended and the undead were all hitting the parking lot at the same time for their cars.

My all consuming, pants-shitting terror was not shared by Lisa, either. This was just a Tuesday for her. If, in fact, today was a Tuesday. The dead things wouldn't eat her, but *I* was sure as shit a top shelf menu item.

I could see through the windows at the back of the store, and that direction was equally full of dead people. There was only one direction to travel in, and I hated the thought of it. Either we died in this little box of a store, or we fled. Now.

"Let's go!"

We ran out the front doors and hooked a left. There were less dead people this way, but not by much. The street this horde had been coming from ran perpendicular to the street we were on and that was my goal.

We were fifty yards away from my intended escape route when I realized we would never make it. Well, she would, but I would end up just another messy stain on the road to be washed away in the next rain.

Not wanting the entirety of me to be inside the rotting stomachs of some dead folks, my juices washed into a storm drain, I made a tactical decision. It wasn't ideal, but it would keep me alive for a few extra minutes at least.

"This way!" I yelled and grabbed Lisa's wrist. I didn't wait for her to fight me and pull away, or give me shit for touching her, I just pulled.

We sprinted toward the only other structure that might offer protection, vaulted and slid over the hoods of the cars used for a barricade, and ran up the yellow steps of the California Highway Patrol building. A brick wall stood in front of us at the top of the stairs with glass doors to the left and right. We went left and pulled the doors, but they were chained from the inside. Fifteen feet away was another set of doors which we reached just as the first of the dead hit the cop cars. The cars would buy us time, but seconds only.

Turned out it was enough. I yanked the right side of the double doors open, and a dead woman staggered into me. I grabbed her by the shirt, spun, and threw her down the stone stairs, her frail body making snapping sounds as she tumbled to the street. We rushed into the building, and I told Lisa to search for dead people while I figured out how to block the door. There was a heavy chain on the floor, and I looped it through the metal handles securing it in a knot. I searched for something to put behind the door, but the only thing near it was a flagpole. A nylon loop dangled from something at the top of the door, and I reached up and yanked it down. It was a steel shutter, and I finished pulling it down and it clicked into the floor.

Spinning around, I saw that Lisa was running past desks and looking all over. I told her I needed to close the shutter on the other set of doors, but I didn't know how to get to them from here and I don't think she understood what I said. I wound my way through the desks toward the other side of the building. I found an open door that said Communications Center and moved cautiously through it. This side was covered in those ancient bubble skylights, the moon casting ominous shadows inside the office. Everything looked like an evil version of itself in the moonlight. The desks had evil phones, there were evil chairs, and I even saw an evil stapler that wanted to kill me.

But nothing moved. I saw the doors which were now to my left and the shutter was already down. The tumult outside told me the dead had circumnavigated the police car barricade, made it up the steps, and were thumping against the doors and the side of the building. I moved back to the door between the different sides of the buildings and took stock.

Twenty or so desks on the left side, with phones and calendars, mugs and headsets. Clearly a dispatch area. Seemed to be the communications center it was advertised as. The other side looked like a police department, with cop stuff all over the place, a front desk, and eight work desks.

Although there had been a dead woman in here, the place was surprisingly clean. I figured on a room full of dead people with stains on the floor, arterial spray on the wall, and bones and guns scattered about. There must have been a last stand outside, but why hadn't they fallen back into the building and locked the shutters?

Maybe they hadn't wanted to get trapped, just like I was now.

Fuck.

Nothing for it now. Shit had fallen apart outside quickly, and I had done the only thing I could think of at the time to not get eaten. I still felt like a moron. We should have gone around this town. The Independence folks told me it was teeming with the dead, but I thought I was all that.

Guess I'm not. As if to totally jump on board with that last statement, the glass on the outside door shattered and the dead poured two feet further into the building until they hit the shutter. The steel was meant to deter people from entry, not stop tens of thousands of pounds of zombie pressing up against it. Eventually it would fail, and the police station would fill with hungry dead. The place would not look so tidy after that.

I needed to get up on the roof to see how fucked I was. I started looking at the ceiling for trap doors. I noticed Lisa looking up as well, so I told her I was trying to get up to the roof from inside. I had to explain to her what the word "ladder" meant. We couldn't find anything in either of the two big rooms, but there were several doors to try. A couple of bathrooms, a break room, and a room with several copy machines later, and I saw a gray, heavy steel door with one of those little chicken wire windows in it.

It was the jail. I don't like jails. I opened the door into a short hallway and saw three cells down the right side. The last two were empty, but lucky number one had a skinny thing sitting on the floor in the center of the concrete. It stood up immediately upon hearing us and shuffled toward us, sticking its hands through the bars.

Poor bastard. He must have been incarcerated for being drunk, or just an asshole. They hadn't let him out before everything went to shit and he had starved to death. Pity moved me, and I grabbed his rotten shirt through the bars and stabbed the poor guy through the eye. He collapsed and Lisa cocked her head at me.

"*Why kill?*"

Her voice was still creepy AF. "Because I felt bad for him. I put him out of his misery."

"*Misery!*"

She liked to yell her questions. "Yeah, he was an undead. They are all miserable." I could see the cockeyed confusion, so I elaborated. "They all feel bad and want to kill us for it." Likely my most full of shit answer ever, but she seemed to buy it.

There was no ladder or access to the roof back here. Just walls and bars. This place was solid AF, but a deathtrap. We moved back into the main room of the Police Department. I searched for and found a firearms locker, but that bitch was open and empty. There wasn't a shotgun shell or even a .22 round to be had.

The thumping on the metal shutter was a tumultuous terror. The windows were all high enough that the dead could only just reach them, so until they started stacking on each other, they wouldn't be able to breach that way. The doors though... they would give soon. Given enough time, these things would batter their way into a mountain, and knowing that, I had to get us out of here.

I ran past the desks to the rear of the station, my footfalls not nearly as thunderous as the pounding fists. Parting the blinds, I scoured the rear parking lot for a way out. While the tide of the dead was significantly thinner out back, there were still several dozen weaving through the rusting hulks of cars that would never move again. The right side of the building was a hard no, as those parted blinds revealed hundreds of the things streaming down the road from that direction.

Lisa and I moved back through the connecting door into the dispatch area, skirting the cubicles and making it to the outer wall. This window was broken, shards of glass crunching beneath my boots as I stuck my head out into the cold night. Fifty of them ambled about, most moving toward the front of the building where the hoopla was happening. I looked left and saw that there were so many out front that they had started spilling around to the sides of the building. We had thirty seconds before they would have us surrounded.

My courage bolstered by the lack of enemies in this direction, I used my rifle to scrape against the inside of the window, smashing the broken pieces of glass that hung there, then climbed up and glared at Lisa.

"Let's go!" I hissed and crawled through. I jumped six feet to the unkempt grass and weeds, hearing a thump behind me as my infected compatriot hit the ground half a second later.

Our secret out, the things all turned from whatever direction they had been going and focused on us, immediately traipsing toward the unspoiled meat. There was nothing else to do, so we turned right, and ran for it. This was back toward a larger number of dead than was right here, but the spillage from the front had made the decision for us.

Damn she was fast. She outpaced me quickly, and *I'm* fast. She looked over her shoulder as she ran, and I realized that she was going to lead us someplace I might not want to go. That wouldn't do. She wasn't afraid of anything and as such was inadequate in her decision making insofar as leading us, or at least me, into death.

I hissed again, "This way!" shifting direction toward the least of the horde. The thing is, when you're in the middle of a throng of things that all want to get to you, your circle of safety begins to tighten quickly. This was no exception, and I found myself dodging outstretched arms and grasping fingers steadily until one latched onto my pack. It slowed me enough that a second one stepped in from the side and I had no choice but to shoot it with my sidearm.

The shot had been suppressed, but I think the undead in the immediate vicinity had figured out what was up and were coming for us anyway. I had the fervent hope that a couple thousand of the things would beat on the brick of the California Highway Patrol building until their fists had worn down to nubs thinking I was in there the whole time. I had no doubts that cop shop would be full of milling undead within the hour when the shutters gave way. They were too loud to hear the shot, but they might follow the crowd who had.

I shot the first thing that had grabbed me, and it did the most unexpected thing; it let go of me and collapsed. Usually, they kept you in a death grip when you clipped their dome. We came to a tall chain link fence and leapt onto it, skittering up and over like spiders. Dozens of the things came at us, but nothing like what we had just left. Our boots pounded the pavement, and I saw a sign for Los Angeles Water and Power Department.

Los Angeles? WTF?

We emptied into a huge area with dump trucks, a couple of loaders, and several other machines. We had to be sprinting through some kind of department of public works parking lot. Big white building to our right, bunch of trucks to our left, and a swarm of dead on our heels. The only option was straight ahead, but I didn't like it. There were so many in front of us. I glanced left and saw them trickling past the trucks. To the right they were coming out of and from the sides of the building.

I was fucked.

"Lisa," I said with a bit of sadness, "kill as many as you can."

I went to the rifle. I checked the load and felt for extra magazines on my vest. I had four. A couple thousand dead and a hundred and fifty shots before I would have to ditch the rifle and use my sidearm. I had two spare mags for that plus whatever was in the gun, then it would be up to Chauncy.

A scream rent the air to the left and we had our first Runner in twenty minutes. Lisa screamed right back, and I have to say, her scream was every bit as terrifying. The bitch of it is, she ran off to the right leaving the other screamer for me. I swiveled left and saw the thing, a woman in shorts and a T shirt, pushing the dead out of the way as she sprinted through the trucks at me barefoot. All I could think was that if I could just restrain her and talk to her, with a side order of drug therapy, she might join me on my way back to San Francisco.

Or she would kill me in my sleep, I thought, my lower lip jutting out and eyebrows raising in agreement with myself. I gave her one center mass and she fell as she ran, losing all kinds of skin on the pavement she scraped across.

Now, *that* was loud. The shot echoed across the lot and through the trucks. I know it echoed because the second I pulled the trigger, every dead person who had been making noise ceased, and other than the echoing shot, there was dead silence.

It didn't last long. I wasn't going to wait for the quiet to go, so I assaulted it with more noise from my rifle. I kept the rifle to my shoulder as I pivoted back toward the west. A huge dead woman was thirty feet away and I popped her dome like a grape. I moved forward, selecting targets and shooting as I could. I did pretty well, dropping twenty-two with my thirty round mag. I performed a tactical magazine switch that would have made Remo proud and continued firing.

Remo. He would be looking for me by now, likely with Ship, Kat, and Alvarez. I was hoping the kids and Donna would be safe someplace, but they were likely together with Remo's group, looking under rocks and behind dumpsters for me. Would they venture into the city? I had to hope not. Maybe they had seen the empty results of such a futile search and decided not to go.

Ship wouldn't see the search as futile. Actually, he would, but he would go anyway. He and Remo would go into San Francisco to look for me, putting themselves in danger because that asshole Gamboa and his Fuckity Force had kidnapped me. If anything happened to any of my friends because I was pulled from them, Gamboa, Baker and their whole crew of miscreants' lives were forfeit. I would hunt them until Armageddon.

Well, a different Armageddon, but you get it.

But how would I get past Thorne? I thought as I squeezed the trigger. That fucker scared the shit out of me. Hell, all the Runners did. Would Subject Nine and Lisa square off against Thorne and his pack of devils, or would they join forces and just tear into all of us? Maybe I would get back and Thorne would have been so sick of those doctors' shit that he would be using their rib bones as xylophone mallets.

A couple dozen stinking undead were rendered truly dead as I calmly considered how to wreak my revenge. Then my thoughts returned to Donna, Chloe, and Richy, and all my calm fled. If they had gone with Ship and Remo into the city to search...

My blood started to boil as I thought of harm coming to my family. I squeezed the trigger again. Nine, eight, seven, miss, five, miss, miss, two, miss. I ejected the magazine, but just let it clatter to the black pavement, no longer giving a shit about loading later. I was starting to shake with anger and my aim suffered.

Thirty shots later and I was standing under a blue street sign that read: S. Fowler. There were more dead on South Fowler Street now than before I had started shooting. I loaded my last mag and fired at will, the anger at this plague and the undead and Gamboa and those fuckers at the golf course building. Brick, Kinga, Ray Ban, what had they died for? Tim! Why had he had to die? That fucking colonel, what was his name? And all those people at Keesler, dead! Baldy Mountain, Havre, Boston, Bishop fucking Cali-fucking-fornia! Dead! All dead!

I clicked empty, let the rifle fall on its sling, and drew my sidearm. I fired and fired as my ire moved way past the red line. The things were closing, and I knew I was dead. All those people, an entire goddam planet, were dead because of a computer virus. Ones and zeros. I would be just one more. One more after one more until there was nobody left.

One of the things grabbed me and I put the suppressor under its chin and ended it. I dropped the sidearm, thinking it was a bad idea not to have it, but also not giving a shit, and drew my knife. Chauncy gleamed as he flashed in the moonlight, piercing craniums and cleaving wrists.

I heard a Runner screaming. It was one of those sounds you just never get used to, and it terrified me. I stabbed a young boy in the eye and spun to search for the Runner. It was still screaming, and it was incredibly loud and close, but I couldn't find it. I heard it but couldn't find it as I slashed the hand of a dead grandma, skeletal fingers flying. Couldn't find it as my trembling hand released the knife and it clattered to the ground. Couldn't find it as I grabbed the closest walking dead man's head with those same shaking hands and sunk my thumbs into its eyes, pushing as deep as they would go. It was when milky-red jelly squirted across my hands that I found it.

SAME

I sighed myself awake. I opened my eyes but couldn't see anything. Before today, I might have panicked. Today I didn't care. I knew the melancholy would pass and I would need to figure out where I was, but right now, sitting in the cloying darkness, I sighed again.

I had no idea where I was or how I had gotten here, but hey, this wasn't my first rodeo with that. I was like a werewolf with that shit. However, there were several downsides to what I thought had just happened.

The first was that I had no idea how long ago I had flipped my proverbial lid. Could have been ten minutes ago or the day before yesterday. I could look at my watch, but as soon as I clicked the button, green light would explode outward telling everything else that resided in this impermeable darkness where I was.

The second downside was that I generally did vile things in my... *other* condition. Things I couldn't take back or disavow. Things that invariably left me with a shitty taste in my mouth and my mind, and sore all over.

I did have a pretty crappy taste in my mouth, but it was because I was thirsty. I didn't want to make a lot of noise, but I also needed to ensure I was alone or at least safe. I felt about, but my rifle was not within reach, and I couldn't find my sidearm or my combat knife. I did find my multitool and a magazine for my handgun on my vest.

Great, I could pliers someone to death or throw loose rounds at them.

I waited for the pain to come, but it didn't. I felt myself over, feeling for bites or blood. No bites, lots of sticky shit which was likely blood. I stunk to high heaven too, so I could only assume the blood came from people whose circulatory system had ceased its circuitous route a while ago. I flexed my fingers, knees, and elbows, then rotated my ankles and shoulders. I moved my hips around to make sure my back wasn't going to betray me. Seems I wasn't hurt. At least not physically. I felt around the area again and knew for sure I was inside. I could feel items and I was leaning against something soft, like a couch or a comfy chair. I didn't want to reach too far, lest I come across something that wanted to bite me, and I really didn't want to try to move around on my hands and knees, searching for a way out of here like Velma looking for her glasses.

I waited what could have been two minutes or an hour, listening to the darkness with nothing to show for it. My tac light was not on my vest, and my backup light was in my missing pack, so the only light I had would be from the G-Shock watch on my wrist. That was pretty bright, but I didn't think I could use it to navigate from where I was. All it would do was give my position away from up to a hundred yards without showing me anything. But I still needed to see.

I sighed again, covered my wrist as best I could and pressed the button on the watch. I let it shine for a second and saw that it was 03:10. One problem down. I might die in the next five seconds, but I would shuffle loose the old mortal coil knowing what time it was.

Nothing tried to kill me, so I pointed the watch face to my right and turned it on. Surprisingly, the green glow illuminated the edge of one of those U-shaped sectional couches. Leather, either brown or black. I nodded. While leather isn't my favorite choice of sofa, I could really use a sit down on something other than the floor. I panned the light around noticing gray carpet stretching forward into infinity in front of me with odd shapes that I couldn't make out in the emerald light. I panned the rest of the semi-circle and almost shit myself when I saw legs draped over the couch with feet resting on the floor on the left side of the U about four feet away.

I stood, keeping my weak light on the legs. If they moved, I would have to fight. They didn't, so I moved closer panning the glow up. The legs were attached to a body which was attached to a head. Most of a head. The top of it was sprayed across an L.A. Clippers poster just above the body. The thing's left arm hung off the side of the couch almost pointing at a nice Beretta 9mm, just like Martin Riggs had in Lethal Weapon. I let go of the button on the watch and fumbled for the handgun, checking the slide action in the dark.

It was still dead silent in the room, and I had to wonder where all the dead people were. There had been thousands of them and when they get together to party, they're loud. I put the gun on the couch and shined the light on it. The action had felt good, and if the thing had sat on the floor for a few years after this guy had checked out, it should be fine.

It was. I racked the slide back a bit and blew into the barrel to clear some dust, but I couldn't see if I did because I couldn't use the watch and hold the gun at the same time. I tucked the Beretta into my holster and used the watch to make it to a wall. I followed the wall until I found a curio cabinet with some weird little monster figurines. Next to that on the left was a cool desk with an even cooler computer on it. Further left was a TV under which a bunch of LEGO busts of Star Wars characters sat on a long shelf.

We were in a room with no windows, and I figured it was a man-cave basement. There was cool nerd shit all over, LEGO cars and Star Wars ships. Light sabers on the wall. A pinball machine, posters of anime stuff

I didn't know, and some signed sports memorabilia including a Robert Parish 8x11 inch signed poster that would absolutely be coming with me. If I can't make room in my pack for a signed photo of the Chief, I might as well quit living now.

I had missed two casement windows because they were covered with heavy shades and drapes, high up on the sheetrock walls. Left of center in the room were a set of skinny stairs up to a closed interior door. An open door next to that led to a smaller side of the basement with a washer and dryer, tools, a work bench, an open gun safe, an oil tank, and a burner. This must have been nerd-guy's workspace. A doorway in this room led to a few steps and a steel bulkhead door with the bolt driven home. Several candles also sat on a long shelf, so I busted out my Zippo and lit one up. The dead guy and I were alone in here, so I moved around with the candle.

The candle threw loads more light than my watch, so I checked out the gun safe. A lever action rifle stood undisturbed within the safe, as did a couple of pistols and one of the sexiest things I had ever seen. A black rifle with SOCOM 16 on the side in white. I know what SOCOM means, it was a military acronym, but I didn't know what kind of gun this was other than it was beautiful. Eight fully loaded 20 round magazines and a dozen or so boxes of different kinds of .308 ammunition were also in the safe. It was Christmas. The rifle was short of length and had a really nifty padded sling.

I wiped sticky black shit from my face and hands, hung the towels I had stolen over the curtain rods just to be safe, then lit up a dozen or so candles. Without a desiccated dead guy, it would have been kind of homey. There were some clothes folded and stacked in a couple of bins near the washer and dryer. I needed out of these blood-soaked duds, but the jeans were way too small. I pilfered a pair of gray sweatpants and a red T shirt. It was a little chilly in the basement, but not freezing, so I also grabbed an extra-large, Hello Kitty sweatshirt perfectly colored in pink.

A few pairs of ratty socks, some clean underwear (shut it, you take what you can get in the apocalypse) and a kid's blue backpack later, and I was a fashion statement. I wouldn't be blending in with my environment unless it was in one of those multi-colored ball pits, but I would be warm and dry-ish upon my reentry into the world.

But first I had to get out of this nerd cave. I hadn't heard a sound while I was exploring the basement, so I gathered all the magazines and rounds for the SOCOM rifle, and let me tell you, that was heavy, and stuck them in my backpack. The Beretta was the best sidearm, so I took that, but there were only two mags and half a box of 9mm. I also took a chrome snub nose .38 revolver and two boxes of ammo. I was set on ammo for a while, but it was damn heavy. I really wanted the lever action, but the bullets for the thing were as long as my index finger. It said 45/70 on the side of the only other ammo boxes in the safe. The weight would be too much, so I left it behind. There wasn't a single knife to be found.

I sighed at the knife situation and moved to the bottom of the stairs. There were fourteen steps between the door at the top and me. I took them slowly and on the eighth step the pressure of my foot creaked so loud I thought they would hear me in Nebraska. I stood there, waiting like an idiot, for what seemed like a half hour, but in reality had been less than a minute.

Nothing came to eat me, so I moved up the stairs and put my hand on the doorknob. I was all about throwing doors open wide, but something told me to ease this one open, so I did. The first light of morning assaulted my eyes, and I blinked rapidly before I peeked through the slit between the door and the jamb into a small-ish kitchen. It was done in walnut cabinets with baby-puke green paint on the walls. Don't get me wrong, the paint worked in this kitchen, and it seemed homey and nice, with green granite counter tops and stainless appliances.

A small kitchen table sat just to the left of the door, and at that table in a brown chair sat a figure with its elbows on the table and its head in its hands. Without looking up, the figure spoke to me.

"*Same,*" a familiar and still somewhat terrifying voice said. "*You, same.*"

She lifted her head and glared at me with crimson eyes. "*Sleep too much.*"

I stepped into the kitchen and scraped a chair across the floor. Placing the rifle on the table, I sat next to Lisa. "You brought me downstairs?" I thumbed at the door behind me.

"*Yes. You... sleep.*" She looked confused for a moment and contemplated what to say. "*No, not sleep...*"

"I passed out," I offered. "It happens sometimes after... after I do what you saw. I have no control over it."

"*Same. We same.*"

"Yes. We're the same."

"*We're the same,*" she repeated with effort.

I sighed and added, "Thank you for getting me in here." I stood and walked to the back door, which had a window in it. I cautiously parted the musty smelling white curtains for a look-see. Two re-killed specimens were face down in the back yard scrub, their heads no longer in one piece. Another was face up on the small deck. Well, it was facing up. The face was gone, smashed-in recently.

"Where are all the dead people?" I asked.

She stood and walked from the kitchen into a nice little living room. A brown couch sat across from a big TV on the wall. A cute little fireplace with photos on the mantle rested kitty corner against the far walls. She pointed toward the double front windows.

Once again, I cautiously parted the curtains, but this time I looked into Hell. Thousands of the rotting bastards meandered around aimlessly a couple hundred yards up the road. They were moving in and out of buildings and just doing dead people stuff. They were far away, but way too close for comfort. Some pounded on doors and others broke through windows on the houses in that direction. The horde was slowly moving this way.

We needed out of this fucked up town. Out and far away, like, now.

I faced my infected friend. "Ok, we go out the back door, sneak through the rest of the town, and run like hell."

She nodded and we moved back into the kitchen. Her pack was on the floor, and she grabbed it. I grabbed my new one and my new rifle.

The door creaked as I opened it, and we stepped through. A dead woman in what was left of a police uniform latched onto me immediately. I had just "cleared" the back yard, and if Remo were here, he might have shot me.

As a former criminal, I wasn't too thrilled to be around cops anyway, but dead ones really suck. They bite too, and this one wasted no time in sinking her teeth into my backpack. She probably had been aiming for my shoulder or upper arm, but she just straight up missed. She pulled her head back, as zombies do when their teeth are in you, expecting to have a hunk of juicy me in her mouth, but all she had was a tuft of blue nylon.

She had ripped the pack a tiny bit but hadn't the jaw strength to bite out a piece. She let go and went in for another nibble, but I was quicker. I had gotten over the initial WTF of the incident, and I sprung into action. By "sprung" I meant I twisted her away, got my legs tangled with hers, and we both hit the dirt hard.

I was doing everything I could to keep the dead policewoman from getting a piece, and she was doing everything possible to chomp. She was making this *ahhh ahhh ahhh* sound too, like she had burned her mouth on pizza.

We rolled left, and I got on top. Holding her throat with my left hand, I reached around to the side with my right desperately searching for a weapon. I didn't want to take my eyes off the cop, lest she bite one of my fingers off, but I couldn't help but notice that Lisa just stood there, head cocked, staring at us fight. My digits passed over a loose piece of those pink, wavy shaped landscape blocks, and I ripped it out of the ground and smashed it into the side of the dead woman's head. I bent back a fingernail and that shit hurt, but it hurt way less than being bitten by a dead person.

I thumped the thing's dome until it ceased trying to bite me, then thumped a couple times more for posterity.

Ew.

Her dome was a shattered mess of goo and bone, and her damaged brain was clearly visible. I had heard someplace that the brain turns into something with the consistency of yogurt shortly after death, but I can tell you for absolute certain that this thing's thinker was not that. It was healthy. I mean other than it being in an ambulatory deceased person's skull and full of a virus and stuff.

But it wasn't rotten like the rest of her.

I stood, heaving, and turned on Lisa, "What in the actual fuck?" I hissed at her. I pointed down at the re-killed thing, "Why didn't you help me?"

She uncocked her head and righted her gaze from the dead thing to me. *"Helped you yesterday,"* she said and strode past me to the garden fence.

"Helped me yest...?" I sighed. We were going to need to work on our communication. Specifically, when to not let me fucking die. She had been great on that until now, and I had to wonder what had changed.

I used to think funny was love, compassion, and empathy all rolled up in a laugh, but I've grown to believe it can also be snark with a side order of bizarre. This was bizarre, but someday, this shit would be funny. "Hey, 'member them livin' dead fellas that tried to chew on everybody?" "Nah, you trippin', bro. No such thing."

It sure as shit wasn't funny now.

"We go."

"Alright, let's go. How does it look back there?" I clambered past the several bodies in the back yard, and we peered through the vertical slits in the brown fence panels together. A moderate amount of shamblers were ambling about on the street and in the yards to the west. Nothing like what was coming from the southeast, though. There were hundreds of them, and they were breaking into the houses and abandoned vehicles looking for something. Again, likely I was what they wanted. I no longer had any doubts that Bishop was as dead as most other towns, the sole living occupant now me.

Except fuck that because I was extricating myself from this rotten place immediately if not sooner. *Occupant* my ass. I was just passing through, and while I had lost more than I had gained while here, I was still alive. I intended to keep things that way.

A narrow gate, held closed by a loop of wire across the top two poles, was our exit. I pointed at it and Lisa just looked at me.

"Through this gate, then we run. We run until we don't see any more dead people, then we can slow down, but we can't stop until we're far away, got it?"

She grunted in response, a gravelly sound full of loss and pain.

The noise of the horde behind us was getting louder. So much so that the ones in front had started to mosey in our direction, pinching us between smaller and larger groups. It was now or never. Without a word I threw the wire loop over the posts and burst through the wooden door. Lisa followed and we jogged straight at the oncoming dead.

They had seen us, and this shit was on. There were, maybe, a hundred all told, but they were scattered across the landscape unlike the crowd coming up the street to the rear. It was easy to juke their outstretched hands, but the problem was that they were starting to converge, and the point of convergence was me. A line of them formed ahead, with a scattered few we passed turning to follow. I juked a dead mailman and the gray fingers of something in a disgusting dress that could have been a bridal gown. I kicked a little girl in rotten pajamas and was almost grabbed by a dude in jeans with no shirt on. His skin not gray but consisting of a greenish hue. A thing with a handcuff on its wrist still cuffed to a rotting and dangling forearm almost got me, but Lisa pushed it away.

Maybe twenty of the things started to close in on us from about sixty feet in front. The landscape was such that I would not be able to avoid them. It was then I realized we would need bullets for this situation, and I unshouldered my rifle. Now the heft of the backpack would be worth its cost to haul. I knew I had already loaded and charged the rifle, but I pulled the bolt back a bit anyway to check. The safety was in the trigger guard and I nudged it forward with my trigger finger, lined up the little sight nub on the nose of the barrel into the little round hole sight on the rear end, and let a dead bitch have it.

The kick of the rifle was substantially more than that of my M4, but not as bad as the other .308s that I had fired. That was nice. What was nicer was that the noggin on the dead woman I had sighted on simply ceased to exist. No little hole appeared like with my M4 or my sidearm. A cantaloupe-sized hole punched through her dome, and as her head hadn't been much bigger than said melon, *her* melon just went away.

My eyes widened and I turned this black beast over in my hands, gazing at the rifle in wonder. "OH! OH HO, HO, HO, HO!" I said in my own gravelly *this is awesome* voice. I had said it was like Christmas back when I found this in the nerd cave, but I had been wrong. This was all pornography, and I am positively proud to record here that I fired the next six rounds in a state of elated, raging priapism.

I scored six headshots, clearing a path for us to run through, but Lisa had already grabbed a dead thing and was smashing its head into the asphalt of the street. When she had decided that the critter had been sufficiently pulped, she stood back up and we ran like hell before the gap could collapse. We made it.

Unfortunately, the shriek of a Runner pierced the air, and the fucker was already sprinting at us from the door of a small house on the left. It was a kid. A ten-year-old boy, and he was *fast*. I aimed the rifle at him but lost the ability to pull the trigger. What if we could catch him and give him the Gamboa treatment? It was a little boy for fuck's sake, and he wasn't dead. Infected, sure, but could we get him back? Could we at least turn him into another Lisa? Before I had met Gamboa and Baker, and most importantly, Thorne, I would have blown this kid out of his shoes, but that trio of assholes made me consider. My finger wavered on the trigger, but I just couldn't do it. I couldn't shoot this kid. I couldn't...

While I had been stupidly contemplating what to do with the boy, he had reached us. He leapt at me snarling, but a boot lashed out from next to me and caught him in the throat, knocking him away. He clutched at his crushed Adam's apple, gagging, and turning multiple shades. He glared at me through his pain with unabashed hatred. The kid tried to move forward to get to us but collapsed quickly.

"*I save you more than yesterday*," Lisa admonished. She grabbed my shirt and pulled me forward. We ran through the gap toward the mountains to the west, but we would have to get through the rest of Bishop first.

QUEEN TAKES BISHOP

We ran for ten minutes, dodging outstretched arms and grasping fingers until things started to get dicey again. The dead started to become numerous in front of us, but they were spread out like they had been behind the nerd house. The noise of the horde had disappeared, so I could only assume they were far enough behind us that it would take some time for them to catch up.

Most of the things in front hadn't noticed us, but several had started their arduous shamble in our direction. It wouldn't take long before one of them squealed, and then the jig was up.

We emptied out through an overgrown copse of trees and into a large parking lot. I put my hands on my knees and gasped for air thinking the whole time what a friggin' idiot I had been for taking us into this town. I looked up to get my bearings and realized that I was, in fact, an idiot. I had led us directly into a hospital parking lot.

Dear Reader, the two places you don't want to be during the beginning of a zombie apocalypse are a prison and a hospital. I know what you're thinking; ... *but the walls of a prison are sturdy and no undead could get to you and there are guards and guns and...* Yeah, no. Every inch of the prison is built to keep you inside. It's not just the cells that are locked, but every corridor and doorway has a locked steel door as well. What you're not thinking about is that the outbreak happens *inside* the prison as well as outside. So now you have dead prisoners shuffling about and you can't get away from them. If you do manage to get away, you still can't escape because the doors are locked and the guards are either shuffling around with the inmates, or they ran off and left you to starve in your cell. Prisons are bad, trust me, I was in one.

But hospitals... hospitals are the end-all be-all of where not to be during a zombie outbreak. Hospitals also have locked doors, but they have sick and dying people as well, AND they have injured folks. Like *Hey, this guy just bit me* type of injured. See where I'm going with this? Fuck hospitals. Fuck 'em.

Except that is where I dumped us out. Straight into a hospital parking lot. Also, as luck would have it, every single dead person in the area seemed to figure out that an ambulatory lunch was just a stumble away. They were all coming for me, and they came from all directions save one. That one direction was the wide-open ambulance bay of the Northern Inyo Hospital on West Line Street in Bishop California.

So, I ran into the hospital, or rather the attached garage whose massive door was open. I skirted between two ambulances, one of them with an occupant mostly under a sheet. The occupant was strapped down, and it was moving. Two or three dozen other bodies were in sheets or black body bags stacked three or four high on a concrete abutment used to store medical supplies and equipment for the ambulances. They weren't moving.

Jesus, can you imagine the horrors of a first responder during the beginning of this thing? Fighting off "sick" people you were supposed to help in order to get to wounded people only for those wounded people to attack you later? What a shit show. I bet less than one percent of the paramedics and EMTs on the whole planet survived the first couple of days, not to mention doctors and nurses in the hospitals. I was about to find out as Lisa and I ran up the concrete steps, through a steel door with a wooden wedge keeping it open, and into the hospital itself.

It was pretty quiet in the hallway, but it was clear that there had been bedlam at one time. The place was a shambles with instruments knocked over, medication bottles on the floor, and lifeless monitors smashed and dangling.

There were a dozen huge brown stains with drag smears on the tile floor and bloody handprints everywhere. And bones. There were bones strewn all over. One pathetic thing strapped to a gurney right next to the door we had come in stared at us. But that was all it would ever do. It was a partial skeleton with its face and jaw torn off for good looks. Basically, just most of a spinal column attached to half a rib cage, it would never move again.

Black bullet holes stitched across the dingy white of one wall, and I saw two M4s, one on a counter and one on the floor. The one on the floor was covered with dried gore and had no magazine. I wanted no part of it. The other one had a mag with nine rounds and it looked clean. I picked it up and handed it to Lisa, who looked at me like I was made out of cheese.

"Just carry it for me," I told her.

I kicked the little wedge out from under the door and it closed with a click. When I turned back around, I saw Lisa, bent at the waist, her face half an inch from the skull-face of the gurney-creature.

"*Why?*" she asked.

"Why what?"

"*Why not die?*"

"It can't. I don't know if it wants to or not, but it can't unless you destroy the brain."

"*No*," she said, "*you*." She spun insanely quickly and pointed at the bite mark on my arm. It was mostly healed, but it had taken way too long.

"I have no idea," I whispered as I scanned the area. I poked my head inside two rooms and motioned her to follow me. "But I can tell you that people want to know. Not just me, but people who want to cut me open to try to learn from me."

I stuck my head into a third doorway and almost got it bitten off by a dead thing that had been standing there. I jerked back and out of the room quickly, but Lisa was there before I could take the bastard down. She threw it to the floor and did that head smash thing that creeped me out. The dead one stopped moving quickly.

What an idiot. I'm an idiot. "Lisa," I said, "would you please check the rooms as we move forward? I will cover us from the hall. They won't attack you."

She growled or grunted or something, I don't remember because that was the moment something smashed into the door we had closed halfway down the hall. The dead must have filled the garage by now, but I wasn't hanging around to find out.

We, rather she, cleared out rooms as we moved deeper into the hospital. I closed doors as we moved north. We came to a consultation area with some stained couches and overturned tables. There were lots of windows here, maybe eight feet above the ground outside. Nothing would be climbing in those windows, but there were a metric shit ton of nothings outside. The dead were streaming past the outside of the hospital. There were hundreds.

The corridor hooked right and fifteen feet down it was inky darkness. There were windows at the far end, but the next hundred feet would be walked in pitch black. I couldn't see the floor, so there could be creepers or syringes or pepperoni pizza for all I knew.

Fuck pitch black. I used my lighter to illuminate the situation. I could see, maybe a six-foot circle, but that was better than nothing. Unfortunately, the light drew the locals, and they came a-shufflin'. There were only three and we dispatched them quickly.

As soon as we arrived at a spot where the sunlight reached the floor through the windows, I doused the light. Peering through those windows affirmed my fears. The horde I had seen a half hour ago was stumbling about on the hospital grounds. Not only that, but I could hear them inside the hospital. Shockingly, there must be a front door that was also open, although I have no idea where. I could follow the exit signs but really, that would only lead me to the dead.

"Lisa," I said, and she whipped her head around to focus on me. "Do you think you could travel twenty steps or so in front of me and kill any dead things in the way?"

She said nothing. Not even a grunt. She just moved away from me down the hall. She peered into an open doorway and just closed the door. The next one she did the same, but the third she strolled into, and I heard a brief scuffle. She exited and closed the door behind her.

It went like that for about five minutes before we saw the first ones in the hallway. There were eight of them, and our groups had seen each other at the same time. They plodded directly toward us, and Lisa was in amongst them in seconds. She dispatched five in under a minute, knocking them down and smashing their heads into the ground, or just smashing their faces into a wall or a doorframe. The three that got past her came toward me, and I got two of them before she used the M4 as a club and squished the dome of the last one.

My very own pet infected. Simply the best zombie slaying tool I'd had since I travelled in an MRAP a while back.

I glanced through a ceiling-to-floor window at the horde outside. There had to be thousands. Lisa might be able to smoke a few in front of me here and there, but I would never get through that. I felt a presence and jerked my head to the left. She was standing there, staring at the dead just like me. While I was wondering if she was thinking that I would be eaten by the end of the day, I heard a screaming whistle.

A hundred feet away, directly in the thick of the horde, a bunch of the dead and the ground around them just exploded. They blew the fuck up. Body parts and whole dead people flew through the air and the blast wave that knocked over a bunch more shattered the window I was standing behind. I threw my hands up in front of my face and was rewarded by being covered in broken glass. A small trickle of blood made its way down the side of my face as I shook glass beads out of my hair. Safety glass, thank God.

I heard two more whistles, grabbed Lisa's arm, and threw us both to the ground. Two more explosions shook the building followed by several more whistles and more booms. Artillery. Someone was dropping artillery shells on us. The explosions ceased and I dared to stick my head up for a peek. Several decent-sized, smoking craters in the ground had blossomed and surrounding those holes were infected who had been knocked to the ground. Most of them were missing bits, several were on fire, and many would never get up again.

But some did. They stood, and I had to marvel at their resolve. Drop bombs on these motherfuckers and they just brush the dirt off their remaining shoulder and soldier on in their single-minded pursuit of ambulatory vittles. I heard machinery and my wonder continued. Coming down the road, and making a road of their own, were two tank-looking vehicles with no gun turrets. Each had these two arms that stuck out in front of them like big fingers and attached to those fingers were these double vertical cylinders. Behind them were two armored backhoes, two Bradley Fighting vehicles and an LAV, those I knew and had seen in action. The armored vehicles with the guns on them stopped and the tracked things kept going. They moved toward the horde, and then the Beatles started to play. Seriously, they were blasting sixties music.

"and the way she looked was way beyond compare..."

The tracked things waded into the dead people, and it was a slaughter. The cylinder thingies were some kind of grinders, and they pulped anything they touched. On the back of each vehicle were more fingers and each had what looked like a giant saw blade on the back. Think a five-foot wide horizontal circular saw blade. While the grinders were stationarily attached to the front, the blade things spun on axes and were clearly being controlled from inside the safety of the tracked and armored zombie juicers.

Pulp and bits of clothing shot out from behind the cylinders and the steel of the vehicle was definitely going to need a wash. The blades were just as effective and chopped into the necks and torsos of the infected.

I was so enamored with the whole situation that I failed to see several of the rotting bastards sneaking up on me until Lisa was smashing their faces into the ground or swinging the M4 by the barrel. I just glanced over my shoulder, shrugged, then continued to stare at the carnage outside the hospital. Lisa was suddenly standing next to me.

"Save you again," she growled.

The carnage went that way for another half hour or so, but the dead were clearly overmatched. I had another epiphany: with this sort of equipment, we could take back vast amounts of territory that now belonged to the dead. If we coupled that with an army of tamed Runners, humanity could bounce back from this brink we were precariously perched on. I was in too much awe to smile.

I could have cheeseburgers again... A hot shower... a Mountain Dew factory! Little kids flying kites and moms and dads playing with puppies in the park. Working computers, a jacuzzi, a stroll down the street, and above all, the absence of constant terror. For the first time since I saw a dead guard bite into a criminal in the prison yard in Massachusetts a few years ago, I had hope. Hope that my species could win against the dead.

Of course, these guys might just want to kill me and be done with it. There's that. They could be straight up bad guys.

The two juicers stopped, and the backhoes moved in. They pushed the goo that had been ambulatory deceased into three piles, then one of the hatches on one of the juicers opened, and a guy with a big cigar in his mouth popped his head out. He was talking on a radio, but I couldn't hear what he was saying from here. He pointed at the hospital and at the rubble piles of destroyed dead. The Bradleys and the LAV came rolling in and they scanned the area before hatches popped, disgorging breathing humans. Several men and women stood talking in a circle while others formed a rifle perimeter and shot any dead who came late to the party. The whole operation had been efficient and effective.

I couldn't hear them over the diesel powered engines of the big vehicles in front of me, but two dozen vehicles, mostly military Humvees and trucks, but some civilian trucks as well, drove up and made a semi-circle in the field I was staring at. A small group of people walked toward the trucks to the drivers of the juicers and the armor. One guy was clearly in charge.

I turned to Lisa, "We should go say hello."

"*I kill them?*" she asked. She had sounded like she was asking the time.

"No. No, don't threaten them in any way or they will do that," I pointed at the piles of goo, "to us. In fact, when we go down there, I want your face and eyes covered by a bandanna and sunglasses."

We made our way to the stairs and had to kill about six infected before we were at a side door. I wrapped Lisa's face in the blue bandanna I had grabbed from the nerd cave and put sunglasses over her eyes. Fuck it. I took a deep breath and pushed the door open. We left the M4 Lisa was carrying by the exit door and I held my rifle over my head with two hands as we approached the humans.

We didn't get five steps out the door before six heavily armed people, one carrying what had to be a flamethrower, started toward us. They didn't yell in surprise, or tell us to freeze, or lower our weapons. Our groups stopped about ten feet apart.

"Howyadoin'?" one of the men asked in a Boston accent.

I replied in the same accent, "Doin' great if you're not gonna kill us."

They all smiled. "That depends on you," a blonde woman with a nasty scar cutting diagonally across her face said. She was wearing one of those military caps. Not a baseball cap, but something you would see in a sixties war flick or a cap that resided on a train engineer.

"Well, ma'am, if you were gonna kill us, there isn't much we could do about it, and if I was gonna shoot you, I would have done it from inside the hospital. You likely would have turned the whole building into smoking rubble if you were shot at, though."

"Smart fella," she said. She stepped forward and held her hand out. "What's your name?"

I clasped her hand in mine and was about to supply a bullshit name when a Runner shriek pierced the air followed by several more. These people didn't look even moderately concerned.

We released our hands, and the woman spoke into a radio, "We got sprinters at the LZ. Sounds like four or five at least. Keep your eyes open." She looked back at me. "I'm Amy Johns, and I'm the First Sergeant in charge of this little incursion into Bishop. We—"

"What's with this one?" one of the guys asked with a chin wag toward Lisa. "She's kinda... twitchy..."

He let that hang and everybody's focus shifted to her. Three rifles raised a few inches, but nothing pointed at her.

"She's my friend. I met her a week or so back and she's been invaluable. She's saved my life twenty times since we met." I stood in front of her, putting myself between my friend and the business ends of five rifles and a flamethrower. Nothing was pointing our way.

"She was my friend before she was infected, and she's been my friend for three weeks after."

Now the barrels came up. Everything was pointed at us. Jesus fuck that flamethrower was terrifying.

"Step away," one guy said, his rifle pointed at my face.

"Not a fucking chance, douche crust. This is Lisa, and she's a sentient infected Runner."

"I said—" the guy started moving his rifle closer to my face, but the woman in charge cut him off.

"Secure that shit, Blevins. I want to see this."

"But,"

"Shut your mouth but keep your weapons on them." She nodded toward me, "Show me."

"Ok," I said. "But if you shoot her, you'd better fucking shoot me, because I'll kill as many of you as I can before you take me down."

She gave a curt nod, "Noted. Nobody shoots unless it attacks."

"*She*," I corrected. "Unless *she* attacks. Lisa, would you pull down the bandanna and take off your sunglasses please?"

She did. There was no mistaking her for what she was now. There was also no mistaking the fact that every finger that had formerly been on a trigger guard was now on the bang switch.

"Sarge, are you fucking kidding?" Blevins demanded. "What are we doing here?"

Amy was breathing heavily. All she said was, "Jesus..."

I smiled at Blevins. He had not lowered his rifle and the boom hole was ten inches from my nose. I didn't look away when I said, "Say hello to the nice soldiers, Lisa."

"*I kill them*?" she asked, and I thought we were both going to be full of lead poste-haste.

I was still looking into the giant hole on the end of Blevins' rifle. "Not unless they turn into bad guys, then you kill them all. Lisa, what is it you do?"

"S*ave you*," she growled. It was that same growl Runners use when they are tearing into someone, but this had distinct syllables and prose. It had been completely understandable, and I don't know if that reassured or scared the shit out of these people.

"Weapons down," Amy said and everybody but the guy with the gun less than a foot from my face complied.

"Sarge..." he started, and she shouted at him.

"Now!"

He lowered his weapon, and my nuts descended back to where they should be. They had gone on hiatus for a few, and I was glad to have my buddies back.

"Call the old man," Amy said. "He needs confirmation on this."

"Confirmation?" I asked. "So, you guys have seen the Runners getting smarter?"

Amy replied to me, but continued to gawk at Lisa, "Yeah. Yeah, but they still want to kill us. And this is our first time hearing one talk. I've heard them trying to say stuff, but never articulated like this."

With the use of the word *articulated*, I knew this girl was more than just a grunt. She was intelligent. Again, I didn't know if that boded well or poorly for me.

"Jennings!" she barked. "Call!"

"Sorry, Top. I'm on it," one of the guys replied sheepishly.

"Thank you for lowering your weapons," I told her. "As I said, we are not a threat. We're just passing through."

We bullshitted for a few minutes until I heard something I didn't like. An honest to God helicopter came whipping in from the north and set down in the field near the armor. Two fully kitted out dudes, two little dudes that had to be staff nerds, and a guy of medium height who just dripped *I'm in charge*, exited the bird. The two nerds, both of whom looked exactly like Radar from MASH, ducked their heads when they left the helicopter. The other three did not. The five of them moved towards us, and soon salutes were being thrown all around.

The kitted guys had beards, but everyone else was clean shaven, and I knew I had either found a great deal of help or had stepped in a pile of shit the likes of which had come out of a brontosaurus.

The guy in charge got a SITREP from Sergeant Amy and was suddenly standing in front of me. Five ten, crew-cut salt and pepper hair, decent build where you knew he kept in shape, and piercing blue eyes that brooked absolutely no bullshit. He had a .45 on his hip and a machete strapped to his leg. Big time officers didn't carry weapons. They didn't feel the need because they had firepower all around them. This guy did and that spoke volumes. He was flanked on both sides by the operators who had their booger hooks in the correct places for a fight. A hand was thrust forward, and I shook it.

"Lieutenant Colonel Richard Queen, commander of the reinstated Rapid Deployment Joint Task Force, Third Army of these United States."

Well shit, that was a title. I half wanted to ask if the guy came from a George Martin novel.

But I just said, "Cap," in response. "And this is Lisa. Lisa doesn't shake hands. Not yet anyway."

"Good to meet you." He looked past me to Lisa, "And you. Would you like to come back to my command center for a chat?"

"Both of us or just me?"

"Both, of course."

I spun to face my travelling companion. "Lisa, would you like to join the colonel for a spritzer and some canapés?"

Nothing, not even a grunt.

"She's shy. What if we say no?"

He shrugged, "Then I give you a pack full of food and water, couple hundred rounds for your pretty rifle, and send you on your way."

"Just like that?"

He nodded. "Exactly like that. We're not in the business of taking prisoners or conscriptions. That said, I guaran-damn-tee you're safer with us than not."

He was right, of course, but I had someplace I needed to be. I nodded, "Alrighty then. We'll come with you. I could use some civility."

"That we have," the colonel told me.

In five minutes, I was sitting on a Blackhawk helicopter staring at Lisa. She was looking the bird up and down and had hesitated before getting on. I saw what could only be trepidation on her face and that scared the shit out of me. The one thing you could count on from the infected was that they were absolutely, utterly fearless. I'm not talking bravery, where you're terrified and you do what has to be done anyway,

I'm talking about not having the capability to feel fear. If these things could learn to be afraid, then they could learn to take precautions.

The end-all-be-all of a Runner is that they will kill themselves trying to kill you. If they could learn to prepare... well, that was frightening. The look on her face and her hesitation had been fleeting, but it had been there. One of the operators stuck out a hand to help her in the bird, and she just stared at it for a moment before moving past it and climbing in.

We all had headsets, even Lisa. Her head was darting back and forth surveying everything as we lifted off. When we jolted forward, and the earth below us started whipping past, she smiled. A Runner smiled. I bet nobody had seen that before, and I didn't know how to process it.

The colonel read my unease as nervousness, and he spoke through the comms to me. "Afraid of flying?"

"Not usually. It's just that the last helicopter I was in crashed."

"Don't worry, this one was just serviced, and the flight time is seven minutes."

The rest of the short flight was spent in silence, and true to his word, we came upon his camp quickly. "Camp" was a bit of a misnomer. This was a forward operating base on a large island in the middle of a lake complete with massive tents, HESCO walls, towers, an airfield, and two roads. Six tanks, not Bradleys or LAVs, actual tanks, sat with guys crawling all over them. Five more helicopters, two of which were Chinooks with the two sets of rotors, two more Blackhawks, and one skinny one with missiles and shit all over it sat inside their own HESCO fortifications. There was a PT training area with a bunch of people doing jumping jacks like you would see in any movie about the military. This was an honest-to-God Army, and the place was half a mile wide by half a mile long at least. On top of everything, the place was mobile. As long as you set up in a place with sand or dirt, those HESCO barriers could be dumped and re-filled and you were good as gold.

"Jesus," I said. "How many people do you have here?"

"Eight thousand. Two thousand former military and six thousand trained since Rising Day. Every one of them, from Delta to the cooks, are capable fighters. Everyone gives one hundred percent and there has never been a single human on human altercation. We save the fighting for the dead."

I ripped my focus from the parade grounds and looked at the colonel. "How did you do this?"

He smiled. "This is one of sixteen forward operating bases in the continental United States. Unfortunately, the central government is not in country, they are... elsewhere."

"Barro Colorado," I said and wished I had kept my mouth shut. The colonel's jaw hit the floor.

"Now, how the hell do you know that?"

I smiled at him, "Internet."

To my utmost astonishment, he smiled back at me. "We'll have a nice long chat, you and me."

We set down and a small contingent of folks came running. Some played with the helicopter, some gave us bottles of water, and some spoke directly to the colonel as soon as we were out of earshot of the noise of the bird.

We gained six more fully armed escorts and suddenly I didn't feel so spiffy being here. In short order Lisa and I were inside the command tent sitting in chairs across a foldable military table the brass used as a desk. His hands were steepled and he began to talk. He told us about the government and that the new President, the former Secretary of the Navy, was giving orders from the fortified island in the middle of the Panama Canal. He pointed to a map of the US fastened to a freestanding chalk board. It had a bunch of information on it concerning huge swarms of undead, US military FOBs, militias, and other places.

Good ole SECNAV. Yeah, he and I had tangled a while back. I wasn't going to forward that little tidbit to the colonel either. Fucking SECNAV. The prick had sent me on what had amounted to a suicide mission. Which I had survived. Because I'm awesome. Then, he wanted me to come back to his lab of horrors of my own free will to be poked and prodded by scientists. Nope.

The colonel asked me pointed questions and sent for coffee. I told him I hated coffee, and he smiled and asked what I would prefer. I huffed and said water unless he had any Mountain Dew. We kept talking, and in a minute, there were some steaming cups of coffee and two ice cold Mountain Dews.

I fucking loved this guy. He was in command of eight thousand soldiers, one of whom had a refrigerator with some Dews in it. There was love.

We talked about Lisa, and sentient infected. He tried to pry into how I knew so much about them, but there was no way I was telling him about Gamboa and Baker, or my immunity. Fuck that noise.

We were talking about how the oil rig I had been on fell to a bunch of dickweeds called The Triumvirate, when he stopped me.

"The Triumvirate?"

"Yeah. Like Caesar, Crassus, and Pompey? Only this time it was some preacher, a CIA dude, and a military guy."

170

The colonel sighed. "Colonel Bourne. Yes, we are well aware of the now defunct Triumvirate. They were holed up in a stadium in Nebraska. It was overrun."

I shrugged. "From what I hear, Bourne was a stand-up guy. Dallas and Rick, two guys I know and respect, travelled with the guy for a while and if they say he's ok, I believe them. I do know he didn't make it, but that's all." I saw the look on the colonel's face and added, "Did you know him?"

"I did," he said, and that was it.

One of the diminutive Radar-looking guys came over and sheepishly pushed a folder toward the colonel, who excused himself and opened it. He looked at the file, then looked over it at me, then looked back at the file. He turned his head to the left and said, "And this is accurate?"

A wiry guy stepped from the shadows of some piled gear. He wasn't ripped and bearded like the operators, and he didn't exude toughness like they did, but one look at him and I knew he could give two or three of those badass Delta or SEALs or MARSOC a run for their money in a fight. Of all the people in the room this guy was the most dangerous. He was likely the most batshit crazy too.

"Sorry," the colonel said, "this is one of our intelligence assets. His name is—"

"Lynch," I finished for him. "His name is Lynch."

FUCK OFF

A wicked smile creased the face of the wiry guy. He folded his arms and leaned against a piece of equipment like he owned the place.

"You two have met?" asked Queen.

"This one? No. But I know his type. I know who he is and who he reports to. I'm also pretty sure I know what's in the file in your hands."

I put my hands on my thighs like I was going to stand, but I felt something on my shoulder. I glanced at it and noticed it was a rifle barrel. It was attached to a rifle and that rifle was held by one of those bearded operators. He just nodded *no*, and I eased back into my seat with a sigh.

Throughout this entire ordeal, Lisa hadn't made a sound. She just sat there, twitching occasionally. The moment that guy put the rifle on my shoulder, a low growl emanated from her throat.

"Lisa, we're fine. Everything is fine."

"*Not fine*," she snarled and everyone in the room moved a bit away from us except the colonel.

Queen put the open file on the table, spun the photo around, and pushed it at me. It was a photo of yours truly, taken surreptitiously in a gated community in Tennessee. I hadn't seen it before now, but I knew who had taken it.

Ship and a guy named Bob were with me in the photo. I sighed. "Shit. Bob. He didn't make it. But me? Damn, I look good in this one." I placed the picture back on the table, turned it around and slowly pushed it back to the colonel. "I'm in a bit better shape now though, don't you think?"

He smiled. I expected so much more, but he just smiled. He put the photo back into the folder, closed it, stared at Lynch, who still hadn't said a word, and pushed the folder off the table into a wire trash can. I guess the military still has trash cans.

Lynch's smile evaporated and he stood tall. The tension in the room was palpable and it felt like shit was about to get real.

The colonel diffused it quickly. "One of the perks of being in charge of the Rapid Response Force is that I report directly to the President. No secretaries or generals or politicians. Another perk is that I can and often do tell those who think I am inadequate to fuck off." He had been looking at me, but he shifted his gaze to Lynch. "Fuck. Off."

Lynch shook his head and sighed like he was dealing with a gaggle of morons, then stormed out. OK, he didn't actually *storm*, but he wasn't happy.

Everybody but the colonel and me was trying to figure out what the hell had just happened. Oh, and Lisa, she just sat there twitching occasionally and looking terrifying.

I looked at him, perhaps a bit sheepishly, and asked, "How much of that file did you read in the minute you held it?"

"Enough to see that you were in Baldy Mountain when it fell, and that you're immune."

"Immune to what?" someone asked behind me in a *Holy Shit* voice. "Not…"

"Yup," I answered without looking to see who it was. I didn't look back when I held up my arm with a mostly-healed bitemark. "They've gotten me a few times. I'm still here," I added.

"Tell me about Baldy," the colonel asked. "Please."

"Big underground military complex-facility thingie. Lots of labs. They did all kinds of tests on me for a couple of months. Couldn't figure out what made me immune, or even what the plague is. In their infinite wisdom, they brought a couple hundred infected inside the facility to run tests on them. In a shocking turn of events, the dead broke out, ate everybody, and I fled the scene with one other guy, Tim. He died a few months later. Good guy," I added. I wanted to make sure everybody knew that. "A real good guy. A different Lynch brought me there for study. He didn't give a shit about anything, he was just following orders."

"As do I," Queen said. "I gave you my word. You will not be conscripted or detained. You're free to go, but I urge you to stay. If you've been out there this long, and you escaped from an infected Baldy Mountain, you're more than capable."

That felt good to hear.

"How about a counter-offer? I go back to San Francisco, get my group, and come back here? My friends are also… capable. I give you five vials of blood per week, and you can do whatever the hell you want with it."

He stuck his hand out, "Deal."

I shook it, then glanced at the tent flap that Lynch had exited through. "He's going to be a problem."

"Not likely," one of the operators said.

I turned to face him. He looked like the tougher child of a professional wrestler and a bareknuckle brawler. Six-two, thick neck, arms like Hulk Hogan, six-inch brown beard, stubby M4 battle rifle, pistols on his hip and his shoulder. Professional tough guy. You get the picture.

"Listen," I told him, "You're a badass. No doubt about it. You were in the shit before people started eating each other. I know your kind and have several friends you would admire. But this guy is… different. He will kill you inside of fifteen seconds. There won't be any type of fight. He's faster and more trained than you are and although you think he has pipe cleaner arms, he's deceptively strong. Probably as strong as you." The guy visibly scoffed and so did the other one who looked just like him. I held my hands up in supplication, "I'm not trying to be an asshole, I just want you to know what you're dealing with. Don't go head-to-head with him. Take him out from a hundred yards with your rifle, or that's your ass."

"How do you know so much about him?" the colonel asked.

"I had my very own Lynch, once. He stole me from my home on an oil rig and dragged me to Baldy Mountain. He was fucking terrifying," I added. "Every bit of what I just said is true, and he was virtually impossible to kill. He was bitten by an infected while trying to save me, but the only reason he was trying to save me was that he was ordered to keep me alive. Otherwise, I'd be dead."

The colonel nodded and gazed briefly at the tent flap the spook had left through, "I see."

I shook my head, "No sir, you don't. He will kill you or anyone in his way like he was brushing his teeth. He is not your friend, and he's way worse than your enemy because you trust him. Don't. Don't trust him. Also, I guarantee you this; the nanosecond you let me go, he is going to disappear. He's going to track me down and try to drag me to whatever installation the people who made that dossier are from." I pointed at the file in the trash.

"You don't seem overly worried," one of the tough guys said.

"I'm fucking terrified. But this time I have a couple of edges." I could see they wanted me to elaborate. "I know he's coming for me, and all the bullshit you might throw his way isn't going to stop him."

"So, you think he can kill me easily, but you can take him down?" the operator said skeptically.

"*Fuck* no. You both would turn me into multiple chalk outlines, I'm sure. But," I pointed at Lisa, "I have her."

She saw me point at her. "*I kill them? I kill them now?*"

"No, Lisa. These are good people. We only kill the bad ones, remember?"

Her brow furrowed and she twitched like she was trying to reason something out. "*Good people,*" she growled, and the tough guys didn't like it. They were itching to riddle her with bullets.

"Say what you want about bullets and knives," I continued, "they don't scare guys like you and Lynch. But you throw her in the mix and all bets are off. Are you going to stand there and tell me you're not uneasy with her so close?"

"I don't like it," he said.

"Exactly." I pivoted back to the colonel, "So! I go back to San Francisco, grab my people, and come back here. Sound good?"

Queen nodded. "Great. You want a shower and some chow first?"

"I'd love both of those."

A WILLY NELSON SONG

Lisa and I are back on the road. We left Queen and his army a few hours ago. The colonel asked me if I wanted some escorts, but I declined. That may have been the stupidest thing I've ever done. We'll find out soon enough. I asked him if he wouldn't mind giving me a ride to San Francisco in a helicopter, but he said that fuel was rationed, and the next supply drop wouldn't be for another three weeks.

For the life of me I can't understand why he let me go. There has to be some underlying reason, but I'm stumped as to what it could be. There's no way Lynch didn't tattle on him, so I'm wondering if I go back if Queen will still be in charge. His operators are great at following orders, but if Lynch came in with a piece of paper saying he was now in control, those guys would laugh and fill him full of holes.

Well, they would try.

I warned the colonel that Lynch may try to kill him, but he didn't seem bothered by that fact. Actually, it was a bit unnerving how not unnerved he was about Lynch, so there has to be something else I don't know. Maybe they're cousins. Nah, that wouldn't stop Lynch.

We're in a refurbished Dave's Towing tow truck. It was one of the vehicles in Queen's motor pool and he said he could part with it. There's only half a tank of gas, but that should get us at least halfway home. We hooked a left onto a road I missed the name of just south of Lee Vining and are heading west. I just saw a sign for Modesto and it's thirty-seven miles in front of us. Modesto is about ninety miles away from San Francisco.

Queen sent me off with two hundred rounds of .556, and an M4 with five mags. I opted to leave the .308 with one of his hitters and I think the guy wanted to bear my children. I got a new threaded barrel Sig with a hundred rounds, two suppressors, and kept Chauncy, but I also got something from the hitter I gave my rifle to. A SOG SEAL Pup. I'm turning it over in my hands right now as I drive. This one is used and there are deep scratches on the black metal, but the guy had it honed to a molecular edge. It is a thing of beauty, and I can neither confirm nor deny having driven the last twenty miles with a stiffy. I still have the chef's knife on my belt, but the SOG is on the left side of the tactical webbing I'm wearing, right above my heart.

I divvied up the ammo with Lisa, and she's also carrying an extra sidearm, but I didn't think her carrying a rifle would be of any benefit. She will use her unique skills to dispatch any would-be attackers.

I also got a radio in the deal. The guy who gave it to me said it was an AN-PVC or PRG or something with some numbers after it. It says Thales on it, so that's what I'm gonna call it. There's also a large battery with it that is supposed to boost the power which means boosting signal strength. One of Queen's supplemental missions is to place repeaters throughout California in an ever widening circular pattern so the radios will function over longer distances.

I pulled over and focused on Lisa. She was just staring out the window, but her left hand was twirling a piece of her hair. I don't know why but that seemed like something a Runner shouldn't do. I mean, yeah, they're talking and taking orders now, but the hair twirling just seems... off.

"Do you want to drive?" I asked her.

Her head whipped around, and her red eyes bore into my soul. Several times in this journal or in ones before this one, I wrote that I almost shit myself, and Dear Reader, every time I've written that it has been true. Everything down there clenched and I felt a turtle trying to be released.

She was fucking terrifying. *Terrifying.* She would never not be terrifying, and we both knew it. I wanted things to go back to the way they were before zombies, but looking at her looking at me, I knew that was a pipe dream. Humans and Runners would never coexist because people, not Runners, couldn't handle it.

But I would fight that last sentence. I would do everything I could to turn Runners back into people again, but I wouldn't do it with the likes of Baker and Gamboa.

I would leave them out of it because I had an epiphany. Runners aren't evil. They are just *infected.*

I would find a way. I would find a way to cure them. I had done it with Lisa, I can do it with more of them. They would never be who they had been before, but maybe I could help them shed their hatred of the non-infected. Maybe, like Thorne, Subject Nine, and Lisa, they would want to help us instead of wanting to kill us.

"*I drive?*" Lisa growled. She still sounded like she was talking through a mouthful of splinters.

"Would you like to?"

She glared at the steering wheel, back at me, back at the wheel, then looked out the window again.

"*No.*"

I smiled and pushed my foot down on the accelerator. Baby steps.

There was a bent road sign a bit ago announcing that we're on Tioga Road, and we have just entered the mountains. I had known about Tioga Road, but had forgotten it because of recent events. Signs for Mt. Dana, Pothole Dome, and Cathedral Peak are all over the place and our elevation is climbing with every mile. I looked behind me, as I am wont to do, and noticed a glint on the road a few miles back. We hadn't seen a single vehicle once we turned onto this road, so there was likely someone following us. I had been lucky I looked when I had. The sun was in front of us, and we were up higher than the vehicle behind. I would probably have missed the glint if the conditions hadn't been what they were.

I had a sneaking suspicion of who was behind me, and if he was driving, that means that Queen wouldn't let him take a helicopter. I really like Queen. I was thinking what a cool guy he was when a deer suddenly burst onto the road. I braked and swerved but the stupid thing just ran right in front of us. Tow trucks are not little, and it went under the wheels and spit out flopping behind us.

There was no way it could be alive. I felt the wheels go over it. I felt like shit, but I hadn't meant to kill it. Sighing and sad, I stopped the truck and got out. The poor thing was a mess. A female with no horns, its entrails were now extrails, and the steaming things were spread across ten feet of cooling asphalt, right on top of the single yellow line in the center of the road. My intent had been to shoot it and put it out of its misery, but it was already dead. It was neither breathing nor moving.

I sighed again and began my sad, forty-foot trek back to the wrecker. Dammit. There was nothing I could do. I rubbed the stubble on my face and put my hand on the tow truck door. I was about to climb in when I heard something behind me. Currently enjoying the zombie apocalypse, I had no doubts about what was there, so I drew my sidearm and spun in a panic.

No zombie closed on me from inches away as I had imagined. Well, there was a zombie, but it was about forty feet back. It turned its head on a long neck and looked at me with blood red eyes and I knew it was a pus bag. Or it would be. There was no pus yet because it had just died. I had killed it.

The deer stared at me on unsteady legs, purple and grey things hanging from its dripping, ruptured belly, its eyes stained the deep crimson of blood. Its mouth opened and a low rasp escaped. Something purple fell from the creature and hit the asphalt with a disgusting wet splat.

I checked out for a moment as this most certainly did not compute. This couldn't be... Animals did not turn. I had been told that the virus that reanimated the dead only worked on humans. There could be no infected deer in front of me. The virus didn't work on animals. No.

I don't know how many different ways I thought of that same piece of evidence right then. Countless in the span of five seconds, while I tried to rationalize. This had only happened twice before; when I had seen my first dead man walking, and when I had received my fist bite.

I realized how fucked we all were. It was one thing for dead people to hunt the living. It was something else to be holed up in an attic avoiding human zombies only to get swarmed by undead squirrels and spiders. I stood precariously on the edge of an infinite abyss of hopelessness, trying to blink the horror of what stood mere feet in front of me away.

I should have blinked faster, because when I checked back in, the deer was inches away. It stretched its head toward me, mouth wide open and its jaws clamped shut... on empty air because it pitched to my right.

Lisa was on top of the thing screeching, scratching, and pulling. She bit into its neck and pulled back with a furry chunk. The deer didn't much care about the thing atop it, it only wanted the food in front. Lisa pushed it down again and kicked out, breaking the creature's front leg with a horrendous snap.

Still trying to stand, it toppled once again when she gave it a mighty shove. It landed on its side and comically rolled over. Lisa was about to pounce when I told her not to bother.

"Let's just go," I told her.

She got up like nothing was wrong and got in the car. I did the same, and as we pulled away, I felt the thump of the deer as it tried to eat its way to me through the vehicle.

LYNCH

The entire ride through Yosemite National Park had been uneventful. Tioga Pass was anything but straight, with switchbacks and hard turns. There had been a dozen or so turnoffs and scenic overlooks, and we stopped at one so I could piss, and we could stretch our legs. I say "our" legs because Lisa stretched too. New fact: Runners stretch given the chance. At least this one does.

We had only seen a few abandoned vehicles on the trip through the mountains. One had been an overturned tractor trailer. Everything in my head told me not to stop, but we did. Either the trailer had been empty, or it had been looted long ago. A few other cars and pickups were either parked at overlooks or just abandoned on the road. One blue pickup had two dead people in it, pawing to get at us, but other than that, the only living creatures I had seen were birds and a herd of bison.

The bison were beautiful, and not undead as the deer had been. We slowed and stopped a hundred or so feet from them. They were right up next to the road, grazing, and didn't seem to care about us. Lisa asked about them and I told her what they were. She then asked if we could eat them and I told her no, but she still wanted to look. She started to get out of the car, and put a hand on her shoulder, telling her not to. She growled at the touch, then pulled the door closed.

I didn't want Lisa to get punted like a fourth down football. Even a guy from the East Coast like me knows you don't pet the fluffy cows.

There had been a few lodges, hotels, and small businesses, but all of them looked to have been looted, burned, or full of shamblers, so we drove on past. It took a bit more than three hours to travel all the way through the park. The roads were bad and would soon be impassible unless repairs were affected.

We came out the far side of the mountains, and in the distance were small towns as far as I could see. We were on the downward slope of the road, so I got out, stood on the roof, and peered behind us through the binoculars.

Other than a few dozen undead who had started after us about a half mile back, I couldn't see anything. No window glint, no vehicle. But that spy-asshole was back there. I knew he was. He wanted me and he would try to get me and whisk me away to some undisclosed location to be analyzed and poked. He didn't care about me, but I knew he would also kill everything that got in his way to ensure I made it back with him safely. My Lynch, the one who had hijacked me, would have done that, so this guy would too.

The slope on this side of the pass was much more gradual than the steep eastern entrance, so the light from the sun was slowly being swallowed as opposed to the quick rising I had seen in the east. I lowered the binoculars and just stared at the scene in front of us.

I got back in the truck and in five minutes saw signs for Groveland. I guess at some point Tioga Road had turned into Main Street which was also the 120 because in twenty minutes I was pulling off the 120 into the Tenaya Elementary School parking lot.

The school was smack dab in the middle of a forest, with nothing about as far as I could see except trees, which were bending a bit with the wind. We sure as shit hadn't seen any type of town yet. One white minivan sat perfectly parked between the white parking lines, but all the doors including the back hatch were open and looked to have been for a long time. We drove up to the vehicle and it had an occupant belted into the back seat. It was what was left of a kid.

Mostly skeletal but spry enough to reach for me, the pathetic thing mewled and hissed. I swear it was frustrated at not being able to get to me, but the doctors at Baldy had said that me believing the dead could display any emotion was just me projecting.

Chauncy and I got out of the tow truck and advanced together toward the kid. The wind was strong in the parking lot, and it blew bits of sand and debris so hard at me that I had to put my palm up to stop the stinging particles from blinding me. The light was fading fast, and I had to be quick about this if I wanted to find us some secure shelter before the darkness took over. The kid's gray skin and rotten shirt were festooned with gore, and I could only imagine he had gotten a bite in before those in the vehicle had extricated themselves, likely with great haste.

Chauncy flashed and the deed was done. I just couldn't leave the little fella in there to rot away forever. I climbed back into the driver's seat and sighed. Lisa stared at me.

"We need to find a place to park for the night, but I don't want anybody to be able to see us." I drove through the school lot and back behind it. Nestled into the trees on the far side of the learning center sat a huge cylindrical structure that must have been town water storage. This wasn't up on stilts, as you would see a water tower, but was one big structure like for natural gas or fuel storage. Behind that sat a garage, probably for lawn maintenance equipment, with two enormous roll-down doors.

We pulled up next to the building, and I couldn't help but remember almost being the side dish to Baked Horse a la Garage a while back. It wasn't nearly as hot here as it had been in the high desert, but still, I didn't want to get trapped in another concrete box, so I smacked the door with my palm a bunch of times.

Nothing shuffled toward us, and I couldn't hear anything from the structure. I put the butt of my handgun through a small window on a locked human-sized door and flashed my light in to see if there was anybody there wanting to chew on me. The place appeared empty of anything large and ambulatory, but one of the bays had a monster-sized tractor with a ten-foot lawnmower attachment on the front. We were in in a sec and had one of the doors rolling up on its pull-rope in another. I backed the truck into the empty bay, wanting my nose forward in case we had to make a hasty departure.

I pocketed the keys, and we made for the school. We had half an hour's worth of daylight before night crept off with it, so we moved quickly toward the structure. A small median strip of what had likely been grass wound its way between the building and the rear parking lot. Dozens of body bags adorned that strip, some of the plastic displaying the tell-tale signs of animals at one time having been at them. Many of the bags were child- sized.

Lisa only glanced at the bags, her twitchy figure following mine with a quiet "*Uh!*" every few seconds. Runners could be damn silent, but mine hadn't figured that out yet.

I sighed again at the death, and we moved past the bodies to a very open door to the back of the school. Some leaves and other debris sat just inside, but in the waning light, I couldn't see very far. I didn't like the open door. Anything from bad guys, to the walking dead, to a family of otters could have strode in or out of the place with that door like that. I was hoping for otters as we entered the building, and I undid the hook and eye that kept the door open.

I had wanted to remain as quiet as possible during this part of our excursion, but me banging on the door across the lot and the fact that this door slammed closed on exceptionally strong springs nullified that desire. My face burned and I felt shame, but then I realized that the only person who would ever know about this was Lisa, and she one hundred percent did not give a shit. Of course, now you know too, Dear Reader, and if you could STFU about it I would be grateful.

The tac light on my sidearm illuminated a tight hallway full of multicolored construction paper with drawings on it, both taped to the wall and on the floor. I picked up a yellow rectangle of the stuff, angling my light as I peered at the crayon drawing of a rainbow. Well, Dany with one "N", your drawing is a piece of shit. I'm not usually judgy, but this was the worst fucking rainbow in the history of rain. It wasn't a bow it was an upside-down capital "V". For fuck's sake, Dany.

I let the picture drop, and it fluttered casually to the floor. Dany was probably dead now, maybe cocooned in a black plastic bag thirty feet away, and my vicious judgement of his graphical representation of meteorological phenomena had been unwarranted. I felt guilty and I didn't like me. I had no right.

We continued down the hall, Lisa twitching and me trying to tone down my anger. If I got too pissed off, there would be two Runners in the school and that wouldn't do.

It suddenly occurred to me that this would not be the first time for that. Lisa must have seen me Hulk out. She had called me *same*. When we were done clearing this place, I would have to ask about that. I had several questions which I really should have asked on our hours-long journey through Yosemite.

The shadows in the corridor had lengthened to a point where I couldn't see without the light and I was once again faced with the dilemma of either illuminating myself and calling everything to my beacon, or soldiering on in the darkness, blind as a bat.

"Lisa, can you see?" I mean, she was no longer human, right? Maybe cat vision was a thing for the infected.

"*No.*"

Fuck.

"Beacon it is then."

I had seen too many horror movies, and had been living in one for some time, to think I would be able to clear the entire school in the dark, so Lisa and I cleared both sides of the corridor shutting doors as we went. Every door was a half-door with a window on top, but other than some evidence that an animal had been living in one of the rooms, nothing stuck out. The school consisted of one floor, so we worked our way into a classroom close to the back door we had initially come through. The room had a view of the garage and, surprisingly, a view of half the front parking lot.

My pack found a home on one of the desks, as did Lisa's, my weapons within easy reach. I had put a couple of desks on this side of the classroom door. It wouldn't stop anything, but it would be an alarm if something decided to poke its head in.

I took two MREs out of my pack and got them going with the heater. Menu 2 which was beef shredded in barbecue sauce and menu 10 chili and macaroni, which also boasted Warfighter recommended, Warfighter tested, Warfighter approved.

Was I a Warfighter now? I had the requisite training from half a dozen actual Warfighters. Professional tough guys who had killed bad guys on several continents. I had been battling both the undead and dickheads for a few years and I had gotten pretty good at it.

But a Warfighter? No. I was not, and I wouldn't shame myself or those men and women who had sacrificed everything by calling myself one. Those heroes were doing what I'm doing before the end of the world and not out of necessity, but out of patriotism.

I'm just a schlep who got good at staying alive. I glanced at the still-healing crusty shit on my arm. It had been almost a year since Captain Bob had bitten me, and still the wound was there. I had had plenty of help in learning how to stay alive. All those tough guys; Remo, Alvarez, Brick, Kinga, Ship, Ray Ban. They had kept me alive, but the one thing that had superseded all the training I could ever get was this immunity. I had been bitten several times and I'm still alive. But the guys I just listed? They had never been bitten and luck was likely not a factor. Any one of them was excellent, but put them together in a team? Unbeatable.

I huffed and Lisa asked about it.

"I was just wondering if you're hungry," I lied.

"*Always want to eat. Always need to kill.*" I heard her stomach growl, and I believed her.

The flameless heaters on the MREs had done their job, and I passed Lisa the shredded beef. "It's hot," I said as the moonlight showed she was staring at the food. "You said you always want to eat."

She turned away, "*Not eat that.*"

"Why not?"

"*Not same. Smell not same.*"

"Same as what?"

She glanced back at the offered food, then focused on me. "*You.*"

"You want to eat me?"

"*Yes. But you say bad.*"

"It is bad. It's probably the worst thing you can do. I would like you to try this." I pushed the shredded beef toward her on the floor. The wind had picked up, and the big plate-glass windows of the classroom rattled.

She picked it up and stared at her hand before gently putting it back down. "*Food hurts.*"

"It's hot. You have to wait until it cools a bit."

"*Why make it hot then make it cold?*"

I had no answer she would understand.

In the end she ate it. Other than soda, this was the first thing I had seen a Runner consume. Actually, that isn't true. I had seen one take a bite and swallow the shoulder muscle of an undead, and I had to wonder what the doctors had been feeding the Runners at the medical center.

Lisa and I talked for a bit, me asking her questions about what she wanted and what she liked. When she stopped replying I flashed my tactical light in her direction and noticed she was asleep. Another question answered: They do sleep. I had thought they didn't

I had to pee, and I didn't want to wake her. She had watched over me for weeks while I slept, and now it was my turn. I carefully picked up the desks in front of the door and moved into an art room two doors down. The wind was absolutely howling outside, and I could see shit whipping past out there on the parking lot. I relieved myself in the sink and it was glorious. As I was zipping up, the moonlight allowed me a quick glimpse of movement outside. I ducked to the side and moved to the big heater/air conditioner near the window, only the top of my head peering up and over.

I know this is a zombie story, but it was not a pack of undead thousands strong. It was a dark SUV with its lights off slowly gliding into the school parking lot. It stopped and a figure got out of the vehicle. It had made absolutely zero sound, and no lights came on when the door opened.

The person stretched their back and glanced casually around, their hand in front of their face to protect their eyes from the wind. I couldn't see the face in the shadows, but the build was that of a wiry guy in his late thirties. The build, the silence, him being here now, and the fact that his looking about faltered when his face was in my direction all led me to the same conclusion as you just came to: Lynch.

There was literally no way he could see me without night vision. No way. With an almost full moon, me being on this side of a glass window and the wind blowing shit into his eyes it was just not possible. But there he was, staring at me. The stare lasted no more than two seconds, then he moved his head further left. He got back in the vehicle, drove around the parking lot, clearly looking for something, then turned out of the lot and sped off into the night on a westerly course. I realized I had been holding my breath and I puffed my cheeks like a blowfish as I let it out.

Lisa was still sleeping when I got back to the classroom, so I let her continue to dream. I was going to give her until two in the morning for a watch change, but she woke up just before. She started undoing her pants, and I knew she was going to pee right there.

"Wait!" I hissed and she glared at me. "There's a sink a couple of rooms over, do your business in that."

Her upper lip curled into a sneer. *"Business!"*

"Yes, go pee in the sink. That way the… urine… won't be all over the floor where we're sleeping."

"*Business…*" I heard her mumble as she started moving the desks.

She knew it was her turn for watch, so I settled down on the floor for some much-needed shut-eye. I'd wait until she got back before I slept, but man I was tired.

The sun was on the rise when someone toed me with their shoe. Lisa was supposed to wait until an hour or so after sunrise to wake me so, WTF was this about?

I started to stir and felt a slight kick, harder than before but not meant to injure. "Get up."

It was a man's voice. What was it now? Evil douches? A crazed sheriff? More cannibals? I opened my eyes, and it was none of those. You know who it was, Dear Reader.

"Where is it?" he asked, and I had no idea what he meant. I was just able to pierce the shadows and see him roll his eyes. "The infected. Your pet. Where is it?"

I thought up a lie and thought it up quick, "I killed her. She went feral again." I had just Grinched Lynch.

He shook his head. "You're an idiot for thinking it was safe to have that thing near you." The rain had increased in volume and intensity, and it was a struggle to hear him, but I snarked back.

I would have shrugged, but the suppressed pistol in his folded arms told me not to. "Nobody has ever complimented my intelligence."

"I wonder why?" he said sarcastically through another nod. "Maybe you…" His Spidey sense kicked in and he tried to whip his body around, but it was too late. Lisa was on him like a Mississippi duck on a June bug.

She hit him like a derailed freight train, children's desks and chairs flying in all directions from the onslaught of the confrontation. Lynch had been standing directly over me, so it was me they had both tripped over before they had crashed into the furniture.

I heard a suppressed round go off and a heavy grunt, then heard the gun go clattering away, bouncing off table and chair legs. I yanked my very own suppressed weapon out while they grappled. Blood pattered the floor around them and Lisa stepped in it and her foot went out from under her. She pulled Lynch down with her, but he jerked her around so that she hit the ground first, breaking his fall.

This was beautiful. Artwork. A professional killer, likely trained and proficient in every martial art in the world, versus a rage-fueled psychopath, incapable of fear or remorse, and with an incredible tolerance to pain, battling it out during the storm of the century. I was stunned for a moment, watching them, and in that moment, Lisa raked her considerable nails across Lynch's face, four furrows immediately welling up crimson, but the operative grabbed Lisa's wrist and gave it a vicious twist. I heard bones snap, but this infected wonder cared less than not at all about it, ripping her broken hand from his grasp, whipping it around, and jabbing her nails into his eyes and mouth.

I fucking knew how much both of those hurt and I winced inwardly. "Alright, enough!" I yelled and it was like I hadn't said anything. The sound of the storm hadn't drowned me out, they just didn't give a shit about me right now. They rolled and Lisa was atop him, choking him with her left hand while slashing talons with her broken right. Did she just? Oh fuck! Right in the baby-maker! She grabbed his crotch, yanking and twisting like he had paid extra for the cruelest mistress. Lynch bucked upwards like a horse on meth, and she flew over the top of him landing on her side, still clutching his throat but mercifully devoid of his twig and berries. He wasted no time and gave her a savage open-handed poke just below her sternum. I swear to Christ he touched her spine. She gasped for air, and he used that advantage to smash his elbow into her kidney.

If anything, this drove her further into rage-city and she let go of his throat, flipping her hand around and gouging more furrows into his neck and chin.

I stood there like a moron, legs apart, gun trying to track Lynch as they rolled around.

He drove a knee into her side, and she went fetal for a second before he rolled on top of her and grabbed her throat with both hands, thumbs digging into her windpipe as he squeezed for all he was worth. I was ready to plug him, but she grabbed his hands, pulled them apart and his face fell as her head shot forward, her forehead catching him square in the nose.

Blood poured from him and rather than push him away, she leaned in, her ravaging need to rip into his neck all over her face like white on rice.

"Lisa!" I shouted and she glared at me. Jesus fuck she was terrifying.

"*Kill!*" she screamed and turned back to him. This was not a human scream. This was the testicle shrinking howl that demons from the darkest pit used when they were roasting marshmallows over someone's burning intestines and one of the fluffy confections fell off the stick and into the fire.

"No!" I bellowed back and she stopped, teeth bared and ready an inch away from his throat.

He was blinking rapidly, thick blood shooting from his ruined face in thick, red, snotty gouts. I stayed five feet away, aiming my weapon at him. "Get off him, Lisa, and let him up. And if you try anything, CI-asshole, I'll fill you full of all the holes."

She rolled away and was on her feet faster than I thought possible, a nightmarish blur of pure horror. A human would have been cradling their wrist in agony, but she just stood there, heaving. A huge, dark stain blotched her shirt, just above her left hip, and I knew she had also been shot.

He breathed heavily, eying first her, then me, the anger and hatred in his face obvious even with the blood pouring out of him. He blinked, one of his eyes bloody, his tongue probing his lacerated gums. He was covered in Lisa's blood and there was no way he wasn't infected. He was smart enough to know it, too, but I didn't know how he would process that information. He stretched his face to see how bad his nose was, but he still kept his hands up when he asked, "What now?"

And that, Dear Reader, was when the giant horde of undead you've been so desperately wishing for showed up.

ALL OF THEM

The windows on this side of the school faced northwest, and the sun was coming up from behind us, but it illuminated an enormous swarm of infected streaming from the trees and heading southeast. Now that the grapple was over, and desks weren't being tossed about, and the wind had let up for a moment, we could hear the dead quite clearly. The wind came right back and wiped away the unnerving sounds with its staunch power.

Lynch started to get up and Lisa growled so he stopped. I noticed I had gotten within five short feet of him, and realizing what he could do to me, I backed up a few steps. His head slowly swiveled toward the window. I mean, he had ears, so he could hear what was coming.

He faced me, his hands gingerly probing his face and coming away bloody. "You're going to need to give me a gun."

"I'd rather put my dick in a pencil sharpener."

"So, you have a pencil dick?" he instantly replied with a wry grin.

This motherfucker. He had me. In the history of comebacks this was one that should be celebrated, and it had come from a total douche.

"You'd plug me the first chance you got."

"Nope, not you," he told me, then disgustingly spat a bloody gob on the floor. His head swiveled once again, this time focusing on Lisa.

"And that, my infected friend, is why you would kill us all."

He stared hard at the blood on his hands, then stared even harder at the furrows dug into his left forearm. The *pat pat pat* of blood drops hitting the ground from Lisa's gunshot wound made him focus on that, then at the copious amounts of blood on the floor, then at her blood all over him.

"Shit," he sighed.

I nodded, "About sums it up."

He stood, Lisa tensed, and I took another two steps back, the long suppressor with its business end directed at this asshole. He looked out the window and sighed again, drawing his forearm across his still bleeding nose. "You need to live."

"I intend to."

"I'll run for the car and lead them away."

I kept my eyes on him while glancing toward the parking lot, "Good plan, but you'll never make it. They'll be at the building in less than a minute and it will take you three minutes to get to your car because I can't see it. That's if the wind doesn't pick you up and deposit you a mile away."

I pointed behind him to a blue first aid kit on the wall. "Band-Aids and antiseptic in there, probably. But you will only need the Band-Aids."

He sighed again. Of all the people I've seen who knew they were infected, this prick was taking it the best. "So, what's your great plan then?" he demanded.

"It's too late to run. We need to find a place we can hide or fortify what we've got. Barring both of those, we fight until we run out of steam, and they kill us, or we run out of infected, and we win."

Something big flew by the window. A piece of plywood or the top of a table, something like that. Too big for it to not be dangerous. I backed up three more steps, putting half a room's worth of distance between the agent and me, and glanced out the window. The treetops were all being pushed to the point of snapping, and the dead were blowing over. Some rolled into the horde to be tripped over or trampled, but most of the rotting things stayed vertical and plodded toward the school. Toward us.

"We won't be running out of infected," Lynch said. He hawked up a generous wad of bloody phlegm and spat it into a tipped over waste basket six feet away. Six feet. Like, legit six feet, not two feet and I'm exaggerating, six feet. Everything these Lynches did was amazing.

"Roof access?" I queried.

"We'd end up trapped for days if this horde doesn't move on. Besides," he spat again, "the wind might blow us off the roof."

It was suddenly very loud. The sound quickly escalated and drowned out the horrible raspy sounds of the dead. It was the storm. The swarm of gray things slowly laboring toward us all had a severe port list because of the wind. Several had fallen over and were struggling to stand, but the wind kept knocking them down. Suddenly, one of the smaller ones, definitely a little kid, was violently lifted up into the storm and carried away.

I knew it was a tornado when the building started to shake. It was too windy to be an earthquake, but that's what it felt like. I could hear bits of the school tearing off and flying who knows where, but I couldn't see it. I sure as shit hadn't realized that central California got tornados, but there was nothing else this could be, not with this wind.

The sun, which had done its best to poke its way toward us earlier, had retreated back behind some inky clouds, and that's when the hail started. Small pieces at first, like little pebbles, then larger ones as the noise picked up. The rain had turned sideways as well, and blew in from right to left in giant, torrential sheets.

And the dead did not give a shit. I saw one take a huge hunk of ice to the head, and it dropped like a rock, the side of its dome now a concave mess. Pieces of the planet and human built stuff pelted the dead like they were under attack by slingers and the catapult crew of a Roman Legion. The nasty creatures dropped, or the wind took them and still I saw no funnel cloud. The last four paragraphs all transpired in the space of five seconds, as the storm's intensity reached a crescendo.

The three of us had forgotten our fervent need to murder each other and stood transfixed, staring into the full fury of God's sudden and powerful hatred. We stood in a line, each a foot from the next, peering out the crystal-clear window at the wholesale slaughter of the dead by a wind with teeth, as if the very existence of the rotten things was an affront to nature itself, and nature was all done with their shit.

Paralyzing slivers of icy terror started off in my nuts and took the spinal highway all the way to the back of my neck when the window we were staring through simply exploded. Nothing had smashed into it that we could see or hear, the glass had just reached its expiration date and wanted to retire to Florida. Not a single one of its tiny pieces made it into the classroom as everything was whisked away. That action, and the fact that I could feel the wind trying to suck me through the brand-new cavernous hole and into whirling oblivion, galvanized the three of us and we all backed away further into the room. Non-domesticated Runners had no idea of what self-preservation or fear was, but the wide-eyes on Lisa told me they could learn.

"Let's get the fuck out of here!" I shouted and we all booked it through the multi-colored dervish of swirling construction paper back into the corridor.

I'm from Massachusetts, I don't know too much about twisters. Was a brick building safer than a not-brick building in a tornado? It had to be, right? We needed to get into a basement, but if the school had a storm shelter, I didn't know about it. I had an epiphany and scoured the walls for... there it was! An emergency pamphlet thingie on the wall and... SHIT! It said to go outside!

I glanced down the hall through a window and bore full witness to the tempest of the world outside. All kinds of shit whipped by so fast I couldn't tell what it was. I glanced up, thanking all that is holy the school roof was still attached, but it was shaking like hell.

"Here!" Lynch yelled. Lisa and I ran for the door he held open, the inside a black maw of terror. I hesitated at the threshold long enough to hear the roof I was bragging about a second ago tear off, and then I said, "Fuck it," and hustled into the darkness. To his credit, the agent let Lisa in after me and yanked the door closed after him. I clicked on my flashlight and noticed we were crammed into an eight-by-eight landing with an open doorway atop stairs leading downward. I shone my light down the stairs and took the steps quickly, the others following, Lynch closing another door. It was a boiler room and most of the heating stuff looked relatively new. The dead guy in blue overalls that shuffled toward me did not look new, and I plugged him between the eyes with my sidearm. The nametag said Carl.

The sound of the storm raging overhead had diminished significantly, but we could still feel the building taking it like a champ. The room we were in was fairly large, maybe twenty-by-thirty feet, with a small office off to one end. Boiler machinery, some tools, and cleaning supplies were present, some knocked over or spilled by the dead man who had been stumbling around in here for who knows how long.

I pointed my weapon at Lynch. "Lisa, search him." He put his hands up, but she didn't move. It occurred to me that she didn't know how to search him and wouldn't know what to look for if she did.

"*Kill him?*" she growled. I don't think she likes Lynch.

"Not yet."

"*Now? Kill now?*" she asked one second later and took a menacing step toward him.

"I will let you know when to kill him," I told her. "Unless he tries to hurt one of us, then kill him," I added quickly.

Lynch still had the little blue med box, and I holstered my weapon and asked for it. "Lisa, pull your shirt up so I can see your bullet wound. If he moves, kill him." There were two pieces of gauze in the kit but no tape. There was an Ace bandage, so I put the gauze over her holes and wrapped the bandage around her belly. Her middle was tight as fuck and Lisa must have been into sit ups back when she was a human.

Done, I looked to the spook. "Sit," I told him pointing at a garden bench that had no business being in a basement and got to work patching his hurt. Something loud crashed in the school above and we all looked up, me pointing my flashlight at the ceiling.

"Mmm," he murmured and spat blood onto the stained concrete floor. "Mouth hurts like hell."

I made a face showing him the cuts I had received in my very own mouth a while ago. They still hadn't healed all the way. "You won't live long enough, but it still hurts after a month and change."

"So, what now?"

"We wait until the storm passes and the dead move on, then I go back to San Franciso and find my family."

"I meant what about me?"

"You can gently kiss my ass and give me a tickle while you're down there. I would say fuck off and die, but I don't want you to open the door just yet and you've already started on the dying part."

He nodded and, God help me, I felt bad. I sat on the bench next to him and sighed. "Why? Why do you blindly follow orders and kill good people, innocent people, to get a job done?"

"Because the job always saves more than it hurts," he answered without hesitation. "It's the first thing you learn when you get recruited. The very first thing. If you wouldn't strangle a baby to save the world, you get booted from the program."

"That's fucked up."

He shook his head. "It isn't. It's purely sensible, just not everyone can see it, or do what's necessary when the time comes. I know I'm a high functioning sociopath. I know it. That helps me do what I have to do such that the greatest amount of people will live."

I had to admit it made a semblance of sense, and at the end of the day, I do the same thing, just not to his extreme.

But I said, "Still fucked up."

"Yeah? You should have seen when they gave us the babies." He saw me bristle. Good thing too because I was absolutely going to shoot him. "Kidding!" he said and raised his palms. "Just kidding, dude. I don't like killing innocent people. I'll do it without hesitation, but I don't get off on it. Some of us do."

"Whatever. Lisa, if he moves off this bench, kill him." She made no sound of acknowledgement or movements of any kind, but I knew she was itching to finish the fight with a mouthful of Lynch's larynx.

I had patted him down when I had patched him up. I hadn't felt any weapons but that didn't mean he didn't have a rocket launcher or an Abrams tank on him someplace. Not that he wasn't a weapon himself. I didn't cuff him because I didn't have any cuffs, and I might need him to fight off an area code's worth of dead.

Lisa would keep watch on him with her baleful glare while I searched the area, and search I did. The office held a bottle of gin and some nudie magazines, which didn't really fit for an elementary school. Damn, Carl. There were no attack helicopters or light sabers to be found, so the weapons on us would have to do.

The howling of the wind had subsided a bit. I knew this because the school had stopped shaking and the noises of the dead had increased. They were inside the building now. I could hear them crashing and thumping around up there.

"If they get in here, we fight," I whispered. "We'll use the stairway to bottleneck them until we run out of ammo, then it's hand to hand. If they don't figure out we're down here, we wait them out and peek later when they've moved on as a group."

"Not a terrible plan," Lynch said in an equally hushed volume. "I hate being trapped."

I nodded. "Me too. It was you, however, who indicated we should jump into the trash compactor, sight unseen, Princess."

"Sweet reference," he said with a snort.

It was a solid hour later he started to get sick. In that hour, I used whispered tones to ask him questions. How was the world doing? Had he heard anything about Boston? Had he or any of his cronies checked on my parents?

He sighed on that last question. Yes, they had gone after my parents, but not to kill them, to relocate them. They figured I might be more amenable to whatever the hell they wanted to do to me if they had my mom and dad.

But they were dead. Truly dead. Lynch started to go into details, but I asked him to stop. He did tell me that the team who went in search of my parents had put them down. I thanked him for that, and he told me he hadn't been on the mission, but every operative had gotten the same dossier on me.

That piqued my interest, and I asked him what was in it.

It was at that moment that I realized how thorough whoever was in charge had been. This guy knew everything about me. He knew about my family, where I was from, what schools I had gone to, and past girlfriends. He told me about my crime and subsequent incarceration, my escape in a prison bus, and travels across the country. He knew about all my friends, Donna and the twins, Ship and Remo. He even knew about Dimitri Sabotino, the douche sheriff of Havre Montana who had gotten bitten on a mission into a hospital and his ensuing euthanasia by rifle round.

What Lynch had *not* known was that it had been me who had bitten the sheriff, and then told the douche's buddy it had been an undead who had chomped him. Douche had his head blown off but before you judge me, he had deserved it. The sheriff had planned on murdering me to appropriate my truck.

I told Lynch this and he smiled with yet another snort, then vomited black shit all over the painted concrete floor. He drew his wrist across his face, then said, "Mouth really hurts now."

"It's going to get worse."

"I know," he told me. "I've seen it a thousand times."

We chatted about bullshit until he started to get really sick. He had quietly puked a few times into a yellow bucket, but in a testament to his willpower, he never left his seat. In a testament to Lisa's willpower, she stood in the same spot for three hours, twitching occasionally, just staring at him. If he had taken his ass of the bench, Lisa would have eviscerated him. I never took the suppressed handgun off my thighs while we talked.

Lynch had been staring at his shoes, but when he glanced up at me, his left eye had gone completely crimson. I sighed. "Do you want to ride this out, or should I take care of you now?"

"There's a hotel in Alberta Canada, the Monroe," he said to me, completely ignoring my question. "My sister lives there with her husband Gus and their young twins. They're alive and both capable, and the place is fortified. If you ever get out that way, tell her how I died."

I nodded, knowing full well that I would never step foot in Canada. He nodded too, his gaze reverting to his shoes. "Maybe I can—"

I put a bullet through the top of his dome, and he collapsed to the floor. I didn't feel a damn thing, good or bad, for him.

What does that say about me?

LISA

I shut the flashlight off a few hours ago. Didn't want to waste the batteries, so we sat in the dark, listening to a bunch of undead rampage through a dead school. Lisa had remained quiet throughout; the last thing she asked me is if she could eat Lynch.

I had whispered to her that she could not, and she subsequently told me he was dead.

"We don't eat people, even if they are dead. It's... wrong."

"*Bad. Bad to eat people.*"

"Yes, bad."

I risked a minute of battery life and checked her bandages, the flashlight in my mouth. They had bled through, and blood was running in red rivulets down her side. The top of her pants was thick with it, and she would need a new shirt. Damn, she was tight. Her belly looked like it was made of bricks. I had to wonder if Runners muscled up when they got infected. That was something I would need to ask Gamboa and Baker if they ever caught me again. I shut the light off and thought about Thorne.

He was scary, for sure, and always looked at me with menace, but not malice. I think he would kill me if given the order, but not without one. He understood that I was important to those who commanded him.

As we sat in the darkness, waiting for the horde to either move on or break in and kill me, I did a lot of thinking. Kids, wife, friends, places I had been, and the dead. Not the undead, my friends who had died. Such sadness and loss just brings you down, ya know? But not thinking of them makes them really die. The only way to keep them alive is to remember them.

I sighed and nodded in the dark.

We waited another eternity of two hours, and I realized I couldn't hear anything from upstairs. It was time to check. I was halfway up the cement stairs, Lisa in tow, when I had yet another epiphany. WTF was I doing checking? I had a zombie-proof companion who I could muster forth to the front lines. The dead either didn't see her or didn't give a shit about her. She wouldn't lose chunks of herself to them, but I certainly could.

I turned around to ask her, flashed the light on her, and noticed she was leaning forward on the stairs, using her hand on one of the railings to hold herself up. She was infected, so she already looked all kinds of wrong, but she looked more... off. The *pat-pat-pat* noise coming from beside her made me look at her feet.

She couldn't have been standing in that spot for more than a few seconds, and there was already a substantial puddle of blood by her boot. The douche's bullet must have nicked something important. She would never complain or utter any type of pain sounds. She probably didn't even know how serious her wound was. For fuck's sake I had an almost identical bullet hit just a few weeks ago when that asshole SEAL had plugged me just to keep me in line.

But the SEAL had not been trying to make me dead. Lynch had. Her wound was closer to her middle than mine was, and the blood coming out of her bandaged side was steady. While her tolerance to pain was inimitable, she was still subject to the same results of damage that an uninfected human was.

My infected compatriot was bleeding out.

I rushed to assist her, and she cocked her head, staring at me in curiosity. The normal angry red tinge that her face portrayed was a ghastly off-white. A sallow pallor, my grammy used to say. She still looked scary, but she was in trouble.

I helped her back down the stairs and helped her to sit against a row of ancient lockers. "I need to see your wound again," I told her, and she lifted her shirt. I couldn't even tell there was a bandage there. The wrap I had put around the gauze was sagging it was so heavy with blood, and the pad wasn't recognizable.

I had learned a lot of medical shit since the end of the world, but I didn't know if yanking the bandage off her without another one handy was a great idea. I thought not, so I left it. She was always twitching, but now she looked almost like she had the shivers.

I sighed, "You can put your arm down now." I stood and she tried to stand up with me.

"No, you wait here. I'm going to go find some more bandages."

"*I come,*" she told me through chattering teeth.

"No," I told her putting my hand on her shoulder. "It's my turn to protect you." She looked up at me but stayed seated.

"I'll be back in a few minutes, you wait here."

"*Wait here,*" she echoed, and her voice seemed less terrifying. She slumped back against the lockers and fluttered her eyelids. "*Wait.*"

I climbed the stairs and moved through the landing. I put my ear against the metal, but other than the dripping of water coming from under the door I couldn't hear shit. Half the state of undead California could be on the other side of this half inch steel door. I glanced behind me, staring into the darkness of the stairwell. Open the door and I could die. Stay here and Lisa would probably die. Was I really going to risk my life for an infected?

Fuck it.

I pushed on the push bar on my side of the door, and it swung open, letting the bright sunlight in through a section of missing school roof. The door swung further when mottled gray fingers snaked around the edge of it and pulled it wide. A dead thing reached for me, but I juked into the hallway away from her. I got a better look of what waited for me. Nothing to the right, four more dead people to the left. I could do four of them without my sidearm. At least I hoped so. I reached to my hip, looking for Chauncy, but grabbing the first thing that came to my hand. In short order, my Dalstrong, Something-inch, Something Series, Something coated (titanium, maybe?), Something Chef Knife with All-New Finger Guard stuck six of its something inches into dead lady's noggin. She dropped like a rock, taking my pretty chef's blade to the floor with her. I almost hit the floor too, as I slipped in a puddle of rainwater.

Apologies, Dear Reader, I couldn't remember all the titles the knife had, only some of them. I righted myself and let her have the knife for now yanking an eager Chauncy from behind my back. I had completely forgotten about my new-ish SEAL Pup adorning my shoulder like a sexy epaulet. The dead were advancing, and I noticed a fifth had come strolling out of a classroom. The first one was six feet in front of the two behind it and I gave a mighty shove when it reached for me. It stumbled back, taking one of the two closest behind it to the floor right next to the beautiful, pearl blue handle of my occupied chef's knife.

The dead teenager with half a face reached me first, so he was the first to taste ten inches of Chauncy. I laughed in spite of the danger, thinking right then what you are likely thinking right now, unless you have a shitty sense of humor. Chauncy wasn't as big as a machete, but he wasn't just any combat knife either. He was a foot of shiny death, and when the next thing stepped over the two sodden ones on the floor, he swiped at its neck, severing most of it, but not decapitating it. The result was the epitome of cool, as the creature's head flopped first back a bit, then to the side. Like, way to the side. Its head was hanging on by a bit of flesh and the spinal column, but the slash had apparently been enough to do it in, and it fell next to the other two.

I advanced on the two on the floor, who had begun to stand, but they were uncoordinated and slipping on the sopping floor. So was I. My foot slipped forward, and I almost did a split before catching myself. That was enough. I didn't need to slip into the teeth of some dead people, and I sure as shit wasn't limber enough to pull off a full split. I switched

Chauncy into my left hand, drew my sidearm, and each of the remaining three dead dickwads ate a subsonic, suppressed bullet.

Black shit was sprayed in conical patterns in the dirty water on the floor, slowly washing away as the remnants of last night's storm drained to wherever it would end up. I sloshed through it, my boots making small wet splashes as I searched for what I needed.

I had still never seen a tornado, even though I had likely lived through one last night. The sun shone through where the roof used to be, an enormous section of it having disappeared overnight. It was as if there had never been a storm, with the sun out and wispy clouds overhead. I was gazing up as I turned a corner in the corridor and almost into a dead thing. It surprised me, but it also had its back to me, staring into the afternoon sky as I had. Chauncy flashed again and we were down to no dead things. I found what I had been looking for three doors up; the nurse's office.

The roof here was still intact and it looked as if the Tenaya Elementary School nurse had been diligent. A spartan steel cabinet with glass paneled doors held my prizes, and I strode forward, a huge smile on my face. The smile dissipated for a moment when I realized the doors were locked, but hey, I was pretty good at getting into locked places. I had the door jimmied in five seconds and looked upon the booty. Epi pens, a few stainless medical implements, ibuprofen, tons of adhesive bandages for little boo-boos, antiseptic creams, and two boxes of large, adhesive gauze pads. I took everything that would fit into my pack, keeping the gauze pads in my hand to apply to Lisa when I got back to her.

I made it back to the boiler room door and entered it quickly, closing it behind me with a quiet *snick*. I hadn't seen or heard any dead fuckers on my way back. My tac light bobbed as I made my way down the stairs, past the landing, and all the way to the basement floor. Quite a large puddle of smeared blood waited for me by the lockers, but Lisa wasn't sitting in it. I flashed the light around until I found her, standing and staring at a calendar with a horse on it. She looked quite calm.

"You should be sitting down," I told her and fumbled with tearing open one of the gauze pads with my teeth. She turned to face me ever so slowly, odd for her as everything she did was fast. I had been focused on the medical supplies, and when I looked back up, she was plodding toward me.

Lisa, my infected friend and protector, my favorite zombie, had died. She made that sound they make and reached for me. I let out a sob and pushed her away. I dropped the gauze as she came in again, and through wracking sobs, pushed her back several times. Tears stung my eyes, and I had to wipe them away or she would have torn into me. I pushed her one last time and pulled my sidearm. When she came forward the last time, I placed the suppressor against her forehead and said goodbye.

I sat on the bench in the dark and cried like a baby for an hour. I cried for the woman who had tried to help me, and for the infected thing who had saved my life over and over. I missed her terribly already.

When I was done crying, I cried some more. For my SEAL buddies who hadn't made it. For Tim, a nerd who liked painting fantasy miniatures. For Javi, a guy I had met on a ranch in Texas. For my mom and dad, who had come to see me every single Saturday while I had been in prison. I guess we tell ourselves that we cry for others, but really, I cried for me. For my sadness. For my inexorable march into grief.

Then I got angry. Really fucking mad. I knew I wasn't done losing people, but they were done losing me. I had waffled like a bitch over going back to my family. I had thought that I would always have a target on my back, would always keep my family in danger.

But fuck that. The way I see it, I had two options: hide or take the fight to the douches looking for me. I didn't think I could stop the fucked-up remnants of the US government, especially with however many Lynches they had after me, but I could hide. We could find a place without any assholes and hole up there. Live our lives and give a hearty FU to The Man. I had made a deal with Queen, but eventually, the powers that be would swing back around to wanting me in their care. Or worse, they would figure out a cure for all this shit and only give it to those they deemed worthy, lording it over the masses like expensive health insurance.

No. No, I would grab my people and literally head for the hills. The wild blue fucking yonder. Fuck SECNAV, fuck the Lynches, and fuck the cure. They would never find one anyway and didn't need my blood to do it.

There were several dozen dead ambling around outside and I didn't think I could safely dig a grave for Lisa. I gently wrapped her in a heavy blue drape I had appropriated from one of the classrooms. I placed her in the center of the floor of the school basement, with some pretty orange flowers I found right outside the broken back door that hadn't been destroyed in the storm. A fitting tomb for her, I thought.

The dead had noticed me getting the flowers, but I was able to get down to her and place them on her chest, then get back out before they were at the door. There ended up being quite a few of them, likely stragglers from the enormous horde that had slogged through yesterday's storm.

The cinderblock garage had taken no storm damage, and I got into the tow truck and headed east, pulping a few of the shitheads who got in my way on the way out of the parking lot. I was sullen and angry, and I didn't like it. Ten minutes into my journey I held the radio out the window of the truck with the intent of dropping it at fifty miles per hour but hesitated. I realized I had given my word to Queen. I wasn't a liar, but for all the reasons I listed above, it might be a mistake to go back to his army. His army controlled by the old SECNAV who was the new President. Bunch of Lynches potentially running around, maybe trying to spirit me away. In the end, I decided to keep the radio for now and let my people help decide whether we would be new recruits or start our own community far from others. Both choices had interesting draws.

RATS

I continued on the 120 passing through Groveland, Priest (which had an insane set of switchbacks through the hills), and north of Moccasin, until I hit the James E Roberts Memorial Bridge. A barricade had been placed across the bridge, but either people or the dead had torn it asunder and after destroying half a dozen dead (there were always zombies on bridges) and dragging a flipped over UPS truck, I was back on my way.

I passed through Chinese Camp, took a left at Yosemite Junction, and in less than an hour, I was parked in the middle of the road in front of a Denny's on the outskirts of Oakdale California staring at a green road sign. The sign said San Francisco 100. In days of old that would have been an hour and a half with no traffic. In today's world it could take a couple of days to a week, but the traffic would be of a different type.

I saw a raccoon or something scurry across the road a couple hundred yards in front of me. That was promising. If there was a raccoon here, there were probably not too many dead. Then I thought of the deer and shuddered. The critter that just crossed the road had done so quickly and furtively, telling me it had been alive, so that was a good thing.

I looked down the hill into the town below. The streets were carved into rectangular blocks, houses and businesses dotting each one. The streets were black, which was odd. The road I was on was that asphalt that years of sun and weather had colored a purplish blue. Something was odd about the shadows on the roads of Oakdale, something I didn't like. The heat waves on the road mixed with the shadows made it look like everything was moving. It wasn't a horde of dead it was very low to the ground. I squinted, focusing, but I couldn't figure it out. Shrugging, I grabbed the binoculars from my pack.

The streets *were* moving. It was not the dead, at least I didn't think they were dead. It was rats. Hundreds of thousands, maybe millions, of rats. These weren't the fluffy little things you see on a farm or a pet shop, these were city rats, the size of a... a raccoon. I jerked my head to the left, where the creature I had thought was a trash panda had moved into the brush, but I didn't see anything. I raised the glasses to my eyes again and the rats were still there.

Every road seemed to be alive with them. I couldn't tell if they were zombie rats, like the deer, but they didn't seem to be. They didn't have wounds on them that I could tell, and they looked to be doing what rats do; climbing over each other and whatnot.

Could I drive the truck through that? Just squishing them with the tires as I soldiered on? No. No friggin' way. The sheer numbers of them must outweigh the tow truck by a hundred times. I didn't know if rats hunted people, but I knew they would eat people if given the chance. With that many of them, and not having human contact near them for a few years, they would be brazen as fuck.

That meant going around Oakdale. The problem was, I had no idea how to go around Oakdale. There were turn offs and roads both right and left, but I didn't know where any of them went. I busted out my trusty roadmap and took a look. Each of the towns around here had population values listed below the name of the berg, and it was then I noticed I had come out of the poorly populated mountains and into a shit show of congestion. Modesto was right up the road, and that had a population of over 200,000. Most of the other pissant towns around Oakdale were in the twenty thousand range.

But where were they? Had they all gone on zombie vacations? Did they wander off, or did... Holy shit, did the fucking rats eat them? Had an overpopulation of the nasty rodents taken matters into their own hands and fucked shit up?

And did that mean they were zombie rats? If a person ate a zombie, they were dead for sure, but rats? Actually...Runners could eat the dead and not die, did that mean rats could too? The undead deer was wreaking havoc on my mind as I contemplated whether or not planet Earth was going to be under a carpet of rats, possibly undead or, for fuck's sake *Runner* rats, in the next few years.

I had pondered all of that with the paper roadmap splayed across the steering wheel. I put my finger on Oakdale and traced a road south, but that just turned back into the city. A road north split west and I...

What was that? There had been a scrabbling sound on the hood of... I bent the map forward and looked over the top of it through the windshield. At a rat. It sat on the hood of the tow truck using its front paws to clean its whiskers. This didn't look like a zombie rat or even a city rat. It was about six inches long, brown and, honestly, kind of cute. It stopped washing its face, rat-walked up to the windshield, tilted its head a bit, and placed its paws on the glass, sniffing, its little, triangular head bobbing and moving around.

This creature wasn't cute, he was fucking *adorable*! I put my finger on the glass, moving it around, and the little guy followed my finger like a puppy! I was absolutely going back to my family with a pet rat. This little dude was coming with me. I would not judge him if he didn't judge me. He could ride on my shoulder, nibbling my ear while I guffawed at his brown cuteness, his little rat tail curling around my ear while I sang

"Know when to fold 'em!" at the top of my lungs because Kenny Rogers' Gambler album was stuck in the ancient tape deck of this equally ancient tow truck.

I started making undignified little squeaks to him, pawing at the glass on my side while he pawed on his. "Who's a good little dude? Who is?" Then, I looked past him and noticed a moving carpet of thousands of the fucking things scurrying up the road toward me. They would be on me in seconds, and these weren't cute little fellas.

Good feelings gone.

"Hang on, little buddy!" I shrieked and threw the truck into reverse. I stomped on the accelerator and accelerate I did. We shot backwards at a dangerous speed, and following my advice, my new pal held onto the passenger side windshield wiper for dear life, little pink tail stuck straight out behind him in the wind.

When the truck had reached a suitable distance from the black tide of fur and teeth, I spun the wheel, turned my ass around, and headed back east. Two miles back the way I had come, and my furry chum had pooped on the hood. I had scared the shit out of him... I felt bad, stopped the truck, and got out to help him.

"We made it, homie!" I told him enthusiastically. I stuck my hand out, palm up, touching the hood so he could climb on it, and we could vamoose. Giant smile on my face, equally huge smile on his, sun shining! What a day. He crawled over, gave my hand a hesitant sniff, tentatively reached his cute little head forward, and sunk his traitorous little teeth into my pinky. I ripped my hand back, pain lancing through the meat of my finger, just next to the nail. The little dude went flying and hit the pavement pretty hard, rolling and skidding to a stop.

He stood, shook his head, then made a beeline right for me, his cute eyes of a moment ago filled with murder as he scurried quickly to intercept. Clearly this bloodthirsty little bastard was some type of conniving, advanced scout for the rat army. A devious super-spy, Operative of the Alliance type of shit. The bitch of it was, he was still cute AF.

I couldn't bring myself to kick or stomp him. It would have taken half a second and all I would have had to do is wipe his innards off my boot. And he sure as shit deserved it, but I couldn't do it. In the end, I got in the truck and drove east, 180 degrees away from my desired destination. He chased me for two seconds, then stopped and sat on his haunches, cleaning my blood off his whiskers, watching me go.

Other than the nick in my finger and a few dozen potential diseases, the worst thing about the rats was that they made me go a day out of my way. I was forced to make a decision at a crossroads, and I chose north, taking the Golden Chain Highway through the tiny town of Angel's Camp. I headed east again after a bit, and in a few hours, I was staring at an Entering Stockton sign. It was a white sign with a huge red X spraypainted on it. The words: *Dead Here* were also spray painted, the dripping paint reminiscent of slaughter.

This was not a town. This was a city. Little green destination mileage signs hung below the Entering Stockton sign, and one of them told me that San Francisco was a mere 83 miles away. An hour and a half pre-apocalypse, and I would have been staring at the USS Florida if it were still anchored off Alcatraz. Now it could take a week or more.

My tow truck was at a quarter tank as well, so fuel would be a problem in the next few hours. The bigger problem was the city of Stockton. The streets crawled, but not with rats. Thousands of dead people milled around or sat where they liked. Several had noticed me up on this hill, and they were already plodding toward me. There was no way I could drive this tank through them. I might get a quarter mile, but eventually I would get mired in bodies and be forced to exit the truck in the middle of a few thousand hungry corpses.

Nope.

So, I turned around again. I headed north for about forty-five minutes then hooked a left at the city of Lodi to go west. Lodi had a bunch of dead, but it was nothing like Stockton, and it looked rat free. The congestion of both dead and abandoned vehicles was significantly less than the surrounding area, so I made decent time all the way to Brentwood. It was at this point that I realized everything in front of me was city, and I was shit out of helicopters.

San Francisco sat on the northern end of a peninsula, and any way I sliced it, I was going to have to pass through a city. I ran my finger over the map. To the north were San Rafael, Richmond, and Berkeley. Direct west were Oakland and Alameda. South were Fremont and eventually San Jose. All of these were before I even hit the damn peninsula.

The sheriff had been right: I'm screwed. Double screwed as the fuel indicator light on the dashboard had winked on while I gazed at this friggin' piece of paper with landmarks on it.

Fuck it. I'll head due west, climb over Mt. Diablo, make my way over I680 south of Walnut Creek, and try to make it through Oakland with an undead population of almost half a million. I nodded. Sounds like a plan. A stupid plan, but a plan nonetheless.

I made it another half hour before my trusty steed sputtered and died. I left her on the side of Morgan Territory Road, just after a trailhead parking area, and headed west on foot. A sign told me that the mountain was 3,849 feet tall, and it was forty-one miles from San Francisco.

I would go a bit north of the large peak in front of me, but it was still a mountain. I was three hours into my journey when it all went to shit.

BUGS

I'm in the best shape of my life. Seriously, if you're not in good shape in the zombie apocalypse, you're dead or undead. I'm up to eighty pushups at once, and I don't care to reach a hundred. I'm totally sure I could do a hundred, but for what? To get in *better* shape? Nah. I've kept up with my running as well, but my life is usually on the line for that. Running from zombies or cannibals or rednecks.

But damn, if this little mountain wasn't kicking my ass. I was huffing after twenty minutes, and full-on gasping at a half hour. A fallen tree, no branches anymore, looked very inviting, so I had a sit down. I can remember thinking that it was more like a big log than a tree and that the sun and shadows on the west side of the mountain looked beautiful. It was when I was looking down at all the populated area I needed to traverse that I heard it. It was a *them* and there were six. Dead as fuck but still looking to get their groove on, I had to wonder how they had gotten up here. Your average zombie won't go out of their way as they slog on, they will take the path of least resistance or follow the horde. Unless there's food, then they will climb to the moon. But how much food could there have been up here? There was a tower on the top of the mountain next to me, but this smaller mountain didn't seem to have any food for these things.

Except me. My point is, why were they up here? I would ask them, but the answer is unlikely to be forthcoming.

Two of the shambling horrors were kids, and you know how I hate that. I sighed, drew my new SOG, and pushed off the log with my hands to stand. Everybody does that, right? If you're in an armchair, or sitting on a log, you don't use just your legs to stand, you push off, yeah? Well, that's what I tried to do, but my left hand went right through a rotten spot and into the damn log.

I could feel things scuttling around in there and did what anybody would do in that situation: I emitted a high-pitched shriek that sounded like Johnny had pulled Suzie's pig tails, and tore my hand out of the hole.

But I hadn't been fast enough. No, the infected didn't pounce, they were sixty feet away and stomping across some likely government protected grass as they made their way toward me. My hand came away from that black maw of a log with a huge brownish yellow bug clinging to it, and in half a second, the little bastard stung me. He got me right in the meaty part of the back of my left hand, in the direct center right above that little web-jobbie between the thumb and forefinger.

It hurt. It hurt a lot, like someone had jabbed me with a three-foot needle recently pulled from a fire, but the little fucker paid for his indiscretion. I smacked him off my hand with my other hand, but keep in mind I still had my incredibly sharp knife in my right paw. So yeah, in addition to being hunted by six dead people and stung by a scorpion the size of a Post-it note, I gave the back of my hand a decent slash. But, as previously mentioned, Mr. Scorpion met his end right then and there under my boot. Fuck him, his kids, his mom and dad, all the rest of the fuckers in the log, and this little asshole's stinger. Motherfucker was a stain in the dirt and stuck to the bottom of my boot. His stinging days were over.

Those dead people? Yeah, they didn't give a shit about my tribulations and kept right on coming. But fuck if that sting didn't start to burn. That hurt like a son of a bitch, and it was very distracting. Once again, I decided that trying to smoke six dead people while I had been recently injured was a poor idea. I switched hands with the SOG, drew my sidearm, and popped six of the fuckers with seven shots one- handed.

My sidearm was holstered and my knife was back in my right hand as I looked at my left. It was on fire. Actual fire. Ok, so there were no flames, but it burned like you can't imagine. I'm not talking about the slash, I mean the sting. It *hurt*. He had stung me less than a minute ago and the whole area was red like I had burned it with boiling water. That's how it felt too.

Blood oozed and dripped from the knife cut, and when I wiped it away, the fire from the sting turned into the sun. Jesus fuck it burned! I read someplace that you should put ice on a scorpion sting but, well you get it.

I got some gauze out of my med kit and put it on the cut, which was across the hand and into my middle finger. It wasn't horrible but would have needed some sutures or glue pre-apocalypse. I had neither, so I wrapped the gauze around it and clutched it hard. Which sent further tendrils of agony up my arm from the sting.

I was so angry and fucked up at recent events that I actually sat back down on the log before I remembered it housed potentially half a billion scorpions. I shot back up and strode away from the little fuckers, even though I couldn't see them. I had squished their paw-paw, and didn't want vengeful arachnids on me, so I ran for it. I mean, I walked cradling my hand like a bitch, but still.

I got a mile before the pain in my hand forced me to lean against a tree. A tree I looked up and down to ensure no more bugs resided on it. I wanted to lean against that bark for days, but I had to get going. The fire in my arm was worse than when I had been shot on that rooftop. It was a blazing inferno that threatened to shut down my entire system. An all-consuming conflagration under my skin that I could neither push to the back of my mind nor self-medicate as I had taken all my ibuprofen. I did the only thing I could, I pushed off from the tree and slogged like a dead thing toward the west.

A couple of hours later and the agony had retreated some, the pain mixing with a tingly numbness that radiated all the way up my arm into my shoulder and an itch that would piss off poison ivy. A constant throb that reminded me of a toothache combined with a prickle that I couldn't scratch because of the agony it caused. Oh, I tried, but nipped that shit right in the bud when my nails barely grazed my itchy skin and bolts of flaming lightning shot from my pain receptors to my brain.

My fingers were twitching, too. Another half hour and I looked down to see the gauze I had put across my hand had fallen off. I looked behind me, but it wasn't there. I have no idea when it fell off because my damn arm was numb. Hey, at least my hand hadn't fallen off. But it looked like it might.

My paw was red and blotchy near where the little fucker had gotten me, swollen to the point where it might split. I was having trouble swallowing, my belly felt off, and I could feel my heart pounding.

There were no horrible scorpions in California, right? I mean I know there are some kinds of them in Arizona that are unpleasant, but weren't all the nasty ones in Africa or the Middle East? There were none in the US that could kill me, right? Right?

"Right?" I asked nobody and dragged my un-stung forearm across my sweaty forehead. It was when my eyes started twitching that I had to sit down. I more fell down than sat, and I realized I was out of breath. The mountain had kicked my ass, but this was more than that. It was actually hard to get a breath in. I had been able to take in huge gulps before, but now, it was like I was breathing through soup. The air, which was supposed to be thinner up here, was thick as hell and every breath felt like it was only doing half duty.

Millions of undead cannibals shuffling around and I was going to die from a bug bite? Fuck that, I thought, and passed out.

"What?" I croaked and tried to sit up. Nausea replied with an emphatic *no*, and I put my head back down. I smelled fire, heard the crackle, but couldn't see it. Terrific. Now I was in the middle of a forest fire. Killer bugs and hungry zombies weren't enough.

"Terrific," I sighed.

"I don't know about that," a gravelly woman's voice replied, and I sat up quickly, nausea be damned. "Might not want to get up just yet," she added.

"Who're you?" I asked, searching for my weapons. They were not within reach.

"Your guns are close," she told me. "We don't know you, so we moved 'em outa reach until we figured you out. Stinger gotcha, and you had a bad time of it."

"Stinger," I repeated. It wasn't really a question, but it got an answer anyway.

A different voice chimed in, "You were stung by an Arizona bark scorpion. Initially I had thought it was a rattlesnake bite, but your symptoms and the injection site are indicative of a scorpion sting. We treated you accordingly, although we did not administer any antivenom as we did not have any."

It was a kid. A ten-year-old kid was talking to me, and she sounded like Ship. The nausea went on hiatus for a sec, and I was able to sit up. Three other kids and an older woman sat on logs near a fire that was built into a hole in the ground. The top of the hole had a triangular piece of folding metal over it, and not a single bit of light showed through other than where these people wanted it to.

I glanced at my hand, and it was bandaged nicely with a fresh gauze pad and a compression bandage. I was no professional, but it looked like nice work.

"Thank you," I told them and tried to stand.

"Mister," the older lady said, "you stay down, or Dory is gonna put a bolt through you. I mean *through you* too, as her crossbow has a 400 pound test."

"I'm no threat," I said, thinking she had mixed up crossbows and fishing line, and raised my hands. That didn't go over well, and everybody stood. One of the kids did indeed have a wicked looking crossbow, one of those where the bow part of it is pulled all the way back to the body so it looks skinny. Except when it's pointing at you, it doesn't look skinny, it looks fucking huge.

"I'm not going to move, ok? Clearly, you have the high ground here, and I really don't want any more holes in me."

Granny put her hand on the kid's bow but continued to look me over like I was something dangerous. "We don't wanna shootcha, but you need to stay down."

"I'm not going to move, but I feel weird."

"Like I said," she continued, "you had a bad time of the sting. Ain't nothin' for most folks, but some it works over pretty hard. They can kill littles like Casey here." A girl of about six stood with her kitchen knife. Her backpack was as big as she was.

None of these kids looked scared, though, and neither did the woman. I guess they were apocalypse wired and knew they had the drop on me.

"What's your name?" I asked the older lady.

"Petunia Hardcastle."

"You're kidding?"

She raised an indignant eyebrow, "I'm not. What's your name, stranger?"

I opened my mouth to tell her, but two dead men loomed behind her at that exact moment, so I shouted a warning. Several things happened at once right then. Dory, the little know-it-all with the crossbow, depressed the trigger, the bolt missing my noggin by a hair's breadth, one of the undead dickweeds grabbed Petunia, and one of the kids, a boy of maybe twelve, brought an axe handle around into the side of one of the dead guys, making it stumble back a bit.

The other three kids leapt into action, one of them whipping a bicycle chain at the legs of the dead thing that had been pushed back. The chain connected with the shin of the creature and wrapped around, the kid and another yanking on the links. The critter fell backward, and I rolled sideways, searching for my weapons. I found them quickly.

Two more dead people ambled toward us from the tree line, but I had a minute or two before I would have to deal. I checked the load on my sidearm and slid Chauncy into his sheath on my belt. I didn't know where my SOG had gone, but that piece of steel pornography would be mine again.

The dead thing on the ground was taking a beating from the kids, but the one who had grabbed the older lady was winning. She was jerking it around so it couldn't get a bite in, but that also pulled it from the reach of the kid who was trying to club it with her tire iron. Dory had reloaded her crossbow but couldn't get a clear shot, and my vision was swimming when I aimed the pistol at the thing. I really didn't want to shoot Petunia five minutes after we had met, but the snapping jaws of the critter were getting closer to her face.

"Fuck it," I said and strode forward. I put the suppressor against the side of the thing's dome and ventilated it. It collapsed, taking Petunia with it, but I had other worries. Dory's crossbow was trained on me and the other three murderous brats looked... well... murderous. "Kill me later," I told them and moved toward the advancing duo of ambulatory deceased.

I smoked them with the pistol and made my way back to the kids.

"Drop it, Mister," one of the brats growled.

"Shut it, kid," I said and holstered the gun. They had taken my gadgets but had left my belt on me. Petunia was sitting in the dirt, breathing heavy, so I stuck a hand down to her. She stared up at me for a moment, then accepted the hand and I pulled her to her feet.

"Your head's bleedin'," I told her, sounding EXACTLY like Quint talking to Brody on the Orca in Jaws. I had done it on purpose and had nailed it. "Anybody have a Band-Aid for Petunia?"

The boy with the chain pointed at her, "You're bleeding!"

"No shit, Sherlock," I said rolling my eyes. I put my hands up in supplication in front of Petunia, then started to check her over for bites and scratches. She was clean. "Looks like you're gonna make it."

She nodded. "Thank you."

I held up my bandaged hand, "Owed you guys for this." I got woozy right then and needed a sit down. I found my way back to the log and planted my ass on it, thumping it with my hand to ensure I wouldn't fall through into a nest of stingy demons. The kids eyed me the whole way, weapons ready to assassinate me if I sneezed or something.

Dory slowly lowered her crossbow and went to check on Petunia, and in a minute or two we were all sitting around the covered campfire. Petunia and Dory came with three side dishes; Casey, Bobby, and to my everlasting sadness, Lisa. They had been together for a couple of years, the kids getting out of their various cities and towns, meeting up with the retired Park Ranger when they all had the same idea of going to the nearest state park to escape the dead.

Petunia knew these hills up and down, having been a ranger for three decades in this part of the world. The kids all had the same story: Dead parents, dead families, dead dog, run to park. I told them some of my story and that I needed to get to San Francisco.

Petunia shrugged. "Can't."

"Can't what?"

"Can't get to San Francisco from here," she added.

"I have to."

"Can't," she shrugged.

"What are you talking about?"

She stood and so did the kids. "C'mon over here." She strode to a precipice and pointed west. I stood next to her, staring into the distance.

"That there," she started, "is the mighty Pacific. The bright you see is the sun glinting off the city of San Francisco."

"Yeah?"

"All of this," she brought her hand around in a sweeping arc, indicating the area between us and the city, "is filled with millions, and I do mean millions, of the dead. There are tens of thousands of fast ones too."

I sighed. "Yeah, I know."

"Boy, if you ain't flyin' you ain't goin'." She shrugged again, "Can't."

I sucked in a huge lungful of crisp mountain air and let it out in a long sigh. "I have to."

USE THE FORCE

The kids wanted to see people again. Living People. They cozied up to me quickly and began firing off questions. Well, three of them did. Bobby had decided to keep his teeth together, but the other three... Damn, they could talk. They asked me everything. How was the rest of the world? Where was the Army? Was it really safe on Alcatraz? How was I going to get there? Were there any other kids there? What kind of food did they have?

I started laughing and joking with them, but Petunia remained silent. Not only that, but I could see her brooding by the fire. She glanced up and... was that anger? Yeah, she was mad.

"I have to poop," Little Lisa said, and all four kids stood. They strode off to the tree line and disappeared into the foliage.

"Are they safe?" I demanded of Granny.

She harrumphed like I had said I hated crochet. "They know what to do."

"Alright," I began, "Spill it. You're pissy and I don't know why. Did I do something? Do you see me as a threat?"

"Damn right you're a threat!" she hissed, her eyes darting between me and the trees where the kids had entered. I thought I had proved otherwise, and the kids seemed to like me, so what the hell? "You all blabberin' about kids on a safe island and now *my* kids wanna go with you!"

"Whoa there, Petunia. I'm not trying to talk anybody into anything!"

"Don't matter! It's done! They want to go I can see it." She started to cry.

I sighed. "No. No, they absolutely can't come with me. It's unlikely I'll make it, and I'm not going to be responsible for killing a bunch of kids." I reached out my hand to put it on her shoulder, but she shrugged it off.

"They'll just follow you. They've been talking about trying to get through the burbs for months." She meant all the populated area between us and the bay.

"No, they won't. How would you feel about you and the kids living in a military camp surrounded by battle-hardened soldiers, tanks, attack helicopters, and all the food you could want? You'd have to pitch in, but they are good people and they'll take you."

She shook her head. "Tanks 'n planes didn't do much good when this all started."

"That's because they underestimated their enemy. Now they know what it is they're fighting, and they are damn good at it." I rummaged through my pack for the radio and the big battery. I hooked them together and showed her. "You want me to make a call?"

"Who are you going to call?" asked one of the kids, all of whom had snuck up on us.

"Ghostbusters!"

"Huh?" they all asked, and I felt old.

Pentunia looked at her kids, "Do you guys want to go live with a bunch of soldiers? They have tanks and helicopters and guns and food."

The kids looked at each other excitedly, "Are there other kids there?" Lisa asked.

I shrugged. "I didn't see any, but I don't see how they could have a base that big without kids. Besides, they are bringing in people all the time."

"I want to go," Casey said enthusiastically. Lisa and Dory agreed emphatically. Bobby, ever the quiet one, strode to the spot where Petunia had given her "can't" speech and gazed at the dead suburbs.

The other three kids and Petunia began to talk hurriedly, so I stood and made my way to Bobby. I stopped next to him and stared out at the ocean. It looked very far away, but also so damn close.

I glanced down at him, "Don't talk much, do you, kid?"

"You should ask me about my dick, that's a long story."

Ten. The kid was ten and had said the funniest thing I had heard in the entire fucking apocalypse. I burst out laughing and he smiled at me.

"Soldiers, huh?" he asked.

"Yeah. They're capable and they seemed like good people. They weren't forcing anybody to do anything. You'll have to help out, but I'm pretty sure you won't have to do anything awful."

He spat on the ground, never taking his eyes from the dead houses and businesses down in the valley. "Ok," he said and we strode back to the others.

They were all in, even Petunia. They would go if Queen would come pick them up. I grabbed the radio. "RRF actual this is Red Five. Come in RRF actual, over?" The kids looked at each other and then at me. Finally, I was cool. "RRF, come in, over?"

"Red Five this is RRF. Actual is inbound to the comms tent. Wait one, over." The kid's voice was weak, so I turned up the volume.

I waited one. Three actually, before Queen's tinny voice came through, "Red Five this is RRF Actual. Status report, over."

"I've found survivors, sir, four kids and a woman." (I'm dispensing with the overs, Dear Reader.)

Queen came back excited, "Great news, Red Five! Also, our fuel drop came early, and with two cases of Mountain Dew. Where are you?"

"Mount Diablo. Two hundred or so miles as the Blackhawk flies."

"Wait one," he said. "We've got an A/L fueled and ready, Red Five. Flight time is two hours and we can take five passengers."

"Four, sir. I will continue on mission." Now the kids beamed at me. I was really fucking cool. I was the envy of all the kids currently standing near me.

"Negative, Red Five. The A/L has enough fuel to get you where you need to go without Bingo. You want a ride, you've got it."

I looked at the kids, "You guys ever been in a helicopter before?"

END

The big bird was landing a hundred feet away from us in three hours. Two heavily armed dudes got out and ushered us in. A few dead shuffled out of the tree line, and it was disconcerting to know they had been so close. Five minutes later I could see Alcatraz clearly. Five minutes after that I could see it too clearly.

The Rock was lost. The dead crawled over every inch of it, and they were still streaming out of the water. Apparently, many of the inhabitants of San Francisco had shuffled across the bottom of the bay seeking some island cuisine and had set up shop. I didn't see the black tube of the submarine, the USS Florida, where it should have been.

Damn. They were gone.

The bird dipped its nose a bit and we turned right, heading north. I didn't have a headset on, but the bearded operator tapped me on the shoulder and pointed in front of us. I did notice a big black tube. It was just off the coast of another island, and we were headed toward it.

We landed and several people were waiting for us, most of whom were dressed in black and carried military hardware. I noticed Dallas' large frame waving to us and sighed in relief. Remo was there too, and... was that a fucking cane he was leaning on? Then, I noticed Donna and Chloe, and my smile widened.

Briefly.

Donna had her hands on her hips and that meant only one thing: I was screwed. I had half a mind to tell the pilot to drop me off back at Alcatraz. It would have been safer. I was preparing my statement, going over it in my head about how none of this had been my fault and I was kidnapped and stuff as I got out of the Blackhawk, but all my trepidations fled when I saw the apocalypse wife running at me smiling and crying with Chloe hot on her heels.

They impacted me at about two hundred miles per hour, but I took it like a champ, throwing my arms around them both.

I had never been to this island before, but I was home.

We moved away from the sound of the helicopter, Dallas, Rick, and Captain McInerney all smiles when they clapped me on the back. I was a bit hurt that Ship and Remo weren't here, and where were Kat, Richy, and Alvarez?

I asked, and everybody's face fell. "Seyfert and Danny took the rest of our group out looking for you several times. They are in the city now," Donna told me cautiously.

I had half expected that. "What about Richy?" I asked, my face falling. "They didn't fucking take him with them?" I demanded, anger rising.

"Richy's sick," Chloe said, and I remembered he had been scratched by an infected back on Alcatraz. But that had been months ago. If he'd gotten infected, surely he would have turned by now.

"What kind of sick?" I almost whispered.

"Not that!" Donna exclaimed hurriedly. "There's something going around and it's kicking our asses."

I let loose with an audible sigh of relief. Remo had hobbled his way over to us and stuck out a paw. "A bad penny," he said, shaking his head.

I lifted up my shirt, showing my still-bandaged bullet wound. I pointed at his walking stick. "Pussy."

He smiled and we shook hands.

"You made it," someone else said and I turned around. It was Captain McInerney, who was also sticking out his hand.

"I do that sometimes, yeah," I replied with a smile. We shook hands as well. I liked this guy, but after somewhat recent events on Alcatraz and his submarine, I had some trepidations about penalties for the frontier justice Ship had meted out to a bad guy under the captain's watch. Remo was here, so that abated my fear a bit, but Ship wasn't and that needed to be addressed.

He clapped me on the shoulder. "Good to have you back. Spend some time with your family, then we'll have a debrief at 17:00."

"Yes sir." I wasn't military and as such, did not need to "sir" him, but he had earned my respect. He spun on his heel and went to meet with the chopper pilots and the kids who were hopping off the bird.

"Remo," I said under my breath, "what—"

"Five o'clock," he told me.

Richy was ok. Sick AF, but ok. Remo had gotten an infection from where that douche Martingale had shot him. In fact, my whole crew had made it from Alcatraz to Angel Island where we were now. Several of them were in the city searching, but McInerney was going to call them back.

My debrief went as you would think. We were in an office in an old museum on the island. I told McInerney, Meara, and Pitt everything. Gamboa and Baker, domesticated Runners, that I had trained a Runner, rats, and an insanely huge swarm of infected heading west in central California.

But the bastard already knew everything except the rats and the part about Lisa. It was then that two people were escorted into the room.

My eyes narrowed and my blood boiled. I stood up so quickly that my chair fell over, and I reached for my sidearm that I had left in the room claimed by Donna and the kids.

Remo put his hand on my arm. "Easy."

I seethed and the two dickwads in front of me looked nervous, the tall one wringing his hands. I sucked in a breath and sat back down, but I was anything but calm.

I glared at McInerney. "We found them while looking for you," he said simply.

I shifted my glare to the newcomers. If you haven't figured it out, Dear Reader, I was glaring at Drs Gamboa and Baker.

"Look," Gamboa said trying to diffuse my anger, "we weren't—"

I interrupted him, "Can someone please just fucking shoot them?"

"Our research is on hold," Baker almost shouted. "We've encountered a far more dangerous problem."

I folded my arms expectantly, leaning back in my chair for this inevitable doozy.

Gamboa sighed. "It's Thorne," he said. "He's gone rogue. He banded all the other Alphas together and they are... missing. It happened shortly after you left. Shortly after the Alphas left, the Trauma Center was attacked by a horde of undead."

"To be clear," I started with an unmistakable air of superiority, "your domesticated infected decided they were sick of your shit and took off to parts unknown."

Baker was initially taken aback, but she turned defensive quickly. "I don't think we can say—"

Gamboa cut her off, "That is exactly what happened. I believe Thorne went looking for Billy, and Subject Nine wanted to find you."

"Which is exactly what I told you would happen," I sniped smugly.

Both doctors nodded sheepishly.

I looked at McInerney, "So, what now?"

It was his turn for the sheepish look. "We, ahhh... we've lost contact with the search party looking for you in the city."

I blinked. "You're shitting me?"

Pitt bristled, but he didn't come off as condescending when he said, "The captain does not shit people."

I closed my eyes and seethed. There had been a lot of seething out of me since this meeting began. Sorry, debrief. I was being debriefed. Debrief sounds like somebody is peeling my underwear off me.

"So, you need me to go into the city?" I asked quietly.

McInerney truly looked sorry when he answered, "Yes."

ACKNOWLEDGEMENTS

Saying thanks isn't difficult for me, I'm just not good at it. I can write a book sure, you just read one, but expressing gratitude to those who shoulder my crap or even try to help me, that's tough. First and foremost, I need to thank my family. My wife and father recently passed away, and those closest to me stepped up and took care of me when I needed it most. Thank you. My friends Allen Gamboa, Scott Baker, and the lovely Hadley Thorne all of whom I do the weekly podcast Watching Wyrd with: You keep me grounded. Thanks for that.

Thanks, as well to my ARC readers. You ladies and gentlemen make my books better. You tell me if something stinks and point out flaws. So, to Dee Spiliakos, Allan Cordera, Allen Gamboa, Heather Bradley, Robert Walther, Brian Grindle, Ed Thigpen, Jarrett D Mundy, Carol Nilberg, Bobby Lloyd, Sue Crafter, Willadeen Hale Castaneda, Rachel Barrett, and Frank Riley I wish to convey gratitude. (That means thanks.)

Special thanks to Claire Davon who unintentionally gave me one of the best lines in this book, and to Bobbie Jean Murphy who selflessly dug the line out of months of messages because I'm dumb and couldn't remember who to thank.

And, of course, thank you, Dear Reader. You've stuck it out through the whole book, read the acknowledgements, and don't even judge me when I start a sentence with "and."

 SEVERED**PRESS**

 facebook.com/severedpress
 twitter.com/severedpress

CHECK OUT OTHER GREAT ZOMBIE NOVELS

900 MILES
by S. Johnathan Davis

John is a killer, but that wasn't his day job before the Apocalypse.

In a harrowing 900 mile race against time to get to his wife just as the dead begin to rise, John, a business man trapped in New York, soon learns that the zombies are the least of his worries, as he sees first-hand the horror of what man is capable of with no rules, no consequences and death at every turn.

Teaming up with an ex-army pilot named Kyle, they escape New York only to stumble across a man who says that he has the key to a rumored underground stronghold called Avalon..... Will they find safety? Will they make it to Johns wife before it's too late?

Get ready to follow John and Kyle in this fast paced thriller that mixes zombie horror with gladiator style arena action!

WHITE FLAG OF THE DEAD
by Joseph Talluto

Millions died when the Enillo Virus swept the earth. Millions more were lost when the victims of the plague refused to stay dead, instead rising to slaughter and feed on those left alive. For survivors like John Talon and his son Jake, they are faced with a choice: Do they submit to the dead, raising the white flag of surrender? Or do they find the will to fight, to try and hang on to the last shreds or humanity?

SEVEREDPRESS

facebook.com/severedpress
twitter.com/severedpress

CHECK OUT OTHER GREAT ZOMBIE NOVELS

RUN
by Rich Restucci

The dead have risen, and they are hungry.

Slow and plodding, they are Legion. The undead hunt the living. Stop and they will catch you. Hide and they will find you. If you have a heartbeat you do the only thing you can: You run.

Survivors escape to an island stronghold: A cop and his daughter, a computer nerd, a garbage man with a piece of rebar, and an escapee from a mental hospital with a life-saving secret. After reaching Alcatraz, the ever expanding group of survivors realize that the infected are not the only threat.

Caught between the viciousness of the undead, and the heartlessness of the living, what choice is there? Run.

THE DEAD WALK THE EARTH
by Luke Duffy

As the flames of war threaten to engulf the globe, a new threat emerges.

A 'deadly flu', the like of which no one has ever seen or imagined, relentlessly spreads, gripping the world by the throat and slowly squeezing the life from humanity.

Eight soldiers, accustomed to operating below the radar, carrying out the dirty work of a modern democracy, become trapped within the carnage of a new and terrifying world.

Deniable and completely expendable. That is how their government considers them, and as the dead begin to walk, Stan and his men must fight to survive.

 SEVERED**PRESS**

 facebook.com/severedpress
 twitter.com/severedpress

CHECK OUT OTHER GREAT ZOMBIE NOVELS

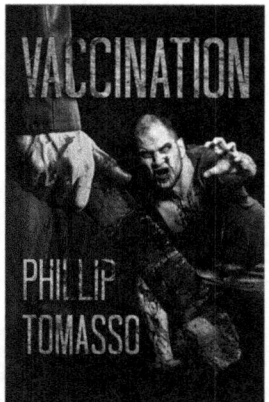

VACCINATION
by Phillip Tomasso

What if the H7N9 vaccination wasn't just a preventative measure against swine flu?

It seemed like the flu came out of nowhere and yet, in no time at all the government manufactured a vaccination. Were lab workers diligent, or could the virus itself have been man-made? Chase McKinney works as a dispatcher at 9-1-1. Taking emergency calls, it becomes immediately obvious that the entire city is infected with the walking dead. His first goal is to reach and save his two children.

Could the walls built by the U.S.A. to keep out illegal aliens, and the fact the Mexican government could not afford to vaccinate their citizens against the flu, make the southern border the only plausible destination for safety?

ZOMBIE, INC
by Chris Dougherty

"WELCOME! To Zombie, Inc. The United Five State Republic's leading manufacturer of zombie defense systems! In business since 2027, Zombie, Inc. puts YOU first. YOUR safety is our MAIN GOAL! Our many home defense options - from Ze Fence® to Ze Popper® to Ze Shed® - fit every need and every budget. Use Scan Code "TELL ME MORE!" for your FREE, in-home*, no obligation consultation! *Schedule your appointment with the confidence that you will NEVER HAVE TO LEAVE YOUR HOME! It isn't safe out there and we know it better than most! Our sales staff is FULLY TRAINED to handle any and all adversarial encounters with the living and the undead". Twenty-five years after the deadly plague, the United Five State Republic's most successful company, Zombie, Inc., is in trouble. Will a simple case of dwindling supply and lessening demand be the end of them or will Zombie, Inc. find a way, however unpalatable, to survive?

www.ingramcontent.com/pod-product-compliance
Lightning Source LLC
Chambersburg PA
CBHW06043 1180626
46817CB00007B/2759